Finders & Keepers

ALSO BY CATRIN COLLIER

Historical

Hearts of Gold
One Blue Moon
A Silver Lining
All That Glitters
Such Sweet Sorrow
Past Remembering
Broken Rainbows
Spoils of War
Swansea Girls
Swansea Summer
Homecoming
Beggars & Choosers
Winners & Losers
Sinners & Shadows

Crime

(as Katherine John)
Without Trace
Six Foot Under
Murder of a Dead Man
By Any Other Name

Modern Fiction

(as Caro French)
The Farcreek Trilogy

Finders & Keepers

CATRIN COLLIER

ORION

First published in Great Britain in 2005 by Orion,
an imprint of the Orion Publishing Group Ltd.

1 3 5 7 9 10 8 6 4 2

A CIP catalogue record for this book is
available from the British Library.

ISBNs 0 75286 700 8 (hardback) 0 75286 701 6 (trade paperback)

Typeset at The Spartan Press Ltd,
Lymington, Hants

Printed and bound in Great Britain by
Clays Ltd, St Ives plc

All the characters in this book are fictitious,
and any resemblance to actual persons living or dead
is purely coincidental.

The Orion Publishing Group Ltd
Orion House
5 Upper Saint Martin's Lane
London, WC2H 9EA

www.orionbooks.co.uk

For Richard Pettit and Victoria Hilliard who married on 19 June 2004 at All Hallows Church, Liverpool. Not only did they have the sense to find and keep one another, they also chose the best man for the post – Ralph Watkins.

Acknowledgements

I would like to thank everyone who helped me research this book and so generously gave of their time and expertise.

Martin Gover, who now owns Craig y Nos Castle Hotel, for giving me a guided tour of the castle, showing me old photographs and relating its history. Without a doubt, Craig y Nos would have been demolished, the fate of so many Welsh buildings of historical importance, if he hadn't somehow found the money and energy to transform it into the sympathetically renovated, impressive hotel, wedding venue and outward bound centre it now is. If Madame Patti could return she would instantly recognize her old home.

All the dedicated staff of Rhondda Cynon Taff's exceptional library service, especially Mrs Lindsay Morris for her ongoing help and support. Hywel Matthews and Catherine Morgan, the archivists at Pontypridd, and Nick Kelland, the archivist at Treorchy library.

The staff of Pontypridd Museum, Brian Davies, David Gwyer and Ann Cleary, for allowing me to dip into their extensive collection of old photographs and for doing such a wonderful job of preserving the history of Pontypridd.

Deirdre Beddoe for her meticulously documented accounts of women's lives in Wales during the last century.

The writer Edith (Mick) Courtney, a former patient of the sanatorium at Craig y Nos, where three of her sisters died of tuberculosis, for sharing her painful memories of life there and also for founding Swansea Writers' Circle, a group that has been instrumental in helping scores of budding writers to take the first faltering steps of their career, including me. Without the encouragement I received from the published and experienced writers of Swansea my manuscripts would probably still be languishing, hidden and unread.

My husband John and our children Ralph, Ross, Sophie and Nick, and my parents Glyn and Gerda for their love, support and the time they gave me to write this book.

Margaret Bloomfield for her friendship and help in so many ways.

My agent, Ken Griffiths, for his friendship, inspiring imagination and sales technique.

Absolutely everyone at Orion, especially my editor, Yvette Goulden, for her encouragement and constructive criticism, Rachel Leyshon, my eagle-eyed copy editor, Emma Noble, my miracle-working publicist, Juliet Ewers, Sara O'Keeffe, Jenny Page, and all the editorial, sales and marketing teams.

And all the booksellers and readers who make writing such a privileged occupation.

And while I wish to acknowledge all the assistance I received, I wish to state that any errors in *Finders & Keepers* are entirely mine.

Catrin Collier,
November 2004

Note

Again, I have taken the liberty of taking my fictional characters and placing them in actual locations.

Madame Patti's home, Craig y Nos Castle, was sold after her death in 1919 to the Welsh Memorial Trust who turned the building into a sanatorium. The death rate for patients admitted with tuberculosis remained at 80 per cent until the advent of antibiotics revolutionized the treatment of lung disease in the 1940s and 1950s.

In later years Craig y Nos was used as a geriatric hospital. It finally closed in the 1990s and although several attempts were made to save the building, gardens and the exquisite small theatre, which Madame Patti had constructed as a miniature copy of Drury Lane, none was successful, and it fell into a sad state of decay until Martin Gover bought it – and the 160 buckets set under the leaking roof.

Craig y Nos Castle and Country Park are part of the Brecon Beacons National Park, a designated conservation area of outstanding natural beauty. You only have to walk through the country park to see why Adelina Patti, who could have lived anywhere in the world, chose to make her home here. The castle, grounds and park are now open to the public throughout the year.

Llanfyllin Workhouse in Brecon was closed after the Second World War and the buildings were used by a local hospital. This in turn closed in the early 1990s and the site was taken over for use by a theological college. There is a website – www.a-day-in-the-life.powys.org.uk – which gives further information on the social history of Powys.

The farm I renamed the 'Ellis Estate' exists under another name and can be seen on the left-hand side of the Brecon Road, 5 miles above Craig y Nos. Local legend attributes the building of the imposing house and outbuildings to a family who lost their fortune in The South Sea Bubble. The estate remains impressive and the wild and beautiful scenery around it has remained unchanged for centuries.

Most of the cottages from which the tenants were evicted during the years of rural depopulation are now inhabited. Some have been bought and restored by incomers, who have come to love Wales as much as the natives and contribute so much to the ever-changing tapestry of Welsh life.

Chapter 1

HARRY BRACED himself for the inevitable judder when the train drew into Pontypridd station. He adjusted his cream felt derby to a jaunty angle, picked up the overnight case and suitcase he had moved from the carriage into the corridor, opened the door and stepped down to be deafened by a scream.

'There he is! Bella, Mam, over here! Harry!' His fourteen-year-old sister, Edyth, hurtled towards him.

'Ow!' He dropped his bags and reeled back when the plaster cast on her left arm caught his cheek.

'Gosh, I'm sorry, Harry. Did I hurt you? Did you have a good journey? Mam and Bella wanted to pick you up by themselves, but I insisted on coming. They said there wouldn't be room for me and your luggage in the car – I told them that they could jolly well get a taxi to take your trunk to the new house. You don't have to bother about it, Mam's arranging for a porter to take it off the train now. Was the summer ball as gorgeous as it sounds? I can't wait until it's my turn to go to grown-up parties. Are you very sad not to be going back to Oxford? No of course you're not, because you're off to Paris on Saturday. Dad – well, not just Dad, everyone's ever so proud of you for getting a First. Oh look, I've got chocolate on your white suit. I didn't realize it was that soft. Do you want a piece?' She opened her hand to reveal four half-melted squares of Five Boys. 'Here, let me get it off.' She pulled a grubby handkerchief from her sleeve with her clean hand, spat on it and dabbed at his lapel, smudging the stain.

'Edyth, don't; you're making it worse. Please, I'll see to it—'

'No, let me,' she interrupted. 'Boys haven't a clue when it comes to getting out stains. Guess what—'

1

'Edyth, stop gabbling like an auctioneer and let Harry get his breath,' sixteen-year-old Bella drawled from behind her.

Both sisters were dressed in fashionable, calf-length, dropped-waist, silk afternoon frocks. To Harry's astonishment Bella looked suddenly and amazingly grown up, in cool, sophisticated cream, with matching accessories and stockings, and amber-coloured cloche hat and gloves. Whereas Edyth – in navy blue, with snagged stockings, her shoes covered in dust – could have just left a hockey field.

Instead of giving him her usual bear hug, Bella offered her cheek. Taken aback, Harry kissed her, then, seeing their mother, ran up the platform and once more dropped his bags. Sali had no compunction about embracing him in public. She wrapped her arms around his neck and held him tight for moment before pushing him back and studying him.

'You look tired.'

'I'm fine,' he reassured her.

'There are shadows beneath your eyes. Too many graduation celebrations?' she said shrewdly.

'I've enjoyed one or two,' he conceded. Like the girls, his mother was dressed in silk. The smart beige outfit she'd worn to his graduation ceremony was complemented by a brown hat, gloves and shoes. 'And talking of celebrations, you three look as though you're going to a party.'

'We are,' Edyth blurted tactlessly.

'Well done, Edyth, for letting the cat out of the bag,' Bella said.

'Harry would have found out soon enough.' Sali frowned at the burgeoning red mark on Harry's cheek. 'Is that a bruise?'

'If it is, it's down to Edyth's cast. And what have you done this time, Miss Courts Disaster Wherever She Goes?' Harry picked up his bag and case again.

'Fell out of the apple tree in the old house,' Edyth answered cheerfully. 'We were flying kites. Glyn's got caught in the branches. He was crying and no one else would climb up to get it—'

'We had more sense,' Bella interrupted.

Edyth stuck her tongue out at her sister 'The doctor said it's a clean break and should heal well.'

'And a trip to the hospital was just what your father and I needed on the day we moved. Your trunk is being sent on to the new house, Harry.' Sali shepherded the three of them towards the ticket collector, who was sitting in his booth at the top of the flight of steps that led down into the station yard.

'You brought my car,' Harry quickened his pace when he looked down and saw the open-topped, five-seater Crossley tourer, which the trustees of his estate had presented to him on his twenty-first birthday.

'I thought you'd enjoy driving it to the old house one last time.' Sali handed him the keys.

'But you've already moved.' A year ago Harry had reluctantly given the trustees of the estate bequeathed to him by his mother's great-aunt, permission to sell the mansion that was part of his inheritance. It had been a hard decision to make as they had lived in it for fifteen years, but the spiralling costs of repairs coupled with the size of the place had made it uneconomical to run as a private house.

'The council took possession of the grounds months ago,' Sali confirmed, 'but they don't take over the house until tomorrow.'

'So we thought we'd have one last "do" there. Your welcome-home from Oxford and bon-voyage to Paris, and our farewell-to-Ynysangharad-House party. It's great for dancing because all the furniture's been cleared out,' Edyth chattered as she ran down the steps alongside Harry. 'I wish I were going to Paris. Uncle Joey says the girls dance the cancan there. And they eat frogs' legs and snails. Can you imagine that? Are you going to eat frogs' legs and snails when you get there?' Edyth charged up to Harry's car, hurdled over the back door and landed on the bench seat in the back.

'I hope you realize that the whole of Tumble Square saw your knickers then, Edyth.' Bella waited until Harry had opened the passenger door for her mother so he could open the back door for her.

'Miss Prissy Bossy Boots,' Edyth chanted the nickname she and their three younger sisters had invented for Bella. She stuck her thumbs in her ears and wiggled her fingers.

3

'Very pretty, Edyth.' Bella settled her handbag squarely on her lap.

Harry listened to his sisters squabbling while he stowed his luggage in the boot of his car. 'You two make me feel as though I've well and truly arrived home.' He climbed into the driving seat besides his mother and pressed the ignition. The engine roared into life. 'How is Dad?'

'Working too hard organizing the miners' strike as well as seeing to his parliamentary duties. I wish he'd take it easy,' Sali answered.

'He wouldn't be Dad if he did.'

'You're right.' Sali had married Lloyd Evans when Harry was four years old. Harry had adored Lloyd then, and they had grown even closer after the five girls had been born, sticking together as the 'men' in the family.

'Mind you, I never thought the miners would hold out alone for so long after the General Strike was called off in May.' Harry stopped the car so a cart could cross from Taff Street into Market Square in front of them.

'If there's one thing I've learned in seventeen years of marriage to an Evans, it's that the miners will carry on every fight until the absolute bitter end.' Sali waved to the doorman of Gwilym James as they passed the Taff Street entrance of the store.

Harry heard a slap, and suspected that Bella had finally lost her temper and lashed out at Edyth. He leaned back towards the rear seat, and asked, 'So who is going to be at this party?'

'Everyone.' Edyth draped her arms around Sali's neck and rested her head on her mother's shoulder. 'All the uncles, the aunts, the cousins, heaps of friends. But you'll be sorry to hear that Bella invited Alice Reynolds—'

'She's a friend,' Bella interrupted.

'Some friend. She only talks to us because she's stuck on Harry. She clung to him like a slug on lettuce at our Christmas party. All slime and simpering smiles—'

'Really, Edyth, I don't know where you get your ideas from. Slugs are disgusting creatures,' Bella said.

'So is Alice Reynolds, and you're beginning to sound more like a school marm every day. I bet you're going to die a dried-up old spinster, Belle.'

'Edyth, enough!' Sali reverted to the 'special' voice she used to silence her children whenever their bickering turned ugly.

'You don't have to worry about me and Alice Reynolds, Edyth, she's a baby.' Harry steered the car through the main gates of the private drive to Ynysangharad House.

'She's the same age as me,' Bella bristled.

'Sorry, Belle, but she's nowhere near as mature as you.' Hoping he'd mollified his sister with the compliment, Harry winked at his mother and slowed the car to walking pace. The afternoon was warm, the garden perfumed with the scent of roses. 'That music doesn't sound as though it's coming from a gramophone.'

'Striking miners.' Sali straightened her scarf and eased a wrinkle from one of her kid gloves. 'A few of them formed a jazz band using instruments donated by the union. Your father asked them to play for us today.'

Harry stopped outside the front door and pulled on the hand-brake. Seconds later a sea of family and friends poured out of the house and engulfed the car.

'Surprise!' Nine-year-old Susie tugged open the driver's door, and his three younger sisters piled on to him.

'Maggie, Beth, Susie.' He kissed each of them in turn.

'I've learned the Charleston, Harry, so you have to dance with me.'

'I'm older than you, Susie, so you have to dance with me first, Harry.'

'And I'm older than both of you, Beth, so that means he'll dance with me first.'

'Edyth and I are older than the three of you.' Bella took the hand of a boy about her own age, who opened the door for her and helped her out of the car.

Before Harry had a chance to ask Bella to introduce him to her friend, a shrill voice resounded above the chatter.

'What about me?' Two-year-old Glyn, his only brother and the youngest member of the family who Lloyd joked was Sali's 'best ever afterthought', was struggling to escape their father's arms.

'What about you, little man?' Harry took him from Lloyd, left the car and set him on his shoulders. He shook his father's hand, kissed his aunts and, surrounded by his cousins, went inside. The band had set up in the hall, so they could be heard throughout the house, and they broke into the strains of 'For He's a Jolly Good Fellow' as soon as Harry walked through the door. Harry stopped and, feeling slightly foolish, stood with Glyn on his shoulders until everyone finished singing.

Sensing his embarrassment, Sali guided him towards the french doors in the dining room. They made slow progress as people continually stopped him to offer their congratulations on his degree and wish him well in Paris. Trestle tables had been set up outside on the terrace, and they were covered with plates of savouries, sandwiches, cakes, jellies and blancmanges.

'Mari's outdone herself.' Harry looked around for their house-keeper.

'She has, but none of us have succeeded in getting her out of the kitchen.' Sali took Glyn from him and handed the toddler a fairy cake.

'I've told the others that I'm first and that's all there is to it.' Harry's youngest sister, Susie, who had all the confidence of a girl twice her age, grabbed his hand and pulled him back towards the house when the band struck up 'Yes, Sir, That's My Baby'.

'What about Maggie and Beth?' Harry asked when they reached the middle of the drawing room where the dancers had con-gregated.

'I told them Mari needed help in the kitchen.'

'And did she?' Harry resolved to pay the housekeeper a visit as soon as he could get away.

Susie just grinned before waving her hands and kicking her legs in an imitation of the chorus girls at the Town Hall.

'Sorry you have five sisters,' Lloyd commiserated when Harry managed to escape into the library five dances later to join the men who had laid claim to the room as a refuge and smoking parlour.

'Sorry Edyth hasn't learned to be more careful with that cast.' He rubbed his arm. 'I haven't been back in Pontypridd an hour and she's managed to thump me twice. Uncle Joey, thank you.' He took the cigarette his father's youngest brother offered him. 'And thank you very much for the wallet you sent me when I graduated. I hope you and Aunty Rhian got my letter.'

'We did.' Joey lit Harry's cigarette.

'And thank you for the pen, Uncle Victor.' He shook his father's younger brother's hand. 'It was much appreciated.'

'First Oxford graduate in the Evans family – you deserve something special. But I don't deserve the thanks, Megan chose it. What would we do without our women?'

'Have more money in our pockets to get drunk on every night?' Joey suggested. He had been strikingly good-looking before the war but the years in the trenches and serious wounds had taken a toll on his health.

'It's just as well Rhian knows you don't mean a tenth of what you say.' Victor passed round a plate of sausage rolls he'd filched from one of the tables outside.

'I won't be the last one in this family to graduate from Oxford. Not with the number of cousins I have.' Harry looked around the room. 'Isn't Granddad here?'

'He complained he couldn't breathe in here so he went outside.' Lloyd handed him an ashtray.

'How is he?' Harry asked. Billy Evans had lost the lower part of one of his legs in a train accident fifteen years before. Forced to leave mining, he hadn't allowed his disability to stop him from moving in with Victor and Megan so he could help Victor out on his farm. But it wasn't only the loss of his leg that had affected his health. Like most miners who had spent twenty or more years underground he had succumbed to 'miner's lung'.

'You know Dad.' Victor swallowed a mouthful of sausage roll. 'He's not one to complain. Even when he's in pain.'

'You're a brave lady venturing into the men's lair,' Joey said archly to Alice Reynolds, who was standing on tip-toe in the doorway.

'I'm looking for Harry. It's a lady's excuse me.'

'Far be it from me to interfere with a lady's wishes.' Joey divested Harry of his cigarette and pushed him towards Alice. Linking her arm into his, Alice led Harry back into the drawing room.

'Please, not near Edyth,' Harry begged.

Edyth was flinging around her one good arm and both legs under the pretext of teaching her younger sisters the Charleston. Harry felt sorry for Maggie, Beth and Susie, who all received a couple of inadvertent kicks from her. He also noticed Bella dancing a practised and more expert version with the boy who'd helped her from the car.

'Bella has a boyfriend?' Harry asked his mother as soon as the dance was over and he'd managed to shake off Alice.

'Gareth Michaels.' Sali glanced across the room at them. 'He's seventeen and so smitten it's painful to watch the way she treats him.'

'Isn't she a little young to be going out with boys?'

'The protective older brother.' Sali looked amused. 'So far he's only taken her to the church social. Perhaps I should remind you how old you were when you escorted your first girlfriend to the theatre.'

'Point taken.' Harry followed Sali back outside. She retrieved Glyn, who was sitting on the grass watching Joey's youngest son and daughters play ball.

'Too much cake isn't good for one small boy, Glyn.' She took an iced bun from him and wiped the crumbs from his mouth. 'I hope everyone is enjoying themselves.'

'Judging by the smiles on their faces, they seem to be. It was a brilliant idea to hold a last party here.' Harry looked up at the house. 'It's a pity it had to be sold but Dad and the trustees were right – a house this size needs an army of servants to run it. And in this day and age it's simply not practical.' He smiled wryly. 'Despite Dad's Marxist ideals, we enjoyed the best of the vanishing world of the privileged.'

'We did.' Sali pressed a plate of sandwiches on a group of colliers who were hanging back diffidently from the table.

'From that look on your face, I can see that I'm not the only one who's sorry to leave,' Harry commented.

'We all are. The girls didn't stop crying for days, and although your father would deny it, I caught him wiping away a tear or two.'

'While you, of course, were indifferent,' Harry teased.

'You know me. I'm sentimental at the best of times. Don't forget, I knew and loved this house long before we lived in it. Some of my happiest times were spent here with Great-aunt Edyth before you were born.'

'Is the new house easier to run?'

'Much,' she said brightly. 'Mari and I manage it with the help of two dailies, although it has almost as many rooms. But they are a lot smaller. Your father sold two of the houses he owns in the Rhondda and paid the builder to extend the original plans so each of your sisters could have their own bedroom. As he said, it's worth the extra expense to stop their squabbling. Now, when they start, we just say, "Go to your rooms" and peace is instantly restored.'

'It's good to be home.'

'You'll be in Paris this time next week.'

'I'll write,' he promised.

'Like you did in Oxford? Letters that ignored the questions I asked in mine,' she reproached. 'You never did tell me how much you drank at the party after your graduation.'

He adopted what he hoped was an innocent expression. 'Not that much.'

'You expect me to believe that?'

'Of course.'

'And Anna?'

'Anna?' He looked blank.

'She's the reason I only allowed two of the girls to drive to the station with me. I thought you might bring her home. You introduced her to us before the ceremony,' she reminded him.

'Oh, that Anna.'

'Given the way and the number of times she kissed you, I assumed it was serious between you two.'

'She's a poet who believes in free love and she's gone to practise her creed with Guy in an artists' commune in Mexico, or perhaps it was Cape Cod. I'm not sure even they knew where they were going,' he said carelessly.

'Guy, your friend who shared rooms with you?' Sali asked in surprise. 'Aren't you upset?'

'About Anna? Good Lord, no. I'm twenty-one, not sixteen, Mam. There have been a few Annas in the last three years.' His mother and stepfather had encouraged him to discuss every aspect of his life openly with them and because they had rarely been disapproving or critical, he told them, if not everything, a great deal more about his life than most of his friends told their parents.

'Lloyd said you weren't serious about her.' (What Lloyd had actually said was, 'Don't get your hopes up of seeing Harry walking down the aisle just yet, sweetheart. She's just another one of his aristocratic flibbertigibbets.')

'Dad was right.'

She changed the subject. 'The builder is progressing well with the house next door that the trustees have bought as an investment for you. Not that they expect you to move in right away. And we put all the furniture you wanted from here in storage.'

'The trustees don't expect me to make a successful career as an artist, do they?' he said quietly.

'I think hope is a better word than expect,' she replied diplomatically.

'I wish they'd see me as a person, not a lump of clay to be moulded into the ideal owner of Gwilym James stores and associated companies.' In some ways Harry had come to resent the wealth that he would inherit in full at the age of thirty and not only because of the interference of the trustees in what he regarded as his personal decisions. He disliked the privileges it brought him, such as his Oxford education. He would have been happier winning a scholarship to an art college on his own merit, and would have tried to get one, if Lloyd hadn't pointed out that if he succeeded, it would be at the expense of a poverty-stricken student who desperately needed the money.

'They don't see you as a lump of clay, darling. And most of them may be elderly and a little old-fashioned, but they are truly fond of you. And although it may not always seem like it, they do have your best interests at heart.'

He slipped his arm around her shoulders and gave her an affectionate squeeze. 'I know, and I also know just how much trouble you had to persuade them to let me spend this next year in Paris.'

'I think your threat to give up your inheritance if they tried to stop you from going to France had more effect than anything I said.'

'It's good to know that you are behind me. Most of my friends' parents have insisted that they start in some business or other after three years in Oxford. Anyone would think all we did there was laze around, drink and have parties.'

'Didn't you?' Sali's question wasn't entirely humorous.

'I admit I had some jolly good times, but they didn't give me a First for my social life. I had to work for it.'

'Of course you did, darling.' She sensed she'd touched a raw nerve. 'And knowing that you wanted to go to art college, not university, made your father and me even prouder of the effort you made. You've dreamed of being an artist for years. It's only right you have the chance to find out if you have what it takes to become one. And now, given the way the food's disappearing, I'd better go and see if Mari needs help in the kitchen.'

Harry noticed Alice Reynolds bearing down on him again. 'And I need to say hello to her. Come on, Glyn,' he picked up his brother again, 'let's go and see what goodies Mari's kept back for us in the kitchen.'

'Welcome home, Master Harry.' Their housekeeper, Mari Williams, who was supervising the colliers' wives Sali had paid to help her in the kitchen, dusted breadcrumbs from her hands, opened her arms and hugged him.

'How's the most beautiful and best cook in Pontypridd?' Harry handed Glyn to his mother and, despite her bulk, swept Mari off her feet.

'I can see that degree of yours hasn't changed you, Master Harry.' She heard her helpers giggling. 'Put me down, you rascal.'

'Seeing as how you asked nicely, I will.' Harry set her gently back on her feet and kissed her cheek.

'What are you after?' Mari eyed him suspiciously.

'Oh, a couple of hours after this party, one of your roasts followed by an iced raspberry bombe would go down a treat, Mari,' he said hopefully.

'Then it's a pity we're having fricassee of tripe and bread and butter pudding for dinner.' They were the only two dishes Harry wouldn't eat.

Sali saw Alice hovering in the passage behind them and whispered, 'If you want to return to the library, use the scullery door.' She raised her voice and pretended she'd just seen the girl. 'Alice, how lovely of you to come and offer to help. There's a tray of cheese patties ready to be carried outside.'

Harry sneaked out of the door and past the stables. A suspicious pall of blue smoke hung above the shrubbery. He crept inside. His Uncle Victor and Aunty Megan's twelve-year-old twins, Tom and Jack, were puffing on a cigarette they were sharing with Eddie, his Uncle Joey's eldest son.

'Got you!'

Jack's eyes rounded in alarm. 'You won't tell on us, will you, Harry?'

'Not if you tell me who you stole this from.' Harry picked up the cigarette Tom had allowed to fall to the ground and held it up in front of them.

'We didn't steal it. Granddad dropped it accidentally, we just picked it up,' Eddie blurted breathlessly. 'Honest, Harry, it's the truth.'

'I believe you, thousands wouldn't. Where's Granddad now?'

'He was sitting on the seat under the chestnut tree.'

He handed the cigarette back to Tom. 'If anyone else catches you, or you start being sick, you didn't see me. Right?'

'Right, Harry,' they chorused.

*

Harry found his grandfather where the boys said they had last seen him, sitting on the bench under the tree, filling his pipe.

'Granddad, I've been looking for you.' Knowing the old man would be embarrassed by a hug, Harry sat next to him and shook his hand.

'I wandered out for some air and caught your cousins trying to smoke dried leaves in bits of newspaper.'

'So you went back into the house, and cadged a real cigarette for them to practise smoking with,' he guessed, recalling the time when he'd been thirteen and Billy had slipped him a cigarette when he had seen him trying to smoke one of his father's cigars.

'It was either that, or risk them poisoning themselves. Besides it's a family tradition. Your father and Victor sneaked their first puffs of tobacco about that age. Your Uncle Joey was an early developer. I caught him with a packet of twopenny tube when he was seven. His mother brought out her carpet-beater when she found out he'd saved his halfpenny a week sweet money to buy them. Not that she used it other than to threaten him.'

'Let's hope Jack, Tom and Eddie don't give the game away by turning green.'

Billy reached for his stick and rose awkwardly to his feet. 'Sad to see the old house go?' he asked, limping on his artificial leg.

'Mam and I were just talking about that.' Harry walked alongside his grandfather as he headed for the door closest to the library. 'It's the sensible thing to do. Are they really going to turn it into a clinic?'

'I think so.'

'I'm glad the War Memorial Committee managed to raise the funds to buy the gardens and grounds outright before handing them over to the town. It would have been awful if the park had been burdened by debt.' Harry held the french door open for his grandfather.

'The people of the town gave every penny they could spare.'

'They wouldn't have managed to meet the price set by the trustees if you and Dad hadn't persuaded the miners' unions to chip in.' The sale of the grounds had given rise to the first serious argument between Harry and his trustees. If the decision had been his, he would have donated the land and gardens. But nine of the twelve trustees had voted against him and all he had managed to do was set the price at slightly below market value.

'Joey's right, a free park dedicated to the dead of the Great War and owned by everyone in the town is a more fitting memorial than any number of statues.' Billy looked proudly towards his youngest son, who was talking to Harry's solicitor, Mr Richards. Joey had enlisted in 1914 and fought in France and Mesopotamia for four years before being wounded and invalided out of the army.

'And here's the man himself, Mr Richards.' Joey buttonholed Harry. 'We were just talking about you and your trip to Paris. Ooh la la. All those artists' models—'

'I'm going there to study.' Harry rose to Joey's bait.

'So you say.' Joey lifted his eyebrows. Away from the influence of his wife, Rhian, his humour tended towards the risqué.

'You putting your car in storage, Harry?' Victor asked, deliberately changing the subject.

'Unless Dad or Mam want to drive it.'

'Not us.' Lloyd handed round a tray of beers. 'I think you were mad to want an open-topped car given the amount of rain we have in Wales. And before you ask, no one has driven it since you returned to Oxford for the summer term apart from your mother when she took it up to the new house and picked you up from the station today. We prefer to sit in the dry when we drive.'

'You have no sense of adventure.'

'Because we don't want to risk pneumonia?'

'Dad, come and dance with me?' Joey's eldest daughter, Rachel, stood in the doorway, Edyth behind her, both with pleading looks on their faces.

'It's times like this I'm glad I have four sons.' Victor watched Lloyd and Joey being dragged into the drawing room as the band struck up 'I'm Sitting on Top of the World.' 'Can I get you anything to eat, Dad?'

'No thanks.' Billy saw Harry slip upstairs and followed him.

The bedrooms had also been stripped of furniture and Harry's footsteps echoed over the floorboards as he walked around the old nursery. He gazed at the seven columns of lines drawn on to the wall next to the fireplace. Each was topped by a name and inscribed with ages and dates in keeping with the family tradition of measuring every child on his or her birthday. All his half-sisters and brother's marks started with age one, his with age six, marked by his mother the year they had moved into the house. He fingered his topmost line, his age, twenty-one, his height neatly inscribed in Lloyd's careful writing beside it – 6 ft 2 in.

He stared at the unpolished square of boards, where a rug had been, and recalled the times he had sat, ostensibly reading on the window seat, while secretly watching his sisters hold dolls' tea parties under Bella's bossy tutelage. The scorch marks that marred the tiles of fairy scenes around the fireplace brought back memories of a traumatic Christmas Eve when Edyth had thrown lamp oil onto a sluggish fire and set the chimney ablaze. But that was Edyth; her well-meaning attempts to be helpful invariably ended in catastrophe.

Harry went to the bay, knelt on the window seat and ran his fingers over the names inexpertly carved there. Mansel James, the father he had never known because he had been murdered before his mother even knew she was pregnant. Edyth James had created the nursery for Mansel – her husband's nephew – when he had been orphaned. And, knowing that he was Mansel's illegitimate child, she had bequeathed her estate to him, to be held in trust until his thirtieth birthday. He had chiselled his own name with his penknife below Mansel's. He remembered doing it shortly after his mother and Lloyd had told him about his birth father and his inheritance.

The photographs that remained of Mansel were identical to his. Mansel had also been tall, slim and fine-featured with slender hands, blond hair and blue eyes. And his mother had once mentioned that Mansel had wanted to be an artist. But unlike him, he had willingly given up his dreams to run his Great-aunt Edyth's businesses.

Was he being selfish in wanting to extend his education beyond the three years he had spent at Oxford by studying art in Paris? He had only read English at the insistence of the trustees who believed that a degree would prepare him to take control of his affairs. They assumed he wanted nothing more than to make money, which he considered peculiar given that he already had more than one man could reasonably spend in a lifetime.

'Am I interrupting?' Billy joined him.

'Not at all, Granddad.' Harry smiled at the old man. 'I came up to say goodbye to my bedroom but got sidetracked.'

'It's understandable if you feel miserable. This is the only home you've ever really known.'

'No, it isn't,' Harry contradicted. 'I remember moving into your house when Mam was your housekeeper.'

'You were a scrap of a half-starved boy. The biggest thing about you was your blue eyes.'

'I was scared to death of you, Uncle Victor, Dad and Uncle Joey. You all seemed so big.'

Billy laughed. 'You soon came round. I hope it all goes well for you in Paris, Harry.'

'Thank you for sounding as though you really mean it.'

'Everyone should have the chance to make their ambition come true.'

'I know I'm privileged.' Harry was very conscious that if it hadn't been for the trust fund he would have had to go down the pit like so many of the boys he had played with as a child.

'I'm not having a go at you, just trying to say that it's good to see you doing something you want to. Victor may have been forced out of the pit when management wouldn't take him back after the nineteen eleven strike, but he should never have gone down there in the first place. He's a born farmer and he loves it. And Joey would never have had the chance to exercise his salesman's charm underground. He's far happier running Gwilym James.'

'Where I'll be sooner or later.'

'Only if you want to, Harry,' Billy advised, sensing a hint of bitterness in Harry's pronouncement. 'Life's too short to waste time doing things you don't want to. Remember that. And now you should rejoin your guests.'

'And be dragged on the dance floor again.' Harry made a face.

'You're determined to be a Harry with a hump today, aren't you?' Billy joked. 'Since when haven't you liked dancing?'

'Since I've been surrounded by babies like Alice Reynolds.'

'Give her a couple of years and she'll be a charming young lady.'

'Perhaps I'm too impatient to wait.' Harry followed his grandfather to the door. 'Thanks, Granddad. You've always been there whenever I've needed someone to talk to.'

'I may have sixteen grandchildren but you're the oldest, and the one I practised on, Harry. You taught me as much as I taught you.'

'There you are, Harry. We've been looking for you everywhere.' Edyth ran up the stairs when she saw Harry and Billy leaving the nursery. 'Mari's made a bon voyage cake; it's got a red ribbon round it . . . Granddad, you all right?'

Harry put his arm around Billy's shoulders when he began to cough, helping him back to the nursery window seat and lowering him on to it. To his alarm, Billy's cough grew sharper and more pronounced, his breathing more laboured. Seeing him fumble in his pocket, Harry produced his own handkerchief.

'Edyth, run downstairs and get a glass of water.'

His sister stared at them, mesmerized.

'Edyth!' Harry looked down at his grandfather as his sister backed towards the door. To his horror, bright red blood was pouring from Billy's mouth. He held his handkerchief to Billy's lips. 'Edyth,' he struggled to keep calm, 'please, go downstairs. Tell Dad to call a doctor.'

She turned and fled. Seconds later he heard a scream and a series of thuds.

Still coughing blood, Billy tried to rise to his feet. He pushed Harry away from him, then fell back and pointed to the door.

'I'm going to get help, Granddad.'

Billy nodded weakly and leaned against the window pane.

Harry ran on to the landing. The band had stopped playing. A crowd had gathered around Edyth, who was lying face down at the foot of the stairs. His mother and Lloyd were crouching over her.

'Dad?' Harry had to call three times before his stepfather looked up. 'We need an ambulance.'

Lloyd was hoarse with shock. 'The phone's disconnected. Joey's gone to fetch the doctor in his car.'

Harry's voice rose precariously. 'It's Granddad. We need an ambulance for Granddad as well.'

Chapter 2

DAVID ELLIS set his back to the majestic sweep of the Brecon Beacons, shaded his eyes and studied the stretch of road that ran in front of his family's isolated farmhouse. It wound from the market town of Brecon, through miles of hills and valleys that were the lonely domain of shepherds, sheep and predatory wildlife; past remote farms, smallholdings and tiny hamlets down through the Swansea Valley to the coast.

A trap was moving along the road at a smart pace. Its varnished panels glittered in the sunlight and the white pony trotting between the shafts was a highly bred, hay-burner. And, as if that weren't enough, the driver was wearing a frock coat and top hat. David knew few men who could afford to dress like that on a Sunday, let alone a weekday, and only one who could afford to buy an expensive new rig. He wasn't a farmer.

David kneed the last lamb that his dog, Merlyn, had rounded up into the dry-stone pen. He fastened the rough gate with a wooden peg, pulled the grubby cap that had been his father's from his pocket, threw it on his head, whistled to the dog and raced across the fields.

He found his eldest sister, Mary, in the yard behind their house. Their six-year-old brother, Matthew, was glaring resentfully at her from a perch on the wall of the pigsty that she was cleaning, their one-year-old brother, Luke, on his lap. Matthew considered himself old and strong enough for farm work, yet Mary invariably set him to watch Luke who had just begun to walk and was into everything he shouldn't be. On the farm that was most things.

'Agent's on his way,' David gasped.

Mary straightened her back and leaned on the broom she was

19

using to sweep out the muck. 'How many lambs do we have ready for market?'

'I've shut a hundred and forty in the pen.'

'Then, there must be close on a hundred left in the hills,' she said anxiously.

'None you can see from the road.'

'If he finds out that we've set them aside—'

'We need at least sixty to replace the ones we lost last winter. And if he takes the rest, we'll starve,' David argued forcefully.

David was only fourteen but he had grown up quickly since their parents had died. Desperate to pay off their father's debts and rent arrears, Mary had no choice but to allow the agent to take and sell off everything of value on the farm and in the house. The only thing she kept that might bring in a pound or two was their mother's wedding ring, and she stubbornly refused to let that go.

She picked up a bucket of water and tipped it over the stone floor of the sty. 'Another couple of these and this will be as clean as I can get it. Then I can move on to the others.'

'Are the sows and their litters in the field?' David asked.

'The sows and thirty piglets.'

'Where have you put the others?'

'I locked them in the tack room behind the stable,' Matthew crowed proudly.

'Let's just hope he doesn't hear them squealing.' Mary saw the trap turn through the arched entrance that cut a tunnel through the house and led into the yard. 'Remember,' she whispered fiercely to her brothers, 'not one word from either of you. Leave the talking to me.'

Desperately wanting to be with Edyth, unwilling to leave his grandfather, Harry was locked in a nightmare dilemma. He had lost count of the number of times his father and Uncle Victor – an ex-colliery first-aider, the closest they had to a medical expert – ran up and down the stairs, dividing their time between Edyth and Billy. Fighting to draw air into his damaged lungs, his grandfather coughed up more blood than Harry would have credited a body could hold.

Mari brought up white linen tablecloths that she had stripped from the trestles, and helped him mop the blood that poured from his grandfather's nose and mouth. But even in his panicked state Harry sensed that she was as torn as he was. Frantic, he murmured meaningless reassurances.

'You'll be fine, Granddad, you and Edyth, you'll be fine, just you see, you'll—'

'Lloyd, she's having a fit!' Sali shouted up the stairs.

'Stay with him!' Lloyd ran back downstairs, Mari at his heels.

'Whatever you do, keep his head up,' Victor ordered before following them out of the door.

Harry continued to support Billy. A few minutes later, his grandfather lost consciousness. He turned his wrist so he could see his watch. Twenty minutes had passed since he'd heard Edyth scream as she'd fallen downstairs.

Bella's voice, high-pitched and hysterical, shrieked, 'Uncle Joey's back. He's brought an ambulance!'

Harry heard the bell ringing. Music had never sounded as sweet, and he weakened in relief. But his waiting wasn't over. Victor came charging upstairs and checked Billy's pulse.

'He fainted some time ago,' Harry whispered.

'The doctor will be up as soon as soon as they've loaded Edyth into the ambulance.'

'She's—'

'Breathing, but unconscious,' Victor interrupted, concern making him terse.

'She'll be all right.' It was more of a plea than a question.

'I hope so,' Victor breathed fervently.

The doctor entered, dropped his bag and crouched over Billy. 'I didn't dare risk delaying the ambulance. We'll need another.'

'I'll send Joey to the Malsters, they have a telephone there.' Victor released his father's wrist.

'Tell them it's a stretcher case for the isolation ward in the Graig.'

'It's TB, isn't it?' Victor looked to the doctor for confirmation.

The doctor nodded as he took a syringe and a phial of morphine from his bag.

Victor left. Lloyd entered, and stood behind the doctor and Harry. All three silently watched Billy slip into a deeper unconsciousness. Ten minutes later Joey came upstairs with an ambulance driver and his mate.

'Can one of us go with him?' Joey pleaded.

The doctor shook his head. 'Straight to the isolation ward,' he ordered the driver before finally looking Lloyd and his brothers in the eye. 'I'm sorry, you can't go into isolation but you can go to the main desk in the infirmary and ask after Edyth. But there's no point in you going there for an hour or two. I won't know anything until she has been X-rayed. I'll meet you there.'

Harry stood back helplessly as the men carried his grandfather out. A few minutes later he heard the sound of a bell again when the second ambulance drove away from the house. He looked around the room. So many happy memories had been overshadowed by this one traumatic incident.

He gathered the blood-stained tablecloths and trailed miserably down the stairs behind his father and uncles.

'I counted thirty-five piglets the last time I called. There's only thirty in the field.' Bob Pritchard, agent for the largest absentee landowner in Breconshire, and universally known as 'Bob the Gob' because his word was law to the tenants from whom he collected rent, glared at Mary.

She wound a strand of black curly hair around her finger. 'The sow rolled on three and crushed them to death.'

'And the carcasses?'

'We fed them to the dogs. They were so broken and bloody they weren't fit for anything else.' Mary slipped one hand behind her back and crossed her fingers. Her father had told her that a lie wasn't a lie if you made the sign of the cross when you told it.

'And the other two?'

She intertwined her fingers until they hurt. 'Were runts. We tried to save them but couldn't.'

Bob pulled a notebook from his suit pocket. 'How many lambs have you ready for market?'

'A hundred and forty, they're in the lower pens in the fields next to the road.' David earned himself a glare from Mary for speaking out.

'A hundred and forty. You've over four hundred ewes.'

'We lost sixty ewes and over a hundred lambs last winter. It was hard—'

'You don't have to tell me how hard last winter was, boy,' Bob snapped. 'I see it every day in the diminishing return on my employer's investments.'

'We should be replacing the ewes but you always take all the lambs.'

'I take all the lambs, Mary, because you have rent arrears of over one hundred and twenty pounds,' he interrupted brusquely. 'I warn you, the landlord won't stand for much more. I've tried to argue your case with E&G Estates, but I've had strict orders from above that the moment your arrears reach one hundred and fifty pounds, I'm to call in the bailiffs and put you, your brothers and sister out on that road in the clothes you stand up in. They wanted me to put the lot of you out when your father topped himself and your mother died, rather than take a chance on a nineteen-year-girl trying to run a place this size. If I'd had any sense I would done just that, instead of asking them to give you some leeway. But I've always been too soft for my own good. Not that you appreciate what I've done for you. You've given me nothing but trouble since the day you took over the lease on the Ellis Estate.'

'I know the law. If you put us out you'd have to give us the tools of our trade as well as our clothes.' David jutted out his chin with a boldness that was pure bravado.

'What tools?' Bob sneered.

'My dog, the farm tools—'

'The dog is livestock,' Bob contradicted.

'Please, David,' Mary begged. 'If we carry on working hard and paying what we owe, Mr Pritchard won't put us out. Will you, sir?'

'That depends on what else you have to send to market when the carts come round tomorrow morning,' Bob replied harshly. 'What do you have besides the lambs and piglets?'

'Must you take all the piglets?' Mary asked. 'They'll only fetch half a crown apiece now. If we fatten them until autumn we'll get at least five shillings.'

'It's not me who makes the decisions. I have to answer to E&G Estates, and they've warned me that my job's on the line. If I don't get the arrears on all the farms I oversee down to a manageable level in the next six months, I'll be out on my ear. The way you're going, most of what you pay is swallowed up by interest and there was one quarter last year when you didn't even cover that.' Bob scribbled a note in his book. 'That's one hundred and forty lambs, thirty piglets. Chickens?' He looked up enquiringly.

'I have twenty plucked, trussed and ready for the butcher, and fifty live.'

'Geese?'

'Ten for the butcher and twenty live goslings.'

'Cattle?'

'Fifteen bullocks and ten milk calves.'

'That the lot?' He gazed at her over the edge of his book.

'It is.'

Bob finished writing his list of figures and looked heavenwards as if he were seeking inspiration before totalling them. 'Going by the prices at last week's market that should fetch forty pounds or thereabouts. And seeing as how it's you, I'll take a chance on the market remaining stable and knock forty pounds off your rent right now.'

'That lot is worth at least double, and you know it,' David remonstrated.

'Prices have halved since last year.' Bob pushed his face close to David's and breathed tobacco and ale fumes at him. 'Haven't you heard there's a depression on, boy? We're all having to tighten our belts.'

'Some more than others.' David stood his ground and parried the agent's glare.

'It's not my fault that your father was a useless waster.'

The boy went white. 'You—'

'David, do you want to see us evicted?' Mary hissed.

Bob turned to her. 'Forty pounds, and that's my final offer. As it is I'm forgoing my agent's commission. I try to help you and all I get is sauce from this one.' He clipped David across the ear. The blow stung and David drew blood when he bit his lip but he remained immobile and defiant.

'Say sorry to Mr Pritchard, David.' Mary slipped her arm around her brother's shoulders.

'I'm damned if I will.'

'Swearing too?' Bob mocked. 'Well, David Ellis, you may soon find yourself learning manners along with your Bible in the work-house. I hear they are expert at beating the arrogance out of heathens like you.'

'Say sorry to Mr Pritchard, David,' Mary pleaded.

'Sorry,' David muttered mutinously.

'Sorry, *sir*,' Bob Pritchard corrected.

'Sorry, *sir*.' David mimicked the agent's voice and inflection perfectly, but his eyes gleamed with undisguised loathing.

Bob made another note in his book and Mary pushed David, willing him to move out of the agent's reach. She was terrified that Bob Pritchard would strike her brother a second time and David would fight back. But Bob snapped his book shut. He looked her up and down. 'I trust you wash yourself occasionally as well as the pigsties, Mary?'

Mortified, she muttered, 'I do.'

'Forty pounds. Take it, or vacate the farm.'

'We'll take it.'

'That will bring your arrears down to one hundred and ten pounds after this quarter's interest is paid. You'd better start looking around for something else that you can sell to make inroads on the rest.'

'We've sold all we can. If you left us more livestock—'

'I've done all I can for you today. But I tell you what I will do.' He gave her a cold, insincere smile. 'I'll take a good look at the books tonight and do some thinking. I'll be back this way mid-morning tomorrow. We can have a chat about your situation then. You'll be here?'

Mary gripped the broom handle tightly as much to stop herself from shaking as for support. 'I'll be here.'

He tipped his hat to her, and sideswiped David's cap from his head on his way back to his trap. 'It's rude to keep your cap on in the presence of your betters, David Ellis. One day you'll get the horsewhipping you deserve. I only hope I'll be around to see it.'

'Don't say another word,' Mary warned as the agent walked out of earshot and David opened his mouth.

'What is there left for you and Bob the Gob to talk about?' David demanded. 'He's taken every stick we had that was worth anything.'

'I think he suspects that we sell eggs and chickens direct to Craig y Nos and the Colonial Stores in Pontardawe, and is after a share of the money.'

'Hand it to him and we may as well walk to the workhouse this afternoon.' David picked his cap up from the yard and flipped it back on to his head. 'At least we'd get three meals of sorts a day there,' he added sourly.

Mary couldn't bring herself to consider the possibility that they might end up in the workhouse as so many of their neighbours had, including Albert Jones, the stockman her father had once employed. It was too huge, too terrifying a prospect, so she did what she always did whenever there was a problem she didn't want to think about, and concentrated on the immediate task in hand. She looked down at the floor of the sty. 'As you're here, pull me another couple of buckets of water from the well, Davy.'

'Can I help?' Matthew asked eagerly.

'If you want,' David answered flatly. He set Luke on his shoulders before picking up the buckets.

Mary watched her brothers cross the yard with a sinking heart. She hoped that they and her sister, Martha, would never find out how low she had sunk to keep the roof of the Ellis farmhouse over their heads. David had the hot Ellis temper, and there was no saying what he would do. And she couldn't bear the thought of Bob Pritchard beating him to a pulp – or making a complaint to the police that would result in him being birched or sent to a Borstal.

Without David, she knew that she would no longer have the heart or the will to carry on fighting to keep the Ellis Estate.

The waiting room in the Graig Infirmary was dark and dingy, the sickly green paintwork above the brown-tiled dado depressing. But it was clean – if the stench of disinfectant was any indication of hygiene. There were only four chairs and, at the men's insistence, Sali had taken one. Lloyd sat beside her, holding her hand, but Victor, Joey and Harry stood, leaning against the wall and staring at the door.

The sister had been furious when they'd arrived *en masse*, an hour and a half after Edyth had been taken from Ynysangharad House, but when Lloyd made it clear that they wouldn't leave until they had seen the doctor she had reluctantly shown them into the cheerless cubicle.

The door opened and all five of them looked up. The nurse held the door as the doctor walked in.

'I told them they couldn't stay—'

'It's all right, Sister. I know this family well. The Mr Evanses have sat on several of the same committees as me.' He fell serious. 'Edyth's fractured her skull. Her brain is bruised and swollen, and she's in a coma. Until she comes out of it there's no way of knowing what, if any, damage has been done. I've taken the liberty of putting her in a private room. She will have her own nurse sitting next to her bed at all times.'

'It's what we would have asked for. Thank you.' Lloyd gripped Sali's hand tighter. 'If it's a question of money—'

'It's a question of waiting, not money, Lloyd. I know that will be hard on you,' the doctor glanced at Harry, 'all of you, but please, be assured she will receive exactly the same care here as she would in any other hospital. Even an expensive one in London.'

'I was hoping that we could nurse her at home,' Sali murmured.

'Until she regains consciousness, I would strongly advise against moving her; it could do untold damage to a patient in her condition.' He gave Sali a small smile. 'I've persuaded Sister to bend the rules and allow you and your husband to see your daughter for a few minutes. But you'll have to be quick – and quiet.'

'We will.' Lloyd helped Sali from the chair and they left.

'How is Dad?' Victor and Joey asked in unison.

'I've been up to the isolation ward. Not that I had any doubt, but it's definitely tuberculosis. He's stopped haemorrhaging, but he could start again at any time.'

Victor paled and Harry knew he was thinking of his sons. TB was rife in the Rhondda Valleys. Virulently contagious, it killed more children and young people than any other disease.

'As Billy lived with you, Victor, I'll arrange for you, Megan, the boys and Betty Morgan' — Billy's one-time neighbour and house-keeper had also moved to Victor's farm to help Megan with her children — 'to have chest X-rays. In fact, it would be a good idea for all of you to have one. Your family as well as Lloyd's and Victor's, Joey. Billy could have been incubating the disease for years.'

'I've heard people talk about the isolation ward here,' Joey said disparagingly. 'It's over-crowded. There aren't enough nurses to see to all the patients.'

'Unfortunately you are right, but like young Edyth, I have arranged for your father to have a private room.'

'But what care can you give him here, Doctor Williams?' Joey pressed, refusing to accept the death sentence that had just been pronounced on his father.

'There is no effective treatment for tuberculosis. As a last resort in some cases we operate, and deflate the most diseased lung in the hope that the remaining lung will recover. Unfortunately, given the amount of dust in your father's lungs, that option is closed to him.'

'There are clinics in Switzerland,' Joey suggested hopefully.

'He would never survive the journey,' the doctor countered bluntly.

'So what can you do for him here?' Joey demanded.

'Other than try to make him comfortable, nothing.'

'Can we at least see him?' Victor asked.

'Visiting is heavily restricted on the isolation ward,' Dr Williams hedged.

'We can't just leave him here, in the workhouse!' Joey exclaimed bitterly.

'Your father is not in the workhouse any more than young Edyth is. He is in the infirmary.'

'Wing of the workhouse, a place full of dying people,' Joey

broke in testily. 'I won't leave Dad here, no matter how ill he is. We'll employ nurses to care for him. He can come to my house.'

'Are you prepared to expose your five young children and your wife to the disease, Joey?'

'No, of course not,' Joey replied angrily.

'Besides, it's not simply a question of day and night nursing. Your father needs a doctor's constant supervision and he can only get that in a hospital.'

'We know that you are only concerned about our father's health and that of our family, Doctor Williams, but there has to be somewhere else that we can send him. Perhaps a clinic or hospital that specializes in lung diseases?' Victor suggested diplomatically.

The doctor thought for a moment. 'There is a sanatorium that offers specialized treatment. I believe it offers the best care not only in Wales, but the whole of Britain, although I'm not sure they'll take a patient in your father's advanced condition. It is called Craig y Nos, in the Swansea Valley.'

'Will you at least ask if he can go there?' Victor looked up when Lloyd and Sali returned. Both were dry-eyed but their eyes were dark with misery.

Dr Williams turned from Sali and Lloyd back to Victor. 'I'll telephone the sanatorium, and talk to the doctor in charge there. I'll let you know what he says.'

'Packing for France?' Sali asked Harry the next morning when she walked into his bedroom to find his trunk open and his clothes strewn over his bed.

'Unpacking to stay.'

She sat on his bed. 'Darling, Lloyd and I have discussed this. We can't do anything for Edyth except pray, follow Doctor Williams's advice, and allow him and the nurses to care for her until she regains consciousness. Hopefully, we will find somewhere that can offer your granddad better treatment than the isolation ward of the Graig, but even if we do, we won't be allowed to visit him very often and possibly not at all. Whether we like it or not, we have to get on with our lives as best we can.'

Harry shook his head. 'I'm not going to Paris while Granddad and Edyth remain in hospital.'

'That could be months in both cases.' Lloyd was in the doorway. 'I've just talked to Victor on the telephone. Doctor Williams has asked us to call into his surgery at four o'clock this afternoon.'

'Can I come with you?' Harry asked.

Lloyd recalled how Harry had sat with his father the day before and how close they were. 'I'm sure he won't mind one more.'

Sali rose from Harry's bed. 'I'll stay here with the girls, and invite Megan and Rhian and their children over for tea. They're bound to be feeling as wretched as we are.'

Dr Williams sent his receptionist to fetch an extra chair when Harry walked in with his father and uncles. He waited until she closed the door before beginning.

'I have spoken to the doctor in charge of the sanatorium I told you about.' He cleared his throat. 'Perhaps it would be better if I started at the beginning. The Welsh Memorial Trust bought Craig y Nos Castle after its owner, Madame Patti, died seven years ago. She was wealthy enough to live anywhere in the world but she chose Craig y Nos because she was very particular about her health, especially her throat and lungs. The air there is supposed to be especially beneficial and healthy, so they've turned the castle into a sanatorium for patients suffering from chest ailments, principally tuberculosis. An old colleague of mine, Doctor George Adams, has been running it for the past five years. He's the foremost expert on lung disease in Britain. But it's expensive—'

'Money's no object when it comes to Dad's care,' Joey interrupted. 'Not if there's a chance of curing him.'

'No one can cure your father, Joey. All Doctor Adams will be able to offer your father, that's if he can offer him anything,' Dr Williams qualified, 'is a more comfortable end to his days.'

Victor swallowed hard. 'But he will take Dad as a patient?'

'He's agreed to look at his clinical notes. I'll put them in the post today.'

'I'll drive there tomorrow and hand them to him,' Harry volunteered. He looked at his father and uncles. 'It makes sense.

One of us should look at the place and talk to the doctor. Dad and Mam can't go, not with Edyth in hospital, and you two won't want to go far from Pontypridd while Granddad is here. If Doctor Adams agrees to take Granddad, all I have to do is telephone you – there's bound to be one in the sanatorium. And then you can make arrangements to transfer him there.'

'That makes sense,' Dr Williams agreed. 'Should Doctor Adams agree to take your father, he'll want to begin treating him as soon as possible. I'll telephone him again later and tell him you're coming, Harry. And you can pick up your grandfather's notes here tomorrow morning before you leave. I'll have them ready for you.'

'Thank you, Doctor Williams. Could you also give me the address of the sanatorium so I can look it up on the map?'

'I can, but you won't miss it. It's on the main road between Swansea and Brecon.'

Glad that he finally had something to do, Harry looked to his father and uncles. 'Then that's decided? I'll leave first thing in the morning.'

Sali had insisted that Lloyd's brothers and their wives join them for tea but none of the adults had eaten much, and when she looked at the plates of sandwiches, cakes, salad and sweet and savoury pies that had been barely touched, she hoped the children had done more justice to the food Mari had laid out for them in the garden parlour.

'A delegation from the union called round the farm just before we drove down here. You know what it's like in Tonypandy,' Victor said deprecatingly.

'We do.' Lloyd handed Sali his cup for a refill.

'They heard that Dad has TB and they said that even with the strike on, union funds could stretch to paying Dad's hospital bills,' Megan finished.

'There's no need,' Harry interposed. 'I'll borrow the money from my trust.'

Lloyd gave Harry a stern look. His stepson's cavalier attitude towards his trust fund as an unlimited source of revenue that he had done nothing to earn was the single source of contention between them. 'As Joey told Doctor Williams, money's no object and the least of our problems. Dad has saved all his life. He'll want to pay his own bills, even if it means selling a couple of the houses he owns.'

'You're determined to take Dad's notes to this sanatorium tomorrow, Harry?' Joey asked.

'Yes,' Harry said firmly. 'As I said earlier, none of you will want to leave Pontypridd while Dad and Edyth are in the Graig. And although I'm not questioning Doctor Williams's description of this sanatorium, it might be as well if one of us sees what they can offer him before we take him there. It will be a long journey for someone as ill as he is.'

'What about Paris?' Rhian asked. 'You were so excited at Easter when you had the letter to say that a place had been reserved for you at the studio you chose.'

'I can go to Paris any time,' Harry said dismissively.

'If they show you around the sanatorium, be careful,' Lloyd warned. 'Tuberculosis is highly contagious.'

Harry shrugged. 'I'm too strong and healthy to catch anything.'

'It's horrible, especially the later stages.' Joey recalled a world he had tried – unsuccessfully – to forget. More soldiers had died of disease, including tuberculosis, in the hospital tents in Mesopotamia than from wounds. 'People waste away to skeletons and cough up their lungs,' he continued. 'It's messy and terrible to watch when the patient is a stranger. We all know how fond you are of Dad and him of you, Harry, but are you sure you know what you're volunteering for, in visiting this place?'

'I haven't overdosed on Keats's poetry or *The Lady with the Camellias*, if that's what you're thinking, Uncle Joey. And I've visited hospitals. I delivered food to some when the General Strike was called in May.'

'And you let this blackleg into your house, Lloyd?' Victor's poor attempt at a joke fell leadenly into the heavy atmosphere.

'The volunteers only kept essential services going, they weren't after anyone's job.' Lloyd stared thoughtfully at his stepson. 'Well, all I can say, Harry, is you're right. One of us should see the sanatorium before subjecting Dad to the journey there. Thank you for taking it upon yourself.'

Harry winked at Bella, the only other one of his generation who had been allowed to eat with the adults. She was very obviously close to tears.

'I wish we could see Dad, if only for a couple of minutes, to ask him how he feels about going to this Craig y Nos,' Victor said feelingly.

'If Doctor Adams does agree to take Dad as a patient, and Harry thinks the place is suitable, we might see Dad sooner than we think,' Lloyd consoled him.

'If everything is as Doctor Williams said, will you stay in the valley until we take Dad to the sanatorium, Harry?' Victor asked.

'That depends on how soon it can be arranged.'

'If they'll take him, we'll bring him down the day after to-morrow,' Joey said firmly. 'I don't think he should be left on the isolation ward of the Graig a day longer than necessary. On Doctor Williams's own admission they can't offer him any treatment.'

'In that case I'll stay. There's bound to be a pub or a farmhouse nearby that rents out rooms.' Harry turned to Megan. 'You're from the Swansea Valley, aren't you, Aunty Megan?'

'Yes, but it's a long time since I've been there, I couldn't recommend anywhere.' Megan was estranged from her family. Her chapel deacon father had warned her that if she married Catholic Victor, he would count her name among the dead, and that he would do the same to her mother, brothers and sisters if they tried to contact her. But instead of deterring her, his threats had made her all the more determined to marry the man of her choice.

'Is the climate there as good as Doctor Williams told us?'

'To be honest, I don't remember it being much different from Pontypridd, but I was only thirteen when I left. There's iron and tinplate works as well as coal pits in the lower valley but the upper valley is pretty. There are woods, a river and a couple of waterfalls. I remember the castle. It's huge and the gardens are beautiful; the river runs through them and there's a small lake. There's even a winter garden. I peeped in there once and saw lemons and oranges growing on trees. But when I was a girl Madame Patti was still alive and living there between tours. She built a theatre in Craig y Nos and gave free concerts for the local people. She had an incredibly clear and haunting voice. The chapel minister told us that theatres paid her five thousand pounds in gold to perform for a single night, and all the kings and queens in Europe would come to hear her, yet she'd sing for us for nothing. After the concerts her servants would give us tea and there'd be a present for every child. Two of my sisters worked there as maids and loved the place and her. For all I know, they could still be at the castle.'

'Sounds pretty, so there's bound to be better views from the windows in the castle for Granddad to look at than there are from the Graig.' Harry pushed his empty cup aside and leaned his elbows on the table. 'I'll drive to the valley tomorrow, find myself a room and try to see Doctor Adams right away. If he is willing to treat Granddad, I'll ask him to show me the room where he will stay, and if it looks all right, I'll telephone you and then you can bring him down.'

'Train would be best,' Victor said decisively. 'We'll book a private carriage so he can lie on the seats. But you'll have to arrange transport from the local station, Harry. He may not be able to sit up in your car.'

'The sanatorium should have an ambulance if we need one.'

'Then it's settled. We'll wait for your telephone call, Harry.' Victor stood.

'Thank you, Harry.' Joey also rose to his feet and slapped Harry on his back.

'Yes, it's good of you to offer to do this, Harry.' Victor watched another tear escape from Megan's eye and squeezed her hand.

'I've a road map of South Wales that you can have.' Lloyd stared ruefully at the boxes piled in the corner of the room. 'That's if I can find it.'

'I'll give you a hand to sort through the packing cases this evening.' Sali handed her handkerchief to Bella, as the tears started to fall from her daughter's eyes.

'Best get an early start, Harry,' Victor advised. 'You know what cars are like. The minute you're the maximum distance from the nearest garage, it will break down.'

'Are you wishing that on me, Uncle Victor?'

'It's happened too often to me to wish it on anyone else. I've been to the Swansea Valley, and Megs is right, – it is a beautiful place but the sheep outnumber the people a hundred to one, and there's nothing there but isolated farms, scenery and the castle. It's twenty-odd miles to Brecon, eighteen to Swansea and there are precious few shops in between. Take a good book if you're intent on staying overnight.'

'Do you think Harry really knows what TB is like?' Victor asked when Lloyd walked him and Joey to the door.

'If he doesn't, he's going to find out.' Joey lifted his hat from the stand. 'That was some homecoming party we gave him.'

'We'll have a party again some other time.' Lloyd tried not to think when that might be.

'Funny to think of little Harry all grown up,' Joey reflected as they walked outside. 'It only seems like the other day that he moved in with us in Tonypandy when Sali became our house-keeper.'

'Some other day,' Victor commented. 'You looked in the mirror and counted your grey hairs lately, Joey?'

'Ready?' Joey opened the passenger doors of his car for Rhian when she brought out his three daughters and two sons.

'I am.' She turned to Sali and Megan. 'See you all very soon.'

Victor opened the doors on the lorry and called impatiently, 'The cows won't milk themselves, boys, Megs.'

Megan hugged and kissed Sali, Rhian and the girls one last time. She was halfway to the lorry when she turned and ran back to Harry. 'You will make sure that this place is right for Dad, won't you, Harry?'

'I promise, Aunty Megan.' Harry picked up Glyn and encouraged him to wave goodbye along with the rest of his family.

Chapter 3

MARY LIFTED the final basket of eggs on to the back of the cart David had harnessed.

Dolly was the sole remaining mare in the stable that had once held two dozen riding, cart and shire horses. Knowing that Mary used Dolly to ferry the produce she kept from him, Bob the Gob had once demanded she send her to market. But even he had to admit that that at twenty-one, Dolly was too old to attract a bid from anyone other than the glue manufacturer, who never paid more than two shillings for an animal. So, he had grudgingly given in to Mary's pleas that they be allowed to keep the horse. But only after reminding her that in return, he expected her to pay a proportion of their rent in hard cash. He also added that it could only be a matter of months before the mare died and she would be forced to give up her clandestine dealings.

Dolly was slow and arthritic but Mary dreaded losing her. She was their only means of transporting produce out of Bob's clutches and, like the ever-present threat of the workhouse, she refused to speculate what would happen when the horse went.

She walked around to the front of the cart where David was sitting, reins in hand, Luke firmly tucked in between him and Matthew.

'There's twelve dozen eggs, six pounds of butter, four cheeses, two dozen chickens and a dozen geese plucked and ready for the oven,' she reminded him. 'You'll make sure that Miss Adams, not Cook – after the way she tried to cheat you last time – has first pick at Craig y Nos. And you'll double-check everything Miss Adams takes and the money she pays you. Take whatever's left to the

Colonial Stores. With luck we should have at least ten pounds left after you've bought our goods.'

'I can barter and look after money as well as you, Mary,' he countered irritably.

'Take care of Matthew and Luke. And only buy what we need; no sweets, no bargains, just flour, salt, tea, sugar, oats, chicken feed, soda and soap.'

'I know what to get,' he snarled. 'Martha, where are you?' he bellowed at the open back door of the house.

'Coming.' Martha ran out in her maid's uniform.

'You'll be walking to Craig y Nos if you don't climb on to the cart this minute.'

'See you all at teatime. You'll be hungry so I'll make a stew,' Mary shouted as David steered the cart through the arch.

She watched them leave before turning back to the farmyard. Ten gallons of milk – over and above what they were contracted to put out in the churns every morning to be picked up by the cart that went into Brecon – waited to be turned into butter and cheese in the dairy. All the churns needed to be scoured and cleaned ready for the evening milking, the cowsheds cleaned, the pigs fed, vegetables dug up for the stew, the sheep checked, and that was without the housework – and Bob Pritchard.

Sick to the pit of her stomach she put the chores in order of priority. Churns first; the longer they were left after they were emptied, the harder they were to scour. And she couldn't take the risk of sending dirty milk to Brecon. The last thing she needed was the dairy withholding payment to the agent for sour milk.

Harry pushed his foot down on the accelerator and watched the needle on his speed dial creep from thirty to forty miles an hour. The sky had darkened; the air felt heavy and portended rain. Yet he was loath to waste any more time by stopping to put up the hood on his car after losing an hour changing his front tyre, which had punctured on the stony track of the Bwlch Mountain that separated the Rhondda and Afan Valleys.

He'd left Pontypridd after an early breakfast in the hope that he would reach the sanatorium before lunchtime and, with luck, arrange an appointment with Dr Adams for that day. But the puncture had delayed him and, suddenly hungry two hours later, he had broken his journey at a roadside pub outside Swansea and bought a pork pie, which he'd eaten in the car while travelling up the road that led into the Swansea Valley.

His Aunty Megan had been right. Once he'd left the industrial area that stretched as far as the small town of Pontardawe behind him, the upper valley was beautiful. But as his Uncle Victor had warned, it was also sparsely populated, except for sheep and cows. The few villages and hamlets he passed through were a fraction of the size of those in the Rhondda. He had seen several inns and pubs but only a couple of dozen shops – mainly grocers, seed merchants and butchers – and after comparatively bustling Pontardawe, most of those had been set up in the front rooms of terraced cottages. If he had passed a garage, he hadn't spotted it, and although he'd been careful to fill his petrol tank and the two spare cans he carried in the boot, the supply wouldn't last long with his tourer barely managing fifteen miles to the gallon.

He glanced at the map his mother had dug out of a packing case, then back to the old coaching inn up ahead. If his calculations were right, he was in the village of Abercrave, only a couple of miles from the hamlet of Penycae and no more than three or four miles from Craig y Nos castle.

He eased his foot off the accelerator and turned into the yard in front of the pub. To his relief a single petrol pump stood in a corner. He parked next to it and hit his horn. A short, stocky, dark-haired young man about his own age walked out of the barn built at right angles to the inn.

'Nice tourer, sir,' he said, brushing his hands together to rid them of sawdust.

Harry picked up the lilt of someone more accustomed to speaking Welsh than English. 'Thank you.'

'We haven't seen many new ones in the valley, not since Madame Patti passed on. Back then we used to get the lot in here. Rolls Royce, Bentley, Mercedes – you name it, we saw and serviced it. That's why my father opened this workshop, to sort out the toffs' cars.' Suddenly remembering he was there to serve, he went to the pump. 'Do you want petrol, sir?'

'I most certainly do. Fill her up, please.' Harry left his car and stretched his cramped legs and arms. 'Am I on the right road for Craig y Nos?'

The man stepped away from him. 'You going to the sanatorium, sir?'

'As a visitor. But if the treatment they offer is as good as my family have heard, and the doctor in charge will take him, my grandfather may become a patient.'

'They say it's the best in Britain for lung disease, sir, but we locals don't go near the place if we can help it.'

'That's understandable. Is it close?'

'About four miles up the valley. You can't miss it. It's a huge place on the right-hand side of the road.' He eased the nozzle from the tank. 'That will be a shilling and a penny halfpenny, sir.'

Harry dug his hand in his pocket, pulled out a fistful of change and handed over two sixpences and two pennies. 'I'm glad there's a garage close by.'

'Only one between Swansea and Brecon, sir,' the man announced proudly.

'Do you do repairs as well as servicing?'

'Yes, sir.' He put his hand in his pocket, checked the coins he drew out and handed Harry a halfpenny change.

'In that case, could you put a new tyre on my spare wheel, please? There's no point in trying to repair it,' Harry warned when the mechanic examined the tyre bolted to the side of the Crossley. 'It's ripped to pieces.'

'I can see that, sir. I have a tyre that size, but it will take me an hour or more to put it on your wheel and it will cost you sixpence for my time and four and fourpence for the tyre.'

Harry unfastened the wheel and rolled it towards him. 'I'll pick it up later.' He extended his hand. 'Harry Evans.'

'Alfred Edwards, sir. Everyone calls me Alf.' He wiped his hand again on the back of his trousers before shaking Harry's hand. 'I served a full mechanic's apprenticeship and I've run the garage single-handedly since my father passed on last year, so if you need

39

anything doing to your Crossley while you're in the valley, I promise you now, I'll do a first-class job.'

'That's reassuring to know.'

'There's not been much call for car servicing since Madame Patti's time because no one other than the doctor can afford one. And although he sends his ambulance down here, as well as his and his daughter's cars, I spend most of my time making furniture.'

'You're a carpenter as well?' Harry asked.

'Not a proper time-served one like my grandfather was, but he taught me a bit. I'm not saying what I make would please the crache, but it seems to suit the farmers round here.'

Harry looked across at the ivy-clad walls of the old pub. 'You live here?'

'My mother's the licensee.'

Harry almost asked if she rented out rooms, then remembered he was still four miles from the castle and there might be something closer. He slipped his hand into his pocket.

'You can pay me when you pick up the wheel, sir.'

'Let's hope I don't have another flat. If I do, I'll be the footsore one walking back.'

'It is only four miles, sir.'

'You're obviously more used to walking than I am.' Harry had never regarded anything above a mile as a stroll. Reflecting how lifestyles influenced attitudes, he climbed into the driving seat, fired the ignition, waved his hand and drove back on to the road.

When he left the last house in Abercrave behind him, grassy, rolling hills, speckled with sheep and an occasional hill farm, rose on his left. On his right, the road sloped gently down to the wooded banks of a river. He followed the twists and turns that led through the few houses that were Penycae. Shortly afterwards, a high wall of dressed stone appeared on his right and above it loomed the towers of Craig y Nos.

His parents had taken him and his sisters on holidays around Wales that invariably included visits to castles. For a small country it had a lot to offer: massive grey stone Norman edifices such as Caerphilly and Oystermouth, which remained impressive even in roofless dereliction; smaller fort types like Carreg Cennen and

Pennard perched on the tops of hills that afforded sweeping views of the surrounding countryside; whimsical concoctions along the lines of Cardiff and Castell Coch, both raised on Norman foundations with so little regard for the original buildings that it was impossible to see beyond the fairytale visions of William Burgess and the Marquis of Bute's fanciful reworkings.

But even his architecturally untrained eye could see that Craig y Nos wasn't old, not in castle terms.

Half was early Victorian Gothic, its towers – one boasting a clock – capped by pyramids. The other half was turreted, and the two styles sat somewhat uneasily together. Yet there was no denying it was imposing, its four-storeyed façade as solid and substantial as that of an English mansion.

He drove into the walled courtyard and switched off his engine. In front of the castle was an elaborate fountain in the shape of a wading bird perched on four gilded fish, forlorn and covered in green slime. He climbed out of the car and ascended a short flight of steps to the main door, rang the bell pull and listened as it clanged into the silence.

He was debating whether or not to pull it again when the door opened. A blonde girl, who would have been beautiful if she hadn't been scowling, looked suspiciously at him. She was wearing a doctor's white coat over a plain black dress, and had a cotton mask pulled down around her neck. 'Can I help you?'

Harry removed his hat. He had expected a uniformed nurse or porter not a slim, young girl with a stern expression. Disconcerted by her icy stare he muttered, 'I hope so.'

'This is a sanatorium. You are risking infection simply by standing there.'

'I've brought my grandfather's clinical notes. Doctor Williams from Tonypandy recommended this place to my family. He has spoken on the telephone to Doctor George Adams.' Harry hoped the name would get him further than the doorstep.

'If you'll follow me to the waiting room, I'll see if Doctor Adams is expecting you.'

'I'm not sure he is, but I'd be very grateful if he could spare me a few minutes.'

She showed Harry into a stone cell set to the left of and just behind the front door. Bare and devoid of chairs, it was a tiny anteroom to a lavatory. The air had been warm and heavy outside the building; inside it was freezing. Harry was rubbing his hands together to keep his circulation flowing when the blonde girl returned.

'Doctor Adams is extremely busy, but he is prepared to offer you five minutes.'

Harry followed her up a second short flight of steps, across a corridor and into an office cum drawing room. A desk and filing cabinets had been placed in front of the window but there were also paintings on the walls and chintz-covered easy chairs and sofas grouped around a fireplace filled with a summer arrangement of dried flowers.

'Mr Evans?' A thin, balding man left the chair behind the desk and approached him, but didn't offer his hand.

'Doctor Adams?' Harry dropped the hand he had extended when the doctor made no effort to shake it.

'I spend my days caring for highly infectious patients, Mr Evans. We have many rules; the one most strictly enforced is to keep all physical contact to an absolute minimum, especially with those who are healthy, yet reckless enough to visit here. Take a seat.' Dr Adams indicated a chair set in front of his desk before returning to his own. 'I have spoken to Doctor Williams. He said you'd be bringing Mr William Evans's clinical notes?'

'I have them here.' Harry handed over the envelope he had picked up from Dr Williams's surgery that morning. He sat in silence while Dr Adams studied them.

'You and your family do realize that Mr Evans's condition is terminal?' The doctor set the notes on his desk and looked Harry in the eye.

Harry felt as though he were condemning his grandfather to death. 'Yes.'

'Clinically we can do little for him.'

'Doctor Williams warned us of that,' Harry said seriously. 'But he also said that you might be able to make him more comfortable.

We were all with him when he haemorrhaged so we know how ill he is. But we also know how over-crowded the isolation ward in the Graig Infirmary is and how over-worked the staff are there. They can do nothing for him. We had hoped to look after my grandfather ourselves. When Doctor Williams said that wasn't possible, my uncle asked him to recommend a good hospital or sanatorium. He told us that Craig y Nos offered the best care in Britain for patients suffering from lung disease.'

The doctor sat back and pressed his fingertips together. 'If we can do anything for your grandfather, and I offer no promises, the best you can hope for is that we make his final days easier and possibly less painful than if he were in an isolation ward in a general hospital.'

'We understand that, Doctor Adams.' Harry struggled to keep his emotions under control.

'Your father is Lloyd Evans the MP?'

'He is.' Harry had learned from experience that the higher the social class, the less likely a person was to be well disposed towards a Labour MP.

'Rank and privilege count for nothing here, Mr Evans. Death is a great leveller.'

'I don't doubt it.' Harry decided it was time to be assertive. After all, it wasn't as though they weren't prepared to pay – and pay handsomely – for the doctor's expertise. 'Please, will you take my grandfather as a patient?' he asked directly.

The doctor shouted, 'Come' at a timid knock on his door.

The door inched open and a scrap of a girl, as dark-haired and dark-eyed as a gypsy, and dressed in a maid's uniform that was far too large for her, crept in carrying a tray set with a teapot, single cup and saucer, milk jug, sugar bowl and a plate of rock cakes. The tray seemed almost as large as her and she was straining to hold it.

'Put it on the table in front of the fireplace, Martha.'

The girl did as she was told, curtsied and backed out of the room.

Both Harry's school and his mother had employed twelve-year-old maidservants during the war when there had been an acute shortage of labour. But Martha looked no more than eight or nine years old. Harry was tempted to ask her age but, aware that Dr Adams might see his question as a criticism, didn't want to risk irritating him any more than he already had.

'I'll tell you what I will do, Mr Evans. I'll let you decide whether or not your grandfather should come here.' Dr Adams picked up a bell from his desk and rang it. 'Miss Adams can show you our private rooms and tell you about the treatment we offer. She is taking a short break from her studies at medical college to further her training here, and although not yet qualified, knows more about lung disease than the average medical practitioner.'

The door opened and the young blonde woman who had shown Harry into the sanatorium stood in the doorway.

'Show Mr Evans the private rooms, and explain the treatments we can offer a patient with tuberculosis and pneumoconiosis.'

'A patient suffering from both?'

'A prospective patient.' Dr Adams picked up a newspaper from his desk.

Sensing that he had been dismissed, Harry murmured, 'Thank you, Doctor Adams.'

'My clerk will advise you of our fees and admittance procedure should you decide we have anything to offer your grandfather. If you wish, Miss Adams will take you to his office after your tour. You can give him the details as to when we might expect to receive him. Mr Evans will need a gown and a mask, Diana.' Dr Evans sat on the sofa, picked up the teapot and poured himself a cup of tea, leaving Harry no choice but to follow Diana Adams out of the room.

'The prospective patient is your grandfather?' Miss Adams opened a cupboard in the corridor and handed Harry a white cotton gown and mask identical to the ones she was wearing.

'Yes.' In all respects bar one, it was true, and Harry saw little point in explaining his complicated relationship to his stepfather's father.

'So he must be,' she glanced at Harry, 'sixty years of age or thereabouts?'

'Sixty-five.' Harry wondered how his grandfather would react to being treated by a female medical student. He also speculated on the relationship between the doctor and Diana Adams. Were they father and daughter? Uncle and niece?

'That is rare. Not the pneumoconiosis – we are treating several miners with the illness – but the tuberculosis. The vast majority of patients who contract the disease are under thirty. But then, your grandfather's lungs would be weakened and susceptible to bacteria.'

'Do you have many patients with both conditions?'

'Your grandfather would be the first.' She halted in front of an iron lift cage and pressed a button.

'You have an electric lift,' he commented in surprise.

'As you see. We couldn't run a sanatorium in a building of this layout and size without one. It wasn't purpose-built.'

Her condescending tone irked him even more than Dr Adams's had, because she looked even younger than him. He couldn't resist biting back.

'Even people in Pontypridd have heard of Madame Patti and her home at Craig y Nos, Miss Adams.'

Unabashed, she continued to lecture him in the same patronizing tone. 'This was the first private residence to have electricity in the country. When Madame Patti lived here, it used to take forty tons of coal a day just to generate the power that was needed to heat and light the rooms. However, she had conservatories and a winter garden that has since been dismantled and taken to Swansea. Given that we have no use for tropical plants or exotic birds, and fresh air plays a vital part in our treatments, our present usage is somewhat less.' The cage descended; she opened the metal grille and stepped inside.

Much as he resented her talking down to him, Harry thought of his grandfather and curbed his sarcasm. He held up the mask. 'Is this really necessary?'

'Not if you want to exhale your potentially lethal germs over patients weakened by disease. Or are prepared to risk inhaling tubercle bacilli, without what little protection that mask affords.'

He tied the mask around his neck, and when she pulled up her

45

own mask, he followed suit, covering his nose and mouth. Hoping to inject a friendlier tone into their discussion, he said, 'Doctor Adams mentioned that you've taken a break from your medical studies to work here.'

'His assistant resigned without giving notice. Given my father's workload, I felt I had no other option but to fill the breach. I will be returning to London to continue my studies as soon as he has found a replacement.'

So she was his daughter. The lift juddered to a halt on the top floor and Miss Adams opened the cage door. They stepped out on to a landing furnished with a desk and chair. A masked woman — dressed in the dark blue dress and white starched veil, cuffs and apron of a nursing sister — sat behind it.

Diana Adams nodded acknowledgement and walked on. 'The private rooms are all on this floor in the old servants' quarters. They were considered to be the most suitable to take two beds.'

'We'd prefer my grandfather to have a room to himself.'

'We will take your family's wishes into account, but occupancy depends on demand. At the moment we have more applications for beds than we can accommodate. But my father is always prepared to assist old friends. And Doctor Williams is a very old friend.'

Harry glanced through the open door of a walk-in cupboard. Two girls dressed in the all-white uniform of trainees were folding linen inside. They stopped to curtsy to Miss Adams.

'As you see, all the staff who work on the wards wear masks, Mr Evans. And you will be expected to wear one should you ever visit your grandfather here.' Miss Adams opened the next door they came to and showed him a cheerless room furnished with two iron bedsteads, set at opposite ends of the room, and a pair of scrubbed pine cabinets. There was nothing else, not even drapes at the windows. The floor-length french windows were wide open. Harry walked through them and out onto an iron balcony that overlooked the terraced gardens.

Far on his left a pond gleamed dull pewter through the leaves of encircling trees, its surface unbroken under a cloudy sky. The river flowed from it, cutting through the shrubberies and flowerbeds that tiered upwards on the opposite hillside as well as towards the house. Hearing footsteps, he glanced directly below and saw beds arranged in rows on the terrace.

'Fresh air, Mr Evans.' Miss Adams stood alongside him. 'As I've already explained, it plays a vital role in our treatment here. It is a proven fact that the sun's rays kill bacteria.'

He glanced up at the sky. 'There's not much chance of the sun's rays killing anything today.'

'The sky is not always overcast.'

'And when it rains?'

'The beds are covered with rubber sheets. The patients remain dry while enjoying the benefit of fresh air, which cleanses, disinfects and strengthens their lungs.'

'Surely damp air cannot be good for chest patients?'

'I see you have no medical knowledge, Mr Evans.' She gave him a withering look.

'The room is rather Spartan,' said Harry.

'All the rooms and wards are minimally furnished so they can be easily cleaned and disinfected.'

'I may not have much medical knowledge but I do realize that much.'

'We insist patients' personal property be kept to an essential minimum and everything brought into the sanatorium be subjected to weekly disinfecting.'

'Even books?' He had a sudden image of his grandfather's beloved books disintegrating in a bath of disinfectant.

'Books are allowed on the understanding that they cannot be passed from patient to patient and that they will be burned when the patient leaves.'

'Burned!' Brought up to value and cherish the printed word, Harry was horrified by the prospect.

'Paper harbours bacteria, as can glass, china and cloth. Everything a patient brings within these walls that cannot be disinfected will be destroyed when he or she leaves.'

'Even personal keepsakes like family photographs?' Harry recalled the photographs that filled every inch of shelf space in his grandfather's bedroom. They went everywhere with him, even when he only spent a single night away. Studio portraits of his beloved wife, Isabella, who had died before his mother had met Lloyd. Family groups of his stepfather and uncles when they'd been boys and young men. Wedding pictures of all three. Studies of him and his cousins . . .

'*Especially* photographs,' Miss Adams emphasized, 'because patients tend to handle them more than any other object.'

Harry made a mental note to warn his father to have the photographs copied and not to allow Billy to bring his gold watch, or any of the books he regarded as precious into the sanatorium.

They moved in to the corridor.

'Have you seen all you want to in here, Mr Evans?'

'Yes, thank you.'

Alerted by voices, Miss Adams opened the door next to the room they had visited.

'Excuse me, Mr Evans.'

An emaciated dark-haired man, who could have been anything between forty and sixty years of age, was sitting up in a bed made with cotton sheets and a single white cotton blanket. He had no pillows and his back was propped against a laddered metal backrest that had been pulled out from the headboard.

A man, gowned and masked like Harry, stood beside the bed. He was holding a clipboard and the patient was sketching on a sheet of paper pinned to it. Interested, Harry stepped forward, but Miss Adams snatched the board from the young man's hands and turned it around before he could look at it properly.

'How many times must we tell you that we cannot take any responsibility for your uncle's health while you persist in flaunting our rules, Mr Ross? You know he should lie flat at all times.'

'Don't shout at Toby, Miss Adams. He tried to stop me . . .' The effort of speaking brought on a coughing fit and the patient sprayed the blanket with bright red droplets of blood.

The ward sister left her desk, pushed past Harry and ran to the bed. She slipped her hands behind the man's back and, while supporting him, helped Miss Adams to return the backrest into the frame before lowering him on to the bed.

'I was only sketching,' the patient whispered when he could finally speak again.

'I saw what you were doing, Mr Ross.' Miss Adams looked to the ward sister. 'How long has Mr Toby Ross been here?'

'Five minutes, Miss Adams. And I warned him not to tire his uncle.'

'There will be no further visitors for Mr Ross today or to-morrow.'

'Yes, Miss Adams.'

Diana turned to the visitor. 'I will ask my father to curtail your visits to your uncle altogether if you continue to encourage him to disobey the rules.'

Meekly he muttered 'Yes, Miss Adams.'

'Out, now!' She held the door open.

'I'll see you later, Frank.' The young man glanced at Harry when he left the room, but Harry failed to decipher the expression beneath the mask.

'Could you leave the board on the window sill so I can look at it, Miss Adams?' the patient pleaded.

'Sister will put it and the sketch in the cupboard in the sluice room, which is kept locked. When Doctor Adams considers you well enough, they will be returned.' Miss Adams folded back the blood-stained blanket. 'Re-make Mr Ross's bed with clean linen, Sister.'

'Yes, Miss Adams.'

Harry noticed the same tone of resignation in the sister's voice as the patient's. The Adamses were clearly in control of every aspect of the staff's lives as well as the patients'.

'Are you in pain, Mr Ross?' Diana asked in a marginally softer tone.

'No.'

'Are you certain?'

'I said no,' he repeated hoarsely.

Miss Adams left the room when the trainees arrived with clean linen. She joined Harry and Toby Ross in the corridor.

'He insisted he wasn't tired, Miss Adams—' Toby began.

She cut him short. 'You will not be allowed to see your uncle again until the day after tomorrow, Mr Ross. And then only if he is well enough to receive you, and you adhere to the rules we enforce

49

for *his* benefit. You will also leave the door to his room open so the sister can supervise your visit.'

'Could I possibly look at the sketch, Miss Adams, just for a moment?' he begged.

To Harry's amazement Miss Adams held out the board. Toby Ross studied it, pulled a small book from his pocket, scribbled down a few notes and a tiny rough sketch.

'Thank you, Miss Adams.' There wasn't a hint of sarcasm in his voice.

'You do realize that our only concern is your uncle's health, Mr Ross?' she said earnestly.

'Of course, and so does he. But you also have to understand, Miss Adams, my uncle's health depends on his art. He cannot survive without it.'

'Which is the only reason we haven't banned you permanently from Craig y Nos. Goodbye, Mr Ross. Don't forget to leave your mask and gown in the dirty linen bin.' She turned to Harry. 'Shall we continue our tour, Mr Evans?'

Mary worked solidly through the morning. She couldn't stop the occasional thought of Bob Pritchard arising while she scrubbed, scoured, cleaned and churned, but she could, and did, drive it out instantly, because she knew that if she didn't, she'd go out of her mind.

The agent had taken at least 80 pounds' worth of livestock and produce for a 40-pound payment they'd never see in cash, and reduced their rent arrears by only 10 pounds because of 'interest payments'. She suspected that next quarter their arrears would be back to 120 pounds – if not more – because no matter how much produce and money they managed to scrape together to give to him, he never reduced their debt to less than 100 pounds.

Bob Pritchard made a show of marking everything he took from them in his book, but she knew he was aware that, like their parents, neither she nor her brothers and sister could read. She suspected he was cheating them, but she didn't dare challenge him. Not when he had the power to throw them out of the only home they had ever known.

His threats weren't idle. He had made them to their neighbours and carried them out. Their stockman Albert Jones and his wife Lizzie, who had worked for her father in better times, as well as two other families who had been their closest neighbours, had been evicted from their cottages by bailiffs called in by Bob Pritchard. They had been thrown out on Christmas Eve when the snow had been lying six inches thick on the ground. The agent had even boasted that they would have had an eighteen-mile walk to the workhouse if it hadn't been for his generosity in providing a cart to take them there. And after they'd left, he had supervised the removal of their possessions and furniture, sending everything to Brecon before boarding up the windows and doors on their houses.

'Didn't you hear me calling?' Bob moved into the doorway of the dairy, blocking out the light.

'No.' Mary dropped the handle of the butter churn and instinctively backed away.

'I'm late because I had to go to Sennybridge to oversee the eviction of a family who were eighty pounds in rent arrears.' He smiled coldly when he saw his announcement had the effect he'd intended. 'Where are your brothers?'

'They've driven down to Pontardawe to pick up our goods.'

He approached; she retreated. He slammed her back into the stone wall, she cried out. He yanked the string from her hair, sank his fingers into her long black curls and pulled her to the door. Once there, he pushed her across the yard and into the house. There was no point in crying out because there was no one to hear and Mary knew better than to struggle or complain.

Stepping into the kitchen ahead of her, he dragged her through to the passage and into the hall at the front of the house.

'That family I was telling you about in Sennybridge. The wife cried like a baby when they took the children away on a separate cart. They may all be going to Llanfaes Workhouse but she knew that the women's wards are in a different block to the children's, and the young ones are usually taken as servants by farmers before the old, because there's more work in them and they're easier to train. It's unlikely she'll see them again. And if she does, it won't be for years, if in this life.' He punched her in the small of her back and she fell, face down, on the stairs. 'Is that what you want for your brothers and sister?'

'No!'

'Don't ever tell me that I didn't give you a choice.'

She rose to her feet and walked up the stairs. He followed and shoved her into the largest bedroom. 'Undress! Down to your skin, you filthy bitch. I won't touch you if you haven't washed.'

She turned her face to the wall, kicked off her broken boots and unbuttoned the working shirt that had been her father's. Dropping it to the floor because there was nowhere else to put it, she unfastened the cotton skirt that, along with her combination underclothes, had belonged to her mother. Like all of the family's clothes, they had been bought in 1919, the last year her family had been free from debt.

'Only sluts don't wear stockings,' he jeered.

'I can't afford them,' she whispered, acutely aware of him staring at her naked back.

'Don't plead poverty to me. I know how much goes from this farm in the direction of Craig y Nos and the shops in Pontardawe. Lie on the bed.'

Trembling, she folded back the top sheet and patchwork quilt she had helped her mother stitch. He unbuttoned his trousers, dropped them along with his drawers and heaved himself on top of her.

Spittle drooled from his fleshy lips, dribbling over his double chin on to her neck, as he fondled her breasts with one hand and thrust the other between her legs.

She closed her eyes and steeled herself for what was to come.

'Fight,' he commanded.

She kept her eyes tightly closed.

'Fight!' He pinched her nipple and she cried out. 'I'll hurt you more if you won't fight.' When she failed to move, he lowered his head and sank his teeth into her breast. Tears started into her eyes but she remained still.

He closed his hand around her throat. 'Open your eyes.'

Terrified by the pressure of his fingers on her windpipe, she did as he commanded.

'Keep them open. If you're too cowardly to fight, the least you can do is look afraid.' It was the last thing he said before he raped her.

Chapter 4

MARY TURNED her back to Bob Pritchard and her face to the wall when he had finished using her. The straw mattress crackled as he shifted his weight and left the bed. She heard the whisper of wool and linen when he buttoned his trousers and straightened his clothes.

'If you want to carry on living here, you should try harder to please me, Mary.' He grabbed her chin in his hand and wrenched her head until she faced him. 'Look at me when I speak to you!'

She opened her eyes but focused inwards, anywhere but on him.

'And you'd better have more livestock ready for market next quarter than you had this one. I'll call in the next time I'm round this way to see how you're getting on.' He released her and she turned back to the wall. The door creaked when he opened it. 'Did you hear me?'

'Yes, Mr Pritchard.'

'*Sir*, always, *sir*, girl,' he reprimanded sharply.

'Sorry, sir.' Her tears soaked into the pillow she'd stuffed with goose-down.

'And a word of advice – keep that brother of yours in check, or I'll be forced to take action.'

'Yes, sir.'

His footsteps echoed down the wooden staircase, the back door slammed, but she didn't leave the bed until she heard the wheels of the trap rattle over the cobbles in the yard. Swinging her legs to the floor, she left the bed, wrapped herself in the bottom sheet and crossed the landing into the narrow room built into the archway that spanned the two halves of the farmhouse. Taking care that she couldn't be seen from outside, she moved to the side of the window and watched the agent drive up the road that led to Brecon.

She felt dirtier than when she spent a day scrubbing out the pigsties and cowsheds. Cleaning up after animals was filthy but honest work. The things Bob Pritchard did to her were foul and degrading, and if it weren't for her brothers and sister, she would have killed herself the first time he'd violated her.

But before her mother had died, she had made Mary promise that she would care for her brothers and Martha until they were old enough to care for themselves. Her mother hadn't needed to elaborate. Martha was young, but not too young to attract the attention of the agent.

She ran down the stairs to the stone scullery behind the kitchen that housed the well. Turning the wheel, she drew up a bucket of freezing cold water. Throwing the scrubbing brush and a sliver of a green carbolic soap into the enormous stone sink that almost filled the room, she rubbed the soap on to the brush and began to scrub every inch of her skin. Her face, her neck, her breasts - still sticky with his spittle – between her thighs, her chest, her arms and legs, and she didn't stop, not even when the scratches she'd raised began to bleed.

'I think I've shown you everything you need to see, Mr Evans.'

'I am grateful for the tour, Miss Adams.' Harry followed Diana Adams along the corridor to a dark-wood staircase.

'The rooms on the floor below were the principal bedrooms when the castle was a private residence. We have turned them into small wards. Some have four beds, some six. But there are no patients in them at present. They are all outside, either on the terrace or the balconies.'

'Yet Mr Ross was still in his room?' When Miss Adams didn't comment, Harry realized the man was too ill to be moved.

Miss Adams led him down to the ground floor. She showed him the modern X-ray equipment and pointed to a closed door labelled, 'Silence – Operating Theatre'.

'Although it's not in use today, it's kept sterile so I can't take you in there.'

'Doctor Williams warned us that it wouldn't be possible to operate on my grandfather.'

'Not if his lungs are also affected by pneumoconiosis.'

'So, all you can really offer my grandfather is fresh air?' Harry only realized how that sounded after he'd spoken. 'I'm sorry, I don't mean that as a criticism. He will be getting precious little of that in the isolation ward of the infirmary he is in at present.'

'Fresh air, the benefit of our medical expertise and the twenty-four-hour care and attention of qualified and trained nurses and doctors in antiseptically clean surroundings designed to prevent the contraction and spread of secondary infections,' she recited as though she were reading from a brochure. 'You know there are no drugs that can cure his condition?'

'Yes.' Harry knew it, but he wished that Miss Adams and her father wouldn't emphasize the fact.

'But there are medicines that will help control his pain and make him comfortable. My father is also a great believer in a healthy, nourishing diet rich in fish oils.' She looked at him, and he noticed that her eyes were darker than his, almost navy blue, but there wasn't any warmth in their depths. 'I would rather that you had not witnessed my argument with Mr Ross, Mr Evans. It may have given you the impression that our rules are unduly harsh. But they are designed not only for the benefit of our patients but also to stop the spread of the disease within our staff and any visitors.'

'I realize that, Miss Adams.' Harry hadn't been quite so irritated by anyone since his schooldays when he'd been subjected to the teachings of masters prone to over-explanation.

'There is one more thing you should see before you come to any firm decision about your grandfather's treatment.'

They left the main building and walked down outside corridors which were obviously recent additions.

They stepped on to a covered, paved yard, surrounded on three sides by what seemed to be workshops of some sort. Harry assumed they had been the stables, outside dairies, stillrooms and storerooms when Craig y Nos had been a private residence.

'This roof was erected by Madame Patti so she could leave and enter her carriage without getting wet. She couldn't afford to catch cold, when her voice was her fortune.'

A middle-aged hunchback with yellow skin opened the door to one of the workshops. 'You need a box, Miss Adams?'

'No, thank you, Fred, not now. I'm showing Mr Evans around the sanatorium.'

Fred touched his cap and retreated, but not before Harry saw that the floor of the workshop behind him was covered in wood shavings and sawdust. A half-finished coffin, resting on trestles, stood in the centre of the room.

'You make your own coffins?'

'Yes.'

Harry took a deep breath. He dreaded the answer but he had to ask the question. 'Do you have many deaths here?'

'Yes, Mr Evans.'

'How many people do you cure?'

' "Cure" ' is not a word my father chooses to use. Tuberculosis weakens the system. What may appear to be a full recovery is frequently reversed when a patient returns to poor living conditions, or a less than healthy way of life. Insufficient rest, drink, poor diet, a strenuous job – one or all of those things can precipitate a relapse.'

'And if the patient returns to an ideal home life, with a good diet and plenty of rest?'

Seeing that he wasn't prepared to be fobbed off, she said, 'Twenty per cent of the patients who have entered Craig y Nos since my father took his post have been certified sufficiently free from infection to be returned to their homes.'

'Two out of ten,' he murmured. That moment he realized he had yet to accept his grandfather was going to die. He was still hoping against hope for a miracle that would save his life.

'I have to visit the children's ward. If you have decided to bring your grandfather here, you will find the clerk in the office. It is the third door on the right down that corridor.' She pointed to her left.

'May I see the children's ward?'

'Why?'

Miss Adams's curt, professional manner had made Harry curious to see how she behaved around children, but he could hardly admit that was his reason. 'I'd like to see the facilities you offer children,' he answered lamely.

'They are exactly the same as the ones we offer adults, but if you want to inspect them, keep your mask over your face. Children are just as contagious.'

They entered a ballroom-sized, light and airy conservatory that overlooked the gardens at the back of the house. Not all of the beds had been pushed outside and Harry blanched when he saw children the same age as his brother, Glyn, and even younger, lying pale, wan and skeletally thin in cots, their faces as white as the sheets drawn to their chins.

'Miss Diana?' a girl called out when they approached her bed. She smiled when Miss Adams turned to her.

'I'll be in to see you – all of you – at teatime. And, I happen to know there's a surprise.'

'Oranges!' one young boy cried hopefully.

'Not oranges, Aled, but something just as nice.' She walked between the rows of cots and beds, and Harry noted that she knew every patient by name and had something personal to say to each of them. All the patients were lying flat on their backs, some in contraptions that resembled straitjackets, and he couldn't help feeling that they must be bored witless with nothing to do other than stare up at the skylights.

He wanted to help, to say something comforting to the children who gazed at him with searching, trusting eyes, but to his embarrassment he couldn't think of a single thing. So intensely grateful for his good health that he was almost ashamed of it, he left the conservatory, turned his back on the rows of beds on the terrace, pulled his mask from his face and walked away from the sanatorium.

Inhaling the 'fresh air' that was all Craig y Nos really had to offer its patients, despite what Diana Adams had said, he strode down the paths and stone steps that linked the flowerbeds and shrubberies, and headed for the river. He crossed a narrow footbridge and looked back at the castle. Its massive grey bulk towered above the trees, seemingly even larger and more imposing from the back. Perched high on the hill overlooking the valley, it dominated the beautiful and lonely countryside.

It was ideally placed for quarantining people with a virulently infectious disease that proved fatal in eight out of ten cases.

Mary returned to her bedroom as soon as she had dried and dressed herself. She stripped the linen from her bed and bundled it downstairs. Dragging the iron bucket to the well, she filled it with water and set it on the range to boil. Hoping that David wouldn't forget to buy soap, she grated the last of what she had into the wooden laundry tub. When the water started bubbling, she poured it in, whipped the suds into lather, threw in the sheets, bolster and pillowcases, and pounded all trace of the smell and sweat of the hated agent from them with the dolly until her arms ached and she no longer had the strength to lift or twist the wooden pole.

Only then did she tip the tub into the stone sink and rinse the bedding in fresh water. After wringing out as much water as she could with her bare hands, she tossed the linen back into the tub and carried it out to the washing line behind the yard. Pegging the sheets, pillowcases and bolster securely with dolly pegs, she hauled the line high and knotted it securely around the nails her father had hammered into the pole.

Exhausted, consumed by loathing for the agent and herself for allowing him to use her, she sank down on the grass. The day was balmy, the sun warm on her bare head and arms. She looked down the hill to the reservoir on the valley floor. Built the year she had been born, it glittered blue and beautiful with the reflected light of the sky and the flickering images of the bare hills that encircled it.

Her father had told her that he hadn't wanted Swansea Council to flood the valley but the agent before Bob Pritchard had told him their landlord had no choice but to sell the council the best grazing land on the Ellis Estate. If he refused, he would have been taken to court, fined more money than most people saw in a lifetime and still lose the land because it was needed to generate electricity for the town of Swansea. Although what a reservoir of water had to do with electricity had been a mystery to her father and remained one to the entire family.

But when all the local objections had been ignored, and the inevitable had happened, her mother said it had been a blessing in disguise because the only thing that could have possibly made the view from the back of their house more beautiful was water. And although Swansea might think it owned Crai Reservoir, it didn't, because the only people who saw it every day were the Ellises. Her mother had come to regard the reservoir as the Ellises' private lake, and so did Mary.

No matter what she did around the farm she was aware of its presence. As the seasons changed so did the reservoir. Its surface, cold, dark and brooding under winter skies, was transformed by the sun. Sparkling and fairy-like in spring and summer, it became wild, windswept and rough when autumn winds blew down the valley from the hills.

Sometimes, she dreamed that she was walking towards it for the very last time, because once she reached its edge, she would carry on walking until the waters closed over her head. And then she'd feel nothing . . . be nothing . . .

A breeze ruffled her washing and a wet sheet slapped her face. Jolted back to the present, she thought of her brothers, shopping in Pontardawe, and Martha working in Craig y Nos. For their sake she had no choice but to carry on.

She returned to the yard and picked up a wheelbarrow and spade from the barn. An hour later she had dug up enough carrots, potatoes, onions and parsnips to make a vegetable stew for their supper, and cut leeks and beans to flavour it. The raspberry canes, which had never done well, yielded enough fruit for a small summer pudding. She stacked the vegetables carefully, balanced the spade on top and wheeled the barrow back into the yard.

A flurry of wings and high-pitched cackling alerted her to a fracas amongst the chickens. One of the Leghorns was attacking a smaller Friesian bird, pecking it savagely and aiming for its eyes. The Friesian was valiantly trying to retaliate, in between dodging its attacker's beak, but it was no match for Leghorn, and blood seeped down its feathers from the wounds on its head.

Mary dropped the handles on the barrow. She saw the vegetables and fruit rolling over the dirty cobbles, but the sight that would have normally appalled her barely registered. She dived on both birds and caught the Leghorn at her second attempt.

Everything went blank until she was conscious of a pain in her leg and she realized she was on the ground. The handle of the barrow was digging into her thigh. Birds were flocking around her, and to her dismay she saw they were pecking at the fruit and vegetables that had taken her over an hour to harvest.

Her hands were warm and sticky. She looked down and saw that she was holding the severed head of the Leghorn in one hand and its body in the other. Blood flowed sluggishly from its neck, soaking her fingers and her skirt. She had wrung its neck and from the mangled state of the head, used more force than necessary.

It had been one of the finest white Leghorns they had bred. Martha had named it Bounty because it had been their best layer. She stared at its dull, lifeless eyes, fingered its clawed feet and began to cry – harsh, rasping sobs that startled the birds and set the dogs barking.

She had no memory of killing the bird. Was she going mad? What if she had attacked a person – Bob Pritchard, for instance? If she hurt him, he would take revenge on her family. Then she recalled his strength. She couldn't hurt him, but she was strong enough to hurt Luke, Matthew and Martha. And even David was a sound sleeper. What if she attacked him one night the way she had the chicken?

She sank her head on to the limp, feathered body and continued to weep. She had never felt so utterly alone. She had her sister and brothers, but she couldn't burden their childhoods by telling them what the agent was doing to her. Much as she loved them, there were times, like now, when she felt the responsibility of caring for them crushing down on her like an enormous weight that prevented her from breathing.

She had no idea how long she sat there cradling the bloody body of the hen amongst the wreckage. She only knew that she had to carry on as best she could. Chickens were too precious to be eaten by her or her family. Even the eggs were hoarded to be sold, and in winter they went without rather than send short measure to the sanatorium or the shop. Whenever she killed a chicken, duck, or goose, it was for market.

But would it be so awful for them to eat one of their own birds? Just this once. She looked down at the corpse and spoiled fruit and vegetables. She couldn't let food go to waste. But neither could she do anything else until she'd set her skirt to soak. Blood stained worse than anything else. She'd change, salvage what she could, pluck the chicken and put it in the stew – or better still, roast it in the oven. She'd tell David that it had been wounded in a fight with another bird, which wasn't so very far from the truth.

She struggled to her feet. She couldn't wash her clothes until David returned with soap, but she could soak them in cold water and salt to bleach the stain. And after she'd changed, she'd prepare the meal. By then it would be time to drive the cows from the fields into the shed for milking. She hoped David would be back to help her. She was tired and what remained of the day stretched ahead, with more work to be done than there was time left to do it in. And all she really wanted to do was curl up in bed, close her eyes and sink into oblivion.

Life would be more bearable if she could see a time, no matter how far into the future, when things would be better. When her family would be able to hold their heads high again because they didn't owe anyone a penny and there'd be no agent to take everything they owned away from them – including her self-respect.

Harry wandered aimlessly around the gardens for over an hour before making his way back to the house. Taking a wrong turn, he was soon hopelessly lost in a maze of modern annexes and old servants' quarters. After ten minutes spent trying to orientate himself, he was relieved to see Diana Adams through the window of a very different ward to the ones they had visited.

It was filled with young women who were all sitting up in beds or on chairs, with cushions plumped behind their backs. Mask pulled down, Diana Adams smiled as she chatted and admired the embroidery and knitting they held up for her inspection. She glanced up and saw him through the window. Leaving the ward, she joined him.

'You are lost, Mr Evans?'

He knew from the tone of her voice that she was annoyed he'd seen her. 'I am.'

'I'll take you back to the main entrance.' She went ahead of him.

'Do those patients have tuberculosis?'

'They did.'

'They've recovered?'

'The patients on that ward are undergoing weekly tests. When we are absolutely certain that they are no longer contagious, and consider them strong enough, we discharge them to their homes.'

'Then they are cured?'

'I told you my father is reluctant to use that word, Mr Evans. But yes, some of them will make up the twenty per cent of patients who walk out of Craig y Nos.'

'How long have they been here?'

'Some have been here since my father took over the management of the sanatorium five years ago, in nineteen twenty-one. Two of the girls have been with us for less than a year, but that is an unusually short stay.'

'A year,' he said thoughtfully. 'You must get to know your patients really well.'

'My father discourages close relationships between staff and patients, Mr Evans.'

It was then Harry realized what should have been obvious from the outset. Diana Adams's offhand manner was a defence mechanism. No one could afford to get emotionally involved with so many terminally ill patients. It would be soul-destroying. But she could let her guard down with those in the recovery ward, because, thanks to her father's treatments and the care they had received in Craig y Nos, they still had their lives ahead of them.

'Miss Adams,' he walked out into the covered yard alongside her, 'would you be kind enough to take me to your father's clerk so I can make arrangements to have my grandfather admitted here tomorrow?'

'Yes, Mr Evans.' For the first time since she had opened the

63

front door to him he saw a hint of sympathy and commiseration in her dark blue eyes.

'I would be grateful if you could recommend a place where I could rent a room tonight.'

'The inn at Abercrave has rooms.'

'The one four miles down the road?'

'It's the only other building in the valley with a telephone, Mr Evans. And there are occasions when we need to get in touch with relatives of our patients urgently. Good day.'

'I won't forget, Dad. You'll be arriving at Penwyllt station at eleven o'clock . . . Doctor Williams has asked Doctor Adams to send an ambulance . . . 'I'll be there as well. I'm sorry there's no change in Edyth. How is Mam coping?'

The crackling on the telephone line drowned out the end of Lloyd's answer. Harry raised his voice in the hope that his stepfather could still hear him.

'. . . Yes, the countryside around the sanatorium is beautiful, Dad. As to whether Granddad will be happy there . . . I doubt it, because he'll be so far away from the family . . . I can't hear you, but I hope you can still hear me. Love to everyone.' The line went dead before Harry finished shouting the last sentence. Exasperated, he replaced the telephone and receiver on the rickety card table.

'Did you get through all right, Mr Evans?' Mrs Edwards asked when he left the tiny room, no bigger than a broom cupboard, which she had grandly referred to as 'the office'. There wasn't even a chair. All it contained besides the table and telephone was a rough set of shelves that housed haphazard bundles of invoices and bills held together by elastic bands.

'Yes, I did thank you, Mrs Edwards. Although I was cut off before I finished.'

'When I booked the call with the exchange, I asked them to give you the full two and a half minutes.'

'I would have liked five.'

'The exchange gives priority to Craig y Nos. They don't like us tying up the line for any longer in case they have an emergency and need to contact relatives.' She lifted the account book she kept beneath the bar on to the counter. 'I'll put the call on your bill, Mr Evans?'

'I'll pay you now, Mrs Edwards.' Harry thrust his hand into his pocket and pulled out a fistful of change.

'When you leave will be fine. I'll add your bar bill to your board and lodge as well, if you like.'

'That's good of you, Mrs Edwards. I'll have a pint of beer now, please.' After three years in Oxford when he'd had to pay for a full term's accommodation in advance, Harry found this attitude to money refreshingly trusting. Mrs Edwards had refused the five shillings he'd offered her for a night's food and accommodation when he'd arrived, on the grounds that she liked her customers 'to be satisfied', adding that if he thought a meal 'wasn't right' she wouldn't charge him for it. And he'd practically had to press the cost of the tyre repair on Alf, who'd insisted he could pay him 'anytime' once he'd discovered that he'd booked into the inn.

'Does the room Enfys showed you suit?' She pulled a dark-amber pint of ale with a creamy head, and pushed it over the counter towards him.

'Enfys?' Harry asked blankly.

'The maid.'

He recalled the red-faced, red-haired serving maid, who'd puffed and panted up the stairs ahead of him, and thrown a bed-room door open before walking on silently down the passage.

'It's fine, thank you, Mrs Edwards.' The room was perfectly adequate but it wouldn't have met with Diana Adams's approval. There were far too many things in it that could harbour germs. The floorboards were covered with rag rugs, the bed was made with a quilt as well as Welsh flannel blankets and feather-filled pillows and bolster. And there was an upholstered easy chair and a writing table in addition to the pine bedroom suite. The furniture was solid and built for durability rather than beauty. Recalling Alf saying that the pieces he made 'seemed to suit the farmers round here', Harry wondered if they were examples of his handiwork. To his amazement the room also had electric light.

'Enfys will serve you supper in the dining parlour,' Mrs Edwards indicated a door in the corridor behind the bar. 'It's steak and kidney pudding, boiled potatoes, peas and carrots tonight, with rhubarb and custard for afters. If you want more beer, there's no need to disturb yourself, just bang the table or call out and Enfys will get it for you.'

'Thank you, Mrs Edwards.'

'I've only one other young man lodging here at present. He'll share the dining parlour with you.'

'And here he is, Mrs Edwards.' A slim man, as dark as Harry was fair, walked down the narrow passageway towards them. 'Good evening.' Juggling the knapsack, easel and folder he was carrying, he freed one hand so he could lift his hat to Mrs Edwards.

'Been off painting again, Mr Ross?'

'You know me so well, Mrs Edwards. A pint of your best, please. Painting's thirsty work.' He set down the easel and folder, turned to Harry and held out his hand. 'Toby Ross.'

Harry shook it firmly. 'Harry Evans.'

'I hope the dressing-down Miss Adams gave me earlier hasn't coloured your opinion of me.' He picked up the pint of beer Mrs Edwards had pulled for him and downed half of it in one thirsty swallow.

'Toby Ross – that was you behind the mask at the sanatorium?'

'It was. Please, call me Toby. I'll dump these things in my room, wash my hands and I'll be with you.' To Harry's astonishment he finished his pint in a second gulp. 'I'll have another with a whisky chaser when I come down, please, Mrs Edwards.'

'He's an artist,' Mrs Edwards confided superfluously after Toby ran up the stairs. 'So's his uncle. He's famous and paints pictures that get put in books. But by all accounts he's in a bad way. That's why Mr Ross spends all his time painting, trying to do as much of his work for him as he can.'

'Frank Ross!' Harry exclaimed.

'I think that's his name,' Mrs Edwards poured a measure of whisky into a glass.

'To think that I met Frank Ross today, and didn't know who he was. He's been my idol for years. You should have seen his exhibition in London two years ago. The way he blended the colours—'

'You met Mr Ross's uncle in the sanatorium! You were in the same room as him?' Mrs Edwards exclaimed in horror.

'All visitors are gowned and masked,' Harry assured her.

'Well,' Mrs Edwards set about refilling Toby's pint mug, 'those precautions Mr Ross is always telling me about had better work, that's all I can say. It's a mystery to me why they had to go and put a lot of infectious people in Madame Patti's castle in the first place. Poor woman would turn in her grave if she could see what they've done to her home. It was lovely in her day, and I should know. The late Mr Edwards and me were up there often enough, serving stout and ale at the parties she gave the locals. If we get any more cases of TB in the valley than we had in her time, we'll know exactly where to lay the blame.'

'The doctor in charge and his staff take every precaution not to spread the disease outside of the castle, Mrs Edwards.'

She sniffed loudly. 'Is the gentlemen's supper ready?' she asked Enfys, who had emerged from the kitchen quarters at the back of the inn with a tray of crockery and cutlery.

Enfys nodded and disappeared into the dining parlour. Harry wondered if she were a mute or simply chose not to speak.

'Thank you again for arranging the telephone call, Mrs Edwards.' He picked up his beer and followed Enfys into the parlour, which was furnished with an enormous oak dresser, long table and ten chairs. The walls were papered in a red stripe that wavered over every uneven bump and lump in the plaster.

Toby Ross joined him a few minutes later, carrying his beer and whisky. He took the chair at the head of the table. 'Cheers.' he lifted his mug and sipped it.

'Cheers.' Harry lifted his own glass.

'So, what were you doing at the sanatorium in the company of the Snow Queen?'

Harry laughed. 'Who christened Miss Adams that?'

'My uncle. He finds it preferable to believe she's incapable of loving any man because her heart has been penetrated by an icicle than to accept her rejection of his advances.'

'Even after hearing Miss Adams call you both Mr Ross and

seeing your uncle sketching, I didn't realize your uncle was *the* Frank Ross. Mrs Edwards just told me.'

'The one and only.' Toby sat back so Enfys could set a plate of steaming steak and kidney pudding and vegetables smothered in gravy in front of him. 'At the risk of being thought rude and repeating myself, why *were* you at Craig y Nos?'

'My grandfather will be a patient there from tomorrow.'

'Tuberculosis?' Toby sprinkled his plate with salt.

'And pneumoconiosis.'

'Then there's no hope.'

'None.' Harry almost choked on the word.

'There isn't for my uncle. Not that I think of Frank as my uncle. He is, but he's only eight years older than me, so we've been more like brothers than uncle and nephew. Especially since he became my guardian after my parents drowned when the *Lusitania* went down eleven years ago.' Toby picked up his knife and fork and cut into the suet pastry.

'Eight years,' Harry repeated in surprise. 'But you can't be much more than twenty-one.'

'Twenty-five. Frank is thirty-three but these days he looks more like sixty. I take it from what you've said that you're familiar with his work?'

'I love it,' Harry enthused. 'I read English Literature at Oxford but I've always wanted to study art. His illustrations for Chaucer's *Canterbury Tales* and *The Shakespeare Folios* were magnificent. I spent hours studying them when I should have been reading the text. But that's not to say his other illustrations aren't as good. It's just that those are my favourites.'

'He's been commissioned to illustrate Malory's *Le Morte d'Arthur*. The publisher almost had a fit when Frank was diagnosed. He wanted to commission another artist, but after some argument he agreed that as long as Frank planned out and oversaw the designs, I could do the actual sketching and painting. That's not to say I have any illusions about my talent. I'm the apprentice to Frank's master. As you saw today, the creation and the ideas are all his. All I do is flesh out his drafts into a poor approximation of what he would do if he were well enough.'

'You've studied art?'

'Three years at the Slade.'

'I would give my eye-teeth and every other tooth in my head to do that,' Harry said enviously.

'The Slade's cheaper than Oxford. So why didn't you?' Toby questioned bluntly.

'It's a long story.' Loath to go into details about his inheritance, he added, 'Basically I went to Oxford to please other people.'

'Frank says life's too short to please anyone other than yourself,' Tony held his fork poised in front of his mouth. 'And given where he is now, he's been proved right.'

'It must be wonderful to spend all your time working on something you're passionate about.'

'It is,' Toby agreed. 'But although I make a somewhat precarious living as an artist I don't consider myself one. Every time I look at one of Frank's paintings or sketches I feel a fraud.' He washed down a piece of pudding with a mouthful of beer. 'But I have been given a few jobs on my own merit, and I like to think they didn't know who my uncle was at the time. Nothing important, just illustrations for children's story books and pantomime posters. Frank couldn't have been prouder of me. But I wish I'd never taken them. They kept me in London while he went off to Paris to hold an exhibition. By the time I joined him two months later he was already coughing up blood.'

'You couldn't have stopped him from contracting the disease.'

'No,' Toby agreed grimly. 'But if I had been around I would have seen and recognized the early symptoms and stopped him from working all day and drinking all night, which is what he always does whenever he lives in Paris. Then, perhaps, the disease wouldn't have taken such a swift hold. Doctor Adams told me there was no hope for Frank the first time he examined him.'

'That must have been tough.' Harry finished his beer and looked around for Enfys.

'Bang your mug on the table and the silent one will appear.' Toby helped himself to an extra spoonful of mint sauce.

'Does she ever speak?' Harry lifted his mug and tapped it on the table.

'Not that I've heard. So you're staying here in the valley?' Toby finished the beer in his glass and handed it to Enfys when she appeared to pick up Harry's.

'Tonight. After that I'm not sure. My sister's ill in Pontypridd and, like the rest of my family, I'm torn between wanting to stay with her and my grandfather.'

'Doctor Adams won't allow you to visit your grandfather often,' Toby warned.

'But I hope to be on hand when he will.'

'What do you want to paint?'

'I'm not sure. And I'm not in your or your uncle's class. I'm only an amateur, and a bad one at that,' Harry qualified hastily, embarrassed at confiding his ambitions to a professional. 'I had planned to go to Paris in the hope of finding out if I have any talent worth developing, but that was before my grandfather was diagnosed.'

'You must have had some idea of what you wanted to study there?' Toby insisted.

'I would have liked to experiment with different techniques. I've finished a few watercolours, mainly land and seascapes, and I've sketched portraits of my sisters.' He gave a deprecating smile. 'You know how it is. My family think I'm brilliant. I know I'm not much of an artist, not yet anyway, and perhaps never will be, but I want to try.'

'I don't know how it is with a family, because since my parents drowned, the only family I've had is Frank and he's a brutal critic. But compared to him I'll always be third rate.'

'So would Beardsley,' Harry added drily.

'You're welcome to whatever little I can teach you when you're here. It will be good to have company.'

Much as Harry wanted to accept Toby's offer, he was reluctant to impose on him. 'I told you I'm an amateur. I'll probably bore you to death.'

'I doubt it. Have you looked at what's around here? If it weren't for Malory, God bless him, and trying to do justice to Frank's ideas on illustrating *Le Morte d'Arthur*, I'd be spending all my days in the bar just so I could talk to another human being as opposed to sheep.

And, as you see – thank you,' he lifted one of the beer mugs Enfys set on the table 'I drink more than is good for me already. Do you have materials?'

'Not with me.'

'Next time you come, bring some. If the weather is good, you can come out with me. I'm painting one of the lanes that leads out of Craig y Nos. It's not the road to Camelot, but by the time I've finished, it will be. How do you think Mrs Edwards would look as the elderly Morgan le Fay?'

'She's far too jolly and nice.'

'I was afraid you'd say that. Besides, I really want to paint her when she's young, before she seduces Arthur. How about the Snow Queen as Guinevere?'

It was the oddest conversation Harry had ever had with someone he'd just met. 'She has the right colouring and she's pretty enough.'

'Pretty and regal, but my uncle is right – her heart has been penetrated by an icicle, and it shows. Which is fine except when she's with Lancelot. Do you think, if I ask her nicely, she'll fall in love for me so I can capture the right expression for their first meeting? Frank insists that painting should be the highlight of the book.' It was an idiotic question but Toby appeared to be perfectly serious.

'Who do you think she should fall in love with?' Harry forked the last morsel of pudding to his mouth.

'You, there's no one else the right age and class around.'

'There's you.' Harry pulled his beer towards him.

'I tried, got absolutely nowhere, and have the ice burns to prove it. In her eyes I am the proverbial dust beneath her feet.' Toby handed Enfys his plate when she came to clear them. 'How are you at seducing women?'

'Useless,' Harry lied.

'This would be in the cause of art.'

'Still useless, even in the cause of art.'

'Then I'll just have to keep looking.'

'For another Guinevere or a man to seduce the Snow Queen?' Harry enquired in amusement.

'Both, if necessary.' Toby stared down unenthusiastically at the bowl of rhubarb and custard Enfys had set in front of him. 'Want to come up to my room and see what I've done? Some of the canvases have already gone up to London, but I've kept sketches.'

'Please.' Harry stood, and Toby followed suit.

'We'll pick up another couple of beers and whiskies on the way.'

Chapter 5

DAVID TOOK the rock Mary handed him and placed it on the lowest layer of the dry-stone sheep-pen wall they were repairing. Whichever way he laid it, he only had to touch it with the tip of his finger for it to move. He pushed it out in disgust and it landed with a thud on the sodden grass.

'This is no good, Mary,' he grumbled, 'I need a flatter one.'

She turned up the collar of her old shirt against the rain, and pulled the peak of one of her father's flat caps over her eyes. The fine weather had ended abruptly at dawn, and rain had teemed down in solid, skin-drenching downpours ever since. 'I'm searching for all the stones that might have been a part of the wall. It looked like a capping stone.'

'It may well have been,' he retorted impatiently, 'but there's a bloody big hole here and I'm a long way from needing capping stones.'

'Don't swear,' she said automatically.

'Our life is enough to make St David swear. Just look at us!' He turned his face up to the sky and closed his eyes as rain streamed into them. 'Grubbing around for stones on the side of a hill in a cloudburst, to mend a wall that was probably built a thousand years ago and has been past saving for the last four hundred. And for what?'

'So the lambs can't escape after you've rounded them up ready for market, like they did yesterday,' she retorted crossly. 'You heard Bob Pritchard's men. He'll knock at least a fiver off the forty he said he'd pay us to compensate for the loss.'

'Those lambs didn't escape. Bob Prichard's men stole them when they went to pick up stock from Pwllcoedlog Farm.'

She sank back on her heels and examined her calloused fingers. 'We can't prove that.'

'We can't prove he's diddling us either, but you know as well as I do that he is.' He wiped his face in the grey blanket that he had thrown over his shoulders to protect his back, not that it was any drier than the rest of his clothes. He lifted the next stone she handed him with both hands and allowed it to fall to the floor of the pen. 'I said flat, Mary.'

'It's difficult to see the difference between the ones that have fallen off the wall and the ones that are just lying around.' She glanced down the hill and through the archway to the open door of the barn where Matthew, with Luke's hindrance, was cleaning out the chicken coops. 'Here, try this one.' She handed him another.

He slotted it into place, and tested it by leaning his full weight on it to ensure that it would provide a firm bed for the next layer. 'Ianto Myles has joined the army.' He spoke casually but she wasn't fooled by his matter-of-fact tone.

'The dairyman's son from Pontardawe?'

'Yes.'

'He's not much older than you, is he?' she asked cautiously.

'Eighteen months. He was sixteen last week and he went down the drill hall the day after his birthday.'

'I'm surprised they took him.'

'They take boys at sixteen,' he informed her authoritatively.

'I'm even more surprised his father let him go.' She lined up three of the flattest stones within easy reach. 'Mr Myles has a good business. He can do with all the help he can get. And Ianto's the eldest, isn't he?'

'If you mean he was set to inherit the business, his father has always promised him he will. But Ianto told me that he didn't fancy waiting around for years for his father to die. He wants to see a bit of the world and have some adventures while he's still young enough to enjoy life.'

'And eighteen would have been too old?' She glanced suspiciously at him. 'You're not thinking of following him, I hope.'

'Why not?' David challenged. 'He'll get board, lodge, boots and uniform provided, and wages at the end of every week. And he'll be able to spend them on whatever he fancies. There'll be no bloody agent following him around to take them off him before they hit his pocket.'

She was too alarmed at the prospect of losing David to reproach him for swearing a second time. 'And officers on his back every minute of every day, telling him what to do, how to behave and what to think.'

'So what?' He dropped all pretence of building the wall. 'They couldn't rule my life any more than the damned agent does already. Did you see Martha, Matthew and Luke's faces when you put that roast chicken in front of them yesterday? The poor kids couldn't even remember the last time we ate meat. We're working farmers and we can't afford to eat our own chickens. Now tell me, where's the bloody sense in that?'

'Don't ever use language like that in front of the little ones.' Shocked by the depth of her brother's bitterness, she began to shake. An icy claw of fear closed over her heart. She brushed a tangle of wet hair from her eyes and stared at him. 'You can't be serious. You can't really be thinking of leaving the farm and becoming a soldier. You're only fourteen—'

'Ianto told me they didn't even ask to see his birth certificate.'

'But all this work we do . . . the Ellis Estate . . . it's for you, Davy . . .' She started at a crash of thunder. A few seconds later she felt as though she were crouched beneath a waterfall.

'Like Dad's father said it was all for him?' David had to shout to make himself heard above the noise of the rainstorm. 'And just like our great-grandfather worked himself to death for our grandfather, and so on, back through all the Ellises until we reach the first one who decided to farm this hellish place. I've been thinking, Mary, what have any of us really got? We certainly haven't got a life. The damned land owns us, not the other way around. All we Ellises have ever done is work ourselves to death for some other bugger's benefit.'

'The first Ellis who came here built the house we live in, and it's a fine place,' she countered forcefully, proud of her heritage.

'It's fine all right, but the roof leaks, the walls are cracked and let in the damp, and the windows are rotten. We've had to sell almost every stick of furniture we possessed, and the way things are, we'll never be able to furnish it again. And although we may live in the house, Mary, we don't own it – there's a big difference.'

'Dad showed you the carving over the lintel, just as he showed it to me. The name of the first David Ellis and his date is up there.'

'Have you ever thought that we only have Dad's word for that?' he challenged. 'He couldn't read those words any more than we can. For all we know it could be Bob Pritchard's great-great-great-grandfather's name up there, and between you and me it would make more bloody sense if it was.'

'Dad told us the truth, I know he did.' Mary was glad of the rain because it hid her tears. 'The first Ellis to come here built the house. He owned everything and left it to his son—'

'Who left it to his son until it was taken away from us in seventeen fifty-four by another greedy landlord. I know the story as well as you, Mary.' He brushed his sodden sleeve over his forehead. 'And look what happened to Dad when he tried to buy it back. I was the one who held his legs when you and Mam cut him down, remember? Is that what you want for me? To be killed by hard work and the swindling landlord and his agent, like Dad?'

'Davy, I had no idea you felt this way,' she protested wearily. 'I thought you understood that we were working to try and keep the farm for you, and for the little ones to have somewhere to live until they grow up.'

'Why won't you see further than the work that has to be done every day, Mary?' He threw a stone aside and it hit one of the few low, scrubby bushes that grew in the pen, breaking a branch. 'The only future any of us will have if we stay here is the workhouse, or tramping the roads. We have to get out and make a living that will keep us and the little ones somewhere else.'

'By soldiering you'll only make enough to keep yourself,' she warned soberly.

'There are other jobs.'

'All both of us know is farming. You said it yourself, we can't even read and write. I'd be lucky to get a job as a kitchen maid. And if I did, what would happen to Martha, Matthew and Luke?'

'The doctor and his family would keep Martha on as a live-in maid.'

'So, what are you saying? That we should put Matthew and Luke into the workhouse?' The silence between them grew tense and unbearable, as the rain continued to pound down, pulverizing them and the earth.

David turned back to the wall when another peal of thunder heralded a second cloudburst. 'And I thought it couldn't get any wetter. Here.' He took the stone she held out to him and thrust it on top of the one he had already placed.

'Davy, you won't really go, will you?' she pleaded.

'Not without talking it over with you first.'

'Talk – or have you already made a decision?' She was shivering more from the prospect of trying to live without him than the freezing rain.

'I haven't decided anything – yet. I heard you talking to Mam before she died. I know she made you promise to look after all of us until we were old enough to look after ourselves.' He held out his hand for another stone. 'Well, you don't have to bother about me, not any more. I can fend for myself. But you can't look after the other three and do everything that needs doing around here, not all by yourself you can't.'

She didn't argue with him. She was too heartbroken by his declaration that he didn't think the Ellis Estate worth fighting for to try further persuasion. All her hopes for a better future when the family might actually live her father's dream of owning their rightful inheritance had been shattered.

And she had struggled too long to keep the family together on the farm to consider what she might do with the rest of her life if they no longer lived there.

Harry woke early the next morning to the sound of rain hammering relentlessly on his bedroom window. There was no sign of Toby at breakfast. Mrs Edwards told him that he had risen early, taken one look at the weather and caught the train into Swansea to buy paints and canvases. Harry breakfasted alone, and afterwards sat in the cheerless dining parlour and tried to read, but he spent more time watching the hands crawl round on his wristwatch than looking at his book.

As the morning wore on, the rain grew even heavier. At a quarter past ten, he dressed in his mackintosh and gaiters, jammed a waterproofed felt hat on his head and crossed the yard to put up the hood on the tourer. He'd garaged it in the old barn, which Alf had turned into a mechanic's workshop.

He drove to the station half an hour before the train was due in. The ambulance was already there, parked outside the station-master's house. He left his car alongside it, pulled up the collar on his mackintosh, angled the brim of his hat to stop the rain from falling into his eyes and headed for the platform. He handed over a penny for a ticket and waited in the doorway of the ticket office.

He heard the train before he saw it. Then he spotted a mist fogging the rain above the trees that bordered the track. The engine slowed, crawling towards the station at a snail's pace before finally drawing to a steam-spitting halt. Doors banged open and half a dozen men and women emerged. They stopped to put up umbrellas before hauling the shopping they had bought on Swansea Market out of the station. Harry caught the whiff of fresh fish and the vinegary tang of cockles as he walked along the train and peered into the carriages in search of his family.

When he was halfway along, he saw his Uncle Joey jump down from a carriage at the end of the train. He turned and lifted out a suitcase. Lloyd leaned out and passed him a wheelchair. Harry ran towards them, reaching them just when Victor emerged carrying his grandfather. Even wrapped in his woollen winter overcoat, with a muffler around his neck and his cap pulled down low, Billy Evans looked fragile.

In the three days since Harry had seen him, his face had shrunk, his teeth suddenly seemed too large for his mouth and his eyes were dark, glittering, pain-filled hollows. Harry had difficulty keeping his voice steady.

'Hello, Granddad.'

Billy looked at him as Victor set him gently in the chair. 'Harry,' he whispered, with a ghost of a smile. 'I've put you to a lot of trouble, boy.'

'No trouble, Granddad. The ambulance is waiting.'

Lloyd picked up the suitcase. Joey folded a blanket over his father's lap, tucking it beneath the shoe on his artificial leg. It said something that Billy didn't protest at his youngest son's fussing. He touched the hand Harry set on his shoulder.

'Lloyd tells me that you've arranged everything in the sanatorium.'

His grandfather's voice was so weak Harry had to crouch down to hear what he was saying. 'And I've found good lodgings at an inn, Granddad. So I can come down to see you as often as they'll let me.'

'Stuff and nonsense,' Billy said with a trace of his old spirit. 'You should be in Paris, painting . . . you should go . . .' The effort of speaking was too much after the journey. He fought for breath, his face turned blue and he fell back weakly in the chair.

'We'd better get you out of this rain before you get soaked, Dad,' Lloyd said.

Lloyd and Joey walked either side of the chair, Victor wheeled it to the gate and Harry hung back, hoping there'd be time for him to tell his grandfather just how much he loved him.

The ambulance driver and his mate hauled the chair, and Billy with it, into the back of their cab, secured the doors and drove off. Harry unlocked his car doors and his stepfather put the suitcase into the boot.

'You'll take us straight to the sanatorium so we can see Dad settle in, Harry?' Joey climbed into the back seat.

'I'll take you there, but they may not let you see him, Uncle Joey.'

'Yes, they will.'

'Not everyone falls prey to your charm, Joey.' Victor sat beside him. 'And the last thing we want to do is upset the people who are going to be caring for Dad.'

'How is Edyth?' Harry asked urgently.

'No change,' Lloyd answered briefly. 'But a word of warning: we had to tell Dad that she tumbled downstairs because he heard her cry and saw the rest of us panic before he passed out. But we've told him she's fine, just collected a few more bruises.'

'Granddad looks terrible,' Harry ventured.

'Doctor Williams warned us that he might not survive the journey,' Lloyd said quietly. 'But we all agreed that he would be better off here than in the Graig.'

'Even Granddad?' Harry pressed.

'Doctor Williams asked him for us, but we already knew the answer. Like most miners, he's been afraid all his life of dying in the workhouse,' Joey answered.

Subdued, they drove the rest of the short distance from the station to the castle in silence. Harry turned into the courtyard. The ambulance was outside the main entrance. He parked opposite it.

'I've ordered lunch for all of us at the inn I stayed at last night, but I told the landlady I couldn't be sure when we'd be there, so she said she'd sort something that won't spoil if we're delayed.'

'Just as well.' Joey opened the car door.

'You're not coming in?' Lloyd asked Harry when he didn't make a move.

'No, Granddad's so weak it will be as much as he can do to say goodbye to you three. As there's no change in Edyth, I thought I might stay over for a day or two, to make sure Granddad settles in all right.'

'And when did you make that decision?' Lloyd asked.

'When I saw him just now,' Harry admitted.

'As you said, you might not be allowed to see him.'

'Even if I'm not, I'll be on hand to make enquiries, Dad. It's only four miles from the inn to this place and they both have telephones. Besides, the weather is foul for driving.'

'It is that.' Lloyd nodded agreement, and shut the door behind him.

Harry turned off the ignition. He watched his uncles and step-father cross the courtyard and mount the steps to the front door. As he suspected, he didn't have to wait long. Ten minutes later the door opened again and all three trooped out.

Joey waited until he and his brothers were finishing their lunch in the dining parlour of the inn, before voicing his opinion on the cavalier treatment they had received in Craig y Nos.

'Was I the only one who took exception to Doctor Adams's attitude?' He looked at his brothers but didn't give either of them time to answer him. 'All we're concerned about is *our* father, yet he insisted he didn't have time to talk to us and ordered us out of the place as though we were tramps who'd come begging at the back door for a handout.'

'I felt the same way at first.' Harry sprinkled vinegar over the remaining food on his plate. The silent Enfys had served them ham, salad and chips; although there was no garnish, the ham had been well carved and the salad and chips were plentiful. 'I thought Doctor Adams imperious, and his daughter condescending, but after talking to the nephew of a patient who has seen them almost every day during the month since his uncle has been admitted to the sanatorium, I've come to the conclusion that neither of them have much time for relatives, but all the time in the world for their patients.'

'How can you be sure about that?' Joey took the vinegar bottle from him.

'I saw most of the wards in Craig y Nos, and although the doctor can't offer a cure or even much in the way of treatment, what little he can do is carried out meticulously. The beds of those strong enough to be moved are wheeled out into the fresh air every day. The place is spotlessly clean and constantly being disinfected in an effort to stop the spread of secondary infections. And when I went into the children's ward with Miss Adams, it was obvious they all adored her. I really believe that although neither she nor her father can be bothered with the social niceties when it comes to relatives, they truly care about their patients.'

'Perhaps it's just as well that you and not Joey made the arrangements for Dad to be admitted,' Victor commented philosophically. 'Tact has never been one of his strong points.'

'No?' Joey demanded caustically.

'No.' As even-tempered as ever, Victor looked his younger brother coolly in the eye.

'Doctor Adams told us that he won't allow Dad any visitors for at least a week, if then,' Lloyd warned, 'but—'

'I'll go over there first thing tomorrow morning to ask about him, and I won't drive back to Pontypridd until they tell me he's recovered from the journey and settled in,' Harry interrupted.

'I warned you there wasn't much life in the upper valley, but it was still a shock to see it again for myself from the train after so many years. If you'll excuse me, I'm going to have a word with the landlady.' Victor finished his beer, blotted his lips in his napkin and folded it beside his empty plate.

'Megan asked Victor to enquire after her family,' Joey explained to Harry after Victor left. 'She hasn't heard anything of them since the Baptist minister moved from the Rhondda to Cardiff eight years ago. And before that it was only the odd snippet of news passed on by his sister in her letters.'

'If he'd mentioned it before I drove down here, I could have asked around for him.'

'I think he'd prefer to make the enquiries himself. You're too young to remember the visit Megan's father made to the Rhondda before she married Victor. But I've never met a man as unpleasant and mercenary as Iestyn Williams before or since. He certainly didn't deserve a daughter like Megan.' Lloyd pushed his empty plate aside and sat back with his beer.

'How is Mam? Really?' Harry asked.

'Keeping busy, working all the hours in the day and more looking after everyone at home and in the store. Doctor Williams has arranged for us to see Edyth twice a week but your mother would much prefer to sit by her bed. And would, if they'd let her.'

'She has to be all right,' Harry breathed fervently.

'She will be,' Joey insisted. 'That one's always been a survivor.'

'All I know is that she's putting years on Sali and me. Any news?' Lloyd asked when Victor returned with four fresh glasses of beer.

'Megan's father is alive, but her mother died five years ago, and one of her sisters the year before that in childbirth.'

'I'm sorry. That is going to be hard for her to take,' Lloyd sympathized.

'For all that the old man's a selfish bully, you'd think one of her brothers or her other sister would have written to tell her about her mother.' Joey was angry for Megan's sake.

'The landlady said it's doubtful the old man told them that their mother had died. It was the talk of the valley when none of them turned up for the funeral. And then again, even if they had known and had wanted to tell Megan, they wouldn't have know where to send a letter.' Victor set the glasses on the table, pulled out his chair and rejoined them.

'If they'd written to our old address in Tonypandy, the letter would have found Megan eventually.'

'It might have, Joey, but from what Mrs Edwards said, I don't think Megan's brothers and sister have any more contact with her father than her. Two weeks after his wife was buried he married again.'

'From what I saw of the way he treated his wife and children I'm amazed he found another woman willing to live with him.' Lloyd took a packet of cigarettes from his pocket.

'There are always women desperate enough to marry anyone who'll put a roof over their head, especially in farming communities where the choice is down to being a wife or a servant.' Victor helped himself to one of Lloyd's cigarettes.

'From what I've seen of life in some rural areas, the farmers treat their wives worse than their servants. At least they have to pay those they employ.' Joey flicked his lighter and lit his brothers' cigarettes.

'As far as Mrs Edwards knows, Megan's brothers are still working on the same farms over Ammanford way that their father sent them to before they were twelve years old. If she's right, they haven't moved on in fifteen years.'

'Aunty Megan said that both her sisters used to work at Craig y Nos,' Harry reminded them.

'The one who died was married to a man who still lives in Brecon, the other to a railwayman, and Mrs Edwards has no idea where she is living.'

'Poor Aunty Megan,' Harry said feelingly. 'I'd hate to lose touch with my sisters and brother.'

'As if they'd let you,' Lloyd commented.

'If you find out anything more about Megan's brothers and sister, or hear where they are, Harry, let us know. Now that her mother's dead, I think Megan might risk writing to them. If none of them are living at home there isn't much that her father can do to hurt them.'

'I'll ask the next time I go to the sanatorium. There might be someone left at Craig y Nos who worked there with her sisters when it was a private house and who knows where the one who married the railwayman is now.' Harry sat back and stretched his long legs out in front of him.

'Be discreet. I'd rather her father didn't hear that she is trying to get in touch with them. Lloyd's right, he's a nasty piece of work.'

Harry stared at Victor in amazement. It was the strongest condemnation he'd heard his uncle make of any man.

Joey pulled his watch from his waistcoat pocket and opened it. 'It's time we were back at the station.' He looked to his brothers. 'Do you think there's a chance that we might persuade the taxi driver who brought us here to drive back more slowly – and safely?'

Diana Adams ran down the stairs of the substantial villa her father had bought as their family home and his refuge from Craig y Nos. Situated opposite the sanatorium, it was ideally placed: close to, yet totally separate from the hospital. Even their gardens were on different sides of the road. One of Dr Adams's chief priorities was to safeguard the health of his remaining family.

It had taken the doctor months to accept his only child's decision to follow in his footsteps and enter the branch of medicine in which he practised. But he still refused to allow his wife to visit them in his office. In his professional opinion, his wife's health was 'delicate'. She was certainly prone to chest infections, and the two maidservants they employed were likewise not allowed near the hospital. Neither were the staff of the sanatorium allowed into the house, which was why Diana had kept Martha Ellis, the kitchen maid from Craig y Nos, waiting in the rain outside the front door.

She went out and handed Martha a battered old Gladstone and an umbrella. 'Now remember, these clothes are for your sister's patchwork quilts. And tell her that it seemed a shame to throw out so many good cotton and linen things when she can give them a new lease of life.'

'I will, Miss Adams, and thank you.' Martha took the bag. It was heavy, and she didn't relish the prospect of carrying it up the five miles of road that separated Craig y Nos from the Ellis Estate.

'My mother and I would love to make quilts, but we simply don't have the time, not with me working in the hospital and my mother having to run this house.'

Martha was only nine years old, but she understood that Miss Adams was trying to be tactful. She had seen the expression on people's faces when they saw her sister and brothers. Not one item of their clothing was in one piece, and Mary wouldn't have had any replacements or cloth with which to patch them if it hadn't been for Miss Adams and the manager of the Colonial Stores in Pontardawe passing on hand-me-downs.

The first thing Miss Adams had given her when she'd walked down to Craig y Nos in search of a job was a uniform, albeit one too large for her. It had been during a particularly desperate winter week. Foxes had burrowed into the barn and killed more than a dozen chickens. Thirty sheep had broken out of the pen and frozen to death on the hillside, and two of their best milk cows had died of fever. For the first time in her life, she had left her bed before Mary and David in the morning, woken Matthew and told him to tell Mary that she'd gone looking for work. She had knocked on the door of every inn and occupied house between the farm and the sanatorium, but had no luck until she reached Craig y Nos.

Cook had given her the same reply that she'd had from everyone else. 'You're too young to work.' But instead of telling her to go back to school – as if any of her family had ever had time to attend school – the middle-aged woman had conceded she was short-staffed. She had sent for Miss Adams who had asked her why she wanted to work. After repeatedly asking her age and listening to her persistently lie that she was twelve years old, she had finally given Martha what she wanted – a job in the castle's kitchens that paid seven shillings a week. And it wasn't just the money. Hardly a week went by without Miss Adams giving her cast-off clothes, shoes or linen, which 'they no longer needed at home'.

Mary had been horrified when Martha had returned to the farm and told them what she'd done. But when her sister had walked down with her to Craig y Nos on the Monday morning she was due to start work, Miss Adams had assured both of them that she would only be working in the kitchens and the areas well away from infectious patients.

'I'm still sorting out the wardrobes, so I may have a few more things for you on Monday, Martha,' Diana said

'Thank you for these and for letting me leave early today, Miss Adams.' Martha held the bag close beneath the cloak Mary had cut down from one of their mother's.

'Go carefully, there's no sign of a let-up in this weather.' Diana looked up at the sky.

'I'll look after your umbrella and bring it back on Monday morning, Miss Adams.' 'No problem, Martha, my mother won't be going anywhere in this. I'll borrow hers. Are you sure that you wouldn't rather go back to the kitchen and wait for a ride? A cart may come along in the next hour or two that's going up to Brecon.'

'There's never much traffic on a Saturday afternoon, Miss Adams,' Martha pulled up the hood on her cloak, pinned the open umbrella on top of it to keep it in place, and started walking.

'See you on Monday,' Diana called after the girl.

Martha waved her hand but didn't look back.

Lloyd glanced out of the door of the station waiting room and made a face at the rain. 'Some summer we're having. You'll be home soon?' he asked Harry.

'As soon as I'm certain Granddad has settled in all right.'

'Ask Doctor Adams when we can visit. He wasn't in a mood to discuss it when we saw him.'

'I will, and I'll telephone every night to ask about Edyth. Give Mam and the others my love, and tell them I might not be with them but I am thinking of Edyth and them all the time.'

The signal clunked down and, hissing steam, the Swansea train inched slowly into the station.

Lloyd dropped the hand he was about to offer Harry. Wrapping his arms around his shoulders, he hugged his stepson for the first time since Harry had turned sixteen. He released him a few moments later and bent to tie his shoelace so no one could see his face. Fighting emotion, Harry shook Victor's hand.

'Take care of yourself, Harry. And remember what I said about being discreet in any enquiries you make about Megan's family.' Victor braved the downpour and ran across the platform to the train.

'Try to have as good a time as this valley can provide, and do as I did at your age – only go out with one girl at a time.' Joey gave him a sly wink before following Victor.

'Tell me where the girls are, Uncle Joey, and I'll ask one out,' Harry called after him. He turned back to his stepfather. 'You won't forget to give Mam and everyone else my love?'

'I won't. You've turned into quite a man, Harry. I'm proud of you.' Lloyd joined his brothers.

Harry watched the train pull out of the station and returned to his car. The grey afternoon was more suited to November than July. He tossed his damp coat and hat into the back, ducked into the driving seat and slammed the door. He had to press the ignition three times before he managed to fire the engine.

He stopped at the junction where the Penwyllt road joined the main thoroughfare that led from Swansea to the market town of Brecon. If Toby had returned from Swansea he would have passed him either on his way to or from the station. What he needed was company, and more lively than that of the farmers and shepherds who frequented the bar at the inn. But he was hardly likely to find that outside of Pontardawe or Swansea, and he didn't feel like driving down into the industrialized lower valley. The weather was depressing enough in a picturesque landscape, let alone one scarred by collieries and metal works.

Succumbing to impulse, he turned right and drove past Craig y Nos, up the valley towards the barren mountains of the Brecon Beacons. He'd heard the scenery was magnificent. Although the clouds were low and the mist thick, he hoped it might clear enough for him to see something of the hills.

But the rain that had been heavy in the valley became a torrential cloudburst when the road narrowed to a winding ascent. With water sheeting down over his windscreen and a thick mist encasing the car, he could see nothing beyond the bonnet of the Crossley. If the road had been wider he would have attempted a three-point turn. As it was, he was wary of the drop that he sensed lay to his left. If he was unfortunate enough to plunge down a bank it could be hours or even days before anyone found him in this remote spot. Regretting his decision to turn right, he had no choice but to reduce his speed and continue to move ahead as best he could.

Martha was cold, wet and bone-weary. Saturday lunch for the patients was cold meat and salad so Saturday mornings could be set aside for cleaning the ranges in the hospital kitchen. As if it hadn't been enough work to scrub out the ovens with powdered bath-stone, and brush black-lead on to every part of the stoves – even those that couldn't be seen – Cook had also ordered her to polish all the baking tins with wire wool.

Her arms ached, her fingernails were blackened, broken and split to the quick, and the bag she was carrying seemed to have doubled in weight since Miss Adams had given it to her.

The fingers on her right hand were numb, so she shifted the bag into her left, and clutched her cloak closer. To her dismay she noticed that the colour had run. Like all her mother's Sunday clothes, it was black, but the rain had run right through it and blotched her grey maid's dress with stains that were too dark to be water. She only hoped that Mary would be able to wash them out.

A thick mist had fallen, obliterating everything more than a foot away. She felt as though she'd fallen into a gulley of cloudy sheep-dip. She certainly couldn't have been any wetter if she had been under water. But as she travelled the road twice a day, and usually on foot, she knew exactly where she was, barely halfway along the five miles that separated the castle from home. It would take her at least another hour to get there.

She pictured the warmth of the kitchen permeated by the welcoming, mouth-watering fragrance of baking bread. Then she imagined the vegetable soup Mary would have simmering on the stove, the smiles Luke and Matthew would give her when she walked in, and Mary's delight at the contents of the Gladstone bag.

Setting her head down against the needles of rain that pricked and stung her face, Martha clutched the umbrella and bag and kept walking.

Harry pushed the car into first gear and dropped his speed from ten to five miles an hour. A small patch of mist ahead of him drifted to the left, clearing a tiny patch of road. He saw something dark in front of him and slammed on his brakes. He willed the car to stop instantly, but it kept crawling forward. There was a sickening crunch, and whatever it was crumpled to the ground.

Chapter 6

'I THINK I'll harness the cart and take it down to Craig y Nos. Dolly doesn't like the wet but if I give her a good rub down afterwards, her arthritis shouldn't get any worse than it already is.' David cradled his cup in his hands, siphoning off the warmth of the tea Mary had made. He had spent the last hour nailing slates back onto the roof of the pigsty and he could barely flex his fingers.

'You're worried about Martha?' Mary shaped the bread dough she was kneading into a loaf.

'No more than you.' He sipped the hot tea slowly. 'It will be impossible to see your hand in front of your face on the hill.'

'That goes for you as well as her.'

'Dolly could walk the road blindfolded, and if I go down in the cart Martha will be home in half the time. She should be leaving work in an hour or so,' he guessed, using this inner clock. They had been forced to sell every timepiece in the house.

Mary glanced out of the window but she couldn't see anything beyond raindrops sparkling against a background of grey mist. 'It's winter not summer weather.'

'Let's hope it will be brighter tomorrow.' David set his empty cup on the table.

'Can I come, Davy?' Matthew asked plaintively from the corner nearest to the range where he was rolling spills from the old newspapers he and David had picked up in Pontardawe. Luke was asleep on a rag rug next to him, worn out after a disturbed night of teething and tears.

'You'll turn into a fish if you come out on the cart in this.' David picked up his cap from the bar in front of the range, where he'd left it to dry.

'If I will, why won't you?'

'Because I'm too big.' David opened the door. 'Don't bring the cows in for milking until I'm back to help you, Mary.'

She set the loaf she'd made on the warming rack above the range to rise. 'In that case, I'll mix some dumplings for the soup and a jam sponge for afters.'

'That's worth coming back for.' Knowing how much he had hurt her by suggesting that he might leave the farm for the army, he gave her a small smile by way of atonement.

Sick to the pit of his stomach, praying he'd hit a sheep for which he could compensate a farmer, Harry opened the car door. He was shaking so much he had difficulty standing upright, and it didn't help that it felt as though he had stepped under a shower head. His hair was plastered to his head in an instant, dripping cold rivulets beneath his collar and into his eyes. And for all that his Craven-proofed coat was guaranteed watertight, his shirt and trousers were soaked before he reached the front of the car.

The body of a young girl was lying in the centre of the road. Her legs were sprawled beneath his car, her eyes closed despite the rain that streamed over her face. A Gladstone bag almost as large as her lay next to her.

Suppressing his initial instinct to scoop her into his arms, Harry crouched down and frantically tried to recall everything he had ever learned about first aid.

He lifted her wrist, weakening in relief when he felt a pulse. He hadn't killed her – not yet anyway. He lifted the sodden hood of her cloak and ran his fingers lightly over her scalp; there was a lump on the back of her head but no blood. He checked her arms and black-stockinged legs.

He couldn't be absolutely certain but apart from the bump on her head there didn't appear to be any other damage. He struggled out of his suit jacket, laid it on the ground, slipped his hands beneath her and, carefully supporting her neck and head, lifted her as gently as he could on to it. It was only when he had laid her flat that he recognised her as the child who had carried Dr Adams's tea tray into his office the day before. He recalled the doctor calling her Martha. He had thought her young then, but she was lighter, frailer and even smaller than he remembered.

Ignoring the rain that had trickled through his clothes to his skin, he carried her to his car, laid her on the back seat and covered her with the travelling rug he kept in the boot. Alarmed when she didn't move or utter a sound, and lacking the knowledge to help her further, he retrieved the Gladstone bag and the umbrella she had been carrying, which had rolled down the hill, and set them on the floor of the car. Then he spent a few seconds checking the road before returning to the driving seat. It wasn't as wide as he would have liked but, by negotiating a six-point turn, he managed to reverse the car. Moments later he was driving as fast as he dared back down the valley towards Craig y Nos.

Diana Adams was running across the courtyard of the sanatorium when Harry drove in. She opened the door, stepped inside and closed her umbrella before shaking the worst of the water from it out on to the steps.

'Miss Adams!' Harry left the car and darted towards her.

'Mr Evans,' she rebuked irritably. 'My father made it perfectly clear to your father and uncles there was absolutely no way that you would be allowed to see your grandfather this evening, or indeed for the next week. He was so exhausted by the journey here that we sedated him in the hope that he'd have a good rest and a visit from you—'

'I haven't come to see my grandfather,' Harry gasped, still faint and unsteady after the accident. 'I knocked your maid down in my car. I didn't know where else to bring her.'

'My maid? I haven't a maid.'

'I think her name is Martha.'

She dropped her umbrella and it clattered to the floor of the porch. 'Where is she?'

He ran back to the car and wrenched open the back door. Diana pushed him aside, leaned inside and checked the child's pulse before running her hands gently over her body.

'I felt her arms and legs – they don't appear to be broken but she has a bump on the back of her head.' Harry continued to stand in the pouring rain behind her, too traumatized to think of anything besides the child.

'Didn't you see her?'

'Not until she was in front of my car and then it was too late. There was a thick mist. I couldn't see further than the bonnet of the car . . .' He bent forward when she lifted Martha from the back seat and took the child from her.

'Take her into my father's office. Put her on the examination couch.' She ran ahead of him. 'Fetch my father at once,' she shouted to a passing nurse.

'Please, can I wait? I have to know how she is,' Harry asked after he had deposited Martha on the couch.

'Go to the waiting room by the front door. I'll send someone there when we've examined her.'

Dr Adams walked past Harry without a word or a look. Diana held the door open, and Harry left. The door slammed shut behind him.

Dizzy and nauseous, he sank down on the top step of the small staircase in front of the office, buried his head in his hands and shuddered as the enormity of what he'd done sank in.

David returned to the kitchen of the farmhouse less than ten minutes after he left. Mary took one look at him and knew something was seriously wrong.

'Dolly's lame,' he announced baldly.

'Is it serious?' Her heart thundered erratically. It was the moment she had been dreading – and expecting. The loss of Dolly would mean the loss of their independence and livelihood. Without the horse the agent would take everything they produced in exchange for knocking 'something' off their rent arrears. There'd be no money to buy the essentials they couldn't produce themselves and they wouldn't be able to survive on Martha's seven shillings a week and what little they could carry down to Craig y Nos and Pontardawe themselves.

'I don't know.' David looked as devastated as she felt. 'It's too dark in the stable to take a good look. I came back for the lantern.'

'I'll come with you.' Mary wiped the flour from her hands in her apron, untied the strings and pulled it over her head. 'Stay with Luke in case he wakes, Matthew,' she ordered before running across the yard after David.

David had lit the lantern and tied on the leather apron he wore when he shoed the horses. 'Hold her head fast.'

Mary wrapped both arms tightly around the mare's head and rested her cheek against the horse's neck. 'Stay still, there's a good girl,' she whispered, looking to David who was at the back of the stall.

Her brother sank back on his haunches and lifted the hoof of Dolly's back left leg between his knees. He scraped along the shoe with his penknife, and pus spurted out. 'There's something caught in here.' He probed further. 'Damned piece of metal. It looks like a nail. She must have picked it up when we went down to Pontardawe last week.'

'Is it bad?' Mary asked anxiously.

'It's not good,' David replied acidly. 'I'll need hot water and soap to clean it out. And something to disinfect the wound.'

'I'll bring the iodine and make an oatmeal poultice to draw out the poison.' Mary patted Dolly's neck. 'Good girl.'

David's expression was grim in the shadowy light. 'What will we do if we lose Dolly?'

'We're not going to,' Mary snapped, avoiding his eyes.

'But—'

'We're not going to, Davy,' she reiterated forcefully. 'The iodine and oatmeal will work.'

'If it doesn't, the vet won't come out. Not when we owe him ten pounds from the time he treated the cows for fever.'

Ignoring him, she said, 'I'll be back as quick as I can with the hot water, soap, iodine and poultice. Do you need anything else?'

David almost added 'a miracle' then saw that his sister was close to tears. 'No, Mary, hopefully that will be enough.'

The little natural light that filtered into the corridor through the skylights was as grey as the rain-filled atmosphere outside. The clock in the tower struck the half, quarter and full hour. Harry heard footsteps behind him as nurses and porters walked up and down the corridor, but although they slowed when they approached, no one spoke to him. Eventually the office door opened. He turned in time to see Dr Adams stride in the direction of the lift. Diana Adams came out and lifted her mackintosh from the hall stand. She started nervously when he rose to his feet.

'Whatever were you doing sitting there in the shadows, Mr Evans?' she demanded suspiciously.

'Waiting.' His voice sounded hoarse and peculiar. 'How is Martha?'

'She has concussion. But she has regained consciousness, and although her speech is slow, as far as we can tell there doesn't appear to be any permanent damage. She will need to be kept under observation but we can't admit her to any of the wards here because of the risk of infection. I will drive her home and visit her there for the next few days.'

'I can drive both of you.'

'I don't think that's wise, Mr Evans. I know her family and—'

Relief brought anger and Harry burst out, 'For God's sake, what kind of a family are they to allow a girl of that age to walk alone on that isolated road in this weather?'

'Keep your voice down, Mr Evans,' Diana said angrily. 'Martha was walking home.'

'Home? There's nothing on that road!'

'How would you know, when all you said you could see was mist? There are farms, cottages and even a couple of old coaching inns.'

'How far away does the girl live?'

'Five miles.'

'Five miles?' he repeated incredulously. 'You employ a girl no more than seven or eight years of age as a maid, knowing that she has to walk ten miles a day, and expose her to all kinds of infection when she's here?'

'She doesn't work on the wards, only in the kitchen, Mr Evans,' Diana retorted. 'And she is not eight years old. She is twelve.'

'I have five sisters between the ages of sixteen and nine, and the youngest, Susie, is twice the size of Martha.'

'I take it that your sisters are well-fed, Mr Evans.'

'I should hope so.'

'Then they are more fortunate than Martha and her brothers and sister. Although they live on a farm they find it hard to make ends meet, a situation with which you are obviously unfamiliar.'

'I know all about poverty—'

'Really, Mr Evans?'

'Yes, really.' Incensed by her mocking tone, Harry lost his temper. 'I lived in the Rhondda during the nineteen eleven strike, and I worked as a volunteer during the General Strike in May.'

'Ferrying goods to poverty-stricken households in your expensive car, Mr Evans?' she said contemptuously. 'There are households that don't see as much money as it cost you to buy it in a lifetime.'

'I don't need to be reminded how privileged I am, or how little money some families have to live on.'

'As you don't see the need for Martha to work, I seriously doubt it, Mr Evans.'

'All I said is that a girl that age shouldn't be working in a sanatorium or walking that distance to get here.'

'Would it surprise you to know that my father and I feel the same way? But we also know that Martha's family couldn't survive without the money we pay her. Now if you'll excuse me,' she slipped on her raincoat, 'I have to get her home before her family send out a search party to find her.'

'I'll take you.' Harry opened the door.

'I told you, Mr Evans, the Ellises will not be pleased to see you. Besides, you need to get back to the inn and change out of those clothes. You're soaked to the skin.'

'I need to face her family and take full responsibility for what I've done,' he insisted. 'And I will drive up there whether you come with me or not.'

'You'd never find the house on your own.'

'There can't be that many. I'll simply knock on all the doors I come to, until I find the right one. They won't all have small girls called Martha living in them who work here.'

'You would do that?'

'Yes.' Harry parried her stony glare.

'In that case I suppose I'd better let you drive us.' Diana took her hat from the hall stand.

'I'll open the car.' Harry ran outside and wrenched open the back door. The Gladstone bag and umbrella still lay, forgotten, on the floor of the car. When he returned to the castle, Diana was in the porch holding Martha, who was swathed in blankets. He took the girl from her and swiftly deposited her on the back seat. She looked up at him in confusion when he settled her. 'Are you comfortable?' he whispered.

She nodded, and he closed the door. He walked around the front passenger side and opened the door for Diana Adams.

She knew he was waiting for her, yet she double-checked her reflection in the hall mirror, adjusted the collar on her light-grey mackintosh, and pulled on her leather gloves and black cloche hat, all the while watching him grow steadily wetter as he stood, hatless and coatless in the downpour. After she'd dressed, she put up her umbrella, walked out of the castle and climbed into the tourer.

He slammed the passenger door behind her, and squelched his way to the driving seat.

'I'll try not drip on you,' he said caustically, when she shrank away from him.

'That would be difficult, Mr Evans. You've already soaked my stockings. Turn right at the gate, I'll point out the house when we get there.'

Although the rain was even heavier than when Harry had driven up the mountain earlier, the mist had cleared and he was able to see the hills rolling upwards on their right. But he found it impossible to gauge their height as the summits were shrouded in low cloud. Just as he'd suspected, on the left a slope slid precariously down to the floor of the valley.

Drenched, bedraggled sheep huddled in clusters alongside the road. Terrified of hitting one of them and nervous after the accident, Harry drove more slowly than usual. The silence between him and Diana Adams grew more oppressive with every passing mile. Even more so every time she turned around to check on Martha, who was lying silently in the back with her eyes closed.

'Is this the house?' he asked, when he saw an isolated building after what seemed closer to ten than five miles. It was a typically Welsh, stone-built, square cottage, with a slate roof, windows either side of a central door and three windows set above.

'If you look more closely you'll see that it's boarded up, Mr Evans,' she informed him curtly.

'So it is. I didn't notice.'

'It's a sign of the times. Rural depopulation. Unemployment is up, wages are down, the price of food has dropped, but not enough to allow people to buy anything beyond the bare essentials. As a result, tenant farmers can no longer afford to pay the rent demanded by the landowners, so they are evicted. And while their family homes are boarded up, they and their families are admitted to the workhouse.'

Sick with worry about Martha, and resenting Diana's preaching, Harry retorted, 'You missed your vocation, Miss Adams. You should have become a lecturer. And I do understand basic economics as they apply to the present situation in this country.'

Diana glanced at him. 'Martha's house is up ahead,' she said in a softer voice. 'You can see the side of it from here. It's behind that copse of trees.'

'That's her house!' Harry stared at the massive building built on an exposed bluff on the left-hand side of the road.

'That's the side wall of the house and the farm buildings behind it. The house itself fronts the road.'

'It looks enormous.'

'It is.'

He lowered his voice. 'How can you possibly say that Martha's family need the money she earns?'

'The Ellis Estate and outbuildings may have been built by her family centuries ago, but they are tenants there now.'

Harry slowed his car to a crawl. The house was even larger than it looked from the side. A slate-roofed arch bridged two buildings, joining them on the second storey. Both were double the size of the cottage down the road and either would have been considered a substantial dwelling in its own right. The arch tunnelled through the house, and opened into a sloping farmyard the size of four tennis courts, enclosed by the house at the front and outbuildings on the other three sides.

'Drive through and park in the farmyard,' Diana advised. 'Martha's family live in the kitchen and we will have to carry her in through the back door. Like most farmers around here they only use the front door for weddings and funerals.'

Harry inched the car through the narrow archway, expecting to see dogs and chickens. But the only ones in evidence were sheltering behind the open door of a barn. The dogs started barking but fell silent when Diana wound down the window and shouted at them. He glanced around the cobbled yard. The buildings were all solidly built of stone and roofed with slate, but their wooden doors had been inexpertly patched with rough-cut timber and six-inch nails. Two or three hung drunkenly on broken hinges, seemingly on the point of collapse.

'The design is more Roman country villa than Welsh farm.'

'You've been to Italy, Mr Evans?'

Loath to admit it after their argument about poverty, Harry conceded an abrupt, 'Yes.'

'Beautiful, isn't it?' she said drily. 'And the Ellis Estate is old, but I doubt it's two thousand years old, Mr Evans.' Without waiting for him to help her out of the car, Diana opened the door. 'But then, the Romans did reach Brecon, and there are the remains of a Roman road and fort not too far away, so you may be right about the foundations.' She stepped out carefully, avoiding the piles of cow dung and chicken manure that littered the cobbles lest she stain her pale-grey, cross-bar leather shoes. After unfurling her umbrella, she opened the back of the car. Startled, Martha looked around in confusion.

'It's all right, Martha, you're home,' Diana soothed.

'Let me take her.'

'I'm not sure that's wise, Mr Evans.'

'You know where we're going, I don't, and it's too wet to argue. Here, she was carrying this.' Harry lifted out the Gladstone and handed it to Diana. He covered Martha with his travelling rug to protect her and the blanket she was wrapped in from the rain.

Diana went to a door set in the centre of the left-hand building.

It was badly in need of a coat of paint. She knocked once and opened it. 'Mary?'

A thin girl of middle height with an abundance of black curly hair tied back with string, and eyes so dark they appeared almost as black as her pupils, ran to meet her. She was dressed in an old-fashioned, ankle-length black skirt, plain black cotton blouse and men's working boots which were several sizes too large for her feet.

'Miss Adams.' She instinctively wiped her hands on her apron, and pushed her hair from her eyes. 'Martha's late. David and Matthew have gone to look for her . . .' She looked past Diana and saw Harry lift Martha out of the car. 'Martha! Oh my God, why are you carrying her? What's happened to her? Martha . . .' Oblivious to the rain, she ran out and folded the rug back from her sister's face.

Diana followed and pulled her back. 'She's had an accident, Mary, but my father and I have examined her and she will be fine after a few days' rest. Come on, let's go into the kitchen and get out of this rain.' Diana held the door open for Harry.

'I just banged my head, Mary,' Martha slurred.

Harry looked around for somewhere to put the girl. The kitchen was larger than any he'd seen in a private house. It was also immaculately clean but he'd seen better furnished church halls. The flagstones on the floor had been scrubbed white. If the walls had ever been plastered, they were bare stone now. A log fire burned in the open range, and a baby lay asleep on a rag rug in front of it. A wooden crate stacked high with logs was pushed against the wall to the side of the hearth; a rickety table stood within a few feet of the fire, two benches set either side of it. That was it. There was no dresser, no easy chairs, only a few pieces of crockery and half a dozen pots and pans neatly arranged on wooden shelves in a niche next to the range.

Mary grabbed her sister and tore her from Harry's arms.

'She really will be all right, Mary,' Diana assured her, seeing the panic in her eyes.

'Put me down.' Martha began to struggle, and Mary set her next to one of the benches. Martha sank on to it and slumped, head in hands, over the table.

'You said the boys are out looking for Martha?' Diana reminded. 'If you know which way they've gone, we'll try to find them. The weather's wild out there.'

'They've gone down the mountain track.'

'Where's that?' Harry asked, hoping to be of use.

'It's a lane that cuts down the mountain on the left-hand side of the road as you head back the way we came.' Diana laid her hand on Martha's forehead.

'I'll see if I can find them.' He went to the door.

'Who are you?' Mary eyed Harry suspiciously.

'I'm sorry, I should have introduced you, Mary.' Diana stood between them as though she were effecting a formal introduction at an afternoon tea party. 'Miss Mary Ellis, Martha's elder sister – Mr Harry Evans. He's a relative of one of our patients, Mary. He drove me and your sister here.'

Harry extended his hand. 'I'm terribly sorry, Miss Ellis. I wish we could have met under better circumstances. I caused your sister's accident. There was a mist. I didn't see her until she was in front of my car—'

'You knocked my sister down in a motor car!'

'I'm afraid I did. But as I said, I didn't see her—'

Mary didn't give him the opportunity to explain further. She flew at him and grabbed him by his collar. Yanking him towards her, she lashed out, tearing his skin with her nails.

'Mary!'

Harry heard Diana shout, but he didn't attempt to defend himself. One of the principles Lloyd had instilled in him, especially after the birth of his sisters, was that no man ever hit a woman, regardless of the situation. Too terrified to try to keep Mary at bay in case he inadvertently hurt her, and too choked to cry out, he stood and took the punishment she meted out.

'Mary, it was an accident. Mr Evans didn't mean to hurt Martha and she is going to make a full recovery.' Diana closed her fingers around Mary's wrist, but the girl dug her nails even deeper into Harry's neck, throttling him.

The room dimmed, Harry's lungs burned along with his throat. Grey shadows crept upwards from the floor.

101

'Mary, if you hurt Mr Evans, you'll be prosecuted. Think about your brothers and sister. What will they do without you to look after them?'

The baby opened his eyes and wailed.

Harry never knew whether it was Diana's threat or the cry of the child that permeated Mary's rage. But, to his relief, she loosened her hold and Diana Adams managed to prise her fingers from his throat. He fell back against the wall, gulping in air. Something warm and wet trickled down his cheek and neck. He lifted his hand to it then saw his palm was covered in blood.

'Are you all right, Mr Evans?'

Diana Adams was looking at him. Too choked to speak, he nodded.

Mary went to her sister and stroked her head. 'I can feel a lump, and Martha doesn't look all right to me.' She glared accusingly at Harry.

Diana lifted the baby from the rug. His body was unnaturally warm, his cheeks flushed. On the premise that the girl was less likely to attack Harry again if she was holding the child, she thrust the baby into Mary's arms. 'Luke needs you, Mary. And Martha needs to rest. Why don't I help you to put her to bed while Mr Evans goes out to look for David and Matthew? And after we've seen to Martha, I'll examine Luke. He seems feverish.' She signalled to Harry with her eyes but he didn't need the hint; he was already backing towards the door.

'Luke's cutting more teeth. He'll be fine when they come through. He always is.' Mary lifted the baby on to her shoulder and patted his back.

'It is just as Mr Evans said,' Diana added. 'There was a mist. He didn't see Martha until she was in front of his car. And he couldn't have been driving very fast. If he had been, Martha's injuries would have been much worse. After a day or two's rest she'll be back to normal.'

Harry was grateful for Diana's support, especially after the heated words they had exchanged earlier. 'I'm sorry,' he croaked, his throat so sore he could hardly make himself heard. 'It was an accident. I really didn't see her.' He reached into his pocket and pulled out his wallet. 'Obviously I'll pay for Martha's treatment and cover her wages while she's ill.' He removed a five-pound note and held it out to Mary.

'Keep your filthy blood money.' She knocked the note from Harry's hand. 'And get out of my kitchen! Now!'

Diana retrieved the money from the floor and handed it back to Harry. 'I won't be long,' she whispered.

Harry went outside. Glad to be alone, he latched the door behind him and leaned against it. His sisters could be boisterous when the mood took them, especially Edyth – he uttered another silent prayer that she would recover – and they had gone through a phase of emulating Douglas Fairbanks's swordfights after visits to the picture houses. But none of them had ever attacked him as violently as Mary Ellis.

Rain gusted over him on a cold blast of wind. The cuts and scratches on his face and neck throbbed painfully to life. He dabbed at them with his handkerchief, took a deep breath to steady himself and headed for his car. When he reached it, two boys walked through the archway. One was shorter than Martha, the other taller, but it was difficult to ascertain their ages as they were wrapped in grey blankets that covered their backs and most of their heads.

The taller yelled a command. A sheepdog ran up to Harry and sank its teeth into his ankle.

Crippled by the pain, Harry struggled to free himself. He shouted, 'Please, call your dog off.'

'Hold, Merlyn! If you don't move the dog won't hurt you.' The boy tossed his blanket aside and walked up to Harry. 'This your car?' He was as dark-haired and wild-eyed as Mary, and looked even more aggressive. Harry knew that he had found the girls' missing brothers without even looking.

'Yes.' The dog's teeth were no longer sunk into his leg, but Harry could still feel its jaws closed around his ankle. Anxious to diffuse the tension, he forced a smile, but it wasn't returned. The boy was younger, smaller and lighter than him, but he suspected that his physical inferiority wouldn't stop him from throwing a punch any more than it had his sister.

'What you doing here?'

Harry crossed his arms across his chest because it was the least hostile stance he could think of adopting. It was still raining steadily but he was so wet anyway it simply didn't matter. 'I drove Miss Adams and Martha up here from Craig y Nos. Martha's had an accident—'

'What kind of accident?' The boy's face was so close, Harry could feel the warmth of his breath.

'A road accident,' Harry answered evasively. 'But she's going to be fine. Miss Adams is with her now.'

'If you brought her home, what you doing lurking in the yard?'

'I came out to look for you,' Harry explained patiently. 'Your sister said you'd gone down the mountain track to look for Martha.'

'If you had been looking for us we would have seen you on the mountain. You're a thief, that's what you are,' the boy declared angrily. He looked for confirmation to the younger boy, who nodded vigorously.

'I've only just left the house, so I hadn't time to go down the track.'

'You were looking for chickens and eggs to steal.'

'If I was looking for things to steal, I'd sneak into the yard not drive my noisy car in so you'd hear the engine.' The dog's jaws tightened on his leg and Harry leaned against the Crossley for support. The boy appeared immune to both sense and argument, and he braced himself to receive another bite.

'Only a bloody toff talks the way you do and wears clothes like that!' David took aim and sent a stream of spittle towards Harry's feet. It hit the toe of his shoe on the foot the dog was holding. 'If you're not here to steal, then the agent must have sent you, and everyone knows he's a bloody thief.'

'No one sent me. And I haven't a clue what agent you're talking about. I told you I drove Martha home—'

'Liar!' The boy finally lashed out and punched Harry in the stomach. The dog growled and closed his jaws.

Harry had been expecting the bite. He'd even had time to tense his muscles to receive the punch, but he didn't bargain for the force the boy used or the strength that was surprising in someone so small and slight. He groaned involuntarily as he straightened his back and the dog tightened its grip.

'David, Matthew, is that you I hear talking?' Diana interrupted from the back door.

'Miss Adams?' Both boys turned to her.

'Call Merlyn off Mr Evans, David, there's a good lad. Mary needs you two inside.'

'Did you come here with him, Miss Adams?' The older boy poked a grimy finger into Harry's chest.

'Yes, David, I did.' She put up her umbrella and, stepping carefully again, crossed the yard to the car.

'He,' David jabbed Harry again with his finger, 'said that Martha's had an accident.'

'She has, but she's all right now. And I'll be up in the morning to make sure she stays that way.' She looked at Harry. 'Are you all right, Mr Evans?'

'I will be when he calls his dog off,' Harry muttered between clenched teeth.

'David?' She appealed to the boy.

'Good dog, Merlyn, heel.'

'Thank you,' Harry breathed gratefully, rubbing his ankle. He believed that Diana Adams was actually enjoying his discomfort.

Diana turned back to David. 'I'll pick up the eggs for the sanatorium every day until Martha's well enough to come back to work.' She glanced from him to Matthew. 'Both of you had better get inside and change quickly before you catch cold. Mary's enough on her plate with nursing Martha. And Luke's teething has given him a slight fever. Go on, off with you.'

David finally opened the back door and ushered Matthew into the house, but gave Harry one last antagonistic glare from the doorstep before slamming it shut.

'Thank you,' Harry murmured. 'Two attacks from two Ellises in as many minutes are as much as I can cope with.'

'He hit you?' Diana asked.

'I know better than to tell tales after I've played with rough boys in the school yard,' Harry rejoined flippantly.

'Did he hurt you?'

'Not anywhere that can be seen.' He picked a dock leaf from a clump that was growing at the foot of a horse's mount and wiped his shoe.

'You should pick another and wipe your face.'

'Is that medical advice?'

'It's a foolish doctor who dismisses all the old country remedies out of hand. And the Ellis boys aren't vicious, just over-protective towards their sisters.' Diana opened the car door and climbed inside. She shook her umbrella, closed it and set it at her feet.

Harry winced when he sat beside her. 'After seeing the children, I wouldn't like to meet the parents.' He ran his hands through his hair brushing out as much water as he could.

'They have no parents, Mr Evans.'

'They run the farm themselves?'

'They have done for the last year. Although it's anyone's guess as to how much longer they'll be able to carry on. It's common knowledge in the valley that they owe a fortune in rent.'

'So that's why the boy accused me of being sent by the agent,' he mused. 'But they're so young.' He started the car and drove out of the yard.

'I wouldn't let them hear you say that should you ever meet them again. Mary's nineteen, David fourteen, and they consider themselves quite grown up enough. Given the responsibilities they have taken on, they have every right to. I've seen farmers in better circumstances than the Ellises give up and take their families to the workhouse.'

'Did their parents leave them?'

'In a manner of speaking. They are both dead. You've a dog-bite that could turn septic and from what I saw of your face in the kitchen, your cuts need to be properly cleaned and dressed. So you'd better drive me back to my house so I can do just that.'

He lifted his hand from the wheel and fingered his throat and face. 'I've had worse and lived.'

'I dare say, but if they get infected, they'll spoil your pretty looks.'

'Pretty?'

She smiled mischievously. 'I've forgotten how touchy men can be about that word. I meant handsome.'

'Really?' he enquired sarcastically.

She dropped her mocking tone. 'We seem to have got off on the wrong foot, Mr Evans.'

'If we have, do you think that is my fault or yours?'

'I'd say about fifty-fifty.'

'I'm big enough to apologize for misjudging you earlier.' He dropped down a gear as they descended the steep hill. 'It's obvious from the state of that kitchen that those children are living hand to mouth and you only employ Martha to make sure that some money goes into the house.'

'I'm amazed you thought my father capable of exploiting a child after seeing our work at the sanatorium.'

'I was upset, angry and feeling guilty after the accident. I'm sorry for what I said. What more can I do other than apologize?' he asked.

'Nothing this evening, Mr Evans. Turn right into the drive just before the hospital entrance. I'll dress those cuts for you and tend to any other injuries you've sustained, including the ones that can't be seen – that's if you're not too embarrassed to take your shirt off in front of a female medical student.'

Chapter 7

MARY LADLED out three bowls of soup. She set two in front of her brothers and mashed the vegetables in the one she had poured for herself with a fork, before taking Luke from David.

'So, the toff came in here.' David lifted a spoonful of soup to his lips and blew on it to cool it.

'How many times do you want me to tell you that he did?' Mary sat opposite her brothers and settled Luke on her lap.

'You haven't told me what he had to say for himself.'

'Not much.'

'So why did you let him in?'

'I told you,' she reiterated impatiently. 'He carried Martha in. Miss Adams said his name was Mr Harry Evans and he's related to one of the patients in the castle.'

David took the crust from the loaf she had sliced and dunked it into his soup. 'He's rich. You only have to look at his clothes to see that. And he had a car.'

'I saw it.' Mary handed Luke a finger of bread, but he screwed up his eyes and threw it down in a fit of temper.

'Martha said it costs a lot of money to keep someone in Craig y Nos.'

'I suppose it does.' She was too busy fighting to keep Luke on her lap to pay much attention to what David was saying.

'So if he does have a relative in there, he must be paying a lot of money to Doctor Adams.'

'I suppose so.' Ashamed of the way she'd flown at him, the last person Mary wanted to talk about was Harry Evans. She dipped a teaspoon into the soup, lifted out a thin portion and held it to Luke's lips. He pushed it aside with his fist and shook his head vigorously from side to side. 'Come on, darling,' she coaxed, 'you have to eat. If you don't, you'll be ill.'

'As he's rich, he should pay for knocking Martha down in his car.' David tore the rest of his bread into pieces and dropped them on top of his soup.

'He offered. I threw his money back at him.'

'What did you do that for?' David retorted angrily.

'Because I didn't want him to think that he could buy us. Like . . . like . . .' she faltered, not wanting to say anything that would make her brother hate the agent any more than he already did.

'Like bloody Bob Pritchard, with his endless "generous" extensions on our rent arrears?' he growled.

'Language!' Mary glanced at Matthew who was sitting low on the bench. His mouth was barely level with the table, and although he was eating, it was obvious from his eye movements that he was listening intently to every word that was being said.

'Well, I'll tell Miss Adams when she comes tomorrow that we *do* want Mr Harry Evans's money,' David declared feelingly. 'It's only right that he pays Martha's wages until she can work again. And we'll take whatever else he's willing to give us.'

'Martha's wages, maybe, but I don't think we should take anything else off him. Not for an accident. It's not as if Miss Adams will charge us anything for seeing to Martha.' Mary gave up trying to feed Luke. She held a cup of water to his lips and he drank greedily. When he finished, she lifted him on to her shoulder and held him there with one hand, freeing the other so she could eat.

'What was he doing driving up here in the rain and mist anyway?' David helped himself to another slice of bread.

'How should I know?' Mary answered irritably. Luke was so hot; his tiny body burnt hers, even through the layers of clothing that separated them. She couldn't bear the thought of him and Martha both being ill at the same time. As it was, she was behind with the cheese- and butter-making, and she needed to kill and pluck at least a dozen chickens before the next market day. And there was Dolly . . . would the poultice work? She gripped her spoon tightly. It simply had to! She looked at David. He was holding his spoon over his bowl, apparently deep in thought. 'Is the supper all right?'

'Yes. Why shouldn't it be?' he snarled.

'No reason. You're not still thinking about that man, are you?'

'A toff like him could do a lot for us.'

'Like what?' she questioned cautiously.

'He could look at the agent's books for one thing, and tell us if Bob Pritchard is really diddling us.'

'I can't believe that you'd want to talk to a total stranger about our private affairs.'

'Why not? He owes us something for knocking Martha down. I told you, Mary, I've just about had all I can take from . . .' he saw fire flash in her eyes and tempered his language, 'the agent.'

'And what would you do if Mr Pritchard refused to show him the books?'

'He wouldn't dare refuse a toff.'

'Maybe not, but he'd be angry with us afterwards for asking Mr Evans to do it. You know he would. And then he'd take it out on us. He could evict us. Promise me you won't say a word to Mr Evans about it, Davy?'

'Only if you promise to tell Miss Adams that we want him to pay Martha's wages until she can work again. As well as take anything else he offers,' he added strongly. 'Promise?' he repeated when she didn't answer.

'I promise,' she answered reluctantly. She moved her head back and looked at Luke. 'I'll take him up and tuck him in between Martha and me. If either of them is ill in the night I want to be on hand to see to them.'

'And tomorrow?'

'I said I'd talk to Miss Adams, didn't I?'

David knew better than to push his sister further than she was prepared to go. He finished the soup in his bowl and left the table. 'I'll check on Dolly. If she's all right I'll clear up here and put Mathew to bed if you want to stay with Martha and Luke.'

'Thanks, Davy.'

'And don't worry about the morning milking, stay with Martha.' He reached across the table and ruffled Matthew's curls.

'It's time this one took over. I'll soon teach him to get the cows in and milk them by himself.'

Matthew bristled with pride, but all Mary could think of was David's threat to join the army. Didn't he realize there was no way that he could train six-year-old Matthew to replace him on the farm? No more than she could do his work as well as her own.

The bathroom in the Adamses' house was cold, and Diana's fingers were even colder. Harry shuddered when she unfastened his collar and tie, opened the top buttons on his shirt and bathed the cuts on his throat.

'Did I hurt you?'

He thought she looked positively gleeful at the notion, and lied rather than add to her pleasure. 'I flinched because your hands and the iodine are cold.' He tensed when she upended the bottle on a fresh ball of cotton wool.

'It doesn't sting?'

'A little,' he conceded.

'You're lucky Mary only took the top layer of skin from your face and neck. If she'd gone for your eyes, she could have blinded you.' She examined his wounds before cleaning them again. 'I doubt they're deep enough to give you permanent scars, but the iodine will make you look as though you're wearing war paint. I could bandage you, if you like.'

'That won't be necessary, thank you,' he said firmly.

'Now the dog-bite.' She knelt in front of the stool he was sitting on and watched him remove his sodden shoe and sock before pressing the skin around his ankle. 'I always knew Merlyn was well trained. You've two neat rows of teeth-size bruises but there are no breaks in the skin.' She wiped the area with cotton wool and iodine.

Unable to quell the feeling that she was relishing his discomfort, he rose to his feet as soon as she'd finished. 'If I don't go now, I'll be late for supper at the inn.'

'If you changed out of your wet clothes and borrowed my father's robe, you could have supper here.'

'Pardon?'

'It's the servants' night off,' she continued matter-of-factly, 'so you'd have to take pot-luck. My repertoire is somewhat limited, but Cook generally leaves fruit, smoked salmon and salad, and I make an excellent Manhattan cocktail.'

'And your parents? Wouldn't they object to you inviting a stranger for supper at the last minute?'

'They are in Swansea. The Mackworth Hotel holds a supper dance every Saturday night and they dine there, dance afterwards and stay over until Sunday morning, when they stop off to attend morning service on their return journey. My father calls it his weekly dose of civilization.'

'And if there should be an emergency in the sanatorium?' Harry was alarmed at the thought of what might happen to his grandfather if he was taken ill during the night.

'I am here and the local doctor is on standby should I need his assistance.' She looked coolly at him. 'So do I get you the robe or not, Mr Evans?'

His throat went dry. If the invitation had come from one of his female fellow students in Oxford he would have known exactly what to do. But he was finding it difficult to see past Diana Adams's starched medical image.

She turned her back on him, plugged the iodine bottle with a cork and replaced it on a shelf. 'Not quite the Saturday night invitations you have been used to, Mr Evans? But then, this is a quiet valley.'

'This is only the second evening I've spent here.'

'You're not bored yet?'

'I would have preferred a boring afternoon to the one I've just had.' He picked up his jacket, which was soaking wet.

Her mouth twitched. 'Are you afraid of me? Or of what might happen if we ate supper together, Mr Evans?'

He never had been able to resist a dare. 'Do you have a telephone that I can use to call Mrs Edwards at the inn, Miss Adams?'

'Downstairs in the hall, Mr Evans. I'll start running your bath while you speak to her.'

'That's right, Mrs Edwards,' Harry concurred. 'My things are still in my room because I've decided to extend my stay at the inn for a day or two. I hope that won't cause any problems.'

The landlady's voice crackled down the line. 'We've no other booking for that room at the moment, Mr Evans. Can we expect you back tonight?'

'Yes.' Harry was conscious that he was speaking on the sanatorium line, and anyone who picked up a receiver in the castle would be able to listen in. He was also very aware of Diana moving around upstairs and probably eavesdropping on every word he was saying. 'I'm not sure of the time because I'm having supper with a friend.'

'A friend, Mr Evans, in Swansea?' she enquired artfully.

'No, Mrs Edwards, in the valley. I may be late, but don't worry, I have the key you gave me.'

'The back door's never locked.'

'Thank you, Mrs Edwards. I have to go, my supper is ready. Goodbye.'

Not at all sure he'd done the right thing in accepting Diana's invitation, he walked up the stairs. Water was still running in the bathroom. When he opened the door, clouds of steam wafted out to greet him. He closed it, noticed there was no lock and hoped Diana was right about them being alone in the house.

He unbuttoned his sodden shirt, and peeled it off, as well as his trousers and underclothes. He was turning off the tap and testing the water when the door opened behind him. He turned and froze.

'You don't mind if I share your bath with you, do you, Mr Evans?'

Diana Adams was standing naked in the doorway, one leg poised in front of the other, her head thrown back, her arms extended and her hands gripping the door frame. It was a classical pose that reminded him of the statues he had seen in Rome. But she was no marble or bronze Venus, or Aphrodite. Her flesh was ivory, blushed with the palest tints of rose. Even her nipples were a light shade of pink. Her breasts were surprisingly full given her slender waist and limbs, her thighs softly rounded, her hair glittering, like spun gold under the electric light . . . and to his shame he couldn't

113

stop staring. He felt his cheeks burn as colour flooded into them. 'Miss Adams . . .' he stammered.

'Diana.'

'The huntress,' he murmured unthinkingly.

'And, like the huntress, I find the predatory approach saves time.' She walked towards him; he stepped back. 'I'm sorry. Have I misjudged you?'

He said the first thing that came into his head. 'I have a bruise.'

She ran her fingers lightly over his abdomen. 'So you do. I have some salve that I can rub on that – later.'

It had been a long time since Harry had thought of himself as an innocent when it came to women. Even before Oxford, where he had met educated, emancipated fellow female students, like Anna, fully conversant with all the modern birth control methods that enabled them to practise their philosophy of free love, there had been a girl with whom he had been besotted. Until he had discovered that she was bestowing her favours as freely on his fellow sixth-formers as on him.

But Diana Adams was more domineering, demanding and adventurous in her lovemaking than any women he had ever encountered. Before he had time to kiss her, she had taken the initiative, rousing him to a pitch where he felt that he was not so much making love to her on the bathroom floor, as being consumed by her there.

Afterwards, at her suggestion, they bathed together, taking it in turns to wash and explore one another's bodies, before going downstairs, he in her father's bathrobe, she in a flimsy silk gown.

The maid had lit a fire in the drawing room. They cobbled together a makeshift picnic in the kitchen and carried it in on trays before making love again at a slightly less frenetic pace on the hearthrug, in between drinking gin cocktails and eating smoked salmon sandwiches.

He was lying back, naked and exhausted, when she loomed over him and dangled a grape above his mouth.

'Don't tell me you're too tired even to snap at it?' She brushed it over his lips.

He opened one eye. 'You've killed me.'

'I hope you're in heaven not hell.'

'Definitely heaven.' He smiled lazily, reached up and stroked the hair away from her forehead.

Evading his touch, she rolled over on to her stomach and propped herself up on her elbows. 'That was fun, Harry.'

'It was,' he agreed sleepily.

She lifted her cocktail glass to him. 'Here's to the beginning of a lovely and loving friendship. Now,' she slipped her robe back on and set a plate of grapes between them, 'Tell me all about yourself, starting with the day you were born.'

'I can't remember it.'

'Do you have brothers and sisters?'

'Five sisters.' He fell serious when he thought of Edyth, and imagined her lying still and unconscious in the Graig Infirmary while he and Diana had been making love. The image brought a sour taste to his mouth.

'You don't like them?' she asked, misreading his expression.

'I adore them, when they don't gang up on me,' he replied, taking refuge in flippancy. 'They are all younger than me,' he added, not wanting to talk to Diana about Edyth – yet. 'I also have a brother, Glyn, who is only two.'

'I would love to have brothers and sisters.'

'You're an only child?'

'I wasn't.' Something in the tone of her voice warned him not to pry further. 'Damn!' She was on her feet before the telephone rang a second time. Tying the belt on her robe, she ran out of the drawing room to answer it.

Harry reached for the robe he'd borrowed. He was so tired he wasn't sure if he was disappointed or relieved by the interruption. But he did know that he felt completely drained – by the acrid taste of guilt after the accident, by Mary and David Ellis's attacks but most of all by the totally unexpected and pleasurable demands Diana Adams had made on his body.

He had the oddest sensation that he'd wandered into a surreal dream. Any moment he'd wake in his rooms in Oxford, the shrill ring of his alarm clock vying with the shouts and arguments of his fellow lodgers as they fought for the bathroom. His grandfather would be fine and he'd be looking forward to a short trip home, followed by a summer in Paris . . .

Diana returned, the thin robe tied tightly at her waist and a frown creasing her smooth forehead.

'Problems?' he asked, when she started piling their plates and uneaten food back on the trays.

She stared at him as though she had forgotten he was there. 'I'm needed across the road, and before you ask, it's not your grandfather. It's one of the children.'

'I'm sorry, is there anything that I can do?'

'I only wish there was something I could do,' she murmured soberly.

'It's time I was leaving anyway.'

She glanced at the carriage clock on the mantelpiece. 'At a quarter past nine? You go to bed this early, you, dull boy?' She pushed her feet into her slippers and picked up a tray.

'It's been a long day and I have wet clothes that need seeing to. I don't think my landlady would appreciate me dumping them on her at midnight.' He carried the second tray into the kitchen for her.

'Leave those,' she ordered, as he started piling dishes on to the board next to the sink. 'The maid will see to them in the morning.'

He followed her up the stairs to the bathroom where they had left their clothes. She picked up his shirt and trousers from the floor and draped them over the bath. 'You can't possibly put these back on, they're sodden. Borrow some of my father's. I'll explain that I brought you back here to see to your cuts and gave you a change of clothes rather than see you risk pneumonia.'

'No, thank you,' he said unequivocally. 'It would lead to too many questions. Mrs Edwards is a kind woman, but if I turned up in your father's clothes she may put two and two together and get the right answer. And that, Miss Adams, wouldn't do your reputation any good at all.'

'Perhaps you're right,' she smiled. 'But you have to promise me that you will have another hot bath as soon as you get back to the inn. We can't risk you going down with anything that will prevent a repeat of what just happened, can we?' She slipped her hand inside his robe and tickled him before retrieving her suspender belt from the chair and hooking it around her waist.

'Yes, Doctor,' he answered with mock humility.

'Are you patronizing me?' she asked, not entirely humorously.

'You don't like taking what you dish out?' he teased. Removing the robe, he hung it on the hook on the back of the door and reached for his underclothes. He wrung them over the bath before he put them on, but he still cringed when they clung to him, cold and clammy. Trying to forget his discomfort, he took solace in watching Diana roll on her stockings.

'My parents go to Swansea every Saturday night, but the hotels there hold supper dances on other evenings.' She stepped into a waist slip and reached for her brassière.

'The slow waltz and the foxtrot?' he asked absently, fighting with his wet shirt.

'It may amaze you to know that the natives have been seen doing the Charleston in the Patti Pavilion. But they have a jazz band in residence there on Friday evenings.'

'And you go there?' He stepped into his trousers.

'Occasionally, when I have company.' She slipped her dress over her head. 'My father doesn't like me travelling on the train by myself late at night.'

'Would he mind you driving down there with me the next time I'm in the valley?' He picked up her one remaining garment from the chair, her knickers, and held them out to her.

'I've lived alone in London for three years, Mr Evans. My father's concern is only for my safety, not the company I keep. Although I don't think he'd object to you.' She trailed her fingers over his flies, took her knickers from him and dropped them into the linen bin. 'You'll be at the sanatorium with Mr Ross tomorrow morning?'

'I will.' His shoes squelched when he tied his laces.

'I'll let you know what kind of a night your grandfather has had then.'

'Thank you, and thank you for earlier – and this.' He fingered his throat when she walked him down the stairs and into the hall.

'Don't, or you'll infect those cuts.' She knocked his hands away from his face. 'Remember, change out of your wet clothes and into a hot bath as soon as you reach the inn. And don't wash that iodine off your face or ankle for at least two days, or you may find yourself even more at my mercy.'

Harry wondered if he had imagined the entire episode when he climbed into his car. Surely he couldn't have just made love with Diana Adams? Not the Snow Queen whose heart had been frozen by an icicle?

'I've hung up your clothes in the old stillroom, Mr Evans. They can drip there until Enfys can see to them on Monday morning. We'd never hear the end of it if word got out that I allowed washing to be done here on a Sunday. The ministers preach against this place enough as it is. But I must say I've seen drier hauled out of a tub, so I hope you have others you can wear. If this storm holds, it might take us a few days to get them properly aired, even on the kitchen pulley.' Mrs Edwards lifted a mug down from the hooks screwed into the wood above the bar and held it questioningly in front of Harry.

'Yes, please, I would like a pint of beer, Mrs Edwards. And don't worry about my clothes. I brought a change, which is just as well if this weather is typical of the Swansea Valley. And I can always take the ones I was wearing back home wet.'

'When it rains here, it rains,' Mrs Edwards said philosophically. 'You warm now?'

'Finally. All I needed was a hot bath and dry clothes.'

'I don't like the look of those scratches on your face.'

'They'll heal in a day or two, Mrs Edwards,' Harry said. 'And they only look odd because I called into the sanatorium to have them treated. They put iodine on them and in the waiting room well away from the patients.'

'That will teach you to stay away from stray dogs.'

'It will.' Harry compounded the lie he'd told the landlady about being attacked by a stray dog when he'd left his car on the mountain.

The only place in the inn that had a bath was a lean-to scullery. It was Spartan, comfortless and draughty, even after the chilly, white-tiled and mahogany splendour of the Adamses' upstairs family bathroom, He hadn't lingered there long. He had washed hurriedly in warm water before dressing in an identical flannel suit to the one he had worn earlier.

'You can't be too careful with your health, that's what I say, especially if you insist on running in and out of TB hospitals.'

Hoping to avoid another discussion of Mrs Edwards' favourite topic – the lethal, disease-ridden air of the sanatorium that she was convinced clung to everyone who walked in or out of the place – Harry changed the subject. 'Is Mr Ross back from Swansea?'

'Like you, he telephoned to say that he had run into a friend, was having supper with him and would be back on the last train. He asked if Alf could go over in the trap to pick him up at quarter to eleven.'

Harry saw Alf serving behind the bar and took the hint. 'I won't be going to bed early, Mrs Edwards, so I'll pick Mr Ross up from the station.'

'That would be good of you, Mr Evans. I know you've had supper but do you fancy a snack?'

'No, thank you, Mrs Edwards, beer is fine.' Harry glanced around the bar. He was used to the pubs in the Rhondda that filled early on Saturday nights and stayed full all evening. It was ten o'clock, prime drinking time in Pontypridd, yet there were only half a dozen farmers and labourers clustered around the fire that blazed in the enormous, old-fashioned hearth.

Mrs Edwards saw him looking around. 'Not many want to walk down from the hill farms on a night like this.' She nodded to her son. 'I'm off to the kitchen with these dirty glasses.'

'No Enfys tonight?' Harry asked.

'Saturday night is her courting night. She leaves at seven.'

Try as he might, Harry couldn't imagine the silent Enfys courting. 'Is it serious?'

'Should be, she's been stepping out with Mervyn Jones for eighteen years next month. And Saturday night suits him and me. We only have our regulars like you and Mr Ross in then. Travellers never stay over at weekends.'

'Eighteen years and no sign of a wedding?' Harry was amused.

'Mervyn's a second son. He has to save for his own farm.' There wasn't a trace of humour in Mrs Edwards's voice.

Harry carried his beer to a quiet corner, sat down and studied the men gathered around the fire. Their faces were lined and weather-beaten, their conversation slow and sporadic as if they were unused to voicing their opinions. And as they were speaking in Welsh not English, he could understand little of what was being said.

He sat back, enjoying the warmth of his dry underclothes, shirt, waistcoat and jacket after spending most of the afternoon soaked to the skin, and thought of the two boys who had gone out on to the rain- and wind-swept mountain to look for their sister, with nothing more than thin blankets around their shoulders for protection.

Diana's comment that he didn't understand poverty had hurt because his parents had never tried to shield him from the grimmer side of life. He knew dozens of families in the Rhondda and Pontypridd who lived close to the breadline, and occasionally below it. But somehow poverty in an isolated farmhouse, miles from the nearest village, seemed much worse than poverty in a street of terrace houses where neighbours might be noisy and interfering, but were also generally charitable and well-meaning.

'Here you are, Mr Evans. I know you said you didn't want anything, but these cockles are fresh up from Swansea market today. And nothing goes as well with a pint of beer as a plate of cold cockles boiled in vinegar water, or so my late husband, God rest his soul, always used to say.' Mrs Edwards set a bowl and a fork in front of him.

'Thank you, Mrs Edwards, they do look good.' He picked up the fork.

'Another pint of beer?' She took his empty mug from the table.

'Please, and a drink for Alf and yourself.'

She glanced over to the bar where Alf was chatting to the farmers who could make their drinks last twice as long as the average customer. 'That's very kind of you, Mr Evans. I'll have a glass of stout and I know that Alf would appreciate a pint of cider.'

Harry rose to his feet when she returned with the drinks and pulled a chair out for her. 'Won't you join me, Mrs Edwards?'

'I don't mind if I do, Mr Evans. The bar's the only place in the inn that's busy on a Saturday night and the weather's put paid to that tonight. Are the cockles all right?'

'Excellent, as was lunch today.' Harry waited until she'd sat down before returning to his chair. 'My father and uncles appreciated you putting yourself out for us.'

'No trouble, Mr Evans. Has your grandfather settled into Craig y Nos?'

'We weren't allowed to go into the ward with him.' Harry knew the declaration would reassure her, and he wanted to steer her on to another topic of conversation. 'Do you know anything about the family of children who live on the big farm on the mountain above Craig y Nos?' He tried to make his enquiry sound casual, although he had no doubt that news of the car accident would spread before too long.

'The big farm – you mean the Ellis Estate?'

'Yes.' The room suddenly went quiet, and Harry realized that although he could only speak a few words of Welsh, his fellow drinkers had a grasp of both languages.

'Why do you want to know about the Ellises?' she asked.

'I happened to meet them today and I was curious to know how such a young girl and her brothers came to be running a farm of that size.'

'That's simple, their mother and father are dead.'

'And we all know whose fault that is.' A short, thickset man, who looked as though he'd never see seventy again, left the group in front of the fire and stomped over to their table.

'Come on, Dic, you can't go saying things like that.' Mrs Edwards glanced uneasily over her shoulder.

'I'll say what I like. It's still a free country for all that the crache are employing scoundrels to buy up every inch of it and put good people out of their houses to starve.'

Harry rose to his feet, pulled out a chair and offered the gnarled old man his hand. 'Harry Evans.'

'Dic Johns.' He shook Harry's hand briefly.

'Can I buy you a drink?'

'Pint of cider.' He thrust his glass at Harry.

'Dic used to be the shepherd on the Ellis Estate,' Mrs Edwards explained.

'And David Ellis was the best bass and friend a man could have until the crache, damn their thieving souls,' he curled his lips, took aim and spat across the room into the fire, 'did for him.'

Alf, who had been watching Dic, brought a pint of cider over to their table. He gave it to Dic and nodded to Harry. 'I'll put it on your tab, Mr Evans.'

'Thank you, Alf.'

Harry knew the question he was about to ask would be seen as prying from an outsider, but he had to know. 'How did David Ellis die?'

Mrs Edwards closed her eyes briefly as if she couldn't stand the thought. 'He killed himself.'

'The crache killed him,' Dic contradicted vehemently, slamming his glass down on the table.

'Dic—'

'All right, Mrs Edwards, I'll grant you, David Ellis tied the noose, but we all know what made him do it.' He looked at Harry. 'What happened to David Ellis happened to a lot of good people around here back in nineteen nineteen.' He wrapped both hands around the pint of cider Harry had bought him as if he were afraid that it was going to be snatched from his hands. The war was over; everyone thought better times were coming. The landlords of the farms and estates around here wanted to sell, and by law they had to give the sitting tenants first refusal. The farm was doing well, so David Ellis took out a mortgage to buy it. Then the Depression came. When he failed to make the payments, the bank sold the estate out from under him for half of what he'd paid them. And to the same landlord who'd owned it in the first place. The landlord's agent went to collect the rent every week, and when the Ellises couldn't pay he started taking their furniture. Some of it had been in the family for five hundred years and David Ellis couldn't stand the shame. It was the shame that drove him to hang himself.'

'That must have been dreadful for his family.' Harry went cold at the thought of the desperation that had led the man to take his own life. It was no wonder that Mary Ellis and her brother were so protective of their sister.

'He did it in the barn. His wife and daughter found him. By the time I heard about it in the hills, they'd buried him outside the wall of the churchyard next to all the other suicides and babes who'd died before they could draw breath, or be baptised. Mrs Ellis told me she couldn't pay me. I didn't have the heart to tell her that I hadn't been paid since her husband had bought the estate. So I found myself a job lower down the valley. I'm at Pen y Cae now. It's all right. But the people aren't like the Ellises. I'd worked for the family, man and boy, for close on forty years, and my father and grandfather before me.'

'When did Mrs Ellis die?' Harry asked.

'Just over a year ago, bringing a babe into the world,' Mrs Edwards informed him sadly.

Harry remembered the baby lying on the rag rug in front of the fire.

'I thought the agent would put the Ellis children out but he did worse.' Dic stared moodily down into his glass. 'He stripped the place of every stick they had left that was worth a brass farthing. And it's my guess that as most of their furniture was hundreds of years old, it was worth a lot more. Not that those babes saw any of the money. It all went into the agent's pocket.'

'You can't say things like that, Dic.' Mrs Edwards looked around nervously again.

'Yes, I can, and I'll say it twice as loud in case any of Bob the Gob's cronies are here. It all went into his pocket.'

'The younger girl, Martha, lied about her age to get a job as a maid in Craig y Nos.' Mrs Edwards sipped her stout.

'How old is she?' Harry asked.

'Eight, nine, I don't know for certain. But I can tell you she's a few years shy of twelve and no one should employ a girl that young, let alone in a sanatorium.'

'Miss Adams makes sure that they don't work her too hard.'

Mrs Edwards sniffed loudly to let Harry know what she thought of that. 'I feel sorry for them. Everyone round here would like to help them but they're an independent lot. And the eldest girl, Mary, is a fool if she believes she can keep that estate going until her brother's old enough to take over.'

'Even if she does manage to keep the tenancy, there'll be nothing left for young Davy to inherit by the time the agent's finished with them,' Dic pronounced bitterly. 'Ask any man around here. Like most farmers, David Ellis paid for his land ten times over and all he got for his trouble was a parish funeral and a plot six feet by two outside the churchyard. Not even inside under the family slab with his father and grandfather.'

'Miss Adams told me that the Estate had been built by the Ellises.' Harry offered his cigarettes around the bar.

'The name David Ellis and the date, sixteen twenty-four, are carved into the arch over the front of the house, and there are Ellis graves in the churchyard that go back even further.' Dic finished the cider in his glass. 'They say the Ellises were aristocracy round here back then. But in seventeen fifty-four another David Ellis had to sell up to re-stock the farm when disease killed every one of his sheep. The man who gave him the money took the deeds to the Estate and that left the Ellises tenants where they had once been freeholders.'

'For all we know that could be a story, Dic,' Mrs Edwards admonished.

Dic clutched his empty glass. 'My dad told me it was true and he never told me a lie in his life.'

'It was that story that made David Ellis all the more determined to buy the place. I remember him coming in here the day he went to the solicitor's to sign the deeds. He and Mrs Ellis were so happy. They bought the children tea to celebrate.' Mrs Edwards smiled sadly at the memory. 'He put down every penny the family had, five hundred pounds, as a deposit against the fifteen hundred pounds the farm cost him. When the bank sold the Estate out from under him for seven hundred and fifty pounds it left him owing two hundred and fifty pounds, as well as the capital on the mortgage and the interest on the payments he hadn't been able to make. The rent was fixed at a hundred and fifty pounds a year and those children have been living hand to mouth ever since.'

'I warned them.' Dic took a cigarette from the packet Harry offered him. 'So help me God, I warned Mary Ellis to pack up, move on and make a life elsewhere for her and the little ones when her mother passed away. But would she listen? "There's always been a David Ellis running the Ellis Estate," she told me. "And our David will be the next one, you'll see." '

'Poor thing, she's deluded, but you can't blame her, living up there with only her brothers and sister for company. She has nothing to think about except her father, the wrongs he suffered and the Estate.' Mrs Edwards cleared away Harry's empty bowl. 'There are more cockles out in the kitchen if you want them, Mr Evans.'

'Save them for tomorrow, please, Mrs Edwards.' Harry left his seat. Even if it hadn't been time for him to drive to the station to pick up Toby, the story of the Ellises' misfortune had quite taken his appetite.

Chapter 8

DIANA ADAMS was stepping out of a Bentley when Harry drove
Toby into the courtyard of Craig y Nos the following morning. In
sharp contrast to the day before, the weather was glorious. The
wind had dropped, the newly washed greenery sparkled with
reflected sunlight and it was pleasantly warm with the promise of
more heat later in the day. Harry and Toby were both dressed in
white flannel suits, white shirts, ties and straw boaters. Determined
to make the most of the weather, Toby had asked Mrs Edwards to
pack them a picnic. Harry had also taken down the hood on his
tourer.

'How is my grandfather?' Harry drew alongside Diana and,
recollecting what had happened between them the night before,
gave her a broad smile.

'Still very weak after his journey,' she replied in her brisk
medical voice, glancing pointedly from Toby to a gardener who
was raking a nearby flowerbed. 'The sister reported that he slept
well, although he had little appetite for breakfast.'

'Can I see him?'

'Not today, but you can ask again tomorrow.'

'Just for a few seconds?' he pleaded.

'No.'

'I'd like to give him these.' He lifted a basket of strawberries
from the back seat. He had bought them from a roadside stall in
Penycae.

'I'll see that he gets them and I'll tell him that you were asking
after him.' She took the basket.

'How is my uncle?' Toby eyed Harry and Diana suspiciously as
he left the car.

'He was feverish first thing this morning. All he could talk about was you and an illustration that you promised to finish by today. He was so concerned about it that my father decided it would be detrimental to his health if he didn't see it. You have finished the painting?'

'Of course.' Toby leaned over the back of the car and lifted out a portfolio, set between two boards and tied with string.

'We know he'll work himself into a state if we don't let him see you, but no more than five minutes – and that painting won't leave his room if you allow him to touch it,' Diana warned.

'Of course.'

'And I know your attitude to time. Not one second more than five minutes, Mr Ross. I have already briefed the ward sister, so don't try exercising any of your charm on her. It will be wasted.'

'It always is on the women around here. They simply don't appreciate me,' Toby lamented with theatrical mournfulness.

'Treat your uncle carefully, he really is worse, Mr Ross,' Diana said seriously.

'I promise you, I'll show him the illustrations and leave.'

'Are they good?' Diana called after him as he ran to the front door.

'How can you doubt it?' Toby disappeared inside.

'Nice car.' Harry looked at the Bentley.

'My father's. My runabout is being serviced by Alf Edwards.' Diana opened the back door and lifted out a basket of eggs.

'I dreamed about you last night,' he whispered.

'There are open windows, Mr Evans,' she murmured, 'and people have ears, but I enjoyed our time together too.' She raised her voice to conversation level. 'I've just returned from the Ellis Estate.'

'How are Martha and Luke this morning?'

'Martha's speech and movements are still slower than normal, but that is to be expected. It will take a few days, possibly even a week or two, for the full effects of the concussion to wear off. And Luke is a different boy. Two brand-new teeth have arrived to drive away the grizzles. Mary is relieved.'

'I'm sorry to hear that Martha's no better. Is there anything I can do?'

'According to David Ellis, plenty.' She curled her lip in distaste. 'He told me to tell you that he expects you to pay Martha's wages until she is well enough to work again.' She set the baskets on a low wall.

'I offered—'

'He knows you did. He also knows that his sister refused to take your money and he's furious with her for throwing it back at you. But be warned, David is very different from Mary.'

Harry fingered his iodine-stained scars. 'Not that different.'

'Oh, he is. Mary's only aggressive when she thinks her brothers and sister are being threatened. David will take every penny that he can squeeze from you, and he'll try to squeeze a lot.'

'It's only right that I compensate Martha for lost wages until she can work again,' Harry insisted.

'As long as you keep it to compensation, Mr Evans. You are not responsible for the family's plight.'

'I heard how they came to lose the farm last night in the pub.'

'It's a tragic story, but then I've heard a number of those since my father took up this post. It hasn't been easy for us to accept that there is nothing we can do to help the tenant farmers around here except give them our worthless sympathy. Mary Ellis is exceptionally single-minded and a fighter, but I don't doubt she'll eventually be evicted, as all her neighbours have been.'

'After yesterday, you don't have to tell me about Mary Ellis being a fighter.'

Diana's smile broadened. 'You're not reluctant to face her again, are you, Mr Evans?'

'Frankly, yes. I really feel that I owe them money but I'd rather post it,' he replied honestly. 'Or you could take it up there tomorrow?'

'I'm not an errand girl.'

'Can you spare me half an hour now?' he pleaded.

'Sorry,' she repeated, looking anything but. 'I'm far too busy this morning to chaperone a coward.'

'It's a bodyguard I need, not a chaperone. Come on,' he coaxed, 'it's a nice day, the sky's blue, the sun is shining. Mrs Edwards has packed a picnic that Toby and I can stretch to feed a guest. Don't you feel like a run-out?'

'I've had my run-out for the day, and I've far too much to do to here to waste any more time visiting.'

'Then I'll wait for Toby.'

'You expect him to protect you?' she smiled mischievously.

'I'll ask him to keep the car's first aid kit in readiness while I talk to the Ellises.'

'If I might make a suggestion, why don't you drive down to the village and buy another basket of those strawberries? Martha loves them.'

'Don't they grow any on the farm?'

'I know it was raining yesterday, *Mr Evans*,' she said loudly for the gardener's benefit as he moved on to a flowerbed even closer to them, 'but didn't you notice what a bleak spot the Ellis Estate is in? It's as much as Mary can do to grow a few potatoes, carrots and cabbages in the sheltered area in front of the house.'

'Martha really likes them?' He pressed the ignition.

'She does. Just a moment, a strawberry has dropped on your back seat, it will stain the leather.' She dropped her voice to a whisper when she leaned over the car. 'Are you staying in the valley tonight?'

'I'm living day to day. One of my sisters is ill and I may have to go home at a moment's notice. But I am reluctant to leave until I know that my grandfather has settled in.'

'If your grandfather is well enough, I'll ask my father if you can see him tomorrow.'

'Thank you. I'd appreciate it if you would.'

'And if you'd like to go for a walk this evening, I'm off duty at eight and I usually go for a stroll alongside the river from the sanatorium up to the hills. The scenery is very pretty around there.'

'I'll look forward to seeing it, Miss Adams.' He gazed into her deep-blue eyes.

'Away from the hospital, I allow my friends to call me Diana.' She raised her voice. 'There, I have the strawberry, Mr Evans.' She flicked the offending berry on to a flowerbed.

'And you consider me your friend?' He gave her the smile that he flattered himself had melted a few female hearts.

'Not yet, but after another evening like yesterday's, I might,' she whispered.

'You'll tell Toby I'll be back for him in ten minutes.'

'I will.' She waved him off.

In the hope of ingratiating himself with the Ellises, Harry bought a large basket of raspberries as well as one of strawberries. He returned to the sanatorium to find Toby sitting on the doorstep, his chin resting on the edge of his portfolio, a disconsolate expression on his face.

'Your uncle is worse?' Harry guessed.

'He looks dreadful. I didn't see him yesterday and I can't believe the deterioration in just two days.' Toby flung his portfolio into the back of the car and slumped in the passenger seat. 'It's ghastly to watch him grow weaker by the day.' He looked intently at Harry. 'I'm not sure how much more I can take.'

'If he can take it, so can you.' Harry was aware that if Dr Adams did allow him to visit his grandfather he would soon be facing the same ordeal.

'You're right, of course. I can't leave him, not now. But I tell you something: if there is a God and I come face to face with him in the hereafter, I'm going to give him a piece of my mind. Frank's brain is sharper than it's ever been, his creative ability is undiminished. He has ideas and passion enough to create hundreds if not thousands more paintings and illustrations that would dazzle the world and give pleasure to untold millions who appreciate art. And he hasn't even the strength to hold a pencil, let alone do anything with it.'

'How did he like your illustration?' Harry asked, trying to lift Toby's spirits.

'He didn't entirely, but then he never does. He made a few suggestions for improving it, but not as many as usual. And that's not a sign I'm becoming more skilled as an artist.' Toby turned and checked that the portfolio was secure in the back. 'Raspberries as well as strawberries? We'll be sick if we eat all those.'

'They're not for us. I bought them for that little girl I told you about.'

'The one you knocked down?'

'I was hoping you'd call in the farm with me. But if you want me to drop you off somewhere first so you can start painting right away, I will.'

'As I'm in no mood to start work right away, a spin up the valley sounds just the sort of time-wasting exercise I need. Besides, I can always fool myself that I'm scouting locations for the next illustration.'

Harry pushed the car into low gear when they started climbing upwards. 'Are you looking for something in particular?'

'Frank wants me to paint the lake next, so I need a stretch of pretty water and a shapely arm to rise out of it to hold Excalibur. I have the sword in my room, as the last illustration Frank completed was Arthur wielding Excalibur for the first time in battle. You should see it, Harry. It's a huge, magnificent canvas. It's bound to be exhibited at the Academy.'

'I'll make a point of going next May.'

'We'll go together, if you like.' Toby fell silent, and Harry sensed that he was thinking of what would happen to Frank before next May.

'I spotted a reservoir below the farmhouse last night that might do for your lake,' he said in an attempt to distract Toby.

'A reservoir?' Toby exclaimed disdainfully. 'How unromantic. I can tell you now, it will never do.'

'You haven't seen it,' Harry remonstrated.

'I don't need to. I need a proper, natural lake. And as all anyone will see of the lady is her arm, it will have to be a very beautiful and young one, with no wrinkles, a slim wrist and manicured nails.'

'Won't the skin on the tips of the fingers have water crinkles if the lady lives in the lake?'

'Idiot, the hand will be out of the water.'

'For how long?'

'As long as it takes Arthur to see it.'

'And of course, your Excalibur is the genuine article?'

'Absolutely.' Toby fell in with Harry's mood. 'As verified by

Merlin himself, who, incidentally, was a marvellous old shepherd who wandered into the bar one night. Frank wanted him painted with Nimue at the moment of her betrayal. Nimue was a model he used in Paris, so I was able to follow his sketches of her. Merlin was all mine, and it took me four days of following him around the mountains before I managed to portray him to Frank's liking. But I have yet to find my Morgan le Fay. However,' he gave Harry a sly glance, 'from the way you looked at the Snow Queen this morning and, more importantly, the way she looked back at you, I have hopes of seeing her transformed into Guinevere in love some time soon.'

'What look?' Harry asked warily.

'The "sick calf in love" look, and if I had any doubts, the guilty one that's on your face right now have dispelled them. So what gives between you two? Tell Uncle Toby all.'

'There's nothing to tell.' What had happened between him and Diana had been so sudden and unexpected, and was so new that the last thing Harry wanted to do was talk about it.

'Don't believe you,' Toby chanted maddeningly.

'She freezes me out in exactly the same way she freezes you out.'

'Still don't believe you,' Toby sang out.

'All right,' Harry conceded when he realized Toby wasn't going to give up. 'I had supper with her last night after she dressed the cuts on my face.'

'My oh my, you don't waste any time.'

'I'm sure she only invited me because she's bored witless by the lack of social life in the valley.' Harry deliberately tried to sound casual. Even after she had invited him for a walk that evening, he could scarcely believe what was happening between them. And he wasn't at all sure where their relationship was leading, or even if they had one.

'There's always church this evening.'

'You're going?'

'I wouldn't miss it.'

Harry looked sideways at Toby. 'I wouldn't have taken you for the religious sort.'

'Oh cynical one.' Toby pulled a packet of cigarettes from his shirt pocket and stuck two into his mouth. 'The truth is I need to paint a room in the Castle of Corbin – you know the scene where the maiden appears to Lancelot in a dream, shows him the Holy Grail and foretells the achievements of Galahad? Well, there's a corner of the vestry that's absolutely perfect for the castle. It has old stone walls with leaded glass windows set at shoulder-height. They're ideally placed to convey ghostly rays of golden light on the maiden. I asked the vicar if I could use it, and he agreed. Unfortunately his wife overheard me so somehow or other I also found myself agreeing to use their daughter as the maiden.' He lit both cigarettes and pushed one into Harry's mouth.

'And when are you painting her in the vestry?' Harry drew on the cigarette before removing it.

'Tomorrow morning. Her father wouldn't allow me to paint her on a Sunday, and her mother, who never, never stops talking, not even to draw breath, is chaperoning us. Join me?' he said hopefully. 'You could paint your own Grail scene. They're very popular in galleries right now,'

'Liar. Besides, if I see my grandfather I hope to drive back to Pontypridd tomorrow.'

'Oh, my good kind Lord.' Toby hung over the side of the car.

'Get back in before you fall out.' Harry grabbed the bottom of Toby's jacket and hauled him back.

'Do you see that?'

'Crai Reservoir. It's the one I told you about and you insisted would never do for your lake. Go on, admit it's pretty.'

'Pretty?' Toby rolled his eyes heavenwards. 'Forgive him, oh great creative ones. It's not his fault that he lacks an artistic soul. It's nothing as ugly as a reservoir, you philistine, it's an Arthurian lake.'

'I saw it marked on a map before I drove down here. It's a reservoir that was built by the town council of Swansea in nineteen o-seven—'

'Now you sound exactly like Diana Adams.' Toby blew a plume of smoke in Harry's direction but it was carried away by the breeze. 'Are you going to marry her and breed a column of solemn-faced lecturers who'll think it their duty to bore the world?'

'You can be an ass at times, Toby,' Harry grumbled.

'After you've done whatever it is you want to at the farm, bring the picnic hamper down, will you? I'll get a head-start on a couple of sketches.'

'You expect me to haul that hamper all the way down to the reservoir?'

'I'll give you my spare sketchbook and an art lesson in return. And there is no reservoir, only an Arthurian lake, and it will be known to all as such by the time I've finished with it.' Toby dared him to say otherwise before turning back to absorb the magnificent view.

Harry had only known Toby Ross for a few days, but he had already discovered that there was no point in trying to talk to him while he was creating paintings in his mind's eye, so he concentrated on the road and the majestic, magnificent scenery of sweeping hillsides that rose and fell around them.

But as they approached the Ellis Estate, he couldn't help agreeing with Diana Adams that, for all its beauty, it was a bleak and lonely spot.

Harry dropped Toby off at the entrance to a track signposted 'Crai Reservoir'. Studiously ignoring it, Toby strode off, haversack on shoulder, sketchpad and pencil in hand and a look of intense concentration on his face as he studied the vista below him. Harry carried on to the farm, but instead of driving into the yard as he had done the night before, he turned the car around and parked on the road opposite the house. Taking the two baskets of fruit, he walked through the arch into the farmyard.

Dogs started barking as soon as he set foot on the cobbles, but to his relief, he noticed they were securely penned. Chickens scratched between the cobbles and wandered in and out of the barn. Ducks waddled around a small pond, splashing water over the weeds that encroached at the sides. Two enormous sows snorted and scuffed in an open sty that fronted the outbuildings at the far right-hand corner of the the yard. The doors to a cowshed and milking parlour opposite him stood open, a freshly swept pile of manure heaped in front of them, but the stalls were empty and there was no sign of any of the Ellises. He was halfway to the back door in the hope of finding someone in the house, when he heard a noise in an outbuilding on his left.

He knocked and the door swung open. Mary Ellis was standing in front of a trestle table, turning the handle on a butter churn.

'I'm sorry, I didn't mean to startle you,' he apologized, when she jumped back nervously.

'I heard the dogs but there's a puppy that starts them off and he barks at nothing . . . Mr Evans! Your face! Did I do that?'

He touched his cuts and bruises lightly. 'They only look this way because Miss Adams put iodine on them to prevent them from getting infected.'

She glanced at him in confusion before looking down at the table. 'I wasn't expecting you to return.'

'I saw Miss Adams this morning. She told me that your brother thought that I should pay Martha's wages while she's too ill to work. And I quite agree with him.' He set the baskets down, pulled his wallet from his inside jacket pocket, opened it and extracted two white five-pound notes. He held them out to her.

Avoiding his gaze, she shook her head. 'We couldn't possibly take that much, sir, Martha only earns seven shillings a week.'

'It's not just Martha's wages, Miss Ellis. It's also the upset and pain I've caused her and your family. Please.' He folded the notes, placed them on the table and pushed them towards her. 'Nothing will make me feel any the less guilty, and this is no more than Martha deserves.'

She hesitated, and he sensed her wavering.

'It's not charity, Miss Ellis; it's compensation for Martha. Sensible people would see it that way.'

'Perhaps just one, sir.'

'Please, take both, and my name is Harry, not sir. I'm not that much older than you.' She made no effort to pick up the notes. 'Miss Adams said that your sister is still suffering from the effects of concussion.'

'She is.'

'I am sorry to hear that.' He pointed to the baskets. 'I brought her some fruit.'

'That is kind of you, sir.'

'Not at all.' Aware that he was making her uneasy, he backed out of the doorway.

She stared down at the banknotes before slowly, almost unwillingly, pocketing them. 'Thank you for the fruit.' She dropped the handle of the churn and picked up the baskets. 'I'll take these into the scullery and draw some water so Martha can clean them.'

'Would you like me to carry the baskets for you?'

'No, sir.' Her refusal was emphatic.

Sensitive to her disquiet, he said, 'Is it all right if I leave my car parked outside your house for a few hours? My friend has walked down to the reservoir and I'm going to join him.'

'What has he walked down there for?' There was resentment as well as suspicion in her voice.

'He's an artist, and he wants to paint a picture of it.' She looked confused, so he added, 'He wants to put it in a book as an illustration.'

'Our reservoir? In a book?'

'You may not realize it after seeing the mountains and reservoir every day, but your house is in a very lovely spot.'

'We like it,' she bit back defensively.

'So do I, all the more after living in a city for the last three years.'

Weighed down by the baskets, she joined him in the yard. 'I've never been to a city.'

It was the closest they'd come to a normal conversation. Wary of provoking further unease or aggression, he settled for a bland, 'Never?'

'I went to Swansea a few times with my mother, when she was alive. She used to sell our butter and cheeses to the farmers' wives who had stalls on the market. She used the money they gave her to buy our clothes. But Swansea's only a town.'

Harry glanced at her black cotton skirt and blouse. Both were patched with material of a lighter shade, and she coloured when she saw him looking at her. Hoping to alleviate her embarrassment, he asked, 'and what did you think of Swansea, Miss Ellis?'

'It was noisy and dirty.'

'Most industrial towns in Wales are. They wouldn't be anything else with all the coal mining that goes on here. But they do have their advantages. Theatres, dance halls, picture houses, shops, art galleries . . .' He recalled how poor the Ellises were and how ridiculous it was to talk about picture houses, plays and the theatre to a girl who couldn't afford to pay her rent. 'Is there a picture house or theatre in the valley?' he asked, wondering if he dare suggest that he take Martha, and any of the other Ellises who wanted to go as further atonement for knocking her down.

'There's a theatre in the sanatorium. Madame Patti used to give concerts there. My father and mother took me when I was little. But it hasn't been used since she died.'

'You don't have any picture houses?'

'There may be one in Pontardawe, and there are magic lantern shows in the chapel vestry sometimes. But it takes us so long to walk down there and we're so busy in the evenings; we haven't been for a few years.'

'The farm must take all your time,' he sympathized.

She went into the scullery and left the baskets of fruit next to an enormous stone sink before going to the kitchen door. 'I have to start making the dinner now.'

He touched his boater. 'Would you mind if I came up to enquire after your sister again?'

'There's no need. Miss Adams said Martha will be fine.'

'Then, if you prefer, I'll make my enquiries with Miss Adams in future.' The girl was obviously frightened of him and he decided that it might be as well if he sent more fruit up with Diana.

'David, you're back early.' Mary looked past Harry to her brother, who strode into the yard with his sheepdog and Matthew trotting at his heels.

The dog growled when David pointed an accusing finger at Harry. 'I stopped shearing when I saw his car parked outside the house.'

'Mr Evans called to give us money.'

'At least a fiver, I hope.' David glared at Harry and made no effort to silence his animal. Harry had never been afraid of a dog in his life, but after being attacked the day before, he stepped back warily.

'He gave me ten pounds, David,' Mary murmured.

'Merlyn!' David snapped, and the dog fell silent. If David was surprised by Harry's generosity he showed no sign of it. 'It's no more than Martha deserves after what he put her through.'

'I was just asking Miss Ellis if she would allow me to call and enquire after your sister's health again . . .' Harry debated what he should call David Ellis. 'David' was too familiar, boys under sixteen should be addressed as 'master', but there was nothing of the child about David Ellis. Fortunately, David interrupted him.

'As long as you know that we expect you to carry on paying for what you did to Martha until she's better.'

'David, that's bad manners,' Mary said.

'How much more do you want me to pay?' Harry asked.

'Her wages.'

'I think the ten pounds will cover those.'

'The doctor's bills,' David added.

'Miss Adams has told me that she won't charge you for her visits.'

'She's not a proper doctor,' David said truculently.

'Then when you call a proper doctor, please tell him to send his bill to me.' Harry slipped his card case from his pocket, opened it and handed David one. 'That's my home address. I'm staying at the inn in Abercrave at the moment. The doctor can leave a message for me there if he calls in the next day or two.'

The boy took the card. 'He will.'

'I'll wait to hear from him.' Harry touched his cap again. 'Miss Ellis, it was good to make your acquaintance. I only wish it could have been under better circumstances.'

Toby added a few lines to his rough sketch of the reservoir and the surrounding hills before shading his eyes and studying the scene for a full minute. Then he closed the book. He glanced across to where Harry was sitting, sketching surrounded by the tins and boxes he'd lifted out of their picnic hamper. 'It sounds like your young David Ellis is a right charmer.'

'He's not "my" David Ellis.' Harry gazed critically at the clump of grass he'd drawn in the foreground of his landscape. 'And I can't say that I wasn't warned. Diana Adams told me this morning that he was going to try and get all he could out of me.'

'Good for you for fighting back. A lesser man would have simply handed him more money.'

'You think I should have given them more than ten pounds?' Harry asked seriously.

'Ten pounds plus a face full of scratches and bruises is more than enough for an accident that was as much the girl's fault for walking in middle of the road in a storm as yours.' Toby opened his knapsack and stuffed his sketchbook inside. 'So, what are we eating?'

'Ham and cheese sandwiches, pork pie, pasties, cheese straws, salad, apple turnovers and two of the biggest slabs of fruit cake I've ever seen. Oh, and four bottles of beer.' Harry handed Toby a plate.

'Thanks, I'll take a piece of pork pie, a ham sandwich, cheese straw, salad and a bottle of beer. You do have an opener?'

'On my trusty penknife.'

Toby sat next to Harry. 'You know the major and most serious problem with the poor is that when you put baksheesh into their hand, they come to expect it on a regular basis.'

'That a proverb or did you just come up with it?' Harry pulled a handful of green salad from a tin box lined with greaseproof paper, and sprinkled it on to his plate, before handing the box over to Toby.

'I came up with it. And it's born of bitter experience. You start giving those children handouts, they'll come to rely on them, and before you know it, you'll either be keeping them or they'll be in the workhouse. And if they're incarcerated, you'll be wracked by guilt even though you are not responsible for them. It wouldn't surprise me if that grasping little beggar asks you for another ten pounds next week – and should you be idiotic enough to give it to him, another tenner the week after that.'

'If he does, he'll get short shrift.'

'You say that now, but what will you do if he tells you that Martha is worse?'

'I'll ask to see her.'

'And if she is?' Toby pressed.

'Diana Adams says she'll make a full recovery and I believe her.' Harry demolished a cheese straw in two bites. 'From the way you're talking, it sounds as though you've doled out charity once too often yourself.'

'I did, with a young model in Paris. It was the closest I've ever come to a serious disagreement with Frank. And much as I hate to admit it, he was right and I was wrong. He said it would end in disaster, it did, and I'd rather not talk about it. So,' Toby dusted the crumbs from his hands and looked enquiringly at Harry, 'let's see that sketchbook I gave you.'

Harry handed it over.

Toby opened it. 'Not bad, not bad at all.'

'Really?' Harry would never have admitted that he was looking for a compliment. He only hoped that Toby wasn't being sarcastic.

Toby pulled a pencil from his knapsack. 'If you extend this line, shorten this one and add a bit more detail here . . .' A few seconds and pencil strokes later, he had completely transformed Harry's sketch.

'One minute's work and you've made it come alive,' Harry said despondently.

'Don't forget it took four years of hard graft at the Slade to learn those tricks, and make no mistake, they are tricks.' Toby handed the book back to Harry and picked up his ham sandwich.

'I'd like to say it was just a doodle, but I really thought I was making headway,' Harry complained.

'You were.' Toby consoled. 'And I know just how you feel. There have been times when Frank has taken my efforts apart in the name of constructive criticism and left me thinking that I'd never produce any work worth a penny damn.'

Harry set the book aside and spread mustard over his slice of pie. 'Can I see what you've done?'

'Later, when I'm past the taking notes stage and know exactly how my lady's arm is going to look coming out of the lake – when I find it. The arm, I mean. The lake is perfect, as are the surrounding hills. I can just see Arthur and Merlin riding over the crest of that hill on their trusty white steeds, draped in red tapestry stitched by the adoring court ladies, and looking down on this wild and lonely place – I'd have to paint out the farmhouse, of course.'

'Of course,' Harry agreed drily.

'I told you all the ideas are Frank's, but that's not to say I won't run this one past him.' Toby finished his sandwich, lay back, crossed his arms behind his head and stared up at the sky. 'This really is glorious. I wish . . .'

'What?' Harry prompted when Toby remained silent.

'That this moment would last for ever. That nothing would ever change.' He sat up suddenly, and pulled the sandwich box towards him. 'The weather, you, me, eating like kings in this peaceful place with nothing to do but try to produce art – whatever that word means. That publishers who demand at least two illustrations every Monday morning be content with what they have, without nagging me to hurry up and send more.'

Harry wasn't fooled by Toby's mention of publishers. He knew that he was thinking of Frank and looking ahead to a time when his uncle would exist only in memory.

He imagined his grandfather and sister lying in strange rooms, in strange beds surrounded by people who, for all their professional expertise and well-meaning attempts to care for them, were still strangers.

And he resolved to demand that he be allowed to see his grandfather first thing the following morning, whatever Dr Adams said.

Chapter 9

'IF YOU wanted the hamper to weigh less, you should have eaten more.' Toby grabbed the second handle and helped Harry haul it up the last fifty yards of hill that stretched between them and the main road.

'After that walk my stomach tells me I should have eaten less, not more.' Harry left the hamper with Toby and opened the boot of his car. 'Here, put it in.'

Toby heaved it next to a pair of rubber galoshes and a mackintosh. 'I see you're well prepared.'

'I wish I'd had the foresight to unpack them from my bag and put them in the boot yesterday.'

'Leave them there, and we're guaranteed to have great weather for the next week or two.' He glanced at his wristwatch. 'Half past four; we're in good time to get back to the inn and have a drink before we change for evensong. You coming with me?'

'To have a drink? Do you have to ask?'

'To evensong, you idiot.'

'My face is a mess and I have letters to write,' Harry prevaricated. After being forced to attend religious assembly every morning, and church three times every Sunday at his boarding school, he had come to resent the waste of time spent in communal worship. He would have much rather used it to read or listen to music on his gramophone.

He'd been happier with his mother's more relaxed attitude in the school holidays. He'd occasionally attended services in St Catherine's with her and his sisters, but she had never criticized him when he had preferred to stay home and play chess with Lloyd.

As a Marxist, his stepfather only attended religious services on family state occasions and then under duress.

'Letters – what letters?' Toby challenged.

'The usual letters, to family and friends,' Harry answered.

'And you can't write them later this evening, or tomorrow?'

'Be honest, would you even think of going to evensong if you didn't want to paint the vestry?'

'That's below the belt.' Toby looked across the road at the arched entrance to the farm. Mary Ellis, wearing a black varnished straw hat, an unseasonably thick shawl thrown around her thread-bare cotton skirt and blouse, walked through, carrying a baby dressed in a white knitted suit. He lifted his hat to her.

Harry followed suit. 'Good afternoon, Miss Ellis.'

'Mr Evans.' She glanced behind her at her brothers. David and Matthew's wild curls had been slicked down with water and flat caps, and they were both wearing shiny, darned and threadbare suits. David's was too large for him, Matthew's too small. White-faced and shaky, Martha walked between them.

'How are you feeling, Martha?' Harry asked in concern.

'Better, thank you, sir,' she slurred.

'Not by much,' David growled.

Mary risked annoying her brother by adding, 'We all enjoyed the strawberries and raspberries you gave Martha, Mr Evans.'

'Are you going somewhere?' He closed the boot of the car.

'Chapel.'

'Isn't it a little early?' Toby suggested.

'Our horse is lame so we have to walk there.' David made it sound as though Toby was responsible for the horse's injury.

'Please, let me give you a lift.' Harry opened the back door of the car, took Toby's portfolio and their knapsacks from the seats and carried them around to the boot. He stowed them away carefully before slamming it shut a second time. He looked across the road. None of the Ellises had made a move towards the car, and all five were standing, watching him.

'I am driving down to Abercrave. You are going that way?'

'Yes,' Mary answered diffidently.

'Then please, get in. You really won't be putting me to any trouble.'

He couldn't have sworn with any certainty that David Ellis said it, but he thought he heard him hiss, 'Pity' as he pushed past him and climbed into his car.

Harry ran out of conversation while he could still see the Ellis Estate in his rear-view mirror. Toby wasn't so easily deterred. He made several attempts to instigate a discussion, starting with the change in the weather, and when that elicited monosyllabic responses, he tried talking about livestock. But as the only thing Toby knew about cows, pigs and sheep were their shapes from a painter's point of view, and as the Ellises weren't prepared to tell him more, he eventually gave up. It was left to Matthew to break the ice when they were speeding down the hill.

'This car can go faster than Dolly.'

'Is Dolly your horse?' Harry was glad he had a question to ask.

'Yes, but she was slow even before she went lame. Why did you poke me, David?' he said with the artful innocence of a child.

'I didn't. Don't make up stories,' David snarled.

'Stop it, you two,' Mary cut in sharply.

'David's still poking me, and I've done nothing,' Matthew whinged.

'Do you like cars?' Harry smiled at the boy in the mirror. 'I'm sorry, I don't know your name.'

'I'm Matthew.'

'Do you like cars, Matthew?'

'I like to look at them, but this is the first time I've ever been in one.'

'And we're going to cause a right stir, turning up in the village in this, especially with his face all painted with iodine,' David muttered sourly.

'I wouldn't think so,' Harry contradicted. 'It's common for drivers to give people lifts where I come from.'

'That's where you come from,' David said. 'It's not common around here.'

'Only because not many people have cars,' Mary said quietly.

'Miss Adams always stops to give Martha and me a ride if she is travelling our way.'

'And all the carters stop when they see someone walking on the road,' Matthew added. 'A car is a sort of cart, isn't it?'

'A rich man's cart,' David muttered darkly.

Harry adjusted his rear-view mirror and saw Martha sitting very still with her eyes closed. 'As you're going to be early for chapel, why don't you come to the inn with us?' he suggested, earning himself a peculiar look from Toby. 'Mrs Edwards serves very good lemonade; we could all have a glass. She may even have some cake or biscuits.'

'You going to chapel?' David asked belligerently.

'Church.' Toby rolled his eyes upwards when he saw Harry looking at him.

'I might have known you two would be church,' David observed, determined to find fault with everything Harry and Toby did.

'There's not a great deal of difference between church and chapel.' Toby felt in his pockets for his cigarettes. 'The people who worship in them all pray to the same God.'

'You ever been in a chapel, mister?' David demanded.

'Yes,' Toby answered.

'To a service?'

'No, but—'

'Then how would you know there's not much difference between them?' David crowed.

'Because they look roughly the same. And you're wrong about Harry. Only I am going to church,' Toby informed him. 'Harry is—'

'Chapel,' Harry broke in to Toby's amusement. Martha looked as though she had fainted, and he couldn't bear the thought of the girl walking five miles back to the farm after the service. 'I would be grateful if you would show me where it is. And afterwards I could drive you home, if you like. I want to make a sketch of the reservoir in the fading light.'

'You're painting an evening landscape?' Toby slipped his tongue into his cheek.

145

'Yes,' Harry countered.

'Just as long as you remember the advice I gave you about getting too involved with your subject, Harry.' Toby found his cigarettes and opened the packet. 'Do you smoke – David, isn't it?'

Harry knew he'd been wrong and David had been right when every head in the congregation turned as he walked into chapel with the Ellises ten minutes before the service was due to start. There was an escalation of whispering among the women sitting in the pews, but the most piercing glares at his scarred face and condemnatory comments came from the seats at the front of the chapel reserved for the deacons.

He stood back and allowed Mary and her family to file into the Ellis pew ahead of him, first Mary carrying Luke, then Matthew, Martha, who looked as though she should be in bed, and finally David.

Although his mother was a churchgoer and both his uncles' families Catholic, he had visited chapels for the christenings, weddings and funerals of his family's friends, so he knew roughly what to expect from the service. Irritated by the continued murmurs and stares in their direction, and longing for a cigarette, he turned his attention to the building. But after examining the plain whitewashed walls, unadorned dark-wood pulpit and hymnal notice with its removable numbers, he was bored. The beaded eyes of the vivid blue bird perched on the hat of the woman in front of them were more interesting. Whichever way he turned, they appeared to be eyeing him, and he wondered if it were a real stuffed bird, or one created by a milliner out of odd feathers she'd found lying around.

The service began. The singing, like most in Welsh chapels, was impressive, as was the organist's playing. The minister, a tiny, wizened man who looked as though he could be blown over by a gust of fresh air, had an uncommonly loud voice that he used to full advantage when he delivered an interminable and tedious sermon on the desirability of the tithe system in relation to chapel income.

When he thought no one was watching him, Harry glanced down the pew. Mary Ellis sat bolt upright, her eyes fixed on the minister. Luke, who fell asleep soon after they sat down, stayed

146

asleep. Matthew was playing with a home-made catapult he'd hidden beneath his hymnal. Martha could barely stand to sing the hymns, and whenever David opened his hymnal, Harry noticed that it was always on the wrong page, but it didn't matter because the boy was word perfect.

When the collection plate came around, he slipped in two shillings and sent it on, earning himself a thump in his side from David. It was only then that he saw the edge of a copper penny protruding from the boy's fist.

Wondering if he'd ever do anything right where the Ellises were concerned, Harry was glad when the minister declared the service over and the organist began playing a mournful instrumental that sounded like a requiem to accompany the congregation's exit.

He stepped back to allow the Ellis family to precede him. An elderly deacon stood beside the minister at the door. Just like the minister, he was a small, withered scrap of a man. He also looked as though he'd never had a bath in his life, but in contrast to his neighbours, his clothes were new and expensive, and he was wearing a gold watch chain that Harry presumed was attached to a watch.

A young woman who might have been his granddaughter stood behind him, easily the best dressed woman in the congregation. Harry recognized her black silk frock, silk-trimmed cloche hat and black patent cross-bar shoes as the height of current fashion. An enormous bow with a garish centre of diamanté, at odds with the elegant cut of her outfit, decorated the belt at her hips. But it was her jewellery that attracted his attention. A Victorian gold and blue enamelled fob watch was pinned to her chest and an unusual antique gold locket hung around her neck.

'Mary Ellis!' the deacon exclaimed when Mary stepped into the porch.

Mary stopped in her tracks and held Luke closer to her.

'You bring a strange man into our chapel—'

'Please, allow me to introduce myself.' Harry pushed through the crowd until he stood between Mary and the deacon. He held out his hand to the minister. 'Harry Evans. Pleased to make your acquaintance, sir. My grandfather is a patient at Craig y Nos, and I am lodging with Mrs Edwards at the inn so I can remain close to him. I trust you have no objection to my worshipping here when I visit the Swansea Valley?'

A few murmurs and nods of acknowledgement greeted Harry's announcement, and he recognized a few faces from the bar. The minister had little choice but to respond to his courteous approach by shaking the hand he offered.

'Mr Penry.'

'Pleased to make your acquaintance, Mr Penry, sir.'

Although Harry avoided looking directly at the deacon, he was conscious of the hostile glare he was sending his way. He offered him his hand. 'Harry Evans.'

'Mr Williams.' The man gave Harry a limp, damp handshake.

'You are a Baptist, Mr Evans?' the minister asked.

'My family is from Pontypridd but I have been studying at Oxford for the last three years,' Harry replied evasively. 'My tutor was Doctor Esau Morgan.'

'Doctor Morgan? You know Doctor Esau Morgan?' The minister beamed at the mention of the name. Esau Morgan had been Harry's English tutor, but he was also a leading Baptist and composer of many rousing hymns. A fact Harry had totally disregarded until that moment.

'Extremely well, sir.' Harry returned the minister's smile. 'An erudite, learned man and leader in his field. And an inspiring teacher.'

'Indeed.' The minister nodded enthusiastic agreement. 'You are very fortunate to know him personally, Mr Evans. I know him only by repute.'

'He helped me considerably with my studies.' Harry turned to David, wrapped his arm around his shoulders and pulled him forward. 'Miss Adams at Craig y Nos introduced me to David Ellis, and he was kind enough to allow me to accompany his family here today.'

'David.' The minister acknowledged the boy before turning back to Harry. 'On behalf of myself, the deacons and the entire congregation, may I welcome you to our chapel, Mr Evans. I hope we will see you again.'

'You most certainly will, Mr Penry. I found your sermon extremely interesting.' Harry kept hold of David.

'It is kind of you to say so.'

'Mr Williams,' Harry turned to the deacon, 'it has been a pleasure to meet you.'

'Has it?' Not so easily won over by Harry's charm as the minister, the deacon glared at Mary. 'You know that Mr Pritchard won't be happy about this, girl.'

'Who is Mr Pritchard, and why won't he be happy, sir?' Harry asked.

'Mr Pritchard is the land agent for E&G Estates. He collects the rents.' The deacon paused so the full effect of his words could sink in. 'When the tenants pay it.'

Harry would have loved to tell the man he was an ill-mannered boor, but he managed to restrain himself. 'And what has Miss Ellis done to make him unhappy?'

'She knows,' the deacon answered mysteriously before turning his back and stomping off. The expensively dressed young woman nodded a goodbye to the minister and followed him.

'Good evening, Mr Penry.' Harry recalled another helpful name. 'I will write and tell Mr Armitage in Pontypridd how much I enjoyed your service.'

'You know Mr Armitage, the Baptist minister in Pontypridd as well?'

'Of course, everyone in Pontypridd does. He is a well respected and charitable man.' Harry tipped his hat to the minister and the ladies. 'David, it's time to drive your sisters and brothers home.'

'Damn Iestyn Williams—'

'David, I told you I won't have you using language like that, especially in front of the little ones,' Mary shouted from the back seat, where she had sat with Matthew, Martha and Luke. Hoping to appease David, Harry had offered him the passenger seat in the front of the car.

David crossed his arms mutinously and muttered a perfunctory, 'I'm sorry.'

Harry looked at him. 'So who is Iestyn Williams and why does

149

he think that he has the right to tell your sister what to do?' he said, too low for Mary to hear.

'He's Bob the Gob's right-hand man.'

'Sorry, I don't understand — Bob the Gob?'

'He's the agent,' David answered abruptly, as if Harry should have known. 'Just because we owe him rent, he thinks he owns us, especially Mary. I told you not to come to chapel with us.'

'David, you, your sister and your family have the right to do whatever you want and go anywhere you want to, with anyone you choose.'

'Not in Bob the Gob's eyes. Or Iestyn Williams. I bet he'll tittle-tattle to the agent first chance he gets. Did you see the locket and watch the deacon's wife was wearing?'

'That was his wife?' It was just as well that Harry was driving slowly, because he turned to David in disbelief.

'They were my mother's.'

'You had to sell them?'

'Bloody Bob the Gob took my mother's jewellery box after she died without even asking. The next time we saw those pieces, *she* was wearing them. The bitch.'

If Mary heard her brother's outburst in the back of the car, she let it pass that time. They drove the rest of the way in silence. When Harry stopped outside the farmhouse, they filed out. Mary and Martha were the only ones to murmur, 'Thank you.'

It wasn't until Harry was passing Craig y Nos on the return journey that he remembered where and when he had heard the name Iestyn Williams. He had met his Aunty Megan's father and his second wife without even realizing it. Perhaps he should have revealed the connection.

Then he recalled what his stepfather and Uncle Victor had said about the man, and decided it was just as well he hadn't known who he was. It wouldn't have done him any good, and he might have done the Ellises even more harm than he already had by attending chapel with them.

'I can just imagine you sitting between David and Mary Ellis in chapel,' Diana laughed. 'Both of them scowling, and you cringing, terrified they'd attack you again, even in a pew.'

'I knew they wouldn't dare hit me in chapel.' Harry sat next to her on the grassy riverbank. He untied his shoelaces, slipped off his shoes and socks, hitched up his trousers and dangled his feet in the water.

'That's a good idea.' She lifted her skirt, unclipped her suspenders, rolled off her stockings and followed suit. 'Ow! It's icy.'

'Now who's being a coward?' Harry leaned back, stretched out his hands to support himself and gazed up at the sun sinking slowly towards the mountains. 'I'd give a great deal to be able to capture that on canvas.'

'You'll have to come here again and try. But then, tomorrow night it will look entirely different,' she said philosophically. 'I've walked along this river almost every dry evening since I joined my father in Craig y Nos, and no two sunsets are ever alike.'

'You said my grandfather had a good day.'

'Yes, but I also said that you are not to nag me about seeing him. My father will decide whether or not your grandfather can have visitors. And he won't give or withhold his permission until the morning when he knows what kind of night Mr Evans has had.'

'I'm sorry. I didn't mean to pressurize you.' He leaned forward and watched the clear sparkling water flow over the brown pebbles on the riverbed. 'I'm worried sick about him. I know it's illogical but it seems disloyal to be sitting here, enjoying this beautiful evening with you when he and Edyth . . . that's my sister,' he explained, realizing there was no point in trying to keep her illness from Diana any longer.

'She's ill as well?' Diana asked in concern.

'And in hospital. She fell downstairs the same day my grandfather haemorrhaged and hasn't regained consciousness since. I telephoned my father after I took the Ellises home this evening, but there's been no change in her condition.'

'No change means no change for the worse, as well as for the better,' she reminded him sympathetically. 'As for being disloyal, I'm sure that neither your grandfather nor your sister would want you to mope. It certainly wouldn't do them – or you – any good.'

He gave her a small smile. 'Thank you for that. You'll make a good doctor.'

'Soon, I hope.' She looked around. 'It's beautiful here. In some ways I'll be sorry to return to London for my final year.'

'When are you going?'

'Just as soon as my father can engage a replacement.'

'You'll come back here when you qualify?' He reached for her hand.

'Perhaps one day but not for a few years.' She squeezed his fingers lightly. 'I intend to specialize in lung disease and my father is universally acknowledged as one of the best practitioners in the field,' she said, 'but I'd like to go to Switzerland and work in one of the clinics there. Some of them are making enormous strides forward in the treatment of tuberculosis.'

He would have liked to ask her where that left him. But although he found her easy to talk to, he felt their relationship was far too new and fragile to make any plans for the future. Instead he kissed her gently on the lips.

'Mmm, that was nice,' she murmured, 'but there's a more secluded and sheltered copse of trees around that bend. You could paddle there.'

'The water is freezing.'

'That's why I said *you* could paddle there.' She wrapped her arms around his neck. 'Carry me.'

He looked at her.

'Please,' she smiled. 'I'm not that heavy.'

'And if I slip and drop you in the river?'

'We'll have to find something to do until my clothes dry out.'

George Adams sat behind his desk, poised, and upright, his attention focused on Harry who was outlining all the reasons why he thought he should be allowed to see his grandfather. Yet the doctor still managed to exude the impatience of a man with more claims on his time than he could possibly fulfil.

'He will have been here for a full two days this afternoon, and I can't see how I could possibly harm him by putting my head around the door of his room and saying a quick hello,' Harry said forcefully. 'And afterwards I'll be able to reassure my family, who weren't here long enough to see your facilities for themselves, that he is being well looked after. Besides,' he added quickly when the doctor looked as though he were about to say something, 'it's not as if my grandfather isn't used to company. He's lived with my uncle, his wife and their four sons for the last twelve years. And we're close, always visiting one another. My father said that he and my uncles are worried about how he's settling in. He rang me at the inn last night and told me—'

'Yes.'

'Pardon?' Thrown by the doctor's interruption, Harry looked blankly at him.

'I said yes, Mr Evans. You can see your grandfather for ten minutes, but on condition you leave immediately if he shows any signs of fatigue. And,' he added firmly, 'you do not touch him.'

Unable to believe he'd heard correctly, Harry said, 'You mean it?'

'My daughter warned me after you called yesterday morning that you would be nothing if not persistent. So you may see Mr William Evans for ten minutes this morning,' the doctor reiterated formally. 'Any future visit will depend entirely on the medical impact this one has on *my* patient.'

'Thank you.' Harry was astounded at his success.

Dr Adams rang the bell on his desk. A nurse appeared in the office doorway. 'Give Mr Evans a gown and mask before taking him up to Mr William Evans's room, Nurse.'

'Yes, Doctor.' The nurse dropped a curtsy.

Harry followed her to the cupboard, slipped the gown she handed him over his clothes and tied the mask around his neck. He pulled it over his nose and mouth when they entered the lift.

The ward sister left her desk when the lift stopped on the third floor. Harry opened the iron cage but she blocked his path.

'Good morning, Mr Evans. Doctor Adams informed me that we could expect you. You understand that you can only stay ten minutes.'

'Yes, Sister.' He would have tried a smile but as it couldn't be

153

seen beneath his mask, he decided it wasn't worth the effort. 'How is my grandfather?'

'As well as can be expected,' she answered in a voice devoid of expression. 'You will leave the door to his room open for the duration of your visit and you will not excite or upset him in any way.'

Harry almost retorted, 'He is my grandfather', then saw her eyes glittering, hard and intractable, above her mask and restrained himself. 'Yes, Sister.'

'This way.'

Harry crossed the corridor behind her. The smell of carbolic and antiseptic was more noticeable than it had been on his first visit. A patient coughed in a room lower down the ward. It was painful to listen to the battle to draw breath and he tried, unsuccessfully, to close out the sound.

'You have a visitor, Mr Evans.' The sister stopped in front of an open doorway. Harry looked in. There were two beds in the room: one was stripped back to the bare mattress; his grandfather lay on the other, which had been wheeled through the french doors onto the narrow balcony.

'Harry, what have you done to your face? And why on earth are you still in this wild spot?'

Relieved, Harry fought his initial instinct to rush across the room and hug his grandfather. Unlike the other patients he had seen when Diana had given him a tour of the sanatorium, Billy was sitting propped up in bed, an open book in front of him, an alert expression in his dark eyes.

'Because I didn't want to go until I'd seen you and could be sure that you'd recovered from the journey and settled in here.'

'As you see, I'm being looked after like royalty.' Billy glanced at the chair that had been placed next to his bed; two legs were on the balcony, two in the room. 'I thought someone might be coming to see me when that appeared this morning. But I had no idea that you'd stayed in the valley. And you still haven't told me how you got those scratches.'

'A playful dog,' Harry lied. He walked over to the bed. 'How come you've persuaded them to let you sit up, when every other patient has to lie down? They even put the young children into straitjackets if they do anything other than lie flat on their backs.'

'It's the pneumoconiosis. If I lie down I can't breathe, so the TB takes second place. Besides it's easier to read sitting up.' He held up his book. '*Tom Jones*; I've been meaning to get around to it for years.'

Harry glanced over his shoulder and, blocking the view of the bed from the sister who had returned to her desk, grasped his grandfather's hand briefly.

'They'll shoot you for that,' Billy whispered. 'Make sure you wash it before you touch anything else.'

'I'm too fit to catch anything,' Harry mouthed.

'I thought the same of myself, so be warned. I'd hate you to catch anything because of me.'

'I won't.' Harry raised his voice to a conversational tone when he sat down. 'You look better than you did on Saturday.'

'I was . . .' Billy turned towards the nurses' station. The sister was writing report cards but he suspected she was listening, so he tempered his language, '. . . on my knees. I don't know why travelling is so exhausting when all you have to do is sit in a railway carriage, but it is. Since then I've done nothing except lie here, eat, drink tea and disgusting oily concoctions, which they insist "will do me good", and read. Reading time has always been a luxury that I've had to steal from working time. Now that it's the only thing I can do, I intend to make the most of it.'

'Any complaints?' Harry asked.

'The food is good,' Billy replied loudly, 'but like all women, the nurses here fuss too much.'

'For a man in your condition, you're very vociferous, Mr Evans.' The sister set aside the card she'd been working on, picked up another and dipped her pen in the inkwell.

'They even let me have a short walk to the bathroom and back this morning.' Billy marked his page with a pipe-cleaner and closed his book. 'There are other miners here, on a six-bedded ward two doors along the corridor.'

'Would you have preferred to have had company?' Harry wondered if they had done the right thing in asking for a private room for his grandfather. Billy had been an outgoing, social person all his life. He had been in charge of all the repairmen in the pit before he had retired from mining, and even when he had helped Victor on his farm, most of his free time had been spent working for the Miners' Union in their eternal quest for better conditions for colliery workers.

'If I feel the need, I'll ask them to move me. But,' Billy glanced fondly at the photographs in the silver frames on his locker, 'good as it is to talk and meet new people, it's better sometimes to lie here quietly, and remember.'

Harry looked at the photographs. There was one of Billy and his beloved Isabella on their wedding day. He was young and resplendent in a dark suit, the winged collar on his shirt set off by a narrow bow tie. Isabella, her Spanish blood evident in her magnificent dark eyes and hair, could have been his sister Bella's twin. Her dress was an elaborate confection of lace-covered bustle and skirt, her bouquet a formal arrangement of roses. But unlike most wedding photographs of the era, they weren't stiffly posed. Instead they appeared to be looking lovingly into one another's eyes.

The second was also of Isabella, taken when she had been a thinner, older woman, her beauty ravaged by time and the cancer that had killed her. She was sitting on a chair in front of a studio backdrop, her three sons standing behind her. It jolted Harry to see how much Lloyd, Victor and Joey had aged since his childhood. The third photograph brought a smile to his face. Lloyd had hired a photographer for Harry's twenty-first birthday party last Easter, and the picture was of the entire family. Billy sitting centre-stage with Harry on his right, surrounded by the entire family.

Billy saw Harry looking at them. 'Thank you for your warning. Your father took the negatives of all three down to the photographer and arranged to have them copied so they won't be lost.'

'I think we must have ordered something like thirty copies of my birthday photograph. Everyone wanted one.'

'It was a good day.' Billy gazed intently at Harry. 'I'd rather not do a soft-shoe shuffle around the subject so I hope you won't be embarrassed if I bring it up. And when I've said all I want to, that will be it. No going back and mulling over the morbid details.' He took a deep breath. 'I've had a good life. A very good life.' He gazed at the photographs. 'I fell in love with an exceptional, wonderful woman who, miraculously, loved me enough to marry me. She gave me three children who turned out to be better sons and men than any parent has a right to expect. The only thing I regret is their mother didn't live to see their wives, because all three would have been the daughters she'd always wanted. My sixteen grandchildren – and in case you can't count, that includes you, because I'll always regard you as the first – look set to change the world for the better. And the General Strike has proved that it needs changing,' he added drily. 'Like most men, I've seen and done some things that I would rather have avoided, but I accept that was down to the times and place I lived in.'

'You, Dad, Uncle Victor and Uncle Joey are the most principled men I've ever met.' Harry struggled to keep his voice on an even keel.

'It's good to know that you have a high opinion of us,' Billy said seriously. 'But it's your time now, boy. And the best advice I can give you is to live every day you're given as if it will be your last, because life flashes past at a much faster rate than you think it will. Do what you believe is right and be guided more by your heart than your head because the head is bound by sense, and the sensible course isn't always the right one. If Isabella had followed her head she wouldn't have married a miner. Richer and better men proposed to her but I struck lucky.'

'From what Dad has told me about you two, so did she.'

'It's a hard life being a miner's wife and mother. Nothing but washing and scrubbing. Your wife, whoever she will be, won't have that problem. But you have to be vigilant, Harry. I have the feeling that the same luck I had with Isabella will soon come your way. And if you don't recognize the right one when she appears, she may slip through your fingers, just as the right one for your Uncle Joey almost slipped through his. But when he was young he was slow on the uptake in matters of the heart. Fortunately for him, Rhian wasn't. There is nothing like a good marriage.'

'I promise you, I'm already on the lookout for my Isabella, Granddad.' Harry felt ashamed when he recalled all the transient, meaningless affairs he'd indulged in at college. And the thought occurred to him that Diana might – just might – be his Isabella.

'There's something else I want to get out of the way, while I have the chance. Your father and uncles know where and how I want to be buried and how I want my estate settled. I told them I don't want any priest canting mumbo-jumbo over me, but I also know they won't get away with holding an atheist funeral in Trealow cemetery. Tell them I knew all along that Father Kelly would persuade them to do it his way. And it's all right, because if the man ever has the sense to dump his religious beliefs he'll make a decent communist.'

Father Kelly was the Catholic priest in Tonypandy, and despite the differences between his philosophy and Billy's, they were closer than most brothers.

'I'll tell them,' Harry assured him.

'Good, you can also tell Patrick Kelly that wherever I am, I'll put up with his prayers for Isabella's sake, but she was such a saint she doesn't need them. However, I'm such a sinner I can do with all the help I can get to try to reach the same place as her.' He fell serious. 'She was a devout Catholic all her life, it's right that there should be a priest present when they open her resting place to put me in. One thing more before we close this subject for good. Knowing your mother, Megan, Rhian and my granddaughters, there'll be a few tears when I'm gone. Remind them that I hated the sound of crying when I was alive. Life's too short to grieve. Tell them to remember the good times, and move on to the good times that lie ahead.'

'Mr Evans.' A shadow fell into the room. The sister was in the doorway.

'You'll remember, Harry,' Billy pressed.

'I'll remember, Granddad. I wish I could explain how much you meant to me when I was growing up.'

'I already know, boy, so there's no need to discuss it. Go home, don't hang round here.'

'I'll go home but I'll be back.'

'The next time you come we'll talk about your painting and what you intend to do with the rest of your life,' Billy replied gruffly.

'Mr Evans!' The sister's voice grew sharper.

'Harry,' Billy's voice had weakened, and Harry realized that the ten minutes he'd been allowed was exactly the right amount of time, 'bring some more strawberries the next time you come; they went down a treat.'

'I will, Granddad, see you again soon.'

'Not if you overstay your welcome, you won't,' the sister said firmly. 'Goodbye, Mr Evans.'

'Goodbye, Sister.' Harry didn't look back as he walked to the lift. He knew that if he did, his grandfather would see the unshed tears brimming in his eyes.

Chapter 10

HARRY LEFT the sanatorium, drove down to the village and, suspecting that his grandfather had given most of the strawberries he'd bought the day before to the miners he'd mentioned, bought two more baskets.

'You're beginning to spend more time in this sanatorium than me, Mr Evans,' Dr Adams commented when he saw Harry hand the baskets to a nurse in the porch.

'I was hoping that I could talk to you for a few minutes, Doctor Adams.'

'Make it brief.' The doctor went into his office, Harry followed, but Diana's father didn't offer him a seat or close the door. 'How did you find your grandfather?'

'Much better than I expected.'

'He has responded well to our treatment.' Dr Adams sat behind his desk.

'When can I see him again?'

'Despite appearances, he is very ill. Any activity that tires him is detrimental. And, although they may deny it, all patients find visits tiring, Mr Evans.'

'I realize that. But as I said to you earlier, we are a very close family and we would like to visit him as often as we can, even if only for a few minutes at a time.'

'You've asked me an impossible question, Mr Evans. I could tell you that you can see your grandfather once or twice a week, only to have to turn you away if he should be too weak to cope with a visit.'

'Mr Ross—'

'Mr Ross is working on a project with his uncle,' Dr Adams

interrupted impatiently. 'And he is aware that although I allow him to call every morning, I have no compunction about refusing him entry if his uncle is too ill to see him.'

'Then you would have no objection to my turning up and asking after my grandfather most mornings, even if I can't see him?' Harry asked brightly.

'You're nothing if not persistent, Mr Evans,' the doctor replied flatly.

'Your treatment has been more beneficial than we hoped for, Doctor Adams, but we're all very aware that my grandfather doesn't have a great deal of time. And we would like to spend as much of it as possible with him.'

'Shall we say that you can turn up here and ask after your grandfather no more than three or four times a week, Mr Evans?' the doctor conceded. 'And always first thing in the morning, because patients are generally at their best if they have had a good night's rest. Also, the maximum number of visitors I will allow at any one time is two.'

'Thank you, Doctor Adams.' Harry almost offered him his hand before he recalled the rule about physical contact. 'I will be back as soon as I have returned from Pontypridd to tell my family the good news.'

'Harry!' Bella ran downstairs, threw her arms around him and hugged him as soon as he walked through the front door of his family's new home. He dropped his suitcase and wrapped his arms around her, contrasting her warm welcome with the more re-strained and reserved one she had given him when he had arrived on Pontypridd station.

'You all right, Belle?' he asked solicitously. Her eyes were red and puffy and she was reluctant to let him go.

'I'm fine,' she replied unconvincingly.

'Edyth?'

'No change as of yesterday. Mam and Dad are visiting her in the hospital now. I wanted to go with them but they won't allow more than two to a bed, or children under twenty-one. I ask you. *Children!*' she exclaimed indignantly. 'As if I'm a child.'

He put his head back and listened for a moment. 'The house is quiet.'

'Mari has taken the others down to Uncle Joey and Aunty Rhian's for tea.'

'You didn't want to go with them?' He disentangled himself from her arms and tossed his hat on the stand.

She shook her head. 'No, I had some school work to do and reading for next term and letters to write . . .' Her voice broke, thick with unshed tears.

'It's all right, Belle, I feel exactly the same way,' he sympathized. 'It just doesn't seem right to carry on as if nothing's happened while Granddad and Edyth are lying in hospital.'

'I feel so guilty, Harry.' She opened the door and led the way into the drawing room. 'All Edyth and I did that day was quarrel. I said some terrible things to her—'

'All you and Edyth have done for years is quarrel, and you both say terrible things to one another all the time,' he reminded her gently. 'Everyone in the family knows that neither of you mean what you say. And much as I love Edyth, she has honed aggravation into an art. How many times has she burst out laughing just when she's got one of us so boiling mad we want to slap her?'

'Yes, but now she's seriously ill and they won't even let me see her, and she could be in hospital for weeks.'

'I'd say only until she's well enough to start annoying the doctors and nurses.' He feigned an optimism he didn't feel. 'So, stop torturing yourself with the thought that anything you said hurt her any more than anything she said hurt you.' He walked over to the drinks tray and poured himself a whisky. 'Want a sherry?'

'A small one, please, Harry.' She sat on the sofa and stared at the summer arrangement of dried flowers that filled the hearth. 'You haven't said how Grandfather is, and after listening to Mam and Dad's bulletins on Edyth this week, I'm almost too afraid to ask.'

He handed her the sherry he'd poured. 'All things considered, Granddad was amazingly well when I saw him this morning.'

'Really? You're not just saying that, Harry?' Her eyes brightened when she looked up at him.

'Really,' he confirmed. 'As he said to me, all he has to do is read, eat, drink and be looked after. Although he did complain that like most females, the nurses fuss too much.'

'That sounds like Granddad.'

He sat next to her on the sofa and reached for her hand. 'Edyth will get better, Belle. I just know she will,' he insisted emphatically, refusing to think of the alternative.

'I wish you'd been around these last few days to convince me. But even if Edyth does recover, Granddad won't, will he?'

He couldn't bring himself to lie to her, not even to give her a few more days or weeks of hope. 'No, Belle, he won't.'

'And that's horrid. I can't imagine him not being there when I want to talk to him. He's . . . He's . . .'

Harry set his drink on a side table, took hers from her and hugged her again. 'We all love him and we're all going to miss him, Belle. But he's not dead yet.'

'Do you think they'll let me see him?'

'That may be difficult. The doctor will only allow him to have visitors when he's well enough and even then only two at a time. But we might be able to arrange something.' He was reluctant to promise her anything. His grandfather had fourteen grandchildren besides them, all of whom would undoubtedly want to say goodbye to him, and that was without his stepfather, mother, uncles and aunts.

She gulped back her tears. 'It's all so ghastly. This summer nothing's happening the way I thought it would. Edyth and I made so many plans. We were going to press a collection of wild flowers and fill a sketchbook with scenes from around Ponty as a Christmas present for Dad. And we were going to take the little ones by train to the fields at Creigau to pick primroses . . .'

The front door opened and closed, and their parents' voices drifted in from the hall. Harry handed Bella his handkerchief. She wiped her eyes and blew her nose before they went out to meet them.

Shocked, Harry saw that his mother's hair had streaks of grey that hadn't been there when he'd left for the Swansea Valley. But she was smiling. She opened her arms to both of them. 'She's awake,' she cried. 'Harry, Belle, Edyth's awake.'

'And she knew both of us.' Lloyd swept Bella off her feet. 'So you can stop crying, Belle, and prepare yourself for some more teasing when she gets home.'

'You're not just trying to make us feel better, Harry? Dad really is in good spirits?' Lloyd asked for the twentieth time when he and Harry sat alone together over coffee and brandy in the dining room after dinner. Bella had gone upstairs to help Sali put the younger girls to bed, and Lloyd and Harry suspected, to write cards and letters to Edyth and their grandfather.

'He really is.' Harry was exhausted, and not just by the long drive from the Swansea Valley. He'd spent half an hour talking on the telephone to Joey and Victor, answering their endless questions about his grandfather and reassuring them that he had settled into the sanatorium and responded well to treatment. And afterwards he'd had to satisfy his parents' and sisters' thirst for news. It had been a relief to read Glyn a bedtime story in the quiet of his bedroom before dinner. 'I didn't like to ask earlier when Mam and Bella were still here – is Edyth going to make a full recovery?'

'Doctor Williams said it's too early to tell.' Lloyd ran his fingers through his hair, pushing it back from his face.

Harry knew his stepfather. The gesture indicated he was worried. 'Does he think there might be a problem?'

'I had a private talk with him when your mother was with Edyth. Not a word to your mother?'

'Of course not,' Harry promised.

'There's damage to Edyth's spine. As yet, she has no feeling in her legs. It could return but—'

'Are you saying that she could be crippled?' Appalled by the thought, Harry slumped back in his chair. Edyth had been born a tomboy. Ever since she'd taken her first steps, she'd been out and about, riding her horse or bicycle, climbing trees, charging round with their cousins on Uncle Victor's farm, doing crazy – and generally dangerous – things, like playing tag with the animals.

'As Doctor Williams said, it's early days, but I'd rather you didn't mention the possibility to your mother or Dad. He still doesn't know about Edyth?' Lloyd asked.

'I haven't said a word.'

'Don't,' Lloyd warned.

'You only have to look at Mam to see the strain she's under,' Harry commented soberly.

'Her hair.' Lloyd made a face as he sipped his brandy. 'It was a shock to both of us. It happened overnight.'

'If you're talking about me, I always said that girl would turn me grey.' Sali came in with Bella.

'She's certainly done that, sweetheart.' Lloyd reached for her hand when she walked past his chair. 'Brandy?'

'Please.' Sali smoothed Harry's hair away from his forehead when she sat down. 'How are you bearing up under all this strain?'

'I'm fine.'

'It's not too late to go to Paris. Your tickets are open until the end of next month, and if you write to the studio—'

Harry shook his head. 'I'm staying.'

'Here or the Swansea Valley?' Lloyd asked.

'Moving between the two, now that Doctor Adams is prepared to let me ask after Granddad three or four times a week. I think I'll manage to see him as long as he's well enough to receive visitors. But I would also like to see Edyth.'

'Doctor Williams isn't prepared to allow anyone other than us in to see her for the next week, possibly even longer, but we can give her your love. Thank you, darling.' Sali took the brandy Lloyd handed her.

'I don't see why Doctor Williams won't let me see her,' Bella argued forcefully. 'After all, I'm the closest to her in age.'

'Sorry, Belle, but he was quite firm on that point. He said young people come into contact with far more contagious diseases than adults and he can't risk Edyth catching anything while she's in her present weakened state.'

'But to look on the bright side, darling, Edyth will be home the minute she's well enough, and now she's come out of her coma, that can't be long,' Sali said confidently.

'When are you thinking of going back to the Swansea Valley, Harry?' Lloyd asked.

'I'd like to call into the sanatorium the day after tomorrow. And because early morning is the best time for visiting, that means leaving tomorrow afternoon. I thought I'd call in on Uncle Joey in the store and Uncle Victor at the farm on the way.' Harry felt slightly guilty. He wanted to see his grandfather – but there was also Diana.

'You'll need an extra suitcase to take all the letters, cards and gifts the children have been making,' Sali warned.

'Ask Doctor Adams if Joey and Victor can visit him at the week-end?' Lloyd opened the cigarette box, and offered it to Sali and Harry. 'They said they were hoping to go down, and your mother and I will visit—'

'Just as soon as Edyth is better and home.' Sali took a cigarette. 'You have no idea how good that sounds after the strain of the past few days, Harry.'

Harry didn't dare look at his mother or glance at Lloyd, lest his mother intercept his look and read his thoughts. She always had been far too intuitive for his liking.

Harry returned to the inn late the following evening. Just as his mother had predicted, he was loaded with cards, letters and gifts from the family for his grandfather: jars of homemade jam and preserves from Mari, and Billy's old housekeeper, Betty Morgan; letters from his older cousins, and crayon pictures from his younger ones; copies of the latest books from Joey, Victor and Lloyd; wool-work slippers stitched by Rhian; a cardigan Megan had knitted; and a dressing gown his mother had bought.

Not knowing how long he would be in the valley, he had also stopped off in Swansea and stocked up on art supplies. Even if Toby was too busy painting his Holy Grail scene in the vestry to give him any hints or tuition, he decided that he might as well put the time between visits to his grandfather to good use. And as he had discovered for himself, with Diana's help, the valley was very beautiful.

*

'You're ready to show your uncle the Grail painting?' Harry asked in surprise when Toby loaded the covered canvas into the back of his car early the following morning.

'I want his opinion on the colours I've used before I finish it. In my room, not the vestry,' he qualified. 'Hopefully, even if he wants them changed, I won't need to go back there or listen to another word that spills from that woman's mouth. Talk about verbal dysentery. However, if Frank doesn't like the composition, I'll look for another background and model before I return there.'

'No doubt you left the vicar's wife and daughter grief-stricken,' Harry joked as he climbed into the driver's seat.

'They can join the club.'

'What club?'

'The club of women who have met me, and had to learn to live with the brutal reality that, to them, I will remain forever unattainable,' Toby recited in Shakespearean mode.

'You do have a vivid imagination.' Harry laughed.

'We can't all be as fortunate as you with the lovely Diana. You given any thought to where you're going after you visit your grandfather?' Toby sat beside him and slammed the car door.

'I thought I might try my hand at translating my sketch of the reservoir into a watercolour.'

'Arthurian lake, you mean.' Toby yawned and stretched his arms above his head. 'Depending on what Frank says, I'll either come back here and work on the canvas, or go on with you. I showed Frank the preliminary sketches of the lake and he's more or less decided where the arm and sword should go. If I ask the Snow Queen nicely, do you think she'll let me paint her arm with the sword?'

'How should I know?'

'I was hoping you'd sit with us and bestow loving glances on her while I paint. That way she won't get bored. Don't tell me you're getting more strawberries,' Toby remonstrated when Harry stopped at the roadside stall.

'My grandfather likes them.'

'He's going to turn into one if he eats the amount you buy.'

'It's a short season.' Harry bought two baskets. His grandfather had always been generous, and he didn't doubt that there were other patients besides the miners who would enjoy them.

'You're back, Mr Evans, and loaded.' Diana Adams stopped Harry in the corridor. Gowned and masked, he and Toby were heading for the lift on the ground floor.

'As you see.' He held up the strawberries and bag of letters and books. 'Presents for my grandfather. How is he?'

'In surprisingly good spirits, and the presents will be given to him at the ward sister's discretion. We have rules about cluttering the patients' rooms.'

'I remember, and I promise faithfully that I will give everything to the sister. Have you seen Martha Ellis?'

'I have, and she's almost back to normal.'

'That's good news.' Harry couldn't stop looking at Diana.

'See you outside later, Harry, and don't forget to ask about the arm.' Toby turned the corner of the corridor.

'The arm?' Diana murmured.

'Toby wants to paint your arm holding a sword. It will be coming out of a lake,' Harry explained.

'Me as the Lady of the Lake.'

'Your arm, at any rate. Any chance of a walk tonight?' he whispered after a nurse passed.

'My parents have a dinner party. Maybe tomorrow.' She held up a file as her father approached. 'If you'll excuse me, Mr Evans.'

'Of course, and thank you for the progress report on my grandfather.'

Billy's bed had been wheeled out on the balcony again. Just as before, Harry found him sitting up and reading.

'Behave, and they might give us an extra five minutes,' Billy said when Harry sat beside his bed.

'Is that you hoping or the sister promising?' Harry asked.

'The sister agreeing after she's been nagged to death,' she answered, without looking up from the papers on her desk.

Billy closed his book. Always a quick reader, he'd finished *Tom*

Jones and was halfway through a combined edition of *Three Men in a Boat* and *Three Men on the Bummel*. 'How is everyone at home?'

'All the better for hearing that you have settled in here,' Harry replied guardedly. 'I saw Uncle Joey and Uncle Victor – they're both coming here this Saturday. The aunts wanted to come with them but Doctor Adams won't allow you more than two visitors at a time. I brought you some more strawberries and a bucketful of letters, drawings, cards and books from Dad and the uncles. I gave them to the sister—'

'Who will pass them on when she sees fit and not before,' the sister interrupted.

'Since when were you invited into the conversation?' Billy's friendly tone belied his words, and Harry sensed that a rapport had already developed between his grandfather and the staff.

'Since I recognized that you're the type of patient who needs a firm hand, Mr Evans.' She left her desk and joined them on the balcony. 'And if you are going to have two visitors the day after tomorrow, your visit shouldn't last more than five minutes now.'

'Come on, Sister,' Billy coaxed. 'Five more minutes aren't going to tire me out.'

As before, Harry heard his grandfather's voice weakening. 'I'll talk to him but won't ask him any questions,' he promised.

'Five minutes, Mr Evans, but only on condition that you do the listening and your grandson does most of the talking,' she warned.

Not wanting to dwell on what was happening in Pontypridd lest he inadvertently slip up and say more than he should about Edyth, Harry moved the conversation on as soon as he'd assured Billy that everyone in the family was as well and as happy as they could be without him. So he talked about the people he'd met in the valley: the mother and son who ran the garage and the inn; Toby Ross; and, halfway into the story before realizing that it wasn't a happy one, the Ellises, and how the family had lost their farm.

Turfed out unceremoniously by the ward sister after ten minutes, Harry found Diana Adams waiting by the lift cage.

'Good morning again, Miss Adams.' He gave her a guarded smile.

'Mr Evans.' Her dark-blue eyes gazed into his. 'I trust you found your grandfather in good spirits?'

'Just as you said he would be.'

'My father is pleased with the way that he is responding to our fresh air and dietary treatment.'

The lift arrived. Harry waited for Diana to precede him into it. He closed the doors and she pressed the button. When they were between floors she pressed a red button and the lift juddered to a halt.

'Something to remember me by until tomorrow evening.' She held her finger to her lips before pulling down his mask and hers. Pressing the length of her body against his, she kissed him hard on the mouth. He leaned against the wall of the cage.

She moved back, lifted the gown that covered his flannel suit and unbuttoned his flies. Slipping her hand inside his trousers, she fingered his erection.

'Diana . . .' The half-hearted protest died in his throat when she kissed him again. He cupped her left breast with his right hand. Her nipple had hardened into a peak that he could feel even through the layers of her clothes.

A bell rang in the lift. She released him abruptly, rearranged her gown, pulled up her mask and pressed the button again. The lift continued its journey. He was still adjusting his mask when they reached the ground floor.

Toby was sitting, waiting for Harry in his car. His eyes narrowed when he climbed in and sat beside him.

'You all right?'

'Hot. The lift got stuck between floors,' Harry said truthfully.

'Your grandfather?'

'Looking remarkably well. He said he'd seen your uncle.'

'Incredible, isn't it? Last week I thought Frank was at death's door. Today they wheeled his bed out on the balcony.'

Harry pressed the ignition. 'So where am I taking you?'

'The inn.' Toby made a wry face. 'The good news is that Frank was happy with the composition. The bad, there isn't enough gold in the painting for his liking. Naturally he's absolutely spot on. The

170

illustration would be more stirring and impressive if there was. But hopefully, if I work like hell, I'll be able to finish it today and start on the lake tomorrow. You sure you don't mind dropping me back at the inn?'

'Not at all,' Harry replied easily.

'You going up to the lake afterwards?'

'I thought I might visit the reservoir,' Harry teased.

'You'll never succeed in capturing it successfully on canvas if you persist in calling it that.'

'So you say.'

'And you won't forget that grass is green, the sky blue and water reflects the light from the sky?'

'I'm not that much of a novice,' Harry said testily.

'Given your present condition and mood you might forget.'

'What condition and what mood?'

'The Snow Queen's obviously – how can I put this delicately? – got you going.'

'What makes you think I even met Miss Adams in the sanatorium?'

Toby grinned. 'Your flies are undone.'

Harry glanced down, saw his shirt tail protruding from his flies and turned crimson. He slammed on the brakes, pulled over and buttoned his trousers.

'For someone who said he was hopeless at seduction, it didn't take you long to thaw the Snow Queen. Or did she thaw you?' Toby asked mercilessly.

Mary spent most of the morning working in the dairy. After making six pounds of butter, she turned every one of the four-dozen cheeses that were ripening on the stone shelves. She cleared all the paddles and butter-shapers that needed washing into the churn, stood behind it, straightened her back, took a deep breath and picked it up. Kicking the door open with her foot, she carried it across the yard and left it next to the stone trough in the scullery, ready for washing. On her way back to the dairy to fetch the milking buckets, she saw Martha sitting, elbows on knees, her chin cupped in her hands, on the kitchen doorstep.

'You're not feeling any worse, are you, darling?' she asked in concern.

'No.' Martha stared blindly into space. 'Just tired of having nothing to do.'

'If you feel like doing something, you could go in the barn and check the chicken coops for eggs.'

'I've already done that and filled both baskets.'

'You could pick some beans for dinner.'

'Matthew did that.'

'Miss Adams said you should rest.' Mary lifted the buckets into the yard and closed the door of the dairy.

'I'm tired of resting. I want to do something.' A crotchety tone crept into Martha's voice.

'All the dairy equipment needs scrubbing with soda.'

'That's a horrible job.'

'I know it is. That's why I hoped you'd help me with it.' Mary looked over Martha's shoulder into the kitchen. 'Where are Matthew and Luke?'

'Matthew's taken Luke down to the reservoir. He said I couldn't go because I'd slow him down, although I can walk quicker than Luke, even after banging my head.'

'The baby . . .' Mary dropped the bucket and ran across the yard.

'It's all right,' Martha yelled after her. 'We saw that man down there. He won't let Luke fall in.'

'What man?'

'The man who took us to chapel . . . Wait for me,' Martha shouted when Mary picked up her skirts and ran to the gate that opened out of the back of the yard.

Harry glimpsed movement out of the corner of his eye. He turned around and saw Matthew leave the farmyard by the back gate. His progress was slow, because every few yards the small boy stopped either to set down the baby he was carrying, or pick him up. He was trying to get Luke to walk, but although the child toddled a few steps quite happily, a few was as many as he was prepared to take because he preferred to sit down and play with the grass.

Harry started sketching out the composition of his watercolour and became so engrossed in placing the lake in relation to the surrounding hills that he almost forgot Matthew and Luke until twenty minutes later, when Matthew's shout took him by surprise.

'What you doing, mister?'

'Sketching out a painting,' Harry replied without looking up from his canvas. 'What are you doing down here?'

'This is my family's land, I can go wherever I like on it,' Matthew announced proudly. He dropped the baby behind Harry, and stared at the canvas Harry had placed on his easel.

'I hope you don't mind me being here,' Harry murmured, expecting the boy to be as confrontational as his brother.

'You can stay here, as long as you don't bother our sheep. That's our prize ewe over there.' Matthew pointed to a sheep, indistinguishable to Harry from the hundreds of others that grazed on the hills around them. 'She's had fifteen lambs. And we've sold them all.'

'How is your sister today?'

'She's still not right in the head but Miss Adams came up this morning for our eggs and she said that Martha is getting better.'

'She told me the same thing. Why do you say she's not right in the head?' Harry asked.

'Because she's all mopey and weepy.' Matthew sat cross-legged on the grass, lifted Luke on to his lap and looked over Harry's shoulder. 'Is that square you've drawn up there supposed to be our house?'

'This is only a rough outline of something I am going to paint later.'

'It doesn't look like our house.'

'This is only the plan of a painting. All I am doing now is placing the things on the canvas.'

'What do you mean?' Matthew stared at him through large brown eyes.

'Putting things where they'll be when the painting is finished,' Harry explained.

'Wouldn't it be better to draw them properly in the first place, if that's where they are going to be?'

'Shouldn't you be in school?' Harry asked, his patience wearing thin.

'School's too far away for us to go. Besides, we all have to work on the farm.'

'You're not working now.'

'Am so,' Mathew contradicted. 'It's my job to look after Luke. But I wish David and Mary would give me another job to do. Taking care of Luke is girls' work. They think I'm too young to shear the sheep, do the milking and kill the chickens. But Davy did all those things when he was my age. All I ever get to do besides look after Luke is collect the eggs and dig up the vegetables.' He stared, solemn-faced, at Harry. 'I'm not a baby.'

'I can see you're not.' Harry had difficulty keeping a straight face.

'Don't, Luke.' Matthew pulled the baby away from Harry's open haversack.

'I can also see that Luke listens to you,' Harry said wryly.

'He does most of the time,' Matthew countered defensively.

Harry took his haversack from the child and removed the tin boxes Mrs Edwards had given him that morning. One was labelled 'Sweet' the other 'Savoury'. He lifted the lid on the one marked 'Savoury' to reveal four slices of veal and ham pie set between sheets of greaseproof paper, three layers of miniature cheese and onion tartlets and two cold boiled eggs. He offered the box to Matthew. 'Are you hungry?'

Luke reached out and grabbed a tartlet.

'He is,' Matthew commented superfluously.

'Don't you want anything?' Harry persevered.

'What's that?' Matthew pointed to the veal and ham pie.

'Pie. Try some, it's good.' Harry took one of the four slices and handed it to the boy. He took another for himself and bit into it. 'Painting is hungry work.'

'Painting's not work,' Matthew sneered.

'Not physical work like you do on a farm perhaps,' Harry agreed, 'But it's still work.'

'My dad used to say that sitting on your arse all day scribbling in books isn't real work and what you're doing isn't much different.'

174

'Matthew,' Mary reprimanded breathlessly as she ran up to them, 'how many times have I told you not to use words like that?'

'Arse isn't so bad. Davy says—'

'I'll be having a word with David about what he says when you are around, big ears. And you know you're not allowed to bring Luke down here near the water,' she scolded.

'He can't fall in when I'm holding him.' Before Matthew had finished speaking, Luke had wriggled from his grasp. Lurching forward, he grabbed another cheese tartlet and stuffed it whole into his mouth.

'He'll choke.' Marry lifted him up, but before she could retrieve the tart, Luke swallowed it. He beamed up at her and chortled.

Ignoring Mary's scowl, Harry offered her the tin box. 'As it appears we're having an impromptu picnic, please join us.'

'I have a butter churn to scour, Mr Evans. And I need to get Luke somewhere safe.'

'He is safe here with me and Matthew, and as for the butter churn, if you're short of helpers, I could do it for you.'

'You're used to scouring butter churns, Mr Evans?'

'It would be a new experience for me.' Harry's smile faltered in the face of her stony glare.

'If it isn't done properly the next batch of butter I make will turn bad, the agent won't be able to sell it at market and we'll get even deeper into debt.'

'I'm a quick learner, and if you won't trust me with the butter churns perhaps you'll trust me with something else?'

'He has a car so he could take the cheeses and eggs down to the Colonial Stores in Pontardawe, Mary.' Still pale, but looking brighter than when Harry had last seen her, Martha joined them.

'And move the fleeces from the pens to the storage shed in the yard,' Matthew added.

'David will cart the goods and the fleeces when Dolly's hoof has healed. And you, Martha, are supposed to be resting in the house,' Mary reprimanded.

'David said this morning that there's no sign of Dolly's hoof healing.' Martha sat next to Matthew and Luke on the grass. 'Can I have one of those, please, Mr Evans?' She pointed to the cheese tartlets.

'Of course you can, Martha.' Harry handed her the box.

'Martha! That's begging!' Mary exclaimed.

Sensing that Mary Ellis felt he was undermining her authority with her brother and sister, Harry said, 'It's hardly begging when I offered to share my picnic with all of you, Miss Ellis.'

'I refused.' Mary frowned at Matthew and Martha.

'What's in that box, mister?' Unabashed, Mathew pointed to the one labelled 'Sweet'.

'What it says on the label,' Harry answered.

'What's that?' Matthew persisted.

'Can't you read it?'

'No, mister.'

Harry looked from Matthew to Martha and back to Mary, who turned bright crimson when Martha said, 'None of us can read, Mr Evans.'

Chapter 11

THE SILENCE that followed Martha's announcement was embarrassing, and not only for Mary. Realizing that she was mortified by her sister's revelation and unsure how to respond, Harry searched his mind for something sympathetic to say. He eventually settled for, 'It's hardly surprising that none of you can read considering you weren't able to go to school.'

'Davy says farmers don't need book learning.' Matthew sneaked a second slice of pie from Harry's box.

'That's Davy. I don't want to be a farmer, and I've wanted to learn to read and write for ages,' Martha persisted.

'It wouldn't do you no good,' Matthew declared emphatically.

'Yes, it would. Cook in Craig y Nos is always reading things that help her with her job. Recipes and books on food and how to plan menus and run a kitchen. If I learned, I could get a better job as Cook's helper and perhaps even become a cook myself one day. They earn good money. Could you teach us to read and write, Mr Evans?' Martha asked hopefully.

'Martha! How dare you pester Mr Evans with your begging!' Mary turned to Harry. 'I'm sorry we interrupted you, Mr Evans. I'm sure you have work to do—'

'No, he doesn't,' Matthew broke in. 'He's just drawing pictures of our house and the hills. You can't even tell what they're supposed to be and that's not work.'

'It is for some people, Matthew.'

Harry could tell from Mary's tone of voice that she held the same views on producing art as her brother.

'If Mr Evans taught Martha to read, she could ask to look at the agent's books and see if he is diddling us like you and David think he is.' Matthew demolished the piece of pie in four enormous bites.

'You think the agent is cheating you, Miss Ellis?' Harry handed Luke, who was crawling towards his food tins, another cheese tartlet.

'Matthew, you have no right to tell a stranger about our personal business. Back to the house, and take Luke with you. Go with them, Martha,' Mary ordered sharply. They hesitated. '*Now!*'

Matthew grabbed Luke and began to haul him, cheese tartlet in hand, up the hill. Martha looked to Harry. He sensed she was expecting him to say something, but wary of offending Mary any more than he already had, he remained silent. When he refused to meet her steady gaze she trailed gloomily behind her brothers.

Mary watched them go but she didn't speak to Harry until they were out of earshot. 'I am sorry that my brothers and sister troubled you, Mr Evans,' she apologized stiffly.

'No trouble, Miss Ellis, and if you would allow me to, I would enjoy teaching Martha, and Matthew if he changed his mind, to read and write.'

'We couldn't pay you.'

'No one would pay anyone who wasn't a proper teacher. But I used to help my sisters with their homework when they were younger, so I do have a little experience.'

'We have no free time. Martha will be going back to work as soon as she has recovered, and the rest of us have more to do than hours to do it in around the farm.'

'What about the evenings?' he suggested.

'We go to bed early.'

'Surely not straight after supper?'

'We go to bed after supper and get up at four in the morning. Would you like us to get up at three so you can give us lessons?' she bit back caustically.

'Miss Ellis, I realize you don't know anything about me other than I knocked your sister down in my car, and that is hardly a good introduction. But the fact is, Matthew is right. I don't have any real work to do in between visiting my grandfather while I'm here – that is why I am drawing and painting. And I can only do that when the light is good. So,' he gave her the full benefit of his warmest smile, 'you'd be doing me a favour by allowing me to spend some of my time with Matthew and Martha. Martha is obviously keen to learn—'

'As soon as we can afford to do without her wages she'll be back here, working with the rest of us. Then she won't have any need for book learning.' She turned and walked away from him.

'And the agent's books?' he shouted after her.

She stopped but didn't turn around.

'Do you really think that he is cheating you?'

Mary clenched her fists as though she were trying to contain her rage. 'I don't know.'

'And you won't know unless you can check his figures.'

She finally turned and faced him. 'Why do you want to help us?'

He shrugged. 'I don't particularly. I told you, I'm at a loose end and have nothing better to do than practise my hobby, which I can only do when the light is right.'

'Miss Adams said you have a relative in the sanatorium.'

'My grandfather. He is very ill and I am the only one in my family who can spare the time to stay close to him.'

'How do you live?'

'As you see.' He held out his hands and smiled at her.

'Someone must pay for your food, fancy clothes, car and your room at the inn,' she probed.

'I do.'

'You're rich?'

'No.'

'But you don't do any work, so where do you get your money from?'

Not wanting to mention his inheritance, he said, 'My family give me an allowance.'

'If they pay you to do nothing, they must be rich.'

'No, they aren't. My father and his two brothers were miners when they were younger, but one of my uncles works in a shop now and the other is a farmer, like you.' He chose not to tell her that he owned the shop Joey worked in, Victor owned his farm and his father was an MP. 'All three are very fond of my grandfather, who was also a miner. As I have just finished university and have yet to find a job, the family decided that I should be the one to remain close to him. So, I am stuck here with very little to do after I have made my morning visit to the sanatorium. It's too far to travel from my family's house in Pontypridd every day. I can only spend so much time painting, drawing, walking and reading, therefore,' he gave her another smile, 'as I said, you really would be doing me a favour if you allowed me to pass some of my time with your family.'

'We don't need your charity.'

'The charity would be all on your side, Miss Ellis. The only person I know in the Swansea Valley besides my landlady, her son, and Doctor and Miss Adams, is Mr Ross, whom you met on Sunday. And he has hardly any time to spare as he is busy illustrating a book. Frankly, I find it lonely here. Doctor Adams won't let me spend more than ten minutes with my grandfather when he allows me to visit him at all. I miss my sisters, brother and parents.'

'So you want to amuse yourself with mine?'

'Amuse is hardly the right word, Miss Ellis.' He tried to be diplomatic. 'Martha is so keen to learn, it would be a pity to forgo the opportunity while we both have time to spare.'

'I'll have to talk it over with David.' She turned her back to him again.

'Wait, I'll walk back up with you. You were going to show me how to scrub out a butter churn, remember?'

'Farming is work, not play, Mr Evans,' she called back over her shoulder before carrying on up the hill.

Infuriated by her stubborn attitude, antagonism to 'book learning' and willingness to leave her family in ignorance, Harry stared at the reservoir. Deciding that the vantage point he'd chosen was all wrong, he gathered his things together and moved on.

'Good day?' Toby asked Harry when he came down to dinner that night and joined him in the dining room.

'I made some sketches of the reservoir in the sketchbook you gave me and one on canvas – thank you,' Harry said to Enfys who

180

brought in two pints of beer and Toby's whisky chaser. 'It's not brilliant but as I have an idea of what I'd like it to be when it's finished, I thought I might start painting tomorrow.'

'Then you're staying here?'

'I spoke to my father on the telephone half an hour ago. Both my uncles are travelling down by train to see my grandfather on Saturday morning. So I may as well stay until then so I can visit him again in the morning. That's if Doctor Adams will let me in again. Then I'll drive them back to Pontypridd on Saturday afternoon.'

'Good, I'll have company.'

'About the sketches I made—'

'Get the composition right for a painting, and the chances are it will be successful. Frank's maxim, not mine,' Toby smiled ruefully. 'Do you want me to look at what you've done?'

'Please. I'd really appreciate your comments, even if they're more helpful than flattering.'

'Uncle Toby would be delighted to look at your efforts. What's so funny?' he demanded when Harry burst out laughing.

'You. I doubt that you're anyone's idea of an uncle.'

'I'll have you know, I would have made a very good one if I'd been given the opportunity.'

'You haven't any nieces or nephews?' Harry asked.

'I haven't a relative in the world apart from Frank.'

'I know you said he was your guardian, but I had no idea that you two are all alone.'

'I should have said that he was my guardian by default. We are the last survivors of our unique line of Ross.' Toby downed his whisky in one and reached for his beer. 'You, I suppose, have dozens of relatives.'

'Parents, five sisters, a brother, uncles and aunts, masses of cousins.'

'Five sisters?' Toby grinned.

'You can wipe that smile off your face. First, you're not likely to meet them unless my father brings them down here. And he will only do that if Doctor Adams allows them to see our grandfather. And secondly, they are all younger than me. Bella's the oldest and she's only sixteen.'

'Pity, I like the idea of having a ready-made family of sisters-in-law to cosset me. Thank you.' He leaned back as Enfys set plates of lamp chops, roast potatoes, peas and cabbage in front of them.

'Cosset!' Harry exclaimed. 'That shows you know nothing about girls. They like nothing better than to play at boxing and fencing. Being the oldest and the only boy for years, I was expected to show restraint. Not that they ever did. One slight accidental tap from me and it was "Mam, Harry's playing rough." But whenever I complained about the bruises they inflicted on me, they ganged up and called me a sissy.'

'Poor you.'

'That was the most unsympathetic "poor you" I've heard in my life.' Harry unfolded his napkin and picked up his knife and fork.

'So where's the sketchbook?' Toby held out his hand. 'I promise not to get gravy over it.'

'It's here, actually.' Harry lifted it from the seat of the empty chair next to him.

Toby opened the book out above his plate and turned the pages, studying the sketches in silence in between mouthfuls.

'Well?' Harry demanded, unable to stand the suspense a moment longer.

'You know what you're doing wrong, don't you?'

'If I did, I wouldn't be talking to you about it,' Harry retorted touchily.

'You've been looking for the perfect angle from which to paint the lake.'

'I thought that was the point of making sketches, to see which one is the best.'

'They're all the best. I mean that, Harry, some of these aren't half bad.'

'Is that meant to be a compliment?' Harry asked cautiously.

'Coming from me, high praise indeed. Like Frank, I'm over critical of everyone else's work as well as my own. But then every artist worthy of holding a brush knows there is no such thing as a perfect perspective. And there won't be until he sees whatever he's painting through his own eyes, not some pseudo-critical view he's developed after reading a failed and disillusioned painter's guide to *Art and Its Creation*. You've swallowed too many books on art, and listened to too many opinions, Harry. But not to worry, it's the common mistake of a novice. Take my advice: be brave, bold and courageous, trust your own judgement more and listen to people less. Including me,' he added ironically.

'I can't wait for you to see the canvas I've prepared,' Harry said drily.

'Neither can I.' Toby turned back to the first sketch Harry had made. 'This has potential, but you need to see the scene through your own eyes, Harry. You understand what I'm saying?'

'I think so.'

'One more small thing.' Toby filched a pencil from his shirt pocket. 'Here,' he stabbed at a clump of grass Harry had drawn in the bottom right-hand corner of one of the sketches. 'Every leaf is lovingly pencilled in on the periphery and yet you've a blur in the centre. It's as though you want to draw the spectator's eyes away from the main theme because you're afraid of it.'

Harry considered the criticism for a moment. 'You're probably right,' he said slowly. 'I always feel daunted when I attempt to paint. Terrified that it's going to turn out a mess.'

'We all make messes in the beginning. Even Frank did, and I've seen the canvases to prove it. The thing to remember is that they can always be cleaned off and re-used, or painted over,' Toby grinned. 'On the other hand, you could always move that clump of grass to the centre and make it the main theme of the painting.'

'Now you're making fun of me.'

'I'm not,' Toby protested. 'There's nothing wrong with draw-ing a clump of grass if you can bring a fresh viewpoint and make others see it in an entirely new way.'

'Philosophy of art? You just told me to be brave, bold, courage-ous and trust my own judgement more and listen to people less, including you.' Harry closed the sketchbook and returned it to the chair.

'You make a good pupil, Harry.' Toby jabbed him playfully in his chest with his pencil before returning it to his pocket. 'But don't expend all your concentration on insignificant details because you're afraid to face the blank page. In my experience artists who are terrified of messing up and making a mistake never get really started on their careers.'

'You talking about art or my life?' Harry joked.

'I don't know you well enough to talk about your life. But when it comes to art, my advice is: when you get up tomorrow morning, take a fresh canvas, sketch out what *you* see, start painting, and when you do, everything else will fall into place.'

'You make it sound so easy.'

'That my friend, it isn't. What do you say we give the afters a miss, go in the bar and enjoy a pint or two of Mrs Edwards's excellent ale?'

'Pint or two?' Harry grinned.

'In your case. As you know, I am a man with a larger appetite.'

After Dr Adams had given them permission to visit the following morning, Toby and Harry shouted good morning to the duty nurse and headed for the cupboard where the gowns and masks were kept. They went up to the ward in the lift to receive the customary morning lecture from the ward sister about keeping their visits short and not upsetting her patients.

Harry left Toby outside his uncle's room and walked out on to his grandfather's balcony. Billy, looking as good as he had done the day before, closed his book. Harry noticed he'd moved on from J. K. Jerome and had started reading *The Great Gatsby*, one of the new books Joey had bought for him.

'Harry, it is good of you to call in again today. Did you do any sketching yesterday?'

Harry sat next to his grandfather's bed. 'Yes, and today I intend to start a watercolour. Toby Ross has been giving me some advice.' Harry looked out over the gardens. 'Perhaps I should try to persuade the sister to allow me to bring my sketchbook and paints up here. This view is magnificent.'

'It is,' Billy agreed. 'But I doubt you'll sway her. I had a chat with your painter friend's uncle yesterday.'

'Frank Ross? Isn't he very ill?'

'He's better than he was earlier in the week,' Billy murmured, glancing at the sister's desk. 'Doctor Adams and the nurses made a big fuss about his recovery, but there's no fooling him, or me, or indeed anyone in here. It's the nature of the disease for some days to be kinder than others.'

'This from the man who hasn't been here a week. How are you really feeling?' Harry asked seriously.

'Too happy for morbid talk. I told you I've said all I intend to on the subject. Life is for living, and in my book that means enjoying.'

'How can you possibly enjoy yourself in here?' Harry knew his grandfather was trying to be positive, but he couldn't help feeling angry for him. It seemed so unfair that a man as well loved and respected as Billy should end his days incarcerated in Craig y Nos away from all his family and friends.

'How can I not enjoy myself?' Billy turned Harry's question back on him. 'I have this beautiful garden to look at, books to read, all the tobacco I can smoke, a brandy at bedtime, your visits to look forward to, and more food brought to me in a day than most people see in a week. Not to mention an endless supply of strawberries. So,' he changed the subject, 'did you see that family of children you told me about when you were sketching?'

'Yes.'

'And you'll see them again today?'

'Probably.'

Harry's offhand tone didn't fool his grandfather. 'I know you, Harry; you're already involved with them, aren't you?'

'No, I'm not, and I shouldn't have told you about them,' Harry said guiltily, realizing he'd burdened his grandfather with problems that weren't even his to adopt.

'Why not?' Billy Evans looked at him over the rim of his reading glasses.

'You're ill.'

'I won't argue with you there, boy, but my brain still works, and it's obvious from the way you've been talking about them that you'd like to help them.'

'I don't know why.'

'I do,' Billy answered. 'I don't know anything about the problems the people who work on the land are facing right now, but I do know about poverty, especially the kind that forces a man to forgo all thoughts of educating his children and put them out to work almost as soon as they can walk. Miners and farmers are both victims of this class war. Both work for the benefit of capitalists, who exploit them mercilessly in the name of profit. Given the way you've been brought up, you're incapable of turning your back on anyone in trouble. And from what you've told me, they are in trouble.'

'They can't even read and write,' Harry murmured unthinkingly.

'Well, that's one thing you can help them with for a start,' Billy smiled.

'I was thinking of going down to Pontardawe to buy some readers, slates and pencils for them.'

'Don't!'

Harry looked at his grandfather in confusion. 'But you just said that I should try to help them.'

'Whatever you do, make it seem as though you're not doing them any favours. Charity is hard for anyone to take, doubly so when it's desperately needed.'

'But how am I going to teach them to read without readers?'

'That expensive education the trustees paid for has addled your brains.' Billy picked up his tobacco pouch and began to fill his pipe. 'Don't you remember your mother and Lloyd taking you to the library in Tonypandy when they ran classes for the miners and their families who hadn't had an education? You learned to read alongside some of them.'

'They used newspapers,' Harry murmured, recalling the middle-aged and old men and women who had sat learning their letters with him.

'All you need to start are newspapers, pencils and scrap paper. And if they offer you anything in exchange – a meal, eggs, vegetables – take it. The less obliged you make them feel, the more chance you have of making friends with them.'

'You're right, as usual,' Harry conceded.

'As you insist on staying here most of the time, it will give you something to do besides drink beer in the evenings.' Billy pushed his pipe between his teeth and lit it. He took a long pull. 'There's nothing like a pipe. They give out free cigarettes a dozen times a day because they're supposed to disinfect the lungs in a way a pipe can't, but I don't believe it.'

'Mr Evans?' The sister had left her desk and was standing in the doorway.

'Coming, Sister.' Harry left his chair. 'Uncle Joey and Victor will be here to see you tomorrow, and Doctor Adams said one visit a day is more than you should get so I have been warned to stay away in the morning.'

'Not Lloyd?' Billy looked keenly at Harry.

'As you are only allowed two visitors at a time, they drew straws; he picked the short one.'

'Edyth is all right, isn't she?'

'We've told you she is.' Harry was instantly alert.

'I can't forget her scream or those thuds.'

'Given the practice she's had over the years, Edyth knows exactly how to fall without inflicting too much damage on herself. Not that she always succeeds. You only have to look at her arm to see that. But as the doctor said, it's a clean break, and on the mend.' Harry could feel his face burning. He never had been very good at lying. 'Shall I send everyone your love when I telephone Dad tonight?' he asked, changing the subject.

'Of course, and tell him to ask Joey and Victor to bring any books they no longer want. Not just for me, but the other patients here. Some of those miners I told you about are down to re-reading books for the tenth time. I know you brought a load yesterday, but tell the boys we can use every copy they can spare.'

'Anything in particular?'

'The lighter and more entertaining the better.'

'I've a couple of books of short stories back at the inn you can have.'

'You have finished with them?'

'Yes,' Harry nodded.

'Then give them to the boys when they come to see me tomorrow.'

Harry turned to the sister. 'That takes us up to the two minutes you allowed for our goodbyes, I believe, Sister.' He winked at her, waved to his grandfather and, to his disappointment, left the sanatorium without seeing Diana Adams.

Harry dropped Toby, who hadn't finished adding gold touches to his Grail painting, back at the inn, then he drove on down the valley. He bought newspapers, pencils and a couple of notebooks in Pontardawe. Heading back towards the Ellis Estate, he saw Mary and David wheeling barrows along the road. Both were loaded well past the point of stability, heaped high and overflowing with sheep fleeces. He stopped the car but they ignored him and carried on pushing.

'Why don't you put those in the back of the car, so I can take them to the farm for you?' he shouted after them.

'We're almost home,' David snarled.

'No, you're not; you're over a mile away.'

Mary dropped the handles of her barrow and brushed her hair out of her eyes. 'They're dirty, Mr Evans.'

'I've waterproofs in the back. We can spread those over the seats and pile the fleeces on to it.' He left the car and opened the boot. 'Come on, you've enough to do without making extra work for yourselves.' As soon as he finished covering as much of the leather seats as he could, he took her barrow from her and wheeled it back to his car.

Mary appealed to David, who remained standing, sullenly, in front of his loaded barrow. 'This is only the first load; it will take us all day to ferry the lot from the pen to the farm, and that won't leave us any time for milking or our other chores.'

David rubbed his mouth with the back of his hand, smudging more dirt over his chin and cheeks. 'All right, if you want to let him tell us what to do, go ahead.'

'I'm not telling you what to do, David. Only trying to help.' Harry flinched when he lifted a surprisingly heavy load from the barrow and dumped it on the waterproofs.

'If you really want to help, there are another half a dozen loads like this back in the pen.' Capitulating, David finally turned around and wheeled his barrow alongside Mary's.

'Then we'll go back for them after we've dropped this lot off at the farm.' Harry brushed his hands against the back of his flannel trousers. They felt gritty, greasy and grimy, an odd sensation that was entirely new to him.

'And the barrows?' David reminded him. 'I'll not leave them on this road for anyone to pick up.'

Both barrows were rusting, with squeaky, wonky wheels. They looked as though they were about to fall apart and Harry doubted that any self-respecting scrap merchant would take them. But given Dolly's injury, he suspected they were the only means of carting goods the Ellises had left. 'We'll balance them on top of the fleeces. You two are so thin you'll both squeeze into the front seat.'

'As long as we don't leave them.' David began to unload his barrow.

Harry glanced from the boy to Mary. They were both filthy, which was hardly surprising considering what they'd been doing, but he also noticed black shadows below their eyes that had nothing to do with dirt. 'Why don't you sit in the car, Mary?' he suggested. 'David and I can see to this.'

'Thank you.' She was so exhausted she took Harry's advice without further argument.

Harry finished unloading Mary's barrow and helped David to heap the fleeces from his into his car. Afterwards, it took both of them ten minutes to lift the unwieldy barrows on top of the load and secure them, using fleeces as wedges and seat protectors. With the Crossley piled high, Harry climbed into the driving seat. Mary stepped out so David could sit between her and Harry.

'Your horse is no better?' Harry asked David, after he'd pressed the ignition.

'What's it to you?' David retorted.

'I can see you're both on your knees. It must be difficult to run a farm without transport.'

Mary closed her eyes and leaned against the door. 'Mr Evans is right, David, we can't go on like this.'

'So how is Dolly?' Harry persevered.

'Still lame,' David answered grudgingly.

'Have you called a vet?'

'So he can tell us what we already know?' David sneered. 'Wounds take longer to heal in old animals.'

'Then she is getting better?' Harry glanced at the wheelbarrows balancing in the back, and slowed the car so the speedometer barely registered, before turning through the arch into the farm-yard.

'Park over there.' Ignoring Harry's question, David pointed to the building next to the barn. 'We store the fleeces in there.'

'Mary,' Martha shouted from the open doorway of the house, 'Matthew won't get water for me to wash the vegetables and the bread I've made won't rise.'

'Matthew what?' Mary blinked hard and looked around in con-fusion, and Harry realized she'd fallen asleep in the few minutes it had taken him to drive to the estate.

'You go and see to the children, Miss Ellis.' Harry pulled on the handbrake. 'David and I will unload the fleeces.'

Mary staggered as she stepped out of the car.

'Go into the house like Mr Evans said, Mary.' David followed her and opened the door to the outbuilding. 'We won't have to carry the fleeces so far if you turn the car around, Mr Evans.'

'Call me Harry, and I'll do it.'

'Wait until I pull this water trough out of the way, Harry. That way you can back in even closer.'

It took ten trips and five hours of backbreaking labour to clear the sheep pen of fleeces. By the time David and Harry had dumped the last of them into the car, it wasn't only Harry's waterproofs and the leather seat that were dirty. His hands were black and oily, his white flannel suit filthy, and everything around him – including, he suspected, himself – stank of sheep, a peculiar odorous mixture of greasy unwashed wool, not unlike unwashed bodies, and pungent animal sweat combined with farmyard manure. And to add insult to injury, when he was driving back from the pen they'd emptied, he noticed another three pens, all closer to the road than the one they'd emptied, and all piled high with fleeces.

'Don't we have to take those as well?' he asked David.

'Those are Bob the Gob's.'

'And these aren't?'

'If he knew about them they would be, but we wouldn't survive if we didn't keep something back to pay for our goods. That's if we can get them to Pontardawe in time for the market next week.'

'How is Dolly really?' Harry ventured.

'I'm not a bloody vet.'

Harry was learning to ignore David's defensive hostility. 'No, you're not,' he agreed calmly, 'but you're a good farmer who knows his animals. You must have some idea.'

David watched him as he parked the car in the yard and turned off the engine. 'You won't tell Mary.'

'I won't, but the chances are if you know, she does too.'

'The only thing Dolly's fit for is the knacker's yard.'

'When would you have to get the fleeces to market?'

'The buyers will be in Pontardawe on Wednesday. Mary has a load of ripe cheeses and a couple of dozen birds ready for killing to take down as well as eggs. But if you're thinking of offering to help us, there's no way that you can take the fleeces in the car.'

'Not without making ten trips and that would take all day.' Harry winced. His back muscles had contracted painfully when he stepped out of the car. He'd considered himself reasonably fit, but half a day of physical farmwork had shattered that illusion.

'You could take the poultry, eggs and cheeses though.' David picked up a couple of fleeces from the back of the car and slung them on top of the others in the storeroom.

'I could, and I will if I'm here next week,' Harry murmured. He didn't mind helping the Ellises in an emergency, but he certainly wasn't volunteering to become their unpaid farm labourer. With his grandfather and Edyth ill, his first allegiance had to be to his family.

'You still owe us something for knocking Martha down in your car. But if you're thinking of buying us another horse, don't.'

'I wasn't,' Harry said quickly, 'but if I was, why shouldn't I?'

'Because Bob the Gob would take it. It's what he does with every tenant farm. He takes the decent animals and leaves the old and sick ones. Mary and I try to keep the best of our livestock away

191

from the road because he doesn't wander far from it. But if he sees them, he orders his men to take them.'

Harry secured the last fleece in the outbuilding. 'The agent's taken everything you had of any value, hasn't he?'

'You know he has.' David waited until Harry left the storeroom, then closed and fastened the door.

'And he keeps threatening to evict you?'

'There's no need to harp on about it, Harry.'

Harry recollected what the shepherd, Dic, had said in the inn. He didn't doubt the man's word. And he only had to look around the farm to confirm that the agent had stripped the Ellis Estate of everything that would bring in a few shillings. What he couldn't understand was why the agent still allowed the children to live on the estate when they had run up such large rent arrears. It simply didn't make sense.

Unless everyone was wrong about the man and he was acting out of honourable motives. And far from robbing the Ellises, he was only giving them time to make inroads on their rent arrears. In which case, the time would come when they would clear their father's debts and could look forward to making enough from the farm to live in relative comfort.

There was only one thing wrong with that theory. He hadn't left them any decent animals for breeding stock.

Chapter 12

MARY LEFT the house and crossed the yard just as Harry was opening his car door ready to leave the farm.

'I assumed you were busy in the house, Miss Ellis, and I didn't want to disturb you by saying goodbye. And then again, I'm hardly in a fit state to pay a social call.' Harry ran his grubby and blistered hands through his knotted hair.

'I'm about to wet the tea, Mr Evans, and there's fresh bread and cheese on the table. You're welcome to join us if you want to, and have time,' she added diffidently. 'As for your state, you're no worse than the rest of us. There's no point in dressing in your best clothes to work on a farm, which is something I'm afraid you've done. Your fine suit is ruined.'

'It was an old one,' Harry lied. Mindful of what his grandfather had said about taking everything the Ellises offered, he said, 'And thank you very much for your invitation. You must have read my mind. I'm parched.'

'Did you make the bread, or did you try to make Martha's rise?' David pulled a clump of thorn-infested fleece from his sweater — which was more holes than wool — and tossed it at a chicken.

'Martha's was fine. It's so long since she made a loaf she was just worried that it wasn't rising fast enough.'

'And it's not solid, like the last time she made one when you were busy in the dairy?' David enquired sceptically.

'That was the first loaf she ever made, and she'd prefer you not to harp on about it. Show Mr Evans where he can wash his hands. And feed the dogs before you come in. Their food is ready for them in their bowls. I'll see if Martha has finished setting the table.' Mary turned back to the house.

David checked that the door on the outbuilding was securely bolted. He disappeared into the barn and returned carrying a padlock and key. Threading the padlock through the bolt, he locked it and pocketed the key. 'Just in case the agent or any of his men come snooping around before we have time to sell these on,' he explained to Harry.

'The agent comes snooping round your yard?' Harry didn't know whether to believe the boy or not. There was no doubt that David was paranoid when it came to the agent, angry with the world in general, and surly and suspicious of strangers. But after hearing what the family had suffered during the last few years his attitude was understandable.

'Every time Bob the Gob comes here he notices everything. How many pigs we have, how many calves, what should be ready for market and what will be ready for sale the following month. Sometimes I think the bastard hides in our attic watching every move we make.'

'I'd keep that language for when you and I are alone together and your sisters and brothers aren't around,' Harry advised, softening the reproach with a conspiratorial wink. It wasn't his place to reprimand David, and he doubted that the boy would listen to him even if it was. But after an afternoon spent working with him, he'd decided that it would be easier to help the Ellises if he could persuade David to alter his opinions on some things, starting with his attitude to 'book learning' and Martha's ambition to read and write.

'If I do, I suppose it'll save me from another bollocking from Mary,' David grinned.

Sensing the boy was testing him, Harry ignored the comment. He followed him to the well at the back of the house.

David drew a bucket of water, carried it into the scullery and tipped it into the stone sink. He handed Harry a sliver of green carbolic soap and a wooden scrubbing brush, then picked up a collection of bowls from the windowsill and whistled for the dogs as he returned to the yard.

Harry stooped and plunged his hands into the freezing water. It was so cold it was impossible to work up lather. After a few minutes of futile rubbing, his hands were raw, the dirt that wasn't ingrained in his folds of skin and under his nails scraped off by the hard bristles. He finished by plunging his face into the bucket and brushing the water back through his hair. Afterwards he felt fresher but no cleaner.

He balanced the soap and brush on the edge of the sink for David, took a worn towel from a nail hammered into the stone wall and dried himself. Mary had been right. His cream flannel suit was ruined. Even in the gloom of the half-light that filtered through the tiny, thickset windows in the scullery walls, it looked more grey than cream. Black, brown and grass-stained oily smudges overlapped on the arms and front of his jacket and the knees of his trousers where he had knelt in the pen to gather the fleeces. Burrs, twigs and thorns caught up in the wool had snagged the suiting, dragging and tearing the cloth.

'You didn't come dressed for work,' David declared insensitively from the doorway.

'I was expecting to paint.' Harry took a comb from his inside pocket and slicked his hair back.

'That suit is only fit for the ragbag now.'

'I'll find one to put it in when I get back to the inn,' Harry said drily.

'Mary says flannel makes good floor cloths.'

'I'll bear that in mind.'

The scullery door opened, and Mary looked in. 'You two coming?'

'Right away.' Harry noticed that she had slipped a clean white apron on over her patched and faded black blouse and skirt. She had also succeeded in taming her unruly curls and winding them into a knot that she had secured at the nape of her neck with old-fashioned tortoiseshell pins.

'Then hurry up.' For the first time since Harry had met her she smiled, and to his astonishment he realized that although her mouth was too large, her features too strong and her complexion too dark for conventional beauty, dressed in clean clothes, with neat, tidy hair, she was an extremely striking woman – not a belligerent child. He felt slightly uneasy. She hadn't looked at all attractive with most of her face hidden beneath the varnished straw hat when he'd taken the family to chapel. He recalled Iestyn Williams's warning: *'You bring a strange man into our chapel . . . You know that Mr Pritchard won't be happy about this, girl.'*

Was the agent in love with Mary? Was Iestyn Williams angry on Bob Pritchard's behalf because he had mistakenly thought him a rival for Mary's affections? But Mary and David were obviously terrified of the agent so Bob Pritchard could hardly be courting her.

And he certainly hadn't any ulterior motives for befriending the family, but could his attempts to help them be open to mis-interpretation?

David flicked him with water. 'You going to hang on to that towel all day?'

Harry handed it over. 'Sorry, I was miles away.'

'Sleeping on your feet. Like all toffs you're not used to hard work.' David dried his hands and led the way into the kitchen.

The scarred pine table had been laid with five plates and cups, a bowl of sugar and a pitcher of foaming milk. A loaf of bread baked with coarsely milled flour lay sliced on a bed of crumbs on a board in the centre. Next to it stood a square of yellow farmhouse butter on a saucer and a round cheese that had been cut into triangles like a cake. Martha was sitting on one of the benches with Luke on her lap. Mary was standing in front of the stove, her face flushed with heat as she poured boiling water from an iron kettle into a teapot.

'Please sit down, Mr Evans.'

Harry sat on the end of the bench opposite Martha. She smiled shyly at him and continued to feed the baby with small pieces of buttered bread from her plate.

The door banged open and Matthew staggered in, logs piled high in his arms.

'Here, give them to me.' David took them from him.

'I didn't need help,' Matthew said truculently, emulating his brother's usual attitude.

'I know you didn't, but you do need to wash some of that dirt off your face and hands before you eat.' David dumped the logs in the rough wooden box at the side of the stove, dusted off his hands and sat next to Martha. He tickled Luke under his chin and the baby squealed in delight.

'Don't,' Martha protested when he did the same to her.

'Too grown up for tickles now, Miss Hoity-toity?' David grabbed a slice of bread from the board.

'I have been for years.' Martha moved Luke on to her other knee and sat up primly.

'Harry and I have brought in and stacked all the fleeces in the little barn, Mary, but I don't know how we are going to get them to Pontardawe next week.' David pulled the saucer of butter towards his plate.

Mary knocked his hand away after she set the teapot on the table. 'Where are your manners, David?' She replaced the bread he'd taken on the board. 'The guest is always offered first choice of food.'

'Why?' he demanded, his anger flaring. 'It's not as if one slice of bread is any better than another. Besides, the food is there; he can help himself, can't he?'

'It's not a question of helping himself, it's a question of manners, and yours are appalling, David Ellis.'

'If they are, it's down to them who brought me up,' he bit back savagely.

Ignoring David, Mary took the bread board and held it in front of Harry. 'Bread, Mr Evans?'

'Thank you.' He took a slice.

David snatched a piece before Mary returned the board to the table. 'What's the matter with you, Harry?'

'In what sense?' Harry asked, wary of getting embroiled in an argument between brother and sister.

'You so idle you'd prefer to see my sister hand you a slice of bread than stretch across the table to get it yourself?'

Harry didn't quite suppress a smile, but he knew it was the wrong reaction when Mary glowered at both of them. 'I'm merely observing good manners, as Miss Ellis said.'

'Mr Evans must think we're a load of savages.' Mary held out her hand. 'Tea, Mr Evans?'

'Please.' Harry gave her his cup.

She filled it and passed it back to him before walking around the table and filling her brothers' and sister's cups. 'Help yourself to cheese and butter, Mr Evans.'

'He can take his own butter and cheese and not bread,' David mocked.

'I think your sister is trying to make me feel at home, David.' Harry took a scraping of butter and the smallest segment of cheese.

'Why, when it's not his home?' David asked Mary.

'Mr Evans is our invited guest. And I don't have to tell you what he did for us this afternoon. Have you even said thank you to him?'

'Thank you for your help, Harry.' David had the grace to look slightly ashamed but Harry found it even more difficult to keep a straight face when the boy was being uncharacteristically contrite.

'It was my pleasure, David.'

'You can't call what we did pleasure.'

'Let's just say I enjoyed your company and doing a worthwhile job in the open air.'

Mary finished pouring the tea. She covered the pot with a knitted cosy and set it on the table. Taking the smallest cup from the shelf of crockery, she filled it with milk, placed it before her own plate and took Luke from Martha before sitting next to Harry.

'Did you hear what I said about getting the fleeces down to Pontardawe, Mary?' David took two slices of cheese.

'Yes.' Mary settled Luke before tipping the small pieces of bread Martha had buttered for him on to her own plate. 'But it's pointless worrying about getting them down there before we have to. Dolly might be better by Wednesday.'

'Our pigs have more chance of growing wings and flying out of their sty,' David pronounced dourly.

'The wound in her hoof is healing. I dressed it two hours ago when you were out at the pen and it definitely looked better,' Mary countered defiantly.

'It's deep; walk her down as far as Pontardawe the way she is and she'll never walk back. They'll have to shoot her there,' David said.

'David mentioned that you have cheeses, eggs and poultry ready to take down to the Colonial Stores in Pontardawe, Miss Ellis,'

Harry put one spoonful of sugar into his tea instead of his usual two.

'He did?' The revelation earned David another glare.

'I could take them down in the car for you. I have to go down to the shops next week and Wednesday is as good a day as any.'

'The produce won't bring in as much as the fleeces.' David finished the food on his plate and took another piece of bread.

'I don't know anything about produce prices, but we both agreed that there is no way that I can take the fleeces down to Pontardawe in my car.'

'If Dolly isn't fit to cart them, we've no choice but to offer them to the agent.' Mary held the cup in front of Luke. She kept a tight hold of the bottom while he lifted it to his mouth and drank.

'Bob the Gob won't offer us any more for that extra pen of fleeces than he will for the three we've left for him to pick up. But he will ask where we got them from, because they're proof that we've a damned sight more fleeces than we've admitted to having sheep.'

'David—'

'I'm sorry I swore,' he cut in irritably. 'But there's no need to give me another lecture. Just the thought of that man makes me curse.'

'Can't you sell your fleeces anywhere other than Pontardawe?' Harry laid the cheese on top of the bread he'd buttered and cut it into four triangles. It was only after he'd done it that he noticed the others had cut their bread into squares.

'Like where?' David snapped.

'I don't know, there must be other markets beside Pontardawe.'

'There are,' Mary said. 'Swansea, Brecon, Ammanford – but we'd have the same problem of getting our fleeces there.'

'There are no farmers nearby who would cart them for you?'

'They're all in the same . . .' David looked away from Mary, 'position as us. Every farm within two miles of this place is owned by our landlord and their rents collected by Bob the Gob. He's taken every horse capable of pulling a cart except Dolly.'

'And you can't hire a horse for a day?' Harry asked, trying to be helpful.

'With what?' David questioned acidly.

Harry recalled the ten pounds he'd given Mary but said nothing.

'We don't have any money to hire a horse, Mr Evans,' Mary spoke quietly. 'The ten pounds you gave us went to pay an old vet's bill,' she explained, as if she'd read his thoughts. 'It's been owed since last winter and he warned us no matter how much we needed him, he wouldn't come here again until we paid it.'

'I could lend you—'

'We couldn't possibly pay you back or take anything else from you.' She looked fiercely at David, daring him to contradict her.

'Was the ten pounds enough to pay the bill?'

'No, we had to put two pounds we couldn't afford towards it.' David bit into his bread and cheese as if he were punishing it.

'I was hoping that the money we'd get for the fleeces would see us through until the autumn stock sales. We've always managed to sell a few calves and pigs that we've kept from the agent. But the problem is ours, not yours, Mr Evans,' she said firmly. 'And thank you for helping David get the fleeces into the little barn. We couldn't have managed without you.'

'You would have, it just would have taken you longer.' Wanting to help, but feeling as though Mary had closed off every avenue, Harry changed the subject. 'This cheese is good. The best I've ever eaten, Miss Ellis.'

'It's from an old family recipe.' Mary turned her attention to Luke who was alternately sucking a piece of bread and a stick of cheese.

Harry glanced around the table. The room might be bare, but it was as spotlessly clean as when he had first visited the farmhouse. And Mary Ellis and the children may be living hand to mouth on the slimmest of budgets and the simplest of food, but the cheese really was excellent. And although coarse, the bread was light. Their clothes left a great deal to be desired, but so did his after only one day of working on the farm.

It would be so easy for him to solve their problems by going to the bank in Pontardawe, drawing some money out of his account and buying them another horse. But his grandfather was right; it wasn't easy to help people. The Ellises might be poverty-stricken but they were also proud, and the last thing he wanted to do was take away the one thing they had left beside the Ellis Estate – their self-respect. It would destroy Mary Ellis to accept any more 'charity' from him. And if David was right, his gesture would be pointless anyway, because the agent would only commandeer the animal the minute he saw it, as further payment against their rent arrears.

'More bread and cheese, Mr Evans?' Mary offered him the board a second time.

'No thank you. I won't be able to eat the supper Mrs Edwards has prepared for me if I . . .' Panic-stricken he reached for his watch. The hands pointed to half past eight and he had agreed to meet Diana Adams down by the river at eight.

'Is something the matter, Harry?' David glanced at Mary as he used Harry's name again.

'I've just remembered that I should have been somewhere half an hour ago.' Harry tried to finish the tea in his cup as he rose to his feet. 'Thank you so much for the tea, Miss Ellis, David, Martha, Matthew. I'm sorry I have to leave in such a hurry.' He ran to the door.

The hands on his gold wristwatch pointed to a quarter to nine when Harry parked his car outside the gates of Craig y Nos. It wasn't until he climbed out that he noticed the back seat. His waterproofs were caked in dirt and when he peeled them away he saw that they had done little to protect the leather covering against the fleeces. The hide was scuffed and stained, and he suspected that like him, the whole car stank of sheep, but after only a few hours he was so used to the smell he could no longer recognize it.

He bundled the waterproofs into the boot and glanced at his boater. Picking it up, he decided he would look ludicrous if he wore it with his ravaged suit. He left it in the car and ran headlong down to the river. Diana was walking along the bank, close to the spot where they had made love the day before.

'I am so sorry—'

Her peals of laughter cut his apology short. 'Don't tell me any more, let me guess. You were kidnapped by ruffians who rolled you down the mountain? Or possibly, judging by the smell, imprisoned you in a sheep pen?'

'I saw David and Mary Ellis trying to cart fleeces in barrows. I offered to help them and—'

'Evidently forgot all about time,' she finished for him.

'Yes. Will you forgive me?'

'Happily. I'll even throw in a few words of admiration for your charitable spirit – as long as you don't come near me.' She wrinkled her nose in disgust.

'I really am sorry, I was so looking forward to this evening,' he murmured disconsolately.

'There'll be others.' Her smile broadened. 'And this one isn't entirely wasted. We can talk while you escort me back to the road, on condition that you stay at least six feet away from me – and downwind.'

Harry and Toby were eating breakfast in the dining room of the inn the following morning when there was a knock at the door.

Toby shouted, 'Come in.'

Alf opened it just enough to stick his head inside. 'Mr Evans.'

'Please call me Harry,' Harry pleaded.

'Wouldn't be proper, not with you staying at the inn, sir.' He leaned over and dropped Harry's car keys next to his plate. 'It took me two hours to clean it this morning, sir, but it's still not how it should be. If you'll forgive me for saying so, Crossley tourers weren't built for farmwork, no more than they were built for moving livestock.'

'I didn't carry livestock in it.' Harry felt that he had to say something in his own defence. 'Only a few fleeces.'

'Whatever you did, sir, those seats have taken heavy punishment. I've done what I can but they need several good coats of leather polish, and even that won't take away all the marks on them.'

'Could you fit that in some time today, Alf?' Harry asked hopefully.

'It wouldn't be fair to promise anything, sir. I'm booked up all this week between the carpentry and Doctor Adams's ambulance coming in for a service. But if you want to do it yourself, I can let you have a couple of tins of polish.'

Harry realized that was Alf's way of showing his disapproval. 'I'll pay you for what you've done now, and for a couple of tins of polish.'

'No need, sir, I'll get my mother to put it on the bill.'

Alf left, and Toby raised his eyebrows. 'I believe you should consider yourself told off.'

'I do,' Harry said irritably.

Toby paused with a piece of toast halfway to his mouth and burst out laughing. 'I wish I'd been there to see it.'

'Where?'

'The farm. You moving fleeces in the sad, tattered remains of your cream flannels.'

'Very funny.'

'I was sympathetic towards you last night, wasn't I?'

'So sympathetic I have the head this morning to prove it.' Harry dropped his cutlery on top of his uneaten breakfast and rose to his feet.

'Can't eat?' Toby forked a slice of fried potato on to a piece of bacon.

'Not hungry, and I have to pick up my uncles at the station in an hour. I have time to drop you off at the sanatorium first,' he offered.

'Can I come with you to the station? I'd like to meet them.'

'My uncles?' Harry asked in surprise.

'It would save you a detour. I'll bring my painting gear and walk on up to the lake from the castle.'

'I'm sure my uncles wouldn't mind a short run up the mountain after they've been to Craig y Nos.'

'And after you've dropped me off you can move them both into the front seat so you can cart more fleeces?' Toby arched his eyebrows.

'Full of jokes this morning, aren't you?' Harry lifted his jacket from the back of his chair and slipped it on.

'Don't you want to remodel your remaining suit?' Toby finished the food on his plate.

'It's a lovely morning, Toby. Let's leave it that way.'

'Look on the bright side, Harry.' Toby followed him out into the yard. 'You might see the Snow Queen at Craig y Nos. And who knows? She may even feel like taking a short walk with you when your uncles are with your grandfather.'

To Harry's surprise, Bella walked off the train behind his uncles. The instant she saw him, she ran up the platform, flung her arms around his neck and hugged him so tight he could barely breathe.

'Harry, how's Granddad?'

'He wasn't too bad when I saw him yesterday.' He looked at his uncles.

'She insisted on coming, and nagged and nagged until your father and mother gave in for the sake of peace.' Joey dropped the bag he was carrying and buttoned his jacket.

'How are you, Harry?' Victor shook his hand when Bella finally released him.

'Fine, Uncle Victor.' He looked around for Toby and saw him hanging back, staring at Bella.

'This place is in the middle of nowhere, isn't it?' Bella had knocked her hat when she had hugged Harry, and she took a few moments to straighten it. 'Everyone sends their love and is missing you like mad. Dad says Edyth's already demanding the doctor send her home, so she must be feeling better, and Susie . . .' Bella fell silent when she saw Toby looking at her.

'Bella, may I introduce the artist I told you about, Mr Toby Ross? Toby – my sister, Bella, and my uncles, Mr Victor and Joey Evans.'

Bella shook Toby's hand enthusiastically. 'Are you the one who is illustrating *Le Morte d'Arthur*?'

'Yes, but it's my uncle's commission. He's Frank Ross, the painter.'

'Harry said you've been giving him advice on painting. Good, isn't he? I wish I could draw half as well as him but—'

Harry noticed that Toby continued to stare at Bella while she carried on prattling embarrassingly about his talent. And he hadn't released her hand.

'Miss Evans,' Toby said, when Bella finally finished talking. 'I am very pleased to make your acquaintance, especially as you would make the absolutely perfect Morgan le Fey.'

'Do you always begin conversations this way, Mr Ross?'

'Careful, Bella, he'll be asking to see your arm next,' Harry warned in amusement.

Toby grabbed Bella's hand and pushed up her sleeve when she tried to pull it away. 'Thank you for that, Harry. It's perfect. So as well as Morgan le Fey, you can be my Lady of the Lake, Miss Evans.'

'Really?' Bella finally managed to extricate her hand.

'I have no doubt he'll explain later.' Harry looked to his uncles. 'They're expecting you at Craig y Nos, but Doctor Adams will decide if you can see Granddad or not. And afterwards we'll go back to the inn for lunch. I've warned the landlady there'll be two extra but I'm sure she'll find a meal for Bella. When you have stopped studying Bella from an artist's viewpoint, perhaps we can go, Toby?'

Toby shook Victor and Joey's hands. 'I hope you don't mind me asking on such a short acquaintance, but as your niece would make the perfect model for Morgan le Fey, would you please allow me to paint her?'

'I suggest you ask her, Mr Ross.' Joey picked up his bag again.

'I'll think about it,' Bella took Harry's arm, 'but first I'm hoping that they'll let me visit my grandfather to see if he really has settled into the sanatorium as well as Harry says he has. You are lunching with us at the inn, Mr Ross?'

'I am now, Miss Evans.'

'I don't recall inviting you, Toby.' Harry led the way out of the station.

'An omission your sister kindly rectified.' Toby also held out his arm to Bella.

She looked from her brother to Toby, and linked her arms into both of theirs. 'Tell me everything, and I mean *everything* that you and Granddad talked about when you saw him yesterday, Harry.'

Harry saw Diana talking to the hunchback in the covered yard to the right of the castle when he drove through the gates of Craig y Nos. 'That's Miss Adams; her father is the doctor in charge of the sanatorium. He agreed that Granddad can have two visitors this morning if he's well enough, but I don't know what he'll say about you being here, Bella.'

Toby rushed to open the door for Bella as soon as Harry stopped the car. 'You can ask Miss Adams to intercede on your sister's behalf, Harry, while I show Miss Evans and your uncles the gardens.'

'I thought Joey was a fast worker with girls when he was young, but your friend puts him in the shade,' Victor commented when Toby led Bella around the side of the castle.

'He's overwhelming when he's after a model,' Harry replied.

'Going by the looks he's giving Bella I'd say he's after a lot more than that,' Joey warned.

'But she's only sixteen,' Harry protested. 'And although I never thought about it until Toby said, Belle is dark, striking and pretty enough to make a wonderful Morgan le Fey, but don't tell her I said that.'

'We won't.' Joey looked at Harry's car. 'What have you been doing with this? The upholstery and paintwork are scratched to hell.'

'I'll tell you when we have an hour or two to spare after lunch.'

Victor looked keenly at Harry. 'How is Dad, really?'

'As I said on the telephone to Mam last night, in himself surprisingly good. He has settled in well, and he enjoys reading and talking to the other patients when they give him permission to walk around, which he has done every day since he's been here.'

'Do you think he's well enough for Bella to see him?' Joey asked.

'That's for Doctor Adams to say. He's very protective of his patients. I thought he was too strict at first, but I've noticed if they allow me to see Granddad for ten minutes, he's always tired nine minutes after I've walked in. I'll go and see Miss Adams, and ask her how he is.'

'Pretty girl.' Joey winked.

'She's going back to London to do her final year in medicine this autumn.'

'You're kidding!'

'No, I'm not.' Harry smiled. 'I'll be back in a minute. Just keep an eye on Toby and Bella.'

Harry waited until the hunchback tipped his cap to Diana and disappeared into his workshop. She turned to face him, and he paled at the expression on her face.

'We had a bad night on the children's ward. I've just ordered three small coffins.'

'I'm sorry, Diana.'

'So am I,' she answered in a brisker, less emotive tone. 'Your grandfather is much the same as he was yesterday so your uncles can go on up and see him.'

'My sister's also here. She would like to see him as well,' Harry said, as Toby and Bella walked back towards his car.

Diana frowned. 'She looks young.'

'Sixteen.'

'I'll ask my father. He won't allow her into his room. But if your grandfather is well enough and wants to see her, we can wheel him to the visitors' room, which separates patient and visitor by a glass panel. Mr Ross can take your uncles up to your grandfather while you wait in the room by the porch with your sister. I'll come and see you after I've spoken to my father. Make sure your uncles and sister are gowned and masked.'

'I will.' Harry drew closer to her. 'I'm returning to Pontypridd with my uncles this afternoon, but I'll be back next week. Perhaps we can go out together? Take in a show or go dancing in Swansea?' he suggested hopefully.

She returned his smile. 'I'd like that.'

They walked across the yard.

'Miss Diana Adams – my uncles, Victor and Joey Evans, and my sister, Bella. Don't offer anyone here your hand,' Harry warned when Joey held his out. 'Doctor Adams insists that all the staff keep physical contact to a minimum so germs aren't passed on to patients.'

'Or passed back to relatives.' Diana smiled. 'I'm pleased to meet all of you. Harry and Toby can show you where we keep the masks and gowns. I'm sorry, Miss Evans, you'll have to stay in the waiting room until I've spoken to my father about you, but I promise I'll do all I can to persuade him to let you see your grandfather.'

'She's nice, Harry,' Bella said, as Diana went ahead of them into the castle.

'She is,' Harry agreed.

'Oh – oh,' Joey muttered.

'Oh – oh, what?' Harry demanded irritably.

'Victor,' Joey nudged his brother in the ribs, 'I think our nephew is in love.'

'There's no "think" about it, he is,' Toby chipped in to Harry's annoyance.

'I am not,' Harry refuted irritably.

'Then why do you go walking together?'

'Toby, you are an ass.' Harry held the front door open. 'Bella, wait for me in there, I'll be back as soon as I've shown Uncle Victor and Uncle Joey where they keep the gowns and masks, and I'll bring one back for you, just in case.'

To Harry's surprise, Diana was waiting with Bella when he returned to the cubicle by the front door.

'My father has agreed that your grandfather can see Bella in the visitors' room. You can go on up, Harry, and help him into the wheelchair; the nurse will show you where the room is. I'll take your sister there in a few minutes.' Diana took the gown and mask from Harry and turned to Bella. 'You do understand, what I told you, Miss Evans? You'll only be able to see your grandfather. You won't be able to talk to him.'

Bella nodded, and Harry could see she was fighting emotion. He caught her hand.

'You don't have to see him, Belle.'

'Yes, I do, Harry,' she said fiercely.

Harry ran up the stairs to the ward. Dr Adams was talking to the sister who was standing behind her desk.

'My daughter has pleaded your family's case, Mr Evans. But I stress visits like this will only be allowed while your grandfather is strong enough to receive them. And if he had been at all reluctant to see your sister, she wouldn't get any further than the front door.'

'I understand, sir.'

'The porter will bring you a wheelchair in a few minutes.'

Harry went to the door of his grandfather's room. Reluctant to break in on his uncles' visit, he stood back and waited, but Billy saw him and beckoned him into the room.

'Did Doctor Adams tell you that I can see Bella?'

'Yes.' Harry smiled. 'They're bringing a wheelchair for you so you can go to the visitors' room.'

'I'd rather walk,' Billy retorted.

'I don't envy the nurses who look after you, Dad,' Victor said feelingly.

'Thank you for your sympathy, Mr Evans.' The sister accompanied a porter into the room. 'We've had more troublesome patients than your father in here, but not many.'

Billy sat up and swung his legs out of the bed.

'Wait for us to help you, Dad.' Joey picked up the dressing gown Sali had sent and draped it around his father's shoulders.

'My slippers are in the locker,' Billy said gruffly, his voice suddenly hoarse.

Harry exchanged a worried look with the nurse but she fetched the slippers and put them on his grandfather's feet. Billy left the bed and rose unsteadily to his feet. Victor scooped him up and deposited him in the wheelchair.

'You'll get shot for that. Visitors aren't supposed to touch patients. Besides, I could have managed,' Billy said irritably.

'Wasn't it better you didn't have to?' Victor said. The sister tucked a blanket around Billy. 'Just don't touch your father again, Mr Evans. And wash your hands before you leave.'

'I don't need fussing over,' Billy protested.

Joey gave Harry a conspiratorial smile above Billy's head. The porter wheeled the chair into the corridor, and they followed.

'Perhaps you'd like to go into the other half of the family room with your sister, Mr Evans?' the sister suggested tactfully when they reached two doors set side by side in the corridor wall.

She opened both doors. The porter wheeled Billy through the

one on the left; Harry walked through the one on the right. Although Diana had warned them about the glass partition, he hadn't been prepared for the reality.

The room would have made an average-sized drawing room if it hadn't been divided into two by a three-foot wall topped by a sheet of glass.

Bella was standing in front of it, staring at Billy on the other side of the glass.

'He won't be able to hear you, Miss Evans, but you can wave,' Diana Adams hinted, sensing that Bella wasn't sure what to do.

Bella dutifully waved but Harry could see that her smile was forced and brittle. Billy waved back, turned and said something to Joey and Victor; they both laughed. Then he started to cough. Harry gripped Bella's shoulders hard as bright-red blood began to flow from their grandfather's mouth.

Diana ran out of the door and into the other room. She snapped a command at the porter who wheeled Billy out.

'Come on, sis.' Harry pulled Bella back towards the door.

'I shouldn't have asked to see him. If I hadn't, Granddad could have stayed in bed.'

'He's insisted on getting up every day since he's been here, Belle. You didn't do anything.' Harry looked through the glass at his uncles' grief-stricken faces. 'Come on, Belle,' he repeated quietly. 'There's no point in staying here, let's go downstairs.'

Chapter 13

JOEY, VICTOR and Harry were grim-faced and Bella tearful, as they waited for the train to arrive at Penwyllt station.

'I really think I should stay——' Victor began.

'We've been over this a dozen times, Victor. You can't leave your farm for any length of time. And even if you could, there's nothing for you to do here except hang around the inn and wait for a telephone call that hopefully won't come,' Joey said impatiently. They had spent the entire afternoon discussing his father's condition before deciding to take the sensible course. But like Victor, Joey would have preferred to let his heart rule his head, forget his responsibilities to his wife, children and the store, and stay close to his father in the valley. 'You heard the doctor. Dad's taken a turn for the worst, but he could recover.'

'And he might not.' Bella sobbed and hid her face in her handkerchief.

'Please, don't upset yourself, Belle.' Wishing Lloyd hadn't allowed her to accompany them, Victor slipped his arm around her shoulders and hugged her.

'Granddad keeps telling me that he doesn't want any of us fussing over him,' Harry said quietly.

'You're sure about staying, Harry? Joey asked.

'As I'm the only one with a change of clothes here, I'm the obvious choice,' Harry joked badly. 'Hopefully, Doctor Adams received the message that I'm still at the inn. But like you said, Uncle Joey, there's nothing I can do except wait near a telephone and go to the sanatorium and ask after Granddad tomorrow. I doubt Doctor Adams will let me see him, even if he recovers, but at least I'll get any news first-hand. I'm only sorry I can't drive you home as we arranged.'

'You'll telephone if there's any change?' Victor asked.

'At once, I promise. Come on Belle.' Harry slipped his fingers beneath his sister's chin. 'You know how upset Granddad would be if he could see you crying.'

'I know. I'm sorry . . .' She left Victor and buried her face in Harry's shoulder.

'You heard Toby. His uncle has had four haemorrhages and recovered from all of them,' Harry consoled.

They were all glad when the train finally drew in. Joey walked along the carriages and looked in the windows.

'There's an empty one here, Victor, Belle.'

'Give my love to everyone?' Harry walked Bella to the door.

Too upset to answer, Bella nodded. Victor and Joey shook Harry's hand and helped her into the train.

'You will try to see Granddad, won't you, Harry?' Bella opened the window and leaned out.

'Of course.'

'And you'll give him my special love?'

'He knows he has it. Take care of yourself and Mam, Dad and the others, Belle.'

The station master slammed the few open doors and blew his whistle. The train began to steam gently down the track.

Toby, who'd been hanging back so Harry could say his goodbyes in private, stepped forward and blew a kiss to Bella.

'I saw that,' Harry commented, smiling in spite of his misery.

'How . . .' Toby noticed his reflection mirrored in a glass-fronted poster advertising Nestlé's Cocoa and didn't bother to finish the sentence. 'Your sister is wonderful. The most—'

'Before you say another word, she is too young and my father is *very* protective of her, as he is of all his daughters.' Harry gave a last wave before the train rounded the corner and disappeared from sight.

'I don't blame him. If I had a sweet, innocent daughter like Bella I'd want to keep her away from all men.' Toby led the way out of the station.

'So you know how he'd feel if he could hear you gushing over her.' Devastated by his grandfather's setback, Harry was intensely grateful for Toby's company. His friend's attempts at consolation might be bluff, over-hearty and ham-fisted, but it helped that Toby knew exactly what he was going through.

'I only want to paint her so she can be captured for posterity.'

'So she can go down in history as the evil Morgan le Fey, not Bella Evans.' Harry pulled his car keys from his pocket.

'Morgan wasn't evil, just misunderstood.'

'If I remember my *Morte D'Arthur*, she tricked her half-brother Arthur into sleeping with her, which was incest. She stole Excalibur's scabbard, which also makes her a thief—'

'My Morgan will be young and innocent before any of that happened,' Toby interrupted. 'And the way I'll paint it, all the guilt for the incest will be Arthur's. Do you think your father will allow Bella – why did I never realize what a glorious name that was before now? – to come again next Saturday so I can paint her?'

'You heard Bella. *If* she decides that she wants to sit for you and *if* my mother and father visit my grandfather – heaven only knows how he'll be next week – she'll come. And possibly all the others will too, in which case you may have an audience of my other four sisters. And her full name is not Bella, it is Isabella.' Harry opened his car and sat in the driving seat.

'Isabella.' Toby rolled it off his tongue as if he were a monk reciting a holy word. 'Oh, the agonies of other people's indecisions. I can't bear the thought that she'll say no. Or – heaven forbid – that I will never see her again.' He leaned against the car door and gazed glassy-eyed into the distance.

Harry started the car. 'You sound as though you have fallen in love with her.'

'I have,' Toby murmured.

'On a couple of hours' acquaintance?' Harry mocked. 'You're being even more of an ass than usual.'

'People do fall in love—'

'Bella is only sixteen—'

'Juliet was fourteen.'

'Bella's not Juliet, and my father would never accept that as an argument. He might be the wrong side of forty but he is still strong. And you've seen his two brothers but not when they're angry – or me either, if it comes to that.' Harry spoke lightly, but he wasn't entirely joking.

'Just saying goodbye to her makes me want to write poetry. I have never seen such dark eyes, luscious black hair, or so beautiful and sweet a smile. "She walks in beauty, like the night/ Of cloudless climes and starry skies/ And all that's best of dark and bright/ Meet in her aspect and her eyes—" '

Harry interrupted him mid-quote. 'That, you idiot, is Byron.'

'You can't expect me to put it better than the poet of love at short notice.'

'At any notice.'

'And you can't blame me for falling in love.'

'I can, when the object of your affections is my sister. She isn't used to dealing with Byron-spouting lunatics.'

'I'm serious, Harry. I feel as though I have only just begun to draw breath and live. Please, give me credit for being honest. Face the fact I love your sister. What are you going to do about it? Shoot me?' Toby jumped over the car door and slid down into the passenger seat.

'I will if you scuff my car.'

'I couldn't possibly damage it any more than you did by playing farmer yesterday,' Toby retorted.

'I was not playing farmer and you are changing the subject!'

'There's no need to get angry. I assure you, my intentions towards Bella are strictly honourable.'

'They had better be, not that you should have any intentions towards her at all, given her age.' Harry drove away from the station. 'And for your information, boys are the last thing on Bella's mind. She has two more years of school and when she finishes my parents intend to send her to university.'

'She told me she wants to become a teacher. But don't you see that she is much too pretty for a classroom? I will teach her to paint and we will travel the world together – after we marry,' he added swiftly, forestalling another eruption from Harry. 'Think of all the books we could illustrate. *The Jungle Book* in India, *Moby Dick* when we sail the Atlantic, *Treasure Island* almost anywhere tropical, and there's a whole host that we could do if we holidayed in America. *The Last of the Mohicans*—'

'If my father could hear you, he'd ban you from seeing her again and send Bella to university with a nun as a chaperon.' Harry slammed the gear-stick up a notch.

'You won't tell him I'm in love with her, will you?' Toby asked anxiously.

'I most certainly will tell him that you're idiot enough to believe that you're in love with her.'

'You do and I'll never get to paint her as Morgan. If she does come down next Saturday, you'll be with us the whole time, and I'll behave impeccably. Like the perfect gentleman I was this afternoon. Come on, Harry, I didn't say a wrong word, did I?'

'I don't know. I was taught that it's ill-mannered to listen in on other people's conversations.' Harry turned on to the main road and headed down the valley towards the inn. 'But that's not to say that I won't listen in on anything you say to Bella from now on.'

'I wish I hadn't told you how I feel about her.'

'So do I.' Harry's agreement was heartfelt. 'But even if you hadn't, it wouldn't have made any difference. That sick-calf look on your face when you sent kisses flying through the air at the station said it all for you.'

'Do you think Bella knows I adore her?'

'She'd have to be stupid not to, and Bella is not stupid.'

'Do you think she likes me, even a little bit?'

'She may be young but you're not the first admirer she's had. In fact, there's a boy in Pontypridd who follows her around like a puppy.'

'How dare he?' Toby exclaimed indignantly.

'He dares because Bella encourages him to moon after her.'

'I hate him already, and I've never hated a man I haven't met before.' Toby opened a packet of cigarettes.

'Perhaps I can put you off Bella by cataloguing her faults.' Harry filched one of the two cigarettes Toby had lit and pushed it into his mouth.

'I don't believe she has a single one.'

'From the day she was born she was a bossy boots. Before she could talk, she knew exactly how to cry to get her own way. If people don't do what she wants them to, she flies off the handle. And when Bella gets angry, the only thing to do is duck.'

'A saint would get angry with you.'

'Why?'

'Let's start with your smug, self-satisfying ambition to make the world a better place.'

'Smug? Self satisfying?' Harry was outraged.

'Look at the way you behave with the Ellises. Giving them money, taking them to chapel, ruining your car by turning it into a tractor, and all for no reward beyond what you'll receive from the saints in the hereafter. It's the overwhelming need to feel good about yourself.'

'Are you suggesting that I shouldn't try to help them?' Harry demanded, his temper escalating.

'Frank told me that all do-gooders have ulterior motives they might not even understand or recognize themselves. And that their meddling inevitably ends in disaster for all concerned.'

'All I've done is give the Ellises some money to compensate for the loss of Martha's wages—'

'Come on, Harry. This is me you're talking to. You gave them more money than Martha earns in six months. Money they prob- ably spent on luxuries they could never have afforded to buy for themselves otherwise, and will hanker for evermore. If they'd never had them, they wouldn't miss them, and they'd be more contented people.'

'For your information, they used it to pay a vet's bill.'

'I bet they told you that in the hope that you'd give them more.'

'They didn't. They won't take any more from me.'

'Then you offered,' Toby crowed. 'I warned you . . . God! How did we get on to this? The last thing I want to do is annoy my future brother-in-law.'

'In your dreams and my nightmares. Bella has better taste.' Harry turned right into the yard of the inn.

'Mr Evans, I thought I heard your car.' Alf walked up them covered in sawdust and carrying a chisel. 'Mrs Davies, the cleaner

216

up at the castle, dropped this in for you ten minutes ago. I was about to take it into the inn, but I knew you weren't there and I was halfway through a job.'

Harry's hand shook as he took the white envelope. He turned it over. It was addressed to him in a firm, educated hand.

'It won't be bad news, they'd telephone,' Toby said soberly, all trace of banter gone.

Harry tore the flap open and removed the single sheet of paper it contained.

Dear Mr Evans

We received the message that you have decided to stay at the inn. Your grandfather is resting. It is too soon to make a prognosis but he is breathing more easily and is comfortable and free from pain.

If you'd care to join me, there's a cold supper and white wine waiting. Unlike last week I'm not expecting any emergencies. Eight o'clock?

Yours

Diana Adams

Harry smiled and returned the letter to the envelope. 'Do you know where I can buy a bottle of champagne, or good wine, and a bunch of flowers, Alf?'

'There's champagne and wine in the cellar left over from Madame Patti's day. She kept her own cellar but sometimes her guests would stop off here on their way to, or from the castle. Flowers are something else. There's not much call for them around here, but Mrs Parsons next door to the Post Office is a keen gardener and she sells bunches from time to time. But she knows how to charge. As much as two shillings for a bridal bouquet or so I've been told.'

'Thanks, Alf.'

'Good news, I take it?' Toby asked when they walked into the inn.

'It's not bad.' Harry tapped his nose.

'Mysterious isn't your style, Harry.'

'How do you know what my style is?'

'I'd say the Snow Queen is about to find out.'

'Do you think Mr Evans will come for tea again today, Mary?' Martha asked when her sister cut the bread.

'Mr Evans is busy. He has his own affairs to tend to.' Mary concealed her own disappointment at Harry's absence beneath a veneer of briskness.

'He said he'd be here—'

'No, he didn't,' Mary contradicted. 'He didn't answer David when he asked him if he was coming today.'

'I like him. He's nice.' Martha set the plates Mary gave her in front of the bench seats.

'He was kind to you because he felt guilty about knocking you down but that's all. He's a stranger with his own family and concerns.' The door slammed open, hitting the wall behind it. She looked up in alarm when David stormed in. 'What's the matter?'

'Agent's come with his men to pick up the fleeces. He's counting them now as the men load them on to the lorry. When he saw me working on the pen in the top field he shouted to me to get you.'

'You didn't tell him about the fleeces in the little barn?' Mary asked nervously.

'Do I look daft?'

Mary untied her apron and lifted it over her head. She smoothed her hair without bothering to look at it in the scrap of broken mirror she kept on the windowsill. Anticipating a visit from Harry, she had brushed her hair with more care than usual that morning, and fastened it into a knot with her mother's old hairpins. She hoped it was still tidy but she didn't want to look pretty – not for Bob Pritchard.

'Watch Luke,' she ordered Martha, 'and wet the tea as soon as Matthew comes in. You don't have to wait for David and me.'

'How long are you going to be, Mary?'

'Who knows, Martha?' David said bitterly.

Bob's men were loading the fleeces from the last of the three pens when Mary and David left the house. The agent was standing, book in hand, watching and counting as his men tossed the bundles from one to another until they reached the lorry. He made a note of the number in his book when the final one was thrown in, then he looked at them.

'This the lot?' he shouted, as soon as they were in earshot.

'I told you we only had the three pens full.' David recollected the power the agent wielded and added a surly, 'Sir.'

'How much will you give us for them, sir?' Mary asked.

'That I won't know until they're sold at Brecon market next week.'

'Usually you can give us some idea—'

'Usually I am too bloody soft with you,' Bob snarled. 'You'll get what they fetch and I'll knock it off your arrears. Over here, Mary.' He beckoned her closer. 'Not you,' he barked when David tried to follow his sister.

Mary began to shake as she always did in the agent's company. He led her across the road, away from his men and her brother.

'Iestyn Williams told me about the toff you took to chapel last Sunday.'

'I didn't take him,' she protested. 'He saw us walking there and picked us up in his car.'

'And you got into it. Do you know what happens to girls who accept lifts from strange men, Mary?' he muttered darkly.

'He's not a stranger.'

His eyes glittered. 'Then you do know him.'

'Miss Adams introduced us,' she revealed in a small voice. 'He came up to the farm with her.'

'Why did Miss Adams call on you, and what was he doing with her?' Bob drew himself up to his full height, crossed his arms across his chest and glared at her.

Intimidated, Mary said, 'Martha fell and hit her head. Miss Adams called to see to her and he brought Miss Adams in his car.' She kept back all mention of Harry knocking Martha down and the money he'd given them.

'Do you know his name?'

'Mr Evans.'

'Mr Evans!' he sneered. 'And what is *Mr* Evans doing in the valley? And why is he taking an interest in you?'

'He has a relative in Craig y Nos.'

'And no doubt time on his hands that he doesn't know what to do with. Well, your lease doesn't allow you to entertain people at the farm. You don't own it, the landlord does, and you should be working to pay off your arrears not gossiping with visitors.'

Too terrified to argue, although she knew he'd lied to her about the lease forbidding visitors, Mary nodded an obedient, 'Yes, sir.'

'And I don't want you going to chapel with him again, understand?'

Mary managed another, 'Yes, sir.'

'I'm going into Pontardawe tonight, on business.' He eyed her suspiciously. 'Why are you shaking, it's not cold. You ill?'

'No, sir.'

'I'll be back this way about eleven. Wait for me in the stable.'

Diana opened the door to Harry herself. Dressed in a lounging suit of white silk pyjamas, her fashionably bobbed hair unclipped and hanging loose over her forehead, she looked seductive and desirable.

'How is my grandfather?'

'Better than he was this afternoon. As I said in my note, he's breathing more easily, and if he has a good night I'll try to persuade my father to let you see him in the morning.'

'Thank you.' Harry held out the bottle of surprisingly good, but horrendously expensive Moët et Chandon Mrs Edwards had unearthed from her cellar and two dozen long-stemmed cream roses he had bought from Mrs Parsons. 'An apology for being late yesterday evening.'

'You're completely forgiven, but champagne and flowers are always acceptable.' She opened the door wider. 'Put your car in the garage so it can't be seen from the road. I'll leave the door on the latch. It's such a glorious evening I've laid out supper in the conservatory at the back of the house. In the meantime I'll put these in water,' she took the roses, 'and this,' she glanced at the label on the champagne and smiled, 'on ice.'

Harry hid his car in the garage, closed the door and went into the house. After locking the front door behind him he walked down the central passage that led out of the hall, past half a dozen closed doors and into a huge glass conservatory that ran the entire width of the house. Light and airy, it was furnished with bamboo tables, desks and shelves laden with books and magazines. The chairs, sofas and day beds were padded with cushions upholstered in pale-green linen. A profusion of tropical plants grew in Chinese-style china pots scattered liberally over the grey slate floor. He recognized a banana tree, several palms, orchids and elephant grass. All the windows, including the french doors that led directly into the garden, had been opened, but the air was still, oppressively warm and buzzing with the hum of insects.

'Make yourself at home. You can start by taking off your tie and jacket, it's warm in here.' The heels on Diana's backless slippers clattered over the slates when she carried an ice bucket and the champagne to a table. 'This will take a while to chill. I'll get the one I put in the ice box a couple of hours ago.'

Harry took her advice after she left, unbuttoning his collar and loosening his tie. He wandered to the door and admired the garden, laid out in the traditional English style of neat squares of lawn bordered by flowerbeds.

Diana returned with a second ice bucket and set it on the table next to the champagne. 'Not up to the standard of the one you brought, but I think you'll find it palatable.' She held up an open, frosted bottle of French chardonnay before pouring two glasses. Indicating the table, she said, 'Cold supper as promised.'

'Smoked salmon, potted shrimps, salad and crackers; it looks good.'

She carried the wine over to him and handed him a glass. 'We need a toast. How about "to a cure for tuberculosis"?'

'I'll drink to that.'

'I'm sorry about today, Harry,' she said sincerely. 'We had no way of knowing that your grandfather was about to haemorrhage again. If we had we would never have taken him to the visitors' room.'

'The end is close, isn't it?' It wasn't really a question.

'Like my father, I hate making predictions.'

'You've experience.'

'None of a case of pneumoconiosis and tuberculosis, but if you insist on pressing me, I'd say weeks rather than months.'

'Thank you for being honest.' He sank down on a daybed. She took his wine glass from him and set it together with her own on a side table, before sitting next to him and kissing him.

He kissed her back and wrapped his arms around her. Her breasts were soft, her back firm beneath the silk, but even as his passions rose, misery at his grandfather's condition gnawed relentlessly at the back of his mind.

'There's nothing you can do for him, Harry,' she murmured, guessing where his thoughts lay.

'I know.' He sat forward, leaning away from her.

She stroked his cheek with the back of her finger. 'The first week I worked in Craig y Nos, I walked in on two patients making love in a side ward.'

'That must have been embarrassing.'

'It was – for me. She was only seventeen, he was twenty, and both were very close to death. When they saw me, they made no apology. He told me they found the act of love life-affirming. Defiance in the face of the inevitable.'

'I suppose it is.' He smiled at her.

'Shall we try it?' She rose from the bed and untied the silk rope belt on her trousers. She stepped out of them and her shoes, then unfastened her jacket and allowed it to slide to the floor on top of them. Just as before, the sight of her naked took his breath away.

'Harry, darling. Sweet, darling Harry.' She lay on the bed, pulled him down beside her and unbuttoned his flies.

She helped him undress and in a repeat of the first time they had made love, he allowed her to take control, obeying the instructions she whispered in his ear, placing his hands and tongue exactly where she wanted them, on her thighs, her breasts, her nipples, the flat of her stomach, kissing and fondling every inch of her until her back arched in pleasure, and in return, she caressed him expertly, bringing him to an all-too-swift climax.

Afterwards, passion still roused, he made love to her again, and that time he retained control and understood what she had been trying to tell him. That it was possible to lose all sense of grief, and even self in passion. And when he was immersed in a second, mind-shattering climax he felt that nothing existed outside of the pleasure they brought to one another.

Exhausted, she finally moved away from him and, making no attempt to cover herself, retrieved their wine glasses and handed him his, before nestling close to him.

He summoned up the courage to ask the question uppermost in his mind. 'What's going to happen to us when you go back to London, Diana?'

'In what sense, Harry?'

'Will you see me again?'

'If you're ever in London and want to see me, but that's not what you're asking, is it?' She moved away from him, leaned against the back of the day bed and looked into his eyes.

'No, I thought . . .' His mind searched unsuccessfully for the right words. 'We haven't known one another long but . . .'

'You haven't fallen in love with me, have you, Harry?' she asked soberly.

'You're a very beautiful and intelligent women, no one would blame me if I had,' he answered evasively, suddenly realizing that although he liked Diana, and enjoyed her company and their love-making, his feelings for her were in no way as intense as his grandfather's description of the passion he'd borne for his Isabella.

'Harry, do you remember my telling you that I wasn't always an only child?'

'Yes.'

'I had two brothers and a sister. When my eldest brother was diagnosed with tuberculosis, my father left his post as a surgeon and re-trained at a chest clinic. He worked hard and, as you know, became one of the foremost consultants on the disease in Britain. But he couldn't save my eldest brother, or my younger one, or my sister.'

'Diana, I am so sorry—'

'So you see, we do know how you feel and what you are going through with your grandfather,' she interrupted brusquely, her emotions clearly raw. 'It's not easy for a woman to become a doctor, let alone a consultant, but I intend to do just that. And when old age forces my father's retirement, I will pick up where he left off. You could say that my first and only love is my work. But,' she smiled, and her eyes glittered with mischief, 'as you have found out, I am not always faithful to my first love, and I like sex.'

'I've noticed.' He had meant the remark to sound light-hearted but it fell heavily into the still atmosphere.

'If I misled you in any way, Harry, I'm sorry,' she apologized contritely. 'You are the darlingest, most wonderful boy. Sensitive, good-looking, charitable and sweet-natured. I'm sure that every woman you meet must fall a little in love with you, just as I have done. But I thought you realized when I told you that I had to go back to London that it could never be serious between us. Please don't tell me that I've hurt you, Harry?'

'You haven't.' To his surprise it was the truth.

Taking his glass from him a second time, she leaned over and kissed him. 'Thank you.'

'You're insatiable,' he protested when she moved on top of him.

'Can you blame me, when you're so good at this?'

As they began to make love again, skilfully, if a little mechanically, his mind wandered away from what was happening to his body. He recalled the expression on his grandfather's face when he had spoken about his Isabella and envied him.

He wanted to be part of a close, loving relationship like the one his parents shared and his grandfather had missed since the death of his wife. And, if he was honest with himself, he was even jealous of Toby, because ridiculous as he considered his friend's sudden passion for Bella, at least Toby *felt* something. Diana was beautiful, intelligent and charming, but he wanted more than sex. He wanted to be in love.

If that made him a hopeless romantic, then so be it. He even found it slightly comforting to think that he had outgrown the curiosity that had spurred him into purely physical relationships and was ready for a whole lot more.

Mary lay on the right side of the double bed, looking down towards the uncurtained window that framed a view of the reservoir. She had watched the moon rise over the mountain behind it, and followed its course as it had inched its way higher in the night sky.

She had no idea of the time and no way of finding out, but she guessed that they had been in bed for about two hours. She turned lightly and carefully on the straw mattress so as not to disturb her brother and sister. Luke was sleeping in the middle of the bed, his small fists curled loosely either side of his plump, round face. Martha lay on her side facing him, her hand wrapped loosely around his small body.

She sat up and reached for the shawl that hung over the end of the footboard. Slowly and stealthily she crept through the open door of the bedroom. David and Matthew's steady breathing came from their bedroom next door when she stole out on to the landing.

She moved lightly down the stairs in bare feet, careful to stay on the wall side, away from the banister, because the boards creaked on the outside edge of the staircase. Feeling her way in the darkness, she was glad when she reached the kitchen. The moonlight that streamed in through the window and the glow of the range meant it was easier to see shapes among the shadows. She went to the door and slipped her feet into her father's old boots. She clutched her shawl around her shoulders, muffled the latch with her fingers and lifted it. The voluminous, old-fashioned white cotton nightgown, which had once belonged to Diana Adams's mother, flapped at her heels as she darted across the farmyard and into the stable.

'Anyone here?' Her whisper resounded, alarmingly loud in the darkness. Dolly neighed and she went to her stall. She stroked the horse's neck and the mare snuggled her nose into her arm. She rested her head against Dolly's and then caught a whiff of decay. Crouching down, she ran her hands over the rag she'd tied around Dolly's hoof to hold the poultice.

There was no mistaking the smell. She recognized it from three years ago when her father had been forced to shoot their prize stallion. It was gangrene. And there was nothing she could do for Dolly, herself or her family other than weep.

Chapter 14

'YOU WON'T switch the lights on your car until you leave the drive?' Diana asked Harry when she re-tied the cord on her pyjama trousers.

'No.' Harry shrugged on his jacket.

She followed him to the front door and opened it for him. 'You'll call at the hospital in the morning?'

'Of course.' He hesitated for a moment. 'We could go for a walk tomorrow evening, if you like,' he added diffidently, hoping she wouldn't think he had only suggested it because he wanted to make love to her again.

'Perhaps. Let's take it one day at a time, Harry,' she said softly.

Harry made his way to the car. He drove slowly to the gate. Lights shone in the windows of the upper storey of the castle opposite, illuminating a deserted road. Restless and suddenly beset by an impulse to see the reservoir under the full moon, he turned left and drove up towards the mountain, but he didn't switch on the car's headlights until the Adamses' house was a hundred yards behind him.

He parked in the lane that led down to the reservoir so as not to disturb the Ellises, left his hat in the car and walked down towards the water that flooded the valley floor. The hills, magnificent in daylight, looked even more majestic bathed in moonlight. Their clean, sweeping lines shimmered in the ghostly, silver-grey light. Above the moon, the sky was a deep rich blue-black, pierced by the diamond glints of myriad stars. The water gleamed, still and unbroken, like the surface of a mirror dulled by time, and he imagined it shattering as Toby's Lady of the Lake lifted her arm from the depths and held out Excalibur.

He considered suggesting the idea to Toby. It was ridiculous, the novice having the audacity to tell a professional what to paint. But as he looked down on the quiet scene spread out before him he sensed that he was right. A night scene would make for a more dramatic illustration, and if Malory had written the scene as having taken place in daylight, then it could only have been because the better alternative hadn't occurred to him.

Resolving to bring a torch and sketchbook with him the next fine moonlit night, he took off his jacket, slung it over his shoulder and continued down the hill. The night breeze blew cool against his neck and ruffled his hair. His footsteps crunched over the stone-strewn path and he had the strangest sense that he was somehow violating the place, that the hills resented his presence.

Someone had once told him that the Brecon Beacons had been covered in ancient forest until the advent of the ironworks in Merthyr. The works had created a demand for wood that had resulted in every forest within a thirty-mile radius of the town being stripped bare to feed the furnaces. But now it was difficult to imagine the hills as anything other than the way they were. And having never seen them wooded, the loss didn't seem a desecration.

Rabbits played around him, diving in and out of their burrows, and nibbling grass alongside the sheep. A few ewes lay curled on the ground but more were grazing and he wondered if, like him, they preferred a nocturnal life on fine nights.

When he was almost at the foot of the hill he glanced back at the farmhouse. It was shrouded in darkness and he hoped all five Ellis children were sleeping peacefully. Enjoying the beauty of the night and the quiet scene around him, he thought of his grandfather, as he had been every morning until that day. Unwavering in his resolution to enjoy every pleasure life still offered, even in a sanatorium.

But then he reflected that his grandfather had found his Isabella and his purpose in life. He had dedicated almost every minute he could to the miners' struggle. He hadn't always succeeded in what he'd set out to do, but at least he'd put every effort into trying, which was what he had to do if he was ever going to realize his ambition to become an artist.

He pictured his paint box and mentally mixed and matched the colours in it to the scene around him. Lost in his task, he sank down on to the ground and visualized the painting he would create and show to his grandfather – and Edyth – when he next saw them again.

Mary heard footsteps cross the yard. They halted at the entrance to the stable. She lifted her head and listened. The harsh sounds of heavy breathing were accompanied by the sour stench of beer mixed with whisky and male sweat. The agent had come, just as he'd said he would – and she'd prayed he wouldn't.

'Where are you, bitch?' He stumbled and tripped over the uneven cobbles at the entrance. 'Where are you?' he shouted before falling a second time and setting the metal on the bridles and harnesses that hung on hooks behind the door ringing against the stone wall.

She recoiled and flinched, unable to bear the thought of him touching her, not just then, but ever again.

'Are you here, bitch? Because if you're not I'll go into the house and roust your brothers and sister from their beds.'

The threat was enough to force her to answer. 'I'm here, sir.'

'Stop squeaking like a bloody mouse and show yourself.'

Creeping low on hands and knees, she crawled to the entrance of Dolly's stall and into the next one before rising to her feet. Bob Pritchard stood silhouetted in the doorway. He dived towards her and she fell back. Nauseated by his reek, she instinctively pushed him away from her. He caught her by the waist and threw her down on the cobbles in the empty stall. Winded, she watched his shadowy figure loom over her. She closed her eyes when he thrust his hands up her nightdress and lifted it to her neck.

He mumbled, 'I like it when you fight.'

She retched and fell back weakly. He slapped her hard, across the face. 'Fight, you bitch.'

'Please—'

' "Sir". Never forget the "sir", Mary.' He unbuttoned his trousers and thrust himself into her.

Afterwards, there was only the same degradation, humiliation and self-loathing that she had suffered so many times before. Only this time it was coupled with a desperate desire for an oblivion that would finally end her pain. One even stronger than her sense of loyalty to her family.

Harry was sitting, wondering how best to capture the night shadows that played over the hills, drawing more sweeping and spectacular lines in his imagination than he suspected he would ever be able to translate on to canvas, when he saw someone running down the side of the hill towards the water.

He looked, looked again and rubbed his eyes, wondering if he were seeing a ghost. A girl dressed in an old-fashioned white nightgown, her long dark hair streaming loose behind her, was charging headlong down the hillside directly towards the reservoir. To his horror she didn't stop at the edge, but plunged in.

Stripping off his jacket and his shoes, he sprinted towards the water, but there was no sign of anyone, only a ripple on the surface that could have been caused by the tonight breeze. He hesitated, wondering for an instant if he had dreamed the entire episode. Then he glimpsed a patch of white floating upwards. Without waiting to see more, he dived in and swam towards it.

When Mary splashed into the water its icy wetness came as a shock, bringing the first realization that she was not locked into a dream.

She recalled lying – broken and spent – on the floor of the stall in the stable after Bob Pritchard finished using her. Listening to his diminishing footsteps as he walked out across the yard and through the archway on to the road. And longing to be clean and cold – cold enough to freeze away the feverish, sweat-inducing memory of the clammy warmth of Bob's hands pawing at her, so cold, she could no longer feel his thighs burning into hers and his fingers tightening around her breasts, so cold . . .

She remembered clambering clumsily to her feet, going to the door and leaning against it, seeing the back gate in the yard and stumbling towards it. She had abandoned her boots in the stall, but obsessed with cleanliness and wanting to rid herself of all vestiges of the agent's damp stench that gummed and seared her skin, she had borne the pain of stones cutting into her feet. She had leaned on the gate and gazed down at the reservoir – cool, familiar and beautiful, just as it was in her dreams.

She'd opened the gate, fastened it behind her and run down on tip-toe, gathering speed as she hurtled down the hill. The breeze was fresh, but not chill enough. Her feet hit the ground so quickly and lightly she felt as though she were flying, and now – now the floor of the reservoir yielded, soft and slimy.

It sucked at her feet, gluing them and holding her fast. She struggled, slipped and fell, and her hands and arms were imprisoned as deeply and securely by the mud as her legs. She was left crouching, half in, half out of the water, trapped like a fly stuck to one of the brown arsenic papers that hung from the ceiling of the Colonial Stores in Pontardawe.

Her voluminous cotton nightgown soaked up the water, and even the folds that remained in the air slapped wet against her, hampering her movements. She tried sliding. Backwards proved impossible, but when she pushed forwards, the mud dissolved, the ground disappeared and she lurched, tumbling downwards. There was only time to snatch one short breath before the water closed over her head.

She opened her eyes and found herself in a mind-numbing, milky-grey blackness. Her lungs and ears burned as though they were packed with scalding ice. Frightened, floundering hopelessly out of her depth, she thought beyond herself for the first time since the agent had thrown her to the floor of the stall. She couldn't leave her brothers and sister to face Bob Pritchard – she couldn't – He would destroy them as he had destroyed her.

She kicked out and utilized every ounce of strength she could muster to fight her way up to the surface. But although she could see the transparent sheet that allowed the moonlight to filter through, no matter how she stretched and struggled, it remained beyond her reach. She gradually sank lower and lower, the weight of her waterlogged gown and shawl dragging her downwards towards the mud on the floor of the reservoir that waited to swallow her.

Her eyes stung, but she bore the pain it cost her to keep them open, so she could focus on the moonlight shining through the squall of air bubbles. She had to breathe – there was no air, but she had to . . .

The cold intensified, flooding her lungs, seeping into her joints and bones, paralysing her. She descended into realms where the water was darker, murkier. A small white light burned in the distance. But before she reached it, the glow flickered and died in the blackness.

Harry ran into the water, but as soon as he kicked the ground from under himself and started to swim, he lost his bearings. He trod water frantically, looked around and wondered if he had really seen a woman run into the reservoir or anything pale floating in the water. He had been thinking about the Lady of the Lake. Had he conjured a figment of his imagination into an illusion that had merely seemed real?

A stream of bubbles broke ahead of him. Was it weed, fish? Was he making a complete fool of himself over a mirage? He dived and swam towards the pockets of air but his trousers, shirt and waistcoat weighed him down and held him back. Wishing he'd had the foresight to take them off before he'd plunged into the water, he was exhausted when he reached the place. The bubbles were still breaking but he could see nothing. Taking a deep breath, he allowed himself to sink, opened his eyes and felt as though he were suspended in an enormous pot of grey ink.

He surfaced and gasped for air. The white spot that had seemed so obvious from the bank was nowhere to be seen. Taking a clump of thorn as a guide and aiming for the area as near as he could remember it, he swam to his right.

Seconds later he broke to the surface. Staying there only as long as took him to gulp in a fresh lungful of air, he dived in again – and again. Just when he'd decided that he must have dreamed the woman, he saw ripples on the water and a flash of movement to his left. Kicking out, he stretched towards it.

His hand brushed against cloth. Knotting his fingers into it, he pulled it towards him and a body gently nudged his. Grabbing it by the head, he broke to the surface and lifted it high. It wasn't until he held the nose and mouth clear from the water and brushed long tendrils of hair away from the face that he saw he was holding Mary Ellis. Limp, comatose, she looked dead. Praying he wasn't too late, he gripped her by the shoulders, turned on his back and, careful to keep her head above water, swam backwards towards the bank.

He dragged her over the mud and lay her face down on the grass. His breath rasped, harsh and discordant, as he tried to remember the lifesaving classes he had taken in school.

He opened her mouth, water trickled out, and he felt gingerly inside to ensure her tongue wasn't blocking her airways. He began to massage her back in as close an approximation to artificial respiration as he could recall.

'Come on, Mary. Try! Please try, Mary,' he whispered.

He continued to mutter under his breath for what seemed like hours. Refusing to admit defeat, he carried on even when logic dictated he was working on a corpse. When a gush of water spurted from her mouth, he held his breath and waited. Five long mouth-drying, heart-pounding seconds later, Mary spluttered and coughed. He rolled away from her, leaned on his hands and knees, and vomited up the supper Diana Adams had given him.

Drained by the moonlight, Mary's face was the colour he imagined death to be. He watched her intently. Then slowly – infinitely slowly – her eyelids flickered and she opened her eyes. When she saw him looking at her she closed them again.

'What the hell did you think you were doing?' His voice croaked, thick with shock, bile and the foul taste of stagnant water. When she didn't answer, he grasped hold of her by the shoulders and forced her upright into a sitting position. 'Look at me!'

She opened her eyes again but stared silently at the silver path of moonlight that wavered over the water.

'What did you think you were doing?'

She shook her head, spraying droplets of water in the air.

'You weren't thinking of your brothers and sister, that's for

232

sure,' he said angrily, shaking at the thought of what would have happened if he hadn't decided to look at the reservoir in moonlight.

She began to tremble, and small, grating cries tore from her throat. He crawled over the grass, retrieved his jacket and shoes and returned to her. Anger abated, overwhelmed by pity, he wrapped his jacket around her, and cradled her in his arms the way he had comforted his sisters when they had hurt themselves as toddlers. He smoothed her wet, tangled hair away from her face, and allowed her to shed hot, salt tears onto the shoulder of his sodden shirt and waistcoat.

A wispy, grey-blue cloud passed over the moon and drifted on. A fox called to its mate on the hillside. Half a dozen sheep, startled by an unfamiliar noise or the advent of a predator, bolted over the mountain above them.

'We're both soaking wet, Mary,' he said at last. 'We'll catch cold if we carry on sitting here.'

She looked at him as if he were a stranger.

Realizing she was in shock, he took his jacket from her, untied her shawl, lifted it from her shoulders and wrung it out before replacing his jacket on her shoulders. It had absorbed some of the water and was damp, but it was still drier than her nightgown. Rising, he held out his hand and helped her to her feet before picking up his shoes.

The walk back up the hill was slow and uncomfortable. Their wet clothes chafed, and the breeze cut through the cloth, raising goosebumps. Physically shattered and emotionally drained, neither spoke until they reached the back door.

'Will you be all right now?' he whispered when she depressed the latch.

She nodded.

He gripped her arm, preventing her from entering the house. 'Really?'

'I was keeping some of my father's trousers and shirts for David,' she murmured dully. 'They'll be too small for you but if you put them on I could dry yours before you go back to the inn.'

His first instinct was to return to his car and drive back down the valley as fast as he could. But the image of her floating, more dead than alive in the water, had branded itself on his mind. He remembered what Mrs Edwards and the shepherd Dic had said about her father hanging himself in the barn, and he knew he'd never forgive himself if she harmed herself after he left.

'I'd like dry clothes, thank you.' He followed her into the kitchen, closed the door behind him and went to the stove. Its warmth permeated his saturated clothes, and he stood, watching the water vapour rise gently from his shirt and trousers while she disappeared upstairs. She returned ten minutes later dressed in her black skirt and blouse, a towel wrapped around her head. She handed him a pair of worn and patched men's moleskin working trousers and a thick blue workman's shirt.

He took them, went into the scullery, stripped off his sodden garments, wrung them over the sink, bundled them together and dried himself as best he could in the towel he found there. Mary had been right about the trousers. They were wide enough but the legs ended six inches above his ankles. The shirt didn't reach his waist and the cuffs flapped at his elbows. Feeling like an orphan who'd outgrown his institution uniform, he returned to the kitchen. Mary was sitting on the bench closest to the fire. Still deathly pale and shaking, she was staring into the flames but jumped up when she saw him.

'If you give me your clothes, I'll dry them for you.' She went to the rope that lowered the drying rack from the ceiling.

'There's no need.' He dropped the bundle on the doorstep before closing the door. 'I'll give them to the maid to wash when I get to the inn.'

'What will you tell her?'

'That I felt like a midnight swim in the reservoir. Sorry, bad joke. I'll tell her I slipped and fell in when I was walking around it, looking for a vantage point to paint it.'

'In the middle of the night?' She returned to the bench and sank back down on to it.

'Some of the most beautiful paintings are of night scenes. Take a look at your Christmas cards when you get them at the end of the year.'

'No one sends us Christmas cards. They wouldn't, would they, seeing as how we can't read.' There was no bitterness in her declaration.

'I'm sorry, I didn't think.' He sat on the other end of the bench and, like her, stared into the flames. It was easier to watch their flickering than face the despair etched into her dark eyes. She continued to sit motionless only a few feet away from him, yet he felt as though a chasm had opened between them.

'Why were you there?' Even her voice sounded remote.

'I was thinking about a painting. Trying to decide what colours to use to capture the moonlight on the water.' He glanced across at her. 'It's just as well that I was. Did you mean to drown yourself?'

She bit her lip but didn't move her head.

'You don't know?'

She remained silent.

'I couldn't believe my eyes when I saw you running into the water. Afterwards it wouldn't have taken much to convince me that I'd dreamed it, or seen a ghost. I almost gave up before I found you because I thought I'd imagined the entire episode. What possessed you to run straight into the water?' When she didn't answer him, he tried another direct question. 'Can you swim?'

She looked down and shook her head vigorously before whispering, 'No.'

'Mary, I know things are bad on the farm and for your family at the moment, but if you let me, I promise I will try to help you.'

She finally lifted her head and the anguish in her magnificent black eyes unnerved him. 'If you knew just how bad they were, Mr Evans, and how bad I am, you wouldn't want to help us.'

'Yes, I would,' he contradicted her.

'Even if you wanted to help us, there's nothing you can do. There's nothing anyone can do—'

The latch on the door that led into the hall lifted and David walked in. He had pulled his muddy work trousers on over a blue-and-white striped flannel nightshirt.

'I thought I heard voices.' He glowered at Harry. 'What are you doing here with my sister in the middle of the night?'

'Visiting.' Harry's flippant remark fell leadenly into the charged atmosphere.

'Mr Evans helped me, David.'

'How?' David crossed his arms across his thin chest and looked from Harry to Mary.

Harry glanced at Marry but she refused to meet his gaze. 'I was sitting down by the reservoir, thinking of ways to paint it—'

'In the middle of the night?' David broke in incredulously.

'Yes, in the middle of the night.' Harry turned to David. He sensed that Mary had lifted her head and was looking at him. 'I saw her run down the hill and straight into the water.'

'*What?*' David turned to his sister.

Mary didn't offer a word of explanation. Harry looked at his watch in the firelight and realized it had stopped at two-thirty, presumably the time he'd entered the water, but he still sensed seconds ticking into minutes. 'One of my sisters used to walk in her sleep when she was small. Mary had the same odd look of not being aware of her surroundings, so I waded in after her and fished her out.'

'Mary, is this true?' David asked.

'Yes.' She took the towel from her wet hair and shook it out as proof.

'You've never walked in your sleep before.' David went to the fire box, picked up a log and dropped it on the flames, sending a shower of sparks flying up the chimney.

'I suppose there's a first time for everything.' Realizing that he could barely keep his eyes open and he still had to drive to the inn, Harry rose to his feet.

'You're going?' David asked.

'It's hardly the time to pay a social call.' Harry looked intently from David to Mary. 'You will look after her?'

'Of course I will, she's my sister,' David snapped defensively. 'Why did you do it, Mary?' he demanded, unwilling to allow the matter to drop.

Mary gave Harry a quick, conscious look. 'Like Mr Evans said, I was asleep. I didn't know what I was doing. But I checked Dolly last thing, and I think she has gangrene in her hoof.'

'You think?' There was real fear in David's voice.

'I'm sure,' Mary said reluctantly. 'And you know what that means.'

'We'll have to shoot her.' David gritted his teeth and clenched his fists. 'But that still doesn't explain why you were sleepwalking.'

Mary looked away from Harry and back at the fire. 'I dreamed that I was running down the valley to fetch the vet. Now that we've paid his bill, we can ask him to call and look at her.'

'And throw good money away?' David snapped. 'There's no need to call him. We've both seen enough animals with gangrene to recognize the smell. If you're right, I'll shoot Dolly in the morning.'

'The agent's taken father's gun,' Mary reminded him.

'Only one of them. There's another in the attic.'

'You hid it?'

'I don't tell you everything I do. And the way things are we might need it,' he muttered grimly.

'If we do, it will only be for shooting sick animals and vermin,' Mary warned.

'Do you want me to shoot the horse for you?' Harry volunteered.

'You ever shoot an animal, Harry?' David asked.

'No, but I won prizes for marksmanship in school.' Harry tried not to sound as if he were boasting.

'My father taught me to shoot rocks off a wall before he let me loose on foxes and sick livestock. There's a difference between killing a target and an animal,' David lectured as though he were the man and Harry the boy.

'David, that was rude,' Mary said wearily.

'Thank you for the clothes, I'll get the maid at the inn to wash them before I bring them back.' Harry looked back at David when he was at the door. 'You will take care of your sister?' he repeated.

'I will, and from now on I'll lock the doors at night.'

Harry wasn't sure whether David was threatening to lock him out or Mary in. 'Then I'll say goodnight.'

David squinted up at the sky when Harry stepped into the yard. The pale-grey light that precedes dawn had highlighted the hills to the east. 'I don't know whether we should go back to bed or start work for the day.'

'It might be as well if we both took a look at Dolly before the little ones get up,' Mary suggested.

Wanting to help, not knowing how, and having no excuse to linger, Harry picked up his wet clothes from the step, closed the door and set out to walk to his car.

'You look like a vampire on his way to bed, or rather his coffin,' Toby declared cheerfully to Harry when they drove from the inn to the sanatorium the following morning.

'It's only fair to warn you that if I am a vampire, I'm one in need of sleep and nourishment,' Harry yawned.

'You should have eaten the breakfast the Silent One put in front of you.'

'I was too tired to eat.'

'Well, if that's what an evening with the Snow Queen does to you, perhaps you ought to look for a gentler woman. I couldn't get more than a grunt out of you at breakfast and you've barely said a word since we got in the car.'

'What's there to say in response to your inane chatter?' Harry turned into the courtyard of Craig y Nos.

'Tell all to Uncle Toby.'

'Like what?' Harry pulled on the brake.

'I happen to know that you had a *very* late night with the beautiful Diana.'

Harry glared at Toby. 'How?'

'You drove into the barn at half past three, according to my alarm clock.'

'Then, like you, your alarm clock's an ass,' Harry said.

'My alarm clock keeps perfect time. I take it that both you and the lady don't give a damn for her reputation.'

Harry left the car. 'After I left the Adamses' house last night I drove to the reservoir.'

'You mean the Arthurian lake.'

'I mean the reservoir,' Harry corrected. 'I was restless and too wide awake to sleep.'

'Ah-hah.'

'Ah-hah nothing,' Harry said irritably. 'I simply wondered what the reservoir would look like in the moonlight. There was a full moon last night.'

'I saw it, although unlike you gallivanting here there and everywhere under an open sky, I viewed it through the window of my room when I was tucked up safe and sound between the sheets in my little bed.'

'Toby, I'm just not in the mood this morning.' Harry walked to the door of the sanatorium.

'I can see that. Take Uncle Toby's advice—'

'Don't you know when to stop?'

Deciding a change of topic would be expeditious. Toby tried another gambit. What did you do up at my Arthurian lake?'

Giving up trying to call it a reservoir, Harry said, I looked at it in the moonlight, studied the colours, mixed and matched them in my mind's eye with the watercolours in my paint box. Wondered just how much cobalt blue I'd need to blend with white to get the exact shade of reflected light on the water. Then, when I'd finished deciding on the depth of tints I needed to reproduce the radiance and shadow, I planned the painting. Pinpointed the exact spot the Lady of the Lake's arm should rise holding Excalibur—'

'At night?'

'A night scene would give the painting more dramatic impact.'

Toby considered the idea for a moment. 'It might at that. And I'm the one who's supposed to be illustrating *Le Morte d'Arthur*.' He punched Harry lightly on the top of his arm. 'Just think, the infant teaching the master. You may turn out to be a prodigy after all, Harry.' He lifted his straw boater and bowed as Diana opened the door. 'Good morning, Miss Adams. How are we this dull and overcast Sunday morning?'

'Are you referring to my father and myself, or the royal "we" Mr Ross?' she enquired with a smile.

'As your father is nowhere to be seen, I was addressing you, Miss Adams.'

'I know our acquaintance is slight, Mr Ross, but I believe that you are aware that I am not royal.'

'I stand corrected, Miss Adams. How are *you?*'

'Fine, and too busy to waste time exchanging meaningless banter. Your uncle was bright and alert when I saw him half an hour ago. You can go straight up to his room.' She turned to Harry, 'Mr Evans, if I might have a word?'

Harry followed her to her car. 'My grandfather—' he began.

'Was tired out by the visit your uncles and sister made yesterday. And that is not a criticism of your family. My father examined him when he came back from church this morning. He's noticed that your grandfather will go to great lengths to conceal his exhaustion and any pain he is in, frequently insisting he feels fine when his symptoms indicate otherwise.'

'He has put other people before himself all his life.' Harry pulled his handkerchief from his pocket and sneezed into it.

'You have a cold?'

'No, I just sneezed.'

'If you have a cold you can't possibly be allowed to see your grandfather. A cold on top of his illnesses could lead to further infection—'

'Do you want to take my temperature?' Harry had intended his question sarcastically, but Diana laid her hand on his forehead.

'You don't feel feverish.'

'Because I'm not. I told you, it was only a sneeze.'

'But you will limit your visit to five not ten minutes?'

'Thank you, I didn't think I'd be allowed to see him at all today,' Harry smiled.

She looked at the front door. Toby had already gone ahead into the castle. 'Your grandfather's condition is worse than he wants anyone to know. And I'm including his doctors as well as his family.'

'He hates fuss.'

'Harry, he's dying.'

The fact that she had used his Christian name in the sanatorium jolted him. 'You told me that he has weeks rather than months last night.'

'My father thinks it will be days.'

'Should I telephone my father and ask him to bring all the family down here to say goodbye?'

240

'Ask your grandfather what he would like you to do, Harry.'

'And your strict visiting rules?'

'My father has agreed to try to accommodate your grandfather's wishes — whatever they may be.'

A stranger might not have noticed the change in Billy Evans, but Harry knew him too well. His grandfather's smile was as wide as it had always been, but it was forced. His eyes had lost some of their spark, and although he was sitting upright holding a book, he was leaning heavily against the pillows. Even his speech was weaker than it had been on Friday.

'Harry, good of you to come.'

The sky was overcast, the air heavy. Billy's bed had been pulled out on the balcony as usual, but the bed linen had been covered with a rubber sheet to protect it from rain. Harry moved the chair around so he could sit with his back to the sister.

'It's not good of me at all. This is the highlight of my day.'

'In that case, poor you. Is Bella all right?' Billy asked anxiously.

'Apart from being worried about you, as we all were when you were taken ill yesterday.'

'It was a stupid thing to do.'

'Miss Adams told me to keep my visit to five minutes because you're tired.'

'Miss Adams is as much of a fusspot as the nurses.' Billy closed his book. 'J. K. Jerome's *Paul Kelver*,' he said when he saw Harry looking at the spine. 'Victor knows I need to smile. He and Joey brought me enough books to keep me going for another week.'

'You want me to ask Dad to bring you more next Saturday?'

'He's coming?'

'I telephoned him this morning; he and Mam intend to.' Harry cleared his throat and braced himself. 'Miss Adams says you can have more visitors if you like.'

'I spoke to Doctor Adams. I know the end's close,' Billy said in a matter-of-fact tone. 'If your aunts and uncle and your father and mother want to come, they can, but only if it's convenient. They all have so many other things to do with their time. But none of my grandchildren, not after what happened to Bella yesterday.'

'And the books?' Harry tried to concentrate on the practical.

'I'll let you know later in the week.' Billy's voice dropped to a whisper.

'Are you in pain?' Harry looked around for the sister.

'No, just having trouble breathing. And don't go telling my boys that. They are busy with their wives and families, which is how it should be.'

'They'll want to say goodbye to you.' To Harry's shame, his voice cracked.

The old man's voice might be weak, but his eyes gleamed, bright and alive. 'I told you I've said all I am going to on that subject, Harry. Do you really think that I've left so much unsaid during my lifetime that I need a great theatrical deathbed scene worthy of Dickens, with my three sons, their wives and all sixteen grand-children sitting round me here, and every one of you running the risk of contracting TB?'

'No, Granddad, I don't, because you've always been totally honest with all of us.'

'Thank you for noticing. Also, I'm too fond of all of you to risk boring you. Even doctors agree that forecasting the time of death is an inexact science. It would be too tiresome if you all stood here, said your goodbyes, ran out of things to say and had to hang around foolishly for hours or, who knows, days or weeks. It's bad enough that I upset two of your sisters by haemorrhaging in front of them. I wouldn't dare risk a repeat performance in front of any of my other grandchildren. So promise me? No worrying telephone calls to Lloyd or anyone else in the family?'

'If that's what you want.'

'Promise?'

'I promise,' Harry agreed solemnly.

'And if Victor and Megan and Joey and Rhian want to come down with Lloyd and Sali next Saturday they can. But tell them what I have just told you. I don't think that I have any unfinished business left, not with the family.'

'Or with anyone else, Granddad?' Harry tightened his fist impotently.

'There are a few colliers walking around the Rhondda who promised to buy me a pint in return for the ones I bought them when they were broke and I wasn't but,' Billy winked, 'if you see any of them, tell them I'll expect my reward in heaven, and not from the angels. If I manage to get there, and get in, I'll be waiting to meet them at the gate. And if heaven is half as wonderful as I've heard, there's bound to be a bar that serves a nice drop of ambrosia.'

'I'll make sure it's broadcast from one end of the Rhondda to the other.'

'Good. Now tell me about your family of children.'

'Granddad—'

'Did you see them yesterday after your uncles and Bella left?' The old man shook his head fondly. 'She's grown into a very pretty girl. A real chip off the old block.'

As Bella's colouring was much darker than his mother's and her features more exotic, Harry guessed that Billy was talking about his Spanish-born Isabella. 'She is,' he concurred.

'And she'll soon have the young men chasing after her.'

'She has some already.'

'Really?' Billy eyes sparkled.

'And not just schoolboys in Pontypridd. Toby Ross hasn't stopped singing her praises since he had lunch with us yesterday. He wants to paint her as Morgan le Fey, only as sweet young innocent Morgan, before she did all her evil deeds,' he added.

'And she's agreed to model for him?'

'She said she'd think about it. Don't worry if she does, I'll chaperon her. Toby can't stop talking about her. He says his intentions are strictly honourable but Bella is only sixteen.'

'A year younger than Isabella when I first set eyes on her, Harry. Word of advice, never interfere in true love.' He looked at the photograph of Isabella on his cabinet, pressed the handkerchief he was holding to his mouth and coughed. The linen turned red.

Harry turned and shouted, 'Sister!' but she was already there.

'Out, Mr Evans.' She pushed past him and ran to the bed. Two other nurses appeared.

He looked at his grandfather. Blood was seeping from his mouth. He gave a slight but perceptible nod.

Harry nodded back to let him know that he understood – then left.

Chapter 15

HARRY WAS walking through the stables at Ynysangharad House. Toffee, the first horse he had helped raise from a foal, was kicking the back of his stall. Knock – knock. He felt in his pocket for a carrot or sugar lump, but he had none. He searched his other pockets . . . Knock – knock.

'Mr Evans!'

He sat up with a start, hit his head on the headboard and a sheaf of papers fell from his bed. They scattered over the floorboards. Disorientated, he stared down at them.

'Mr Evans!'

The second shout galvanized him. He lurched clumsily from the bed and wrenched open the door. Mrs Edwards was on the landing, a troubled frown creasing her wrinkled forehead.

'Craig y Nos is on the telephone asking to speak to you, Mr Evans.'

Without waiting to put on his shoes, Harry hurtled past her down the creaking staircase and along the flagstoned passage. He muttered a hurried 'sorry' when he barged into Enfys, who emerged from the kitchen as he was about to enter the tiny 'office'. The receiver was lying on the rickety table. He snatched it up. 'Harry Evans.'

'This is Craig y Nos sanatorium, Mr Evans.'

He recognized Diana Adams's voice. 'What's wrong?'

'Your grandfather has made a temporary recovery. The haemorrhage appeared more serious than it actually was. My father believes that only the upper quarter of the right lung was affected.'

'Can I see him?' Harry pleaded.

'Not until tomorrow morning, and then only if he is strong enough to receive visitors.'

'Please—'

'Mr Evans has been sedated, he is sleeping and we're not expecting him to wake until tomorrow, but if he should, I will tell the ward sister to pass on your concern and best wishes, Mr Evans.'

The line went dead, and Harry realized that there must have been someone in the room with Diana. He hung up. After the sister had ordered him out of his grandfather's room in the sanatorium that morning, he had tried to sit in the waiting room by the front door to wait for news. A nurse had followed him, and told him if anything happened they would telephone, so there was absolutely no point in him staying there.

He had driven Toby up to the reservoir, dropped him off, turned the car around and returned to the inn to wait for a telephone call he didn't know whether to wish for or not.

'Not bad news, I hope, Mr Evans?' Mrs Edwards was hovering outside the door.

'My grandfather has made a recovery – a temporary recovery, Mrs Edwards,' he amended.

'I am glad to hear it. You didn't come down for lunch or tea, and I didn't like to disturb you. Would you like a sandwich now?'

'What is the time?'

'Six o'clock, Mr Evans.'

Harry realized that he'd slept most of the day away. 'A sandwich and tea would be most acceptable, Mrs Edwards, if it's not too much trouble.'

'No trouble, Mr Evans.' She wiped her hands in her apron. 'Would you like Enfys to serve you in the dining room?'

'The bar will be fine, Mrs Edwards, but I'll go upstairs and wash and change first. I can't believe I fell asleep in the middle of the day.'

'You were very late last night, Mr Evans,' she said reproachfully.

'I'm sorry if I disturbed you,' Harry apologized, embarrassed that others besides Toby had heard him arrive back at the inn in the early hours. He ran upstairs and gathered the papers that had fallen from the bed. Too tired after his sleepless night to attempt to draw or paint, and too restless after visiting his grandfather to settle to anything pleasurable, he had returned to his room with the intention of catching up on his correspondence and the monthly reports the trustees of his estate sent him.

He glanced at the topmost page when he stacked the papers and set them on the table. He could recall reading the first paragraph and no more. So much for 'catching up' on business. He could almost hear Lloyd lecturing him.

'Wealth brings responsibilities, Harry. You owe it to the people dependent on the wages your companies pay to make sure that every business you own is run fairly and honestly. And the only way you can do that is by monitoring them. It is time you learned everything there is to know about them and the people who labour for your benefit.'

He set his leather writing case on top of the report so he wouldn't have to look at it. Like all the others he had received since his eighteenth birthday, it was crushingly boring, and he wondered if he would ever find 'business' interesting. He stretched his arms above his head and glanced out of the window at the deserted road. He felt even more exhausted than when he had returned to his room that morning. But he was also unpleasantly warm, sticky and hungry. Taking his towel and soap from his washstand and a clean shirt from his wardrobe, he made his way down to the ground-floor scullery cum bathroom, ran a cold bath and plunged into it.

An hour later, refreshed, his appetite satisfied by two rounds of ham sandwiches and a pot of tea, he set out to fetch Toby. He had deliberately waited until the end of evensong when the chapels and churches would be closed in the hope of picking up the Ellises. After the scene with Iestyn Williams the week before, he didn't want to go to the chapel again.

He drove slowly up the valley and caught up with the Ellises on a lonely stretch of road half a mile up the valley from Craig y Nos. He stopped the car ahead of them and Martha ran up to him.

'Mr Ross is painting the lake today. He gave Matthew and me some of his picnic, but we missed you.'

'I'm sorry, Martha. My grandfather was ill and I wanted to be near a telephone.' Harry left the driving seat, opened the back door and she climbed in. Matthew followed, but David and Mary, carrying Luke, were walking at a slower pace.

'Mr Ross said your grandfather was taken ill this morning, Mr Evans. I hope he is better now,' Mary said when she drew close. She wasn't wearing her shawl, which he presumed was still wet, and her thin black cotton skirt and blouse made her look positively emaciated. There were also deep shadows beneath her eyes as if she hadn't slept for days. David didn't look much better.

'My grandfather's marginally better than he was thank you.' He braced himself. 'Dolly?' he ventured.

'I walked her to the pit this morning and shot her.' David sat in the front passenger seat.

'I'm sorry, I knew how much she meant to you – to all of you,' Harry sympathized. He waited until Mary settled herself in the back seat with Luke before closing the door. He returned to the driving seat, started the car and drove off.

Matthew leaned forward from the back. 'The pit is where we burn our favourite animals, Mr Evans, so they don't have to go to the knackers' yard. Do you think they go to heaven from there? The minister doesn't, because he said in one of his sermons that animals don't have souls. But I think they do.'

'You shouldn't contradict the minister, Matthew,' Martha said primly.

'Why not? He's only a person, same as us,' David chipped in.

'He's an important, educated person,' Martha countered.

'Who wouldn't let us bury Dad in the family grave, old—'

'David.' Mary's voice was weak with exhaustion.

'For what it's worth, Matthew, I think animals do have souls.' Harry was finally able to answer the boy's question. 'And when I get to heaven I hope to see the dogs, cats and horses my family has owned over the years.'

'You're not just saying that, Mr Evans, because David had to shoot Dolly?' Martha pressed.

'No, I really do believe that animals have souls. If they didn't they'd all be the same, wouldn't they? And each one I've met has its own personality.'

'I'm glad you think the same as me, Mr Evans.' Matthew settled back contentedly.

Martha shouted in Harry's ear, 'Miss Adams came up to see me this morning and she said that I can go back to work a week tomorrow.'

'I'm glad to hear that.' Harry glanced across at David, who was sitting, sunk in misery. He knew exactly how he felt. Lloyd had always insisted that any decisions that had to be made about ending an animal's life because of accident or disease had to be made by its owner. The memory of one particular Labrador, Brutus, whose kidneys had failed after eight loyal years, still haunted him. 'Do you still want me to take your produce down to Pontardawe on Wednesday, David?'

David said two words Harry had never expected to hear him utter. 'Yes, please.'

Harry parked the car outside the farmhouse and walked through the yard to the back gate. Toby was standing in front of an easel he'd set up close to the reservoir on the floor of the valley. Harry shouted to him to attract his attention. Toby waved back and pointed to the canvas. Harry pointed to the house. The Ellises had already gone inside, he presumed, to change out of their 'best' chapel clothes.

He returned to his car, opened the boot and took out the cardboard box he had filled with newspapers, pencils, paper scissors and his spare sketchbook. Already he knew the family's routine. As soon as they changed, Mary would most probably start making supper, David and Matthew would bring in the cows for milking, and Martha would be taking care of Luke. He couldn't think of a better time to start teaching her to read.

When it grew too dark to see the newspapers Harry had spread out, Mary pushed a spill into the fire. She waited until it caught, then lit the wick on a homemade tallow candle and set it between

Harry and Martha in the middle of the table. David came in from the yard after shutting the poultry into the barn for the night. He unlaced his working boots, set them in the corner behind the door, put on a pair of knitted slippers and sat alongside Martha, Luke and Matthew on the bench opposite Harry.

'I didn't know people could paint in the dark. That friend of yours down by the reservoir has just lit his lantern, Harry.'

'Toby may have lit his lantern, but he won't be painting. He's probably doing what I was last night, studying the colour of the landscape in the moonlight and wondering how best to capture it in paint.' Harry watched Matthew, who had stayed at the table after supper, to help Martha to cut out letters and words from the papers. Without any prompting from him, Matthew put the first and second letters of his name in order.

'That's the first letter over the door.' David pulled a 'D' towards him with his forefinger.

'That is the first letter of your name.' Harry found the remainder of the letters that spelled out David and put them in front of the boy.

'Then David Ellis *is* written above the door?' He looked to Harry for confirmation.

'David Ellis sixteen twenty-four,' Harry echoed, suppressing a smile at the astonishment on the boy's face.

'I thought it was a story Dad made up.'

'I told you it was your name, David.' Mary finished sweeping the hearth, emptied the dustpan into the fire and sat next to Harry. 'Dad told me that the eldest son of the family has always been called David Ellis.'

'Then that means that your family and a David Ellis has lived in this house for three hundred and two years,' Harry moved the 'h' Matthew had put into his name and pushed in a second 't'.

'Three hundred and two years,' Martha repeated in wonder. 'Is that right, Mr Evans?'

Harry smiled. 'Absolutely right, Martha. Now, look at these sheets of paper. I've written out the alphabet on them, and there's space under each letter for a small picture. I thought you could draw something that starts with that letter under every one to remind you of the sound. Let's see if we can think of things that you have on the farm.' Conscious that although they were silent, David and Mary were also listening to him, Harry pointed to the 'A'.

'That's the "A" from my name,' said Martha.

'It is, and what starts with an "A"?'

'An apple?'

'That's good, Martha, and that is a perfect apple you've drawn,' he complimented when she added a stalk to the top.

'Can you see what we're doing, Matthew?' Harry asked after Martha had drawn a bee, cow, dog and egg. 'Can you think of something that starts with "F"?' He shook his head slightly at Martha who looked as though she were about to speak.

'Fish?' Matthew answered doubtfully.

'We don't see many of those round here. I can't remember the last time we had fish for dinner,' David complained.

'A fork?' Martha was already drawing a hay fork. ' "G" . . .'

'Gate,' Matthew said with more confidence, and when Harry didn't contradict him, Martha drew a gate.

'Looking at those pictures, Martha, I think Mr Ross would be better off trying to teach you to paint instead of me,' Harry complimented.

'That's an "H" like in Martha so it could be a—'

'Hay.' A tear rolled down Mary's cheek.

'J for jam,' Harry continued briskly, assuming that she was thinking of Dolly. 'Now we come to "K".'

'Kitchen,' Matthew shrieked, carried away by the new game.

'Excellent.' Harry ruffled the boy's hair. 'But that will be hard for Martha to draw so let's look at something else that is in the kitchen.' He looked pointedly at the stove.

'Kettle,' Matthew and Martha called out simultaneously.

' "L" for leek . . . mouse, nose, otter, patch . . .'

'We've plenty of those,' David quipped, and the others laughed.

'Quill.' Harry pulled a feather from his pocket that he'd picked up in the yard. 'People used to dip the end in ink and write with these years ago.'

'So that's why there were so many in the old oak desk drawers.

The agent threw them in the rubbish when he took the desk. Do you remember, Mary?' David turned to his sister.

Mary looked so pale, drained and exhausted that Harry quickened the pace so he could finish the lesson. 'Snail, rabbit, trap, udder, vicar, wagon, "X" – that's a hard one. The word that's most often used in the alphabet books for "X" is xylophone.'

'What's a xylophone, Mr Evans?' Matthew asked.

'A musical instrument. Let's cheat, Martha, there's an "X" at the end of fox, so you can draw one of those. And that leaves the last two letters – "Y" for yard and "Z" for zoo.'

'What's a zoo?' Matthew looked to Harry again.

'A place where they house animals from all over the world so people can go and see them.'

'What kind of animals?'

'All sorts.' Harry listed the most exotic creatures he could think of. 'Elephants, camels, zebras, lions, tigers, monkeys . . .'

'We saw a monkey once, in Pontardawe, with an organ-grinder, didn't we, Davy? He was only small but he could make a lot of noise.'

It was then that Harry realized the Ellises had probably never seen photographs of the other animals he'd mentioned. 'There's a wonderful zoo in Bristol. It's not too far by train. You learn to read and write, Martha and Matthew, and I'll take you there as a reward.' He glanced at Mary and David. 'And you two, of course, if you'd like to come.'

'As if we can leave the farm,' David growled, reverting to his customary sour humour.

There was a knock at the door. Mary blanched.

'Who is it?' David moved close to the box of logs next to the stove.

'A weary painter,' Toby answered.

Matthew ran to open it. 'Come in and look at what we're doing, Mr Ross. Mr Evans is teaching us to read.'

Toby glanced at the table. 'So I see. I'm sorry to spoil your evening, but Harry and I will be in trouble with our landlady if we're any later than this for our supper. Ready to go, Harry?'

'Yes.' Harry picked up his hat from the windowsill where he'd left it. 'Thank you for the tea, Mary.' He looked back. David was spelling his name with the cut-out letters just like Martha and Matthew. And he noticed that, like Martha, he hadn't made a mistake in the order.

'You will come again tomorrow, Mr Evans, and teach us some more?' Martha pleaded.

'If your brother and sister don't mind, Martha,' he answered cautiously.

'You'd be welcome, Mr Evans,' Mary murmured.

'You know what time we have tea, Harry.'

As there was no anger, bitterness or sarcasm in David's voice, Harry smiled and nodded. 'Thank you, David, I'll be here.'

'So that's what you did in your room last night. It's not bad, Harry.' Toby stood back and eyed the watercolour Harry had painted.

'Not bad,' Mrs Edwards said as she crossed the yard to Alf's workshop. 'It's brilliant. That moonlight on the water looks real to me, Mr Evans.'

'Thank you, Mrs Edwards. It's the first painting I've done that I'm not ashamed of.' Harry covered the canvas and lifted it into the back of the car.

'You taking it to the sanatorium to show your grandfather?' Toby asked.

'I am.' Harry looked at the shrouded canvas Toby was carrying. 'Can I see yours?'

'It's not finished,' Toby answered evasively.

'I thought your lake only needed a lady's arm holding a sword?'

'I'd still rather you saw it when it's ready for London.'

Harry stood back and crossed his arms across his chest. 'It's that much better than mine?'

Realizing that Harry wasn't going to take no for an answer. Toby unveiled it.

Harry stared for a moment, then let out a low whistle. 'Compared to that, mine's dead. I feel as though I could dive into the water.'

Toby covered it up. 'What you have to remember is I have had four years' tuition at the Slade and a lifetime of watching Frank paint, as well as private tutoring from him.'

'And if I had all that and more, I'd never be as good as you,' Harry climbed into his car.

'That's where you're wrong, Harry.' Toby secured his painting in the back of the car alongside Harry's. 'If you are prepared to put in the work and the hours, you'll improve. You certainly have the talent. Believe you me, the first landscape watercolour I did was nowhere near the standard of yours.'

'And how old were you when you did it?' Harry drove out of the yard on to the road.

'I can't remember.'

'Really?' Harry questioned sceptically.

'You have talent, Harry,' Toby insisted. 'I wouldn't say so if you didn't. What I don't know is if you have the dedication and application to push yourself to the absolute limit of that talent and wring all you can out of it.'

Harry thought about what Toby had said. 'You know something. I haven't a clue if I have or not,' he said seriously.

'Talent is only half the battle,' Toby mused. 'There were students at the Slade who were fantastic, streets ahead of me. But . . .'

'But?' Harry prompted when Toby didn't finish the sentence.

'They preferred to do other things. Drink, womanize, make money. I couldn't understand them then, and I understand them even less now. God knows what drives a man. I only know that I have to paint in the same way that I have to draw breath. And Frank feels just like that as well. Take away our art and you'd take away our lives. No one, and I mean no one, would have made me waste three years of my life studying English in Oxford.'

Billy Evans looked at Harry's watercolour and nodded. 'That's very good, Harry. You certainly have talent, and you should be in Paris, not wasting your time here with me.' He started to cough and saw Harry start nervously. 'But you'd better keep it away from me or you won't be allowed to carry it out of here. You haven't told them at home what happened to me on Sunday morning?'

'Against my better judgement, no, I haven't.' Harry shifted uneasily on the chair at the side of his grandfather's bed on the balcony and moved the canvas behind Billy's bed. 'Dad telephoned the inn last night. Uncle Joey and Uncle Victor are coming down with him to visit you again this Saturday. They're travelling down with Mam and Bella, who has decided to model for Toby.'

Billy's eyes glittered feverishly and his voice was even feebler than it had been the day before. 'Are the boys bringing Megan and Rhian?'

'Yes, and hopefully they'll all be allowed in to see you, but Dad's already warned Bella that she will have to stay at the inn.'

The old man nodded. 'Thank you. I'd hate to risk upsetting her again.' He grimaced as he moved in the bed. 'You making progress teaching that family to read?'

'Yes.' Harry saw the sister hovering in the doorway. Flouting regulations – again – he rested the canvas against the wall, blocked her view of the bed with his body and gripped his grandfather's hand. 'See you tomorrow morning.'

'Good luck, Harry. You can tell me then about the progress your scholars are making. And thank you for showing me your painting and what the scenery around here is like.'

Harry glanced at the sister. 'Take care, Granddad.'

'I'm not planning on having another haemorrhage, if that's what you mean.' Billy winked at him and glared at the sister, who was now smoothing the cover on his bed. 'You've done that three times already this morning, woman, haven't you anything else to do besides fuss over me?'

'No, Mr Evans, I haven't.'

His voice grew marginally stronger. 'Pity. If you did, I might get some peace.'

Harry smiled at the banter and walked to the lift. After seeing Toby's watercolour he wondered if he should start on a second painting of the lake, or try to help David on the farm again.

He had spent all of Monday and Tuesday painting. But the day before, clouds had obscured the sun and muddied the light. Bored, he had walked up to the farm and found David in one of the outbuildings, chopping a pile of logs he had been given by a farmer who had cleared his woodland for grazing.

David had told him that Martha and Mary were out with Luke and Matthew repairing a wall in one of the fields. Harry had offered to help until they returned, and, to his amazement, David had accepted.

He'd taken off his jacket, rolled up his shirt-sleeves and chopped steadily while David had cleaned the pigsties and cowsheds. By the time the others returned, he had cut every log in the outbuilding into stove-sized pieces. He had drunk tea and eaten bread and jam with the Ellises, then given Martha and Matthew another lesson. Mary and David joined them, and although they said very little, he noticed that they took in everything he said.

He'd resolved that when he couldn't paint he'd spend as much time as possible on the farm, deciding that if David couldn't find him work to do, he'd ask if he'd allow him to make small repairs around the place. Any activity had to be better than sitting around thinking about his grandfather's illness.

'I saw that.' Toby watched him rub an aching shoulder muscle as he left the sanatorium.

'What?' Harry returned his canvas to the back of his car.

'You moving your shoulder as if you were a wooden puppet. That will teach you to chop wood.'

'I enjoyed it.'

'I bet.' Toby sat beside him. 'The good news is Frank's reasonably well and approves – more or less, given a few improvements that need to be made – of what I've done so far. So I can start on another lake painting today. The background for the final scene. The wounded Arthur being rowed away by the mysterious ladies after his last battle. Frank's already sketched the barge and ladies, so it will be just the background. I thought I'd paint the lake from the opposite side of the bank I used for the Lady of the Lake. After that, I'll have to do some scouting for the last three illustrations.'

'Only three more to go?' Harry drove on to the main road.

'Including my Morgan le Fey, which your sister will sit for. I told Frank about her and he agrees she'll be perfect. I am going to paint her walking through a wood.'

'I hope you didn't tell Frank how you feel about her.'

'Of course,' Toby countered. 'I've never kept any secrets from Frank.'

'If you know what's good for you, you'll keep your feelings to yourself when Bella's around.'

'The protective brother.'

'Too true. She's—'

'Only sixteen,' Toby finished for him. 'I need a ruined castle, so I thought I'd take the train down to Swansea tomorrow and look at what's left of Swansea Castle. Although my memory tells me that Oystermouth would make a better Camelot.'

'It's more impressive,' Harry agreed.

'You know it?'

'We often holidayed there and on the Gower when I was younger. My grandfather's sister and her husband had a farm there, and we used to rent a cottage from them at Port Eynon.' Harry smiled at the memory. 'We all used to go down, my uncles and their families as well as my grandfather and us. We had some great times.'

'Your aunt isn't there any more?'

'Her sons were all killed in the Great War, and she and her husband died shortly afterwards. My grandfather always said they had nothing left to live for.'

Toby fell uncharacteristically serious. 'I know what it feels like to lose the people you love the most. If it hadn't been for Frank I wouldn't have wanted to go on living after my parents drowned. This half-life of brief morning visits that we have now is no life really, but it's better than none.' He rested his elbow on the sill of the car and sank his chin in his hand. 'I'm dreading losing him.'

'As I am my grandfather,' Harry said softly. 'I can't wait to see your finished book,' he added in an effort to move the conversation on to a more positive level.

'Morgan le Fey, Camelot and, for the final one, my meeting between Guinevere and Lancelot. So if you could have a word with the Snow Queen . . .'

'No.' Harry's refusal was categorical.

'Meanie.'

'That's me. You want the Snow Queen to be Guinevere, ask her yourself. Who are you going to get to model Lancelot?'

'That's easy.' Toby flashed him one of his theatrical smiles. 'As he was the handsomest man in the world, it has to be a self-portrait.'

'You take the biscuit sometimes, Toby.' Harry burst out laughing as he parked the car outside the farmhouse.

'You joining me, or playing at farming today?' Toby retrieved his artist's materials from the back of the car.

'Painting this morning and farming this afternoon. And I'm not playing.' Harry opened the boot. 'I picked up a few things from Alf. I thought I'd have a go at repairing some of the doors on the outbuildings.'

'You what?' Toby stared at him in amazement.

Harry showed him a toolbox and an armful of planking he'd stashed in the boot. 'I used to help my Uncle Victor around his farm in the school holidays. He taught me a bit of carpentry.'

'You're full of surprises, Harry. You'll be telling me that you can kill pigs and milk cows next.'

'I can milk a cow but I've never volunteered to kill a pig.'

'When I've finished *Le Morte d'Arthur* I'll paint you leaning against a gate, gazing lovingly at a bull and chewing a straw. I'll enter it in the academy, and call it *Harry as Farmer Giles*.' Toby perched his boater on his head and set off down the hill, whistling.

'Oi,' Harry shouted after him. 'Why am I always the one who carries the lunch basket?'

If Toby heard him, he ignored him. Harry took out the hamper, slammed the boot shut and followed him.

Late that afternoon, Mary left the house carrying two cups of tea. She offered one to Harry. He rose to his feet, rubbed the small of his back and took it from her.

'It's good of you to fix that door, Mr Evans. We used to keep the chickens in that building until the bottom half rotted away and the foxes got in.'

'I enjoy small jobs like this one, and the door only needed

patching; the top half is still sound.' Harry sat on a mounting block next to her.

'It's a pity David is out haymaking. You could have shown him how to do the job properly. As you probably guessed,' she looked ruefully at the roughly patched doors and windows in the yard, 'he tried his hand at carpentry but because we never had any money for wood or nails, he had to use whatever he could scrounge around here.'

'He did well, considering. And I haven't bought anything,' he assured her. 'I'm only using the off-cuts from Alf Edwards's furniture-making that he had earmarked for firewood.'

'You're sure you haven't paid out any money?' She glanced at him, saw him looking intently at her and lowered her gaze.

'I'm sure.' It wasn't exactly a lie. Harry had told Alf to put everything he had taken from his workshop on to his bill at the inn. 'Mr Ross is going into Swansea tomorrow, but I will be up to take your produce to market after I have visited my grandfather in the morning. Will you come into Pontardawe with David and me?'

'No, someone has to stay at the farm.'

'You don't leave here very often.'

'Only for chapel since Mam and Dad died,' she admitted.

'If David would take care of the farm, you could come to Bristol when I take Matthew and Martha to the zoo.' He sensed her hesitating and added, 'I need someone sensible to help me take care of them.'

'I know you are trying to be kind, Mr Evans, but it wouldn't do for you to get too friendly with us.'

'Why ever not?' he asked, looking into her eyes.

'Because you will visit us only as long as it suits you while your grandfather remains in Craig y Nos. Someday you'll leave here for good, and Martha and Matthew already like you—'

'And I like them,' he interrupted.

'But you are from a different world, and when you go back there Martha and Matthew will miss you. Living here as we do, we don't meet many people, so the people we do know tend to be far more important to us than we are to them. I don't want Martha and Matthew to be disappointed.'

'I promise you, they won't be. And even after I move away I will continue to visit them.'

'You say that now while you are here, and I have no doubt that you mean it – now. But when you go back to your family and your home you will forget about us.'

'Mary, how can you think so little of people?' he asked.

'I may not have left the farm very often in the last two years, Mr Evans, but I did go to Swansea and down the valley before then. I've seen the houses people like you own, and the way you live.' She finally met his steady gaze. 'You may not mean to, but you will forget about us, Mr Evans.'

'I won't, Mary.'

'Yes, you will.'

Not wanting to get caught up in a pantomime argument, he asked, 'What do you mean, "people like me"?'

'People who dress in Sunday clothes every day of the week, go shopping with no thought as to how much they spend, have servants to clean up after them and drive cars. You're rich, we're poor, and Dad always used to say that rich and poor are different breeds. Trying to mix them would be like trying to keep fighting dogs and preening cockerels in the same pen.'

'Mary, you're a person, I'm a person. You want your brothers and sisters to be happy, which is exactly what I want mine to be. You work to that end and . . .' He recalled just how little work, other than the academic type, he had done in his life and fell silent.

'You're educated, Mr Evans. You know all there is to know about books and learning. All I know about is skivvying.'

'That's for now, Mary. You have to believe that better times are around the corner for you and your family,' he persisted optimistically.

'I saw my mam and dad working harder than anyone should have to, and all the while they waited, hoped and prayed for better times, Mr Evans. But no matter how they fought to improve themselves and this place,' she looked around the farmyard, 'things only became worse.'

'That's not to say the same will happen to you.'

'It already has, Mr Evans.'

'You still have the farm and one another.'

'For the moment.' She rose to her feet. 'The milk churns need scouring.' She held out her hand for his teacup. He gave it to her. She turned her back on him and walked into the farmhouse.

Chapter 16

'GOOD GOD, Mrs Edwards, what's going on here?' Toby asked when he and Harry walked into the inn that evening to find the place so jam-packed with strangers they could barely get inside the building. The bar was heaving, the dining-room door was open and every place was taken at the table.

'You blaspheming, Mr Ross, that's what's going on,' Mrs Edwards said sternly.

'Sorry.' Toby gave her an apologetic smile.

'The wool market's being held in Pontardawe tomorrow and the merchants have come to buy fleeces. I'm serving my best dinner: choice roast Welsh beef, peas, carrots, roast and boiled potatoes, with apple tart and clotted cream to follow. But you'll have to wait until the second sitting for yours. We would have kept you a seat at the first if I'd known what time you'd be here,' she admonished.

'That's all right, Mrs Edwards,' Toby said cheerfully. 'The second sitting will give us more drinking time.'

'After washing and changing.' Harry looked around when Toby carried his things upstairs. 'Are there any wool merchants here now, Mrs Edwards?'

'We've four staying the night.'

'Could you introduce me to one of them, please?'

'A wool trader, Mr Evans?' She eyed him suspiciously.

'Yes, please.' Harry had an idea. He wasn't sure if it was feasible, but if it was, it would result in the Ellises having some money to put into their pockets and solve just one of their many problems.

'How many fleeces did you say they had?' Mr Hawthorne, the

wizened, overdressed wool merchant to whom Mrs Edwards had introduced Harry, enquired in a high-pitched, squeaky voice.

Harry did a rough calculation. He and David had made six trips from the pen to the farm and the first time he had loaded the back of the car he had counted twenty fleeces. 'About a hundred and twenty, give or take.'

'Tell me again why they can't bring them down to market?'

Harry picked up the man's glass as well as his own, and held them up to Alf, who nodded as he served customers at the bar. 'They had to shoot their only horse the day before yesterday because it had gangrene. They are living hand to mouth and can't afford to hire another, not even for a day.'

'Times are hard. Very hard.' The man took the brandy Alf set in front of him and sipped it through his teeth. 'But I won't buy fleeces unseen.'

'I am not expecting you to. I could drive you up there now, so you can check the quality.'

'Seeing them is no good. If I wanted to buy them I'd have all the problem of transporting them to the station.'

'Supposing I paid a carter to take them,' Harry offered.

'Why would you do that?'

'Because I know the family and I'd like to help them, but they are very proud. They wouldn't allow me to pay a carter. But if you bought the fleeces, they'd have to go along with any arrangements you made to shift them. Please, Mr Hawthorne,' Harry pleaded, 'they're little more than children.'

'I won't go on any wild goose chases,' Mr Hawthorne countered. 'And I won't pay for any carting.'

'I've already told you that I will. But you have to swear you won't tell them that I'm footing the bill.'

'All right, I'll look at them.' The merchant pushed his empty glass towards Harry. 'But you'll have to arrange a carter first, in case I like what I see.'

'If you don't, I'll have to pay him a cancellation fee,' Harry protested.

'And if I do, and you can't arrange for carting, I will have wasted my time to no purpose.'

263

Hoping that Alf knew a friendly carter, Harry took Mr Hawthorne's glass. 'The barman's so busy I'll take these up myself. Brandy, wasn't it?'

'Double,' the wool merchant replied unsmilingly.

Mr Hawthorne left Harry to park the car when they returned to the inn and, having dined at Mrs Edwards's 'first sitting', he made a beeline for the bar. Harry secured the doors on the barn, washed his hands in the scullery and went into the dining room where Toby was sitting alone, toying with a bowl of apple pie and clotted cream.

'The wanderer – or is it merchant? – returns,' Toby commented.

Before Harry could think of a suitable retort, Mrs Edwards bustled past him.

'I put fresh gravy on your dinner, Mr Evans, because it dried in the oven but that's hardly surprising. It *is* nine o'clock.'

'Thank you, Mrs Edwards.' Harry sat down, reached for the salt and sprinkled it over the potatoes and peas. She was right; his dinner was dry, but he could hardly complain.

'So, you persist in getting more and more involved with the Ellises.' Toby pushed aside the dessert he'd hardly touched, and reached for his whisky chaser.

'I happened to meet a wool merchant.' Harry cut into his beef.

'Happened?' Toby enquired sceptically.

'All right, I asked Mrs Edwards to introduce me to one,' he conceded between mouthfuls of charred beef and powdery, crunchy potato that had been mashed and creamy an hour before.

'And then asked Alf to introduce you to a carter.' Toby sat back in his chair. 'Word's out, Harry. How long do you think it will be before the Ellises find out what you're up to? I've already heard one of the farmers say that Mary Ellis has done well to catch the eye of a toff who can afford to pay her bills.'

'What farmer?' Harry spoke quietly but there was an undercurrent of anger in his question.

'Does it matter? You can't stop people from thinking what they want.'

'I can, if it's damned lies!'

'Harry, even I'm beginning to wonder what attraction the Ellises hold for you. At first I accepted that you felt guilty about knocking Martha down, but now?' Toby shrugged.

'I feel sorry for them.'

'Pity is the worse of all emotions, especially if you're on the receiving end,' he pronounced with all the bitterness of someone who'd experienced bereavement early in life. 'And although we haven't known one another that long, I'd prefer to think that you're not the type who needs to dole out largesse to the under-privileged to feel good.'

'Is that what people are saying?'

'The ones who aren't assuming the worst about you and Mary Ellis, yes.'

Harry dropped his knife and fork on top of his blackened roast potatoes. 'The last thing I want to do is destroy her reputation.'

'I believe you, but not many would around here.' Toby finished his whisky and picked up his beer glass. 'So, was it worth ruining your dinner?'

'Pardon?' Harry picked up his fork again and poked at a slice of beef that had been baked as solid as shoe leather.

'Did you manage to sell the Ellises' fleeces?'

'Hopefully, if everything goes according to plan, David Ellis has sold their fleeces,' Harry corrected. 'Alf introduced me to a carter who's fully booked for market day, but he offered to pick up and take the fleeces to the railway station first thing on Thursday morning for three pounds, which I think is fair because it includes wages for himself and a helper.'

'And which you agreed to pay?'

Realizing a denial was futile, Harry said, 'I gave the wool merchant three pounds to settle his bill. Mr Hawthorne told me that he has agreed to buy the fleeces at a price that suits him and the Ellises.'

'You didn't do the negotiating?'

'I stayed in the car while Mr Hawthorne went into the farm-house. David Ellis might be young but he knows the value of his goods. I can't see him being rooked.'

'So everything has gone exactly as you wanted it to.'

'No, it hasn't,' Harry snapped, 'because it appears that the entire valley knows what I've done. And I had hoped to keep my part in it quiet.'

'You're involved with the Ellises up to your neck, Harry.' Toby shook his head disapprovingly. 'And tomorrow you're going to drive David to Pontardawe so they can deliver their dairy produce to the Colonial Stores.'

'How did—'

'Matthew told me. He spent the afternoon watching me paint the lake while you played carpenter in the farmyard.'

'I offered to take the Ellises' produce and poultry down to Pontardawe because they have no other way of getting their goods to market,' Harry said pointedly.

'And when you and your car are no longer here? How do you expect them to transport their produce then?'

'I don't know.' Harry was honest enough to accept that part of his anger was rooted in the knowledge that Toby was right. Not only in questioning his motives for helping the Ellises, but also the effect his help would have on the family long-term. 'All I know is that I am here, able and willing to help them now,' he muttered defensively.

'I wish you could see that you're not doing them any real favours, Harry.'

'You think I should ignore them, as you do?'

'I think you shouldn't start something you can't finish.'

'Perhaps I will.'

'How — by marrying Mary Ellis?' Toby parried Harry's glare. 'She is extremely attractive beneath the farmyard grime and rags. Or haven't you noticed?'

'I'm surprised you haven't asked her to model for you,' Harry said evasively.

'I've thought of it, but if she doesn't do a week's worth of work every day on that farm, those children will starve. And it's no good me offering to pay someone to take over because there's no one else within walking distance able to do her chores for her.' He hunched over the table. 'Believe it or not, I truly hope that your

266

good deeds don't end the way mine did – in tragedy. But I'm beginning to think that's a very slim hope.'

There was sincerity and sadness in Toby's assertion, and Harry had never been able to remain angry for anyone for long without good reason. 'When are you going to tell me that story?'

'Never, because it's not the sort of story a man tells his future brother-in-law, but mark my words, what you're doing can only end in disaster.'

Toby's warning came back to haunt Harry the following morning when he and David were unloading Mary's butter, cheeses, eggs and trussed poultry from his car. He could feel the eyes of all the people queuing at the counter of the Colonial Stores boring into his back as he ferried the loads to the stockroom behind the shop. Uneasy, sensing trouble waiting to happen, he was carrying in his third and most fragile load, twelve dozen eggs, when a woman's voice rose above the general chatter.

'He's paying to stay at the inn with the Edwardses and that says something, the prices they charge, but he spends most of his time up at the Ellis Estate. And there are no prizes for guessing what Mary Ellis has to give a toff like him, with a car, to do her running around for her.'

Harry stopped and glared at the woman who had set the entire queue cackling. She was middle-aged, fat and slovenly, dressed in a grease- and coal-stained work overall, rolled-down stockings and hairnet, unlike her neighbours, who'd donned hats, coats and gloves to do their shopping in the town.

'Would you care to repeat that?' He was acutely aware of the silence that had fallen over the shop.

'I'd rather hear why you're happy to do Mary Ellis's fetching and carrying. I like a dirty story.'

David tapped her on the shoulder. She turned, and he squared up to her. 'That's my sister you're talking about.'

'And if I am?' For all her show of bravado, Harry detected a tremor in her voice.

'David, I'm sure this . . .' Harry searched for a word other than 'lady' that wasn't derogatory, 'person is aware of the laws of slander.' He set the boxes of eggs he was holding on the counter and removed the notebook and pencil he kept in the top pocket of his shirt. 'If you give me your name and address, my solicitor will be in touch and we will see you in court.'

'It's Mrs Reece Jones.' The assistant closest to them, opened the account ledger and leaned across the counter. 'I can give you her address, if you like, Mr Evans.'

'Please.'

'There's no need for that.' Flustered, Mrs Reece Jones turned scarlet.

'I think there is,' Harry said, and this time he noticed the woman had difficulty meeting his eye.

'I believe that Mrs Reece Jones is very sorry for what she said and would like to apologize to you, Mr Evans, sir. And Miss Ellis and young Master Ellis. Wouldn't you, Mrs Reece Jones?' The manager's voice was cold and hard.

'I—'

'Would like to apologize for spreading malicious and untrue gossip about Miss Ellis and Mr Evans.'

The elderly woman mumbled an approximation of what the manager had said.

'You can't say what you did about my sister, then just add "sorry," and expect her and me and Mr Evans to carry on as if nothing happened.' David dumped the butter he was carrying next to the eggs.

'What do you suggest, David?' The manager walked out from behind the counter.

'If she pays for what she said, perhaps she'll think twice before she spreads any more filthy lies.'

'Who do you think she should pay, David?' the manager asked cautiously.

Given the way David had tried to blackmail him when they had first met, Harry expected David to make a ridiculous demand.

'She should put half a crown into your League of Pity collecting box.' David pointed to the blue, egg-shaped box on the counter.

The women in the queue nodded collective assent. If David had asked for money for himself there would have been an outcry, but charity was different and the League of Pity held children's parties that benefited almost every family in the valley.

'Half a crown! I can't afford half a crown!' Mrs Reece Jones exclaimed. 'I'm a widow——'

'Who should have thought before she spoke,' Harry said flatly.

'You can afford threepence a week, Mrs Reece Jones.' The manager picked up the box and held it in front of her. 'Ten weeks and you will have paid your fine. In fact, that is such a good idea of David Ellis's I think I'll make it shop policy to fine anyone who spreads unsubstantiated gossip about any innocent party in this store from now on.' He turned to Harry. 'Mr Evans, if you'll be good enough to carry those eggs into the storeroom, I'll get the boy to take them from you.'

Harry left David haggling prices with the manager and went in search of Matthew. The boy had pleaded to be allowed to look around the town as soon as they'd arrived, and Harry found him staring wistfully into the window of a sweet shop.

'Martha and I had a sugar mouse each for Christmas. Mine was white and hers was pink, but I've never seen brown or cream ones.' He pointed at the row arranged on a shelf at the back of the window.

'Those are made of chocolate, Matthew. You can get brown and white – or rather cream-coloured chocolate.' It would have been easy for Harry to go inside and buy two bagfuls of sugar and chocolate mice. He was tempted to do that just to see the smile on Matthew's face when he presented them to him. But Toby's words came back to haunt him, as they had done when Mrs Reece Jones had attacked Mary Ellis's reputation in the Colonial Stores. *I think you shouldn't start something you can't finish.*

Toby was right. If he bought the Ellis children a bucketful of sweets and they developed a sweet tooth, who would buy sugar mice for them when he was no longer in the valley? He offered Matthew his hand but the boy pretended not to see it and stuck his fists in his pocket.

'Davy says men don't hold hands, it's sissy.'

'Sorry. David was almost finished when I left the Colonial Stores.

269

Shall we go and see what he wants to do next? And on the way we can call into the stationers so I can buy you and Martha some paper and a new pencil each so you can practise your writing.'

'That would be good, Mr Evans.' Matthew's eyes shone with excitement and Harry trusted that Mary and David wouldn't see pencils as charity. They stopped outside the shop and looked in the window at the goods on display. Notebooks, stacks of writing paper, envelopes, blotting paper, bottles of coloured inks and fans of pencils and pen nibs of various sizes were arranged on narrow shelves alongside expensive boxed fountain pens.

'Can I have a red pencil, please, Mr Evans?'

'You can. What colour do you think Martha will like?'

'Her favourite colour is yellow. We both practised writing our names after you left last night. You will teach us some more today, won't you?'

David's reflection loomed in the glass behind them. 'If he does it will be after you've done your jobs, Matthew, and helped me with the milking.'

'I need to buy some writing paper, and I thought I'd get Martha and Matthew pencils as a reward for the hard work they've put in.'

David nodded a silent agreement but there was a surly look in his eye. He followed Harry and Matthew into the shop and watched Harry purchase writing paper, envelopes, ink, the pencils and two cheap notebooks.

'The price you paid for that lot would keep the chickens in feed for a week,' David grumbled when they left.

Harry decided it would be politic to ignore his comment. 'Is there anything else that you have to do in town, David?'

'No. I've been paid for our produce and finished buying our goods. I've already stacked them in your car.'

'Then you're ready to go back to the farm?' Harry thrust the change the assistant had given him into his pocket.

'I need to check and fix all the sheep pens on the hills. Winter comes early on the mountains. If you drop Matthew and me off at the top of the road close to the first one we'll get started. But that means that you and Mary will have to unload the goods and feed I bought.'

'That's not a problem.' Harry didn't offer to help David mend the sheep pens; he didn't know the first thing about dry-stone walling.

He recalled the evil-minded gossip in the shop. From the brash, confident way she'd spoken about him and Mary Ellis in his presence, he assumed she wasn't the first to spread unfounded rumours about his visits to the Ellises and, despite the manager's efforts, he wasn't optimistic enough to believe she'd be the last.

He made a resolution to leave the family to their own devices but only after he'd completed the repairs to the doors and windows on the farmhouse and outbuildings. As David had said, winter was coming and the wood he was replacing wouldn't stand another season of frost, snow and rain. It was essential the buildings be made watertight. And there simply wasn't anyone other than him available to do it.

The next two days passed swiftly and busily for Harry. He went up to the farm after visiting his grandfather, who continued to deteriorate. He worked on his new watercolour until midday, and repaired the doors and windows in the farmyard in the afternoon. He only saw Mary, who was busy in the dairy, and David, who spent all his time out on the hills in the sheep pens, briefly except when he ate tea with them at the end of the day.

Diana had been busy all week studying in preparation for her return to college, but he persuaded her to allow him to take her to Swansea on Friday evening, and although he gave Matthew and Martha lessons on Wednesday and Thursday evenings, he finished working in the farmyard at four o'clock on Friday afternoon in good time to return to the inn and change.

'It's strange to have tea without Mr Evans,' Matthew commented absently, watching Mary pour the tea as he bit into his bread, butter and blackberry jam.

'He's not one of the family,' David growled. 'Although you wouldn't think it from the way he's been living here the past couple of weeks.'

'He's been kind enough to do jobs for us that should have been done months ago,' Mary said pointedly.

'He's going out tonight, to Swansea, with Miss Adams.' Martha dropped a sugar lump into her tea cup.

'Out with Miss Adams?' Mary whispered, stunned by the revelation and her reaction to it. Although when she thought about Mr Evans and Miss Adams, it was obvious they belonged together. Both educated, both rich, both blonde. She beautiful, he good-looking. People in chapel would refer to them as a handsome, well-suited couple.

'I overheard Mr Evans and Mr Ross talking about it when they were taking their painting stuff out of Mr Evans's car,' Martha continued, oblivious to Mary's shock. 'Mr Evans said he'd booked a table for them in the Mermaid Hotel in Swansea and afterwards he's taking her dancing, to the Patti Pavilion. It must be wonderful to go to a dance with a real orchestra playing real music and see people in their best dancing frocks. I bet the girls even curl their hair and wear scent and jewellery like the young Mrs Williams,' she murmured dreamily.

'I think dancing's soppy,' Matthew said, although the only dancers he'd ever seen were the clog dancers who entertained shoppers at the Pontardawe Christmas market.

Mary's heart thundered against her ribcage. She remembered all the times she had caught Harry looking at her and she, unable to bear the intensity of his blue-eyed gaze, had looked away.

An image of Diana Adams as she had been the last time she'd visited Martha sprang to mind: ducking as she walked beneath the low lintel on the kitchen door; her fair hair gleaming like spun straw in the small-windowed gloom of the farmhouse, her skirt and blouse glossy with the lustre of freshly laundered, top-quality linen. It had been years since anyone in her family had been able to buy expensive clothes, but that hadn't stopped her mother from taking her into Ben Evans's department store in Swansea and showing her the difference between good and cheap clothes. And everything she'd ever seen Diana Adams wearing had been high-priced.

Even Miss Adams's voice was attractive, musical and so obviously educated. Her hands were long, slim, elegant and clean because she'd never had to scrub out a pigsty or cowshed in her life. Miss Adams was everything she could never aspire to be. If ever she needed to be reminded that she was an ignorant, ugly, illiterate farm girl, all she had to do was think of her. Even her Sunday clothes were rags in comparison. Diana Adams was going to be a doctor. All she was good for was exactly what she had said to Harry Evans – skivvying.

No cultured, wealthy man like Harry Evans, who could teach Martha and Matthew to read and write with a patience she had never thought any man capable of possessing, would ever see someone like her as anything other than a servant and a low one at that.

She recalled the feel of his body close to hers when he had helped her up the hill after she had run into the water and almost drowned, his concern and his kindness after his initial anger and shock had worn off. Then she remembered why she had run into the reservoir.

She was used and damaged, the agent's whore – unfit to be a wife to any man.

'Mary? Mary!' David repeated impatiently.

She stared at her brother in bewilderment.

'I was asking if you wanted Matthew and me to move the chicken coops into the shed now that Harry's repaired the door. It would be handy to have the barn back for feed storage. We haven't been able to use it for that since we put the chickens in there because they peck through the sacks.'

'Yes . . .' she stammered. 'I'll give you a hand.'

'No hurry, we'll do it tomorrow morning.' He gave her a hard look before nodding to Matthew. 'Time to do the milking.'

Harry stood in the porch of the Adamses' house and rang the bell. It pealed loudly, echoing through the hall, and he heard the clack of high-heeled slippers walking over a wooden floor.

Diana called, 'It's for me, Sarah.' She opened the front door.

Harry had taken care in dressing. He had arranged for his dinner suit and dress shirt to be sent from Pontypridd and entrusted them to Enfys to be pressed – to his amazement they had been returned in pristine condition. His cologne was the horrendously expensive one he had treated himself to in Harrods the last time he had visited London, and Alf had buffed his dress shoes to a crystal shine.

'A small thank you for everything you have done for my grandfather, and,' conscious of the maid and her parents in the house, Harry lowered his voice to a whisper, 'me.'

She took the boxed flower from him. 'An orchid! How wonderful and extravagant. Did you have to send to Swansea for it?'

'Yes.'

'Then it should be very happy to return there. Would you like to say good evening to my parents?'

Given Dr Adams's usual brusqueness, Harry would have preferred not to, but he stepped over the doorstep and followed Diana into the drawing room he remembered so well, and pretended never to have set eyes on before.

'Good evening, Mrs Adams.' Harry bowed slightly to Diana's mother, an older, thinner and more wrinkled version of her daughter.

'Good evening, Mr Evans.' She glanced up momentarily from the newspaper she was reading, but remained seated in her armchair.

'Good evening, Doctor Adams.'

'Mr Evans.' The doctor rose and, to Harry's surprise, offered him his hand. 'I trust you and Diana will have a good time this evening.' He shook Harry's hand firmly. 'There is no risk of contracting infection in this house, Mr Evans. Diana and I are meticulous about washing and changing our clothes after we leave the sanatorium.'

'Yes, sir. As for the good time, I have booked a table for half past seven at the hotel.'

'Then you had better be on your way. I trust that you will drive carefully, Mr Evans.'

'I always endeavour to, Doctor Adams.'

'Martha Ellis might say different.'

'Father, you know that accident wasn't Harry's fault. There was a thick mist.' Diana handed Harry her white evening coat, which was trimmed with ostrich feathers. He held it out and helped her

274

on with it, watching while she pinned the orchid to her left shoulder. 'Expect me when you see me.' She kissed her mother's, then her father's cheek.

Harry held the door open and they left the house. 'No directives about what time you have to be home?'

'I'm over twenty-one. And my parents trust me. Don't yours?'

'I'm a boy so that doesn't count. Besides, I've lived in college for the last three years.'

'As have I.' She waited until he opened the passenger door of the car for her. 'What about your sister?'

'You only met the eldest. I have five.'

'And your father is stricter with them than you?'

'Much.' He picked up the feather-trimmed hem of her coat and draped it around her slim, silk-stockinged legs. 'Careful, you don't want to catch that in the door.'

'No, I don't, thank you. And I pity your sister. I would hate to be sixteen again. If you'd called to take me out when I'd been that age, my father would have demanded that you brought me home by eight o'clock.'

'You're joking.'

'I am not.'

He started the car, and she pulled her cloche hat over her bob to keep it in place.

'I could put up the hood,' he offered.

'No, don't, I like the feel of the wind in my face.'

'It seems it's not only your patients who are used to fresh air.' He drove out on to the main road.

Their conversation on the journey down to Swansea was intermittent, and he realized it was the longest they had been together without taking off their clothes. Their lovemaking had been so sensational it came as a shock to recognize that outside of passion they had little in common. They both made fairly banal observation on the beauty of the upper Swansea Valley compared to the industry-ravaged lower. But when Diana touched on the miners' determination to continue the General Strike single-handedly, Harry changed the subject.

He respected and loved Lloyd, and knew better than to embark on such a discussion with a privileged, middle-class woman like Diana Adams when his stepfather saw the strike as an essential weapon in the miners' interminable fight for a fair deal from the colliery owners. Instead, he mentioned current topics he'd read about in the newspapers in the hope they'd interest her, like his admiration for Gertrude Ederle, the American woman who had just swum the channel. They went on to talk about sport in general, and tennis and Wimbledon in particular. With the result that when he drew up outside the hotel he knew that Diana played a fair game of tennis but not much else.

He had enjoyed her company, made love to her, and yet there was a gulf between them that was of her making. Given her determination to follow her chosen career, he sensed she would keep that distance between her and every man – however much she liked him. Just in case 'like' spilled over into a love that would sway her from her resolve to follow in her father's footsteps.

For some reason he couldn't quantify he began to compare Diana to Mary Ellis. Diana was poised, socially adept, confident and far easier to talk to than Mary, who restricted her answers to monosyllables whenever she could. Yet, he couldn't help feeling that if it came to a choice between the two women, Mary would make a far better and more loyal girlfriend – and wife. He wondered if the preference was down to Diana's open and free attitude towards sex. But when he thought of the number of affairs he'd had during his college years, he felt hypocritical in the extreme.

But Mary's dark eyes had an innocence . . .

'You all right, Harry? The drive didn't tire you?' Diana asked when the waiter unrolled her napkin and laid it with a flourish over her lap.

'No, why should the drive tire me?'

'It shouldn't, if it was only the drive, although I happen to know that you've been working like a common labourer up at the Ellis Estate every afternoon for the last week.'

He took the menu from the waiter. 'Martha Ellis has been talking.'

'You have quite an admirer there. And an adoring student. She wrote her name out for me when I picked up the eggs from the farm this morning.' She glanced at the menu. 'I'll have the iced grapefruit salad, followed by the lobster with oyster sauce and tomato salad, and for dessert – fresh strawberries, no cream.'

Harry was amazed. Not only had Diana made up her mind in seconds, but unlike most of his other girlfriends, she'd had no compunction about ordering the most expensive dishes on the menu.

'Make that for two, and we'll have a bottle of champagne, please.' He closed the menu he hadn't even glanced at and returned it to the waiter.

'Before you bring the champagne, we'll have cocktails. Manhattans?' Diana raised an enquiring eyebrow at Harry.

Recalling that he still had to drive over twenty miles back that night and that his family would be arriving early in the morning, he said, 'Just one Manhattan, please, waiter.'

'Spoilsport,' Diana muttered when the man left.

'I have to be up early tomorrow.'

'And I have to be up and working in the sanatorium by eight.' She toyed with her fork. 'I confess, I didn't realize my father was a slave-driver when I offered to help him after his assistant left.'

'Why *did* he leave so suddenly?' Harry sat back so the waiter could set their drinks on the table.

'Can't you guess?'

'He found Craig y Nos too isolated?'

She sipped her drink. 'Mmm, just the right amount of vermouth to whisky. No. He contracted tuberculosis.'

'Then he's a patient?'

'His family sent him to Switzerland on the first available boat-train. If he had been working anywhere else, he would have probably disregarded the early symptoms. But even if he makes a recovery he won't be returning to Craig y Nos. Re-infection occurs in a high percentage of tuberculosis patients. The last time my father heard from him he was considering a career in medical research. That way he can at least work regular hours and organize regular meals. And who knows?' She smiled. 'Given his personal interest in the disease he may be the one to find the cure we're all looking for.'

'So, that's why you stepped in.'

'My father advertised but most of the best people are going to Switzerland to work in the clinics there. They are experimenting with innovative treatments that seem to offer the best chance of survival – provided the patient is up to travelling that distance. And before you ask—'

'I know my grandfather isn't. He barely survived the journey from the Rhondda to the Swansea Valley. But my family are grateful to you. Despite the distance from the Rhondda you have made him far more comfortable in Craig y Nos than he would have been in any of the Rhondda or Pontypridd hospitals.' The waiter arrived with their iced grapefruit salads.

She picked up her spoon. 'These look delicious. Harry, you can have no idea how much I have been looking forward to this evening.'

'You do like your work, don't you? You're not just doing it because of what happened to your brothers and sister?'

'I admit they were the reason I wanted to study medicine, but I also love my job,' she assured him. 'Don't misunderstand me, I'm very fortunate to be able to work with my father, and not just because he is my father. I'm learning more than I ever would have in a general hospital in London, and it is rewarding. Nothing compares to seeing a patient who was carried into Craig y Nos sitting up, or walking. But sometimes I feel as though I'm serving a sentence on one of those isolated French penal colonies. Craig y Nos is beautiful, but for all the life I see there, I may as well be incarcerated on Mars.'

'I wouldn't describe the valley people as Martians,' he laughed.

'You're lucky; you have Toby Ross to talk to.'

'And you have your parents, the nurses and some highly intelligent patients,' he countered.

'When they're well enough to talk. Frank Ross and your grandfather are two of the most articulate and interesting, and that's not just an empty compliment.'

'And you'll come back to Craig y Nos after you qualify?' He signalled to the waiter to pour their champagne.

'Not immediately.'

'You'll go to Switzerland?'

'Until my father is ready to hand the reins over to someone else, probably.'

'So you can learn about the innovative treatments they offer?' Harry waited until she lifted her glass and touched it with his.

'And because my lover is opening a clinic there.'

'Your . . .'

'Married lover,' she corrected.

'You said you're married to your job.'

'I am. The last thing I need is a husband. And with George it's all fun and no domesticity, which suits us both. It's not as bad as it sounds. His wife is a hopeless invalid. She's been in a mental institution for years. This way he can remain faithful to her and we can work side by side with no complications.'

'I thought . . . I mean . . .'

'Harry, let's not be coy. Surely you weren't naïve enough to think you were my first lover? Given your expertise, I certainly didn't think I was yours.' She lifted her glass again. 'To you, Harry. The sweetest, kindest boy I know. I hope you soon find a besotted and devoted wife who deserves you.'

Diana proved to be an expert dancer. When she did the Charleston every other person on the floor stopped and formed a circle around her. Harry saw other men eyeing him enviously, and wondered how they would react if they knew that Diana had more than one lover. He smiled wryly. Judging by the looks they were sending her way, they'd probably join the queue.

All he felt when the band played the National Anthem at midnight was relief that the evening was over. Although Diana looked as though she could have danced and downed Manhattans all night, he was tired. A week of working in the fresh air coupled with the emotional strain of his grandfather's illness had taken its toll. He took Diana's cloakroom ticket from her bag, picked up her coat and was waiting to offer her his arm when she was finally ushered from the building with a dozen other stragglers.

'You're an angel.' She stood with her back to him so he could help her on with her coat. 'Shall we walk along the beach?'

'It's after midnight.'

'The moon is waning, the stars are out, the tide's in and the sea looks glorious. Come on.' She slipped her arm out of his, ran down the road and over the slip bridge. Below them the last train from Mumbles to Swansea wound its way along the track next to the coast road. She turned back and smiled at him. 'The perfect end to a perfect evening and a perfect affair.' She kissed him, a surprisingly chaste kiss after all the lovemaking. 'Thank you, Harry, I'm ready to go home and back to London now.'

The only sensation he registered was relief. Outwardly Diana Adams was a woman any man would be proud to marry. But whatever else she was, she wasn't his Isabella.

And that was the moment he realized Mary Ellis was.

Chapter 17

HARRY LEANED his elbow on the side of his car, slid forward on his driving seat and peered through the windscreen. The now familiar countryside of the upper Swansea Valley had been transformed by the darkness. What little he could see of it in the glare from his headlamps was unrecognizable. Shadows took on strange, terrifying shapes, and leapt out unexpectedly when he negotiated blind bends, and the car's lights froze hares, rabbits, foxes and stoats in positions more suited to a taxidermist's studio than nature, contributing to the peculiarly nightmarish atmosphere.

Diana moved beside him. He glanced across at her but her eyes remained closed. She pulled her coat over herself and settled back in her seat. He didn't blame her. If he could have, he would have slept himself. He rubbed his eyes, looked ahead and saw a house he knew. They were entering Abercrave. He had only travelled eighteen miles but it had seemed more like eighty.

Abandoned to his thoughts, he debated his future more seriously than he had done since he'd left Oxford. And, as part of his future – the newest and most vital part – he considered Mary Ellis. He recalled their first meeting. He hadn't realized at the time that it had been worth the stinging discomfort of the iodine to make her acquaintance. She was unlike any other girl he had ever known – totally and completely unique. There were so many words he could use to describe her – fierce, savage, wild, untamed – and all would be accurate.

By the standards of Diana Adams and his sisters she was unkempt, but he preferred to think of her as untouched by artifice or the vagaries of fashion. Raw and untutored, she hadn't a modicum of the refinement or elegance a woman needed to succeed in modern society. But she did have a bewitching, beguiling inno-cence. Something Toby had said only a few nights before came to mind: *Harry, even I'm beginning to wonder what attraction the Ellises hold for you. At first I accepted that you felt guilty about knocking Martha down, but now?*

He'd succeeded in fooling Toby, and even himself, into believ-ing that his visits to the Ellises had been prompted by a charitable desire to help the family. But now he realized that he had only wanted to spend time with Mary Ellis. Beneath the veneer of suspicion and hostility, which he blamed on the tragic and early death of her parents, she was caring and sweet-natured, especially towards her brothers and sister. And she was beautiful – seduc-tively so – with her exotic dark features.

No woman had ever needed a man to take care of her more than Mary Ellis, and he was grateful that he had the money to do just that. He would cosset, educate, nurture, love and spoil her. And his reward would be to watch her blossom after he'd removed her from her life of drudgery.

He began to make plans for the entire Ellis family. First, he'd take them from the blighted, run-down farm, move them to Pontypridd and rent a decent property for them until his house was ready. He would live at home until his and Mary's wedding could be arranged. He'd take them around the Gwilym James department stores and let them pick out anything they wanted, clothes, toys, things for the house . . .

He'd ask Mari to help him find housemaids, a cook and a gardener, so Mary would never have to do housework again. David might be a problem. He could hardly send him to school. An illiterate boy his age would be teased unmercifully, but he'd employ a tutor who could teach him alongside Martha and Matthew. And once the boy reached an acceptable standard David himself could decide what profession or trade he wanted to follow.

He'd enrol the younger two in private schools. His sisters attended the grammar school in Pontypridd. Martha would never pass the entrance examination but there was a convent school in Cardiff. She could board there in the week and come home at weekends, and he would find an equally good school in the city for Matthew.

He would employ a nursemaid to care for Luke, and introduce Mary to the pleasures of urban living – the theatre, picture houses, hotels, restaurants and dance halls. They would go for walks in the new park, and he would teach all of them to roller-skate, ride bicycles and – after the near-tragedy of the reservoir – swim. He would drive them to the beaches he had visited as a child.

His mother and sisters would help Mary to acquire the necessary social graces. They would be pleased and his father would be delighted at the prospect of him finally settling down. *Settling down*. He shuddered.

He couldn't wait to marry Mary and move into his own house, but his plans for domestic happiness didn't solve all his problems. In fact, they created more. He could hardly take the entire Ellis family to Paris and expect them to lead a student's life there. But the last thing he wanted to do was work nine to five, dressing formally every morning in a suit, stiff-collared shirt and tie. But if he returned to live in Pontypridd his trustees would put pressure on him to work in one of his own companies.

The castle wall towered, blacker than the shadows on his right. He turned into the Adamses' drive and turned off the ignition. Diana remained still, her head resting sideways on the edge of the seat. He shook her gently and, conscious of her parents sleeping in the house, whispered her name. She opened her eyes and looked around.

'To quote Madame Patti's most famous song, "Home Sweet Home".'

'I'm sorry, I didn't mean to fall asleep. It must have been that last Manhattan.'

'Or the hours you worked today before we went out.'

She shivered and huddled into her coat. 'What's the time?'

He struck his lighter and held it over the face of his wristwatch. 'A quarter past one.'

'Another four and three-quarter hours before I have to get up.'

'Poor you.'

'It was a lovely evening, Harry, thank you.'

283

He walked around the car and opened the door for her. 'I enjoyed it too. I'll see you again?'

'You'll see Miss Adams again, not the Diana you took out tonight.' She kissed his cheek. 'It's been fun knowing you, Harry.'

'Likewise. Good luck in London.'

'Thank you.'

He climbed back into his car and waved to her before driving out through the gates. Feeling as though he had made the most momentous decision of his life, and needing to think about his future, he drove up to the farm. He parked by the entrance to the reservoir so the sound of his car wouldn't disturb the family and walked towards the lonely farmhouse.

The scene looked picture-postcard peaceful beneath the waning moon, and he started to plan out another picture for when he had finished his second watercolour of the reservoir. Perhaps he could try one in oils? If he took the road as a vantage point, and looked through the arched entrance into the farmyard in daylight, he could portray a glimpse of farm life . . .

Something moved in the archway of the farmhouse. He was surprised to see a pony and trap standing there. The rig looked new even in the muted shadows. He was crossing the road to take a closer look at it when a piercing cry shattered the quiet. It echoed towards him a second time, faint but unmistakable, more human than animal. The sound of someone in pain.

Running stealthily, he charged past the trap into the farmyard, setting the dogs barking. Whistling the way David had taught him to silence them, he waited for them to settle. The stable door was ajar, which he found odd. He hadn't seen any of the Ellises go near it since Dolly's death. He stole towards it and peered inside.

The blackness was devoid of shadow and he recalled there were no windows in the old stone building. He detected movement and scuffling in the stall nearest the door. Then the cry came again, an anguished, muffled scream that culminated in a sob.

He pushed the door wide. Dim grey light flooded in from the yard. A silhouette moved upwards from the floor revealing a second figure beneath it. A fist flew towards him and connected with his jaw. He reeled back, falling awkwardly on the cobbled yard, cracking his elbow and scraping his hand. A crippling electric shock of pain shot down his arm. He watched his assailant waddle out of the stables and realized his movements were hampered by his trousers pulled down around his ankles. The shadowy figure heaved them to his waist and the few seconds he took to fasten his braces gave Harry time to collect his senses.

He saw the second blow coming and rolled to avoid it. Winded, fighting the pain in his arm, he heaved for breath. A flash of white appeared in the stable doorway. He looked up and saw Mary clinging to the frame. It was a glance that cost him pain. A boot connected with his ribs. He groaned and doubled up.

A rasping voice grated, 'Mary, who the hell is this?'

'Please, sir, don't hurt him—'

'I'll kill the bastard!'

Harry grabbed the boot before it connected with his body a second time and wrenched it upwards. His attacker thudded on to the cobbles beside him. Harry rose to his knees and listened. He could hear his assailant's breathing, the creak of the pony moving in harness in the archway and a fox calling to its mate on the hills behind the house.

He tried to stand but it felt as though red-hot knives were piercing his lungs. The slightest movement was torture but he managed to crawl towards the man who had attacked him. He touched his head. The man sighed and turned. He ran his hands over him. Apart from a lump on his temple he seemed to be in one piece, if out cold. Glad he hadn't killed him – whoever he was – he looked to where he had last seen Mary. She was crouched in the doorway of the stable, her head buried in the skirt of her nightgown.

He crept towards her on his hands and knees. 'Mary?'

She shrank back.

'Mary?'

She didn't move, or look up, but mumbled, 'Please, go away.'

'Not until I'm sure that you're all right.'

She finally lifted her tear-stained face, but she couldn't look at him. 'You saw what he was doing to me. I'll never be all right, never again.'

It was only then that he realized she'd been raped.

'Mr Pritchard was the reason my father hung himself.' Mary sat with her legs curled beneath the hem of her nightgown on the floor outside the stable stalls. Harry had tried to comfort her but every time he had drawn close, she had retreated, until she succeeded in boxing herself into a corner between the wall and the wooden partition. So he remained six feet away from her, his legs sprawled on the floor, his back supported by a post.

'Your father hung himself because of the agent?' he murmured in bewilderment.

It had taken Mary years to find someone she could confide in, and now she had, it was as though the floodgate that had dammed all her pent-up misery and shame had finally burst. 'Every woman who lives on the farms Bob Pritchard collects rent from knows what he's like. They're all afraid of him and try to keep what he does to them a secret from their men, but they talk to one another.'

'Then you're not the only one he has raped?'

'The agent's forced dozens of women to sleep with him,' she revealed bitterly. 'My mother knew what was going to happen to her the day my father told her he couldn't pay the rent. She'd spoken to Mrs Jones – Mr and Mrs Jones used to work for us when my father could pay them. They lived in the house down the road before they were evicted. Mrs Jones told my mother that as soon as they were in arrears, the agent came round, offering to stop the landlord from sending in the bailiffs, but only if she gave him what he wanted "in kind".'

'She didn't tell her husband or go to the police?'

'She didn't dare because she knew no one would believe her, except perhaps her husband. And she was afraid that Mr Pritchard would hurt him. As you've found out, Mr Pritchard's strong, but it's not just him. The bailiffs do whatever he tells them to because he pays them. He even boasted to Mrs Jones about the other wives who gave him their rent "in kind". We used to see some of them in Pontardawe and Swansea on market day. They were all ashamed of what he was doing to them. They used to whisper to one another about it, but they couldn't stop him from using them.'

Harry didn't doubt for one minute that Mary was telling the truth. He was appalled by the thought that a man could misuse his position of trust as a rent collector to commit crimes against dozens of women – and to carry on doing so for years – when so many people knew about it. 'I'm beginning to wish I hurt him more than I did,' he said feelingly.

'I knew what he was doing to my mother from the very beginning because I was there when he told her what she had to do if she didn't want us to get thrown out of the house. And the whole time he talked to her, he looked at me. I was twelve years old. My mother told him she'd do whatever he asked, provided he left me alone and allowed us to stay here. From then on, he used to come here once or twice a month and always when he knew that my father would be in Pontardawe or working in one of the far fields. I looked after David, Martha and Matthew while he took my mother into the stable. Then, one day, my father returned unexpectedly. He'd gone down to buy our goods in Pontardawe but Dolly threw a shoe. He went into the stable and saw . . . saw . . . he saw . . .'

'The agent raping your mother,' Harry finished for her, unable to bear the pain in her voice.

'When I saw my father and Mr Pritchard fighting in the yard I shut Martha and the boys in the front of the house so they wouldn't see what was going on. My father accused the agent of raping my mother and threatened to go to the police. Mr Pritchard laughed in his face and said he'd never had to force himself on a woman in his life because they all threw themselves at him. That he had trouble choosing which one to have because every tenant's wife and daughter wanted him.' She dropped her voice until it was almost inaudible. 'He said my mother had begged him to make love to her. And it was true. He always made her ask him to take her into the stable, and he would never go until she said please.'

'That's horrible. The man's a sadist. Can't you see, Mary? The agent didn't need to beat your mother to get her to ask him to take her into the stable, because she was afraid that if she didn't, he'd assault you and evict your family. If that doesn't amount to rape, I don't know what does.'

'There was a woman once, on one of the farms. She'd only been married a few weeks. She complained to the police about Mr Pritchard. He said she'd led him on and when he'd done what she wanted him to she'd asked him for money. And the only reason she'd complained to the law was he'd refused to pay her. Wherever she went afterwards, people used to point at her and call her vile names. No one took her side. They were too afraid that they'd be treated the same way if they did. The minister wouldn't even allow her over the doorstep of the chapel. In the end her husband threw her out. She had nowhere to go except the workhouse. And they sent her off to London to become a maid in a hospital.'

'That is an appalling story. And the fact that the police didn't believe her doesn't make Robert Pritchard innocent. He raped you, your mother and all those other women,' Harry insisted.

'But the police wouldn't see it that way. Just like when that girl complained, they'd believe the agent. He'd tell them that he hadn't forced himself on any of us and we'd made up stories to blacken his name to try to stop the landlord from evicting us because we couldn't afford to pay the rent. And then me, my mother and all the others – the police would say we were prostitutes.'

'You're victims, Mary.'

'I wish I could think the way you do,' she whispered dully.

'Did your father hang himself the day he fought the agent?' Harry hated himself for asking, but he had to know.

'No, a month later. It was horrible. He just stopped talking.'

'To your mother?'

'To my mother, me, Davy – everyone. It was as if he wanted to be dead just to get away from my mother because of what the agent had done to her.' She shuddered at the memory.

'I doubt he wanted to get away from your mother or you, Mary. I imagine that any man would find it impossible to live with the knowledge that he couldn't protect his own wife against a rapist.' Harry felt in his pocket for his cigarettes.

'After my father – after we buried him, my mother found out that she was having Luke. She didn't know if he was my father's baby or the agent's and when she grew big, Mr Pritchard came here. David had taken Martha and Matthew into Pontardawe to buy our goods. I think the agent must have seen them leave the farm.

And that day he dragged me into the barn instead of my mother, he bolted the door on the inside and . . .' She screwed her eyes shut. 'My mother hammered on the door and cried until he opened it. But by then it was too late.'

'You do know that you could have a child?'

'He told me he's too careful to father a bastard on an unmarried girl. The married women are different.' She finally looked at him. 'My mother was having Luke, we had the little ones to think of, I didn't want to . . . I didn't . . . I didn't . . . but he would have thrown us out of the house and we had nowhere else to go . . . and after my mother died, he still threatened to evict us. If he does we'll have to go to the workhouse and then they'll separate us and I wouldn't be able to take care of Davy or the little ones . . .' Her voice rose hysterically.

Harry stole closer to her and reached for her hand. He took it into his, and to his relief she didn't try to pull it away. 'That day you ran into the reservoir. You were running away from the agent?'

'Not him, he'd already left, but what he'd done to me,' she answered in a small voice.

Harry wished she would let him put his arms around her but he sensed that she would find it hard to bear any man to touch more than her hand, not yet, and perhaps not ever again. 'Does David know what the agent did to your mother – and is doing to you?'

'No!' she exclaimed fearfully. 'You won't tell him, will you?'

'No, I won't. But you have to promise me that you won't allow him to rape you ever again.'

'But that would mean we'd have to go into the workhouse.'

'No, it won't, Mary. I'll help you,' he promised recklessly.

'How can you?'

The grey light that drifted in through the gap at the top of the door had lightened to silver while they'd been talking, and Harry could see her face quite clearly. Her dark eyes looked enormous in her pale, thin face, and the thought occurred to him that he had never seen anyone look so desolate or tortured. His mind groped to assimilate the full horror of her suffering – and what she would continue to endure if he didn't help her.

289

But nothing could alter the fact that, far from being innocent, the girl he had been about to propose to had been systematically raped for years by a cruel and callous rent collector.

It was so unjust, so unfair. All the plans he'd made for his own and the Ellises' future came crashing down. He felt as though he'd been allowed to see everything he'd ever wanted, only to have it snatched away at the last moment. He was only sorry that he hadn't killed the man when he'd had the chance.

As if she sensed what he was thinking, Mary shrank back within her nightgown making herself even smaller. 'I told you not to get involved with us, Harry. You can't help us.'

'Yes, I can,' he snapped, disillusionment turning to anger. 'I've never thought much about money, but in this case it can help. I'll pay off your rent arrears.'

'They're over a hundred pounds.'

'I can afford it.'

'You're angry with me, because of what I let Mr Pritchard do to me. You'll never think of me the same way you did before. I am a—'

'Don't say that word,' he ordered her. 'And I'm not angry with you. But I am bloody furious with Robert Pritchard and whoever owns this estate for giving a man like him the authority to exploit helpless women. I'm sorry, I shouldn't have sworn, but when I think about what you and your father and mother have suffered . . .' Harry realized he was frightening her. He took a few moments to light a cigarette and calm himself.

'Even if you paid off all our debts, it wouldn't make any difference. We'd only end up owing you money instead of the landlord.'

'There'd be a great deal of difference. I won't rape you if you can't afford to pay me.'

'I think I've known for some time that we can't afford to carry on living here, not with fewer livestock every season and no help to run the place.' She wrapped her arms around her knees and sank her head down on to them. 'It's hopeless but I wouldn't accept it. David knew. He tried to tell me that there was no point in trying to carry on, but I wouldn't admit that he was right.'

290

'You're worn-out and no one thinks straight when they're tired.' Harry rose stiffly to his feet. His lungs were on fire and the bruises on his arm and back were aching unbearably. 'Stay here. I'm going to see what Mr Pritchard has to say for himself.'

'No . . .'

'I'll be careful.' He pushed open the wooden door, walked outside and looked around the yard. The agent wasn't there and the trap had disappeared. He ran out on to the road. There was no sign of it in either direction.

'He's gone?' Mary stood shivering in the doorway of the stable when he returned to the yard.

'Yes. He must have left while we were talking.'

'Dawn's broken.' She looked up at the sky. 'Father used to say, "A new day a new beginning". But it won't ever be for me again, will it?'

'You're a pretty young girl with her whole life ahead of her.' Harry had said it automatically, meaning to be kind but when he looked at her, he was overwhelmed by the strength of his own love for her. 'I'm tired, Mary, and I'm going to be busy today. My family are coming down from Pontypridd to see my grandfather, but they'll be going back late this afternoon. After they've gone I'll drive up here. We'll talk.'

'There's no point—'

'I say there is,' he interrupted her. 'You will talk to me?'

'If you want me to,' she answered carelessly.

'And you won't do anything silly before then?' he pressed.

'Like kill myself?'

'Like kill yourself,' he echoed.

'I have my brothers and sister to think about.'

'Then carry on thinking about them until I come back, Mary. Together we'll solve your problems. I promise.' He bent towards her, intending to kiss her cheek the way he did his sisters, but she backed away and looked up at him.

'You know all there is to know about me and you're not disgusted?' She stared at him incredulously.

'You're still you, Mary. The same person you were before the agent made you do things you didn't want to.'

291

Tears started into her eyes. He opened his arms and she fell into them. They stood locked together in the yard for as long as it took for the emotion she'd contained for so long to surface.

He led her gently back to the stable, sank to his knees, lifted her on to his lap and rocked her while she cried out all the hurt, anger and bitterness. And the whole time he held her, he fervently hoped that her tears were the kind that healed.

Harry woke with a start. It took him a few moments to recall the events that had led him to the farm and into the stable. He looked around. There was no sign of Mary but the sun had risen and it was light enough to read his wristwatch. The hands pointed to seven o'clock. Something sharp was digging into his leg. He felt in the straw beneath him and retrieved a silver pocket watch. He picked it up and opened it. There was an inscription engraved in the back: 'For Robert Pritchard in return for ten years of faithful and loyal service, E&G Estates.'

He closed it and pushed it into his pocket before climbing to his feet. There were marks on the wall of the stable and he was trying to decipher them when he heard footsteps cross the yard. Mary Ellis joined him. Her eyes were still shadowed but they were dry, and she was dressed in her patched and faded black skirt and blouse, her hair pinned back by the old-fashioned tortoiseshell pins.

'I came to see if you were awake. You said that you had to fetch your family from the station.'

'Not until half past ten. How are you?' he asked solicitously.

'Fine,' she answered in a tone that warned him not to mention what had happened in the night.

'What are these?' He indicated the strange grid on the wall.

'That's our tally line.'

'What's a tally line?' He ran his fingers over the scratches etched into the stone.

'My father started it after the Estate bought the farm back from the bank. Because he couldn't read and write he couldn't list everything the agent took to pay our rent. So he drew this.' She stepped closer to him. 'Those egg-shaped marks with squiggles on the top are live chickens, and those without are the ones the agent took that were plucked and trussed ready for the butcher. These long lines separate the months and at the top is the year. So you can see eight columns of years divided by twelve lines of months. And we're now in the eight month of the eighth year since we lost the farm. Every mark represents ten animals. Next to the chickens, the ones with little straight lines sticking up are the bullocks and these are the pigs' snouts, those with eyes are the lambs, those without the fleeces.'

'So you have a complete record of everything that Robert Pritchard has taken from you to pay the rent?' Harry asked in excitement, hoping that it might give the Ellises the proof they needed to convince the owner of the Estate that the agent was stealing from them. He didn't doubt for one minute that Mary and David's suspicions were correct. And after what the man had done to Mary and all the other women, he'd like to make Robert Pritchard suffer in any way he could.

'Yes, not that it does us any good because we can't match it to the writing Mr Pritchard puts in his book because we can't read.'

'But I can. And I can write this out for you properly. Why didn't you tell me that you kept this record?'

'You didn't ask. And because we didn't want to trouble you with our problems.'

'You'll explain this to me when I come up this afternoon so I can make a proper account book for you?'

'If you want me to. The others are all out. David and Matthew have gone to fetch the cows in for milking, and Martha and Luke are looking for eggs in the barn. They've eaten, but I could make you breakfast, if you like.'

'I'd like that very much, thank you.' He followed her into the kitchen and watched her beat eggs in a bowl and take down a frying pan from the shelf. 'Do the others know that I fell asleep in the stable?'

'Yes, they saw your car parked down the road.'

'What did you tell them?'

'That it broke down in the night and you woke me and asked if you could sleep in the stable until the morning when it would be light enough for you to see to mend it.'

293

'You didn't mention the agent?' He sat at the table.

Tight-lipped she shook her head and he realized she had kept the secret for so long that it was easier for her to blot Robert Pritchard's visits from her mind than acknowledge they happened – until his presence forced her to do just that.

'But David did ask me why you came here again in the night, Mr Evans.'

'I'm Harry, not Mr Evans, so please don't ever call me that again, and you are Mary.'

'Were you trying to paint another picture – Harry?'

'No. I thought you knew I've given up painting pictures to take up carpentry,' he joked.

'You just thought you'd rescue me again?' There was no irony in her question.

'I wasn't expecting to see you. I'd been out.'

'Dancing in Swansea with Miss Adams, Martha told me.'

'I had no idea she knew.' It was a leading question but he had to ask it. 'Do you mind?'

'It's not my place to mind anything that you and Miss Adams do.' She scraped an ounce of dripping from a bowl and dropped it into the frying pan she'd put on the open hob.

'I was with her, but I spent most of the evening thinking of you.'

'Why?'

'I didn't know at the time but I do now.' He choose his words carefully so as not to frighten her. 'I like you very much, and I'd welcome the opportunity to get you know you better.'

'And that's why you decided to visit me in the middle of the night?'

'No,' he laughed. 'I came because Swansea was hot, noisy and dirty, like you said. I wanted peace and quiet and I couldn't think of anywhere more peaceful or quieter than these hills, this farm and the reservoir.'

She tipped the eggs she'd beaten on top of the melted fat and stirred them. Leaving the pan, she went to the table and cut him a slice of bread from the loaf. 'Tea?'

'Please.'

She poured two cups and took hers over to the stove.

'I could take you to a Swansea hotel for dinner and dancing, if you like?' he suggested lightly.

'Me?' She blushed crimson. 'I can't dance, I have nothing to wear and I wouldn't know how to behave in a hotel.'

'I'll buy you a dress and teach you to dance. As to how to behave in a hotel, I'm sure you wouldn't disgrace yourself.'

'I couldn't let you buy me a dress.'

'Yes, you could. It would be a present.'

'No, Mr . . . Harry, I couldn't take an expensive present from a man. It wouldn't be right.'

'Then if you won't let me take you dancing how are we going to get to know one another better?'

'I thought last night would have solved that problem. I'm not worth getting to know.'

'Yes, you are.' He straightened the knife and fork and plate she'd laid in front of him.

'You don't have to be kind to me.' She carried the eggs over and scooped them on to his plate.

'I'm not. And these eggs look perfect.' He smiled at her, and she blushed again. 'So, tonight, when I come up for my talk, if you won't let me take you to Swansea, will you let me take you for a drive in the car?' he persevered.

'I can't leave the little ones.'

'David would look after them.'

'He'd want to know what we were doing. He likes you but—'

'But he's suspicious of me. In that case, we'll just sit and talk, here in the kitchen after I've given Martha and Matthew their reading lesson.'

'What about?'

'Ways to solve your problems – and what the future could be like, if you let it,' he said softly.

'I'm afraid that the only future any of us will see is in the workhouse,' she said bitterly.

'No. Whatever else the future holds for you and your family,

295

Mary, I promise that none of you will have to go into the work-house.'

He looked up at her. And for the first time since he had known her, she returned his smile.

Chapter 18

'DO YOU think Bella will model for me today? I've painted the background, so all I need is her figure; the sketches shouldn't take long, an hour or two at most,' Toby said.

'I have absolutely no idea,' Harry snapped, exhaustion and pain making him irritable.

'What happened between you and the Snow Queen last night? You've done nothing but snarl since breakfast, which is not surprising given your bruises—'

'I have a photograph of Bella, if it will help.' Harry wished Toby would stop talking so he could think about his grandfather – and Mary.

'A photograph?' Toby sneered. 'I need to put her in position in the light, to see the dappled sunshine cast the shadows of the woodland leaves on her face—'

'Please, Toby, no artistic flights of fancy, not now,' Harry begged.

'Sorry, I know you're worried about your grandfather,' Toby apologized.

'I am.' Harry parked the car in the yard outside Penwyllt station. He waved to Alf, who had travelled ahead of them in the inn's carriage. 'You'll wait in the car?'

Toby nodded. Harry went inside as soon as he saw the signal drop.

Bella was the first off the train. 'Great news, Harry,' she said, kissing his cheek. 'Edyth is going to be fine. She's coming home next week.'

Harry looked to his parents for confirmation.

'It's true, darling.' Sali hugged him. 'The doctor said her back will be stiff for a while and she may suffer from headaches for a few months but she will make a complete recovery.'

'It would appear that your sister has more lives than a cat,' Lloyd added, his relief evident in his smile.

'That's wonderful news.' Harry noticed new lines around his stepfather's eyes that he suspected stemmed from the strain of having both his father and daughter ill at the same time.

Harry led the way out of the station. The moment Toby saw Bella, he left his seat, ran to the boot of Harry's tourer, opened it and, when she approached, thrust an enormous bouquet of red roses into her hands.

'A small bribe for my beautiful and heartless Morgan le Fey.'

'Heartless?' Bella looked confused.

'Heartless to have left me with your brother for an entire week when you knew full well how much I burned to start painting you.'

'I haven't said I'd model for you yet,' Bella reminded him.

'You see?' He appealed to Harry. 'Cruel, just like the real Morgan le Fey.'

'When you've stopped flirting with my sister and playing clown to the non-existent gallery, Toby, perhaps you'll allow me to introduce you to my parents and aunts. You know my uncles.'

Toby kissed Sali's cheek, shook Lloyd's hand and was introduced to Megan and Rhian. While they were talking, Harry stepped back alongside Lloyd.

'Because there are more of us than my car will hold, I asked Alf Edwards to bring the carriage from the inn.'

'So I see. You all right, Harry?' Lloyd asked, eyeing him keenly.

'Of course, why do you ask?'

'Because you're walking as if you've come off a horse head-first, and there are bruises on your chin,' Lloyd answered.

'I fell over.'

'Fell or pushed by a fist?' Lloyd raised both eyebrows.

Harry didn't answer. 'The carriage holds six. Alf is happy to drive you to the sanatorium, wait while you visit Granddad and drive you back to the inn afterwards. But the length of the visit will depend on how Granddad is today. And,' Harry looked at his sister, 'after last week, the doctor won't let you in, Bella,' he said tactfully, not wanting to tell her that it was their grandfather who'd rather she didn't visit.

'The last thing I want to do is make him ill again.'

'You didn't make him ill last time,' Victor consoled. 'He would have had that coughing fit whether you'd been there or not.'

'I could take Bella down the garden towards the river, while you go into the sanatorium,' Toby suggested. 'If your grandfather is out on the balcony, she could wave to him from there and Doctor Adams couldn't possibly object because it's nowhere near the patients' terrace.'

'And your uncle?' Harry asked.

'I'll see him afterwards.'

'That sounds like a good idea,' Lloyd agreed.

'Bella, you go in Harry's car with him and Toby.' Sali took charge of the arrangements. 'The rest of us will ride in the carriage.'

'Granddad's dying, isn't he, Harry?' Bella asked when they stood in the yard watching the carriage drive away.

'You know he is, Belle.' He helped her into the passenger seat, leaving the back seat for Toby.

'What I mean is, it's going to be soon.'

'I've seen Granddad every day this week, Belle. And whenever the subject comes up, which isn't often, he insists that he's said all he wants to say to all of us. And, if you think about it, what else is there for any of us to say to him?'

'That we love him.' Bella opened her handbag and scrabbled blindly for her handkerchief.

'He knows we love him, and we know how much he loves us. He doesn't need to be told that we're going to miss him unbearably when he's gone.'

'I can't stand the thought of him not being here . . .'

'None of us can, Belle.' Harry gripped her hand. 'But you have to be brave, and think about Granddad and how he must be feeling. He knows more about loss than any of us. From what Dad and the uncles have said, half of him died with our grandmother. You only have to look at the way he smiles whenever he speaks about her or gazes at her photograph.'

'He obviously adored her.' Bella blew her nose.

'He's been a strong man most of his life, Belle, and he's always been there for us when we've needed him. Now he's ill he hates it, and he hates us seeing him sick and in pain. It would be different if it was a disease he could fight. But he can't, and I think all he wants to do now is die while he still has strength to do it well.'

'You think he wants it to happen soon,' Bella said quietly.

'I do.'

'I need to see him – just one last time.'

'From the garden. Today belongs to Dad, Mam and the uncles and aunts.' Harry pressed the ignition, pulled out and followed the carriage.

Toby, who'd remained tactfully silent in the back of the car, leaned forward and handed Bella his sketchbook. 'I made a few notes from the corridor outside your grandfather's room.'

Bella turned over the page and cried out in surprise. She was looking at a pen-and-ink wash that was a lifelike and perfect portrait of Billy Evans.

Dr Adams was sitting in his office, with the door open. He left his desk when he saw Harry walk in with his family.

'Mr Evans.' He nodded to Harry. 'You can all go up to the ward to visit your grandfather today.'

'He's well enough?' Lloyd asked.

'When I spoke to him this morning, he said he wanted to see whoever came.' The doctor evaded the question.

After slipping on gowns and masks, they all went up in the lift to the ward. They found Billy sitting, propped up in bed, a book in front of him, just as Harry had seen him nearly every day since he'd been in the sanatorium. He was looking out over the garden and waving to Bella and Toby below.

'They make a handsome couple,' he teased Lloyd when he walked in.

'Bella's too young to be a part of any couple.' Lloyd gazed down at them.

'I dare say I would have felt the same way if I'd had daughters instead of sons.' Billy looked at them all. 'How nice of you to come all this way. I asked the nurses for chairs but they only brought three; at least the ladies can sit down. Now, I want to hear all the news from home. Tell me, how are all my grandchildren?'

'Well,' Sali answered. 'Even Edyth, apart from the arm that's still mending.'

'And as soon as it has, she'll be up to more mischief,' Billy said philosophically.

'I hope it will slow her down,' Lloyd said seriously.

'The boys are well, busy on the farm, and they send their love.' Victor drew close to his father's bed.

'Has working for you in the school holidays changed Jack and Tom's mind about becoming farmers?'

'Not yet, Dad, and I don't think it will. Both of them take too much after their father.' Megan pulled her chair close to Billy. 'We've given the nurse some fruit and homemade cake and bread for you.'

'And books.' Rhian forced a smile, although her lashes were suspiciously wet.

Harry hung back, watching Billy steer the conversation on to the everyday affairs of the family, lightening the atmosphere until all three of his sons and their wives were able to laugh.

He glanced at his watch, an old one, because he hadn't had time to take the gold one he'd soaked in the lake to the jeweller's for repair, and to his surprise realized that they had been in the room for twenty not ten minutes. He turned and saw the ward sister behind him. Her attention was fixed on his grandfather and, when Billy leaned back against his pillows and pressed his handkerchief to his lips, she stepped forward.

'And that, Mr Evans, is quite long enough.'

'See how I'm bullied?' Billy appealed to his sons.

'If you behaved we wouldn't have to bully you, Mr Evans.' She went to his bed and took his pulse.

'It's strange to say goodbye without kissing you, Dad,' Sali complained.

'No kisses, no touches,' the sister warned sternly.

'But we can blow kisses.' Rhian touched her fingers to her lips. 'See you again soon, Dad.'

Megan followed suit, and Sali went outside with them.

'See you tomorrow, Granddad.' Harry waved.

'It's good of you to want to stay, Harry, but I'd rather you went to Paris,' Billy said seriously.

'I wouldn't get one-to-one tuition from Toby in Paris.' He joined his mother and aunts in the corridor, pulling the door to behind him. Lloyd, Joey and Victor joined them a few minutes later.

They hadn't had time to say much to their father, but then, Harry reflected, it was as Billy had wanted. Everything that needed to be said had been. His grandfather would leave no unfinished business.

'I believe Bella thought modelling for a book illustration would be more glamorous,' Sali commented when they all went into the orchard at the back of the inn after lunch to watch Toby paint Bella.

He had given her a long purple velvet gown that Frank had bought in a Parisian flea market, and draped a gold curtain over her shoulders to act as a cloak. After festooning her with brass necklaces and brooches and a pair of enormous brass earrings, which he'd assured her he'd paint as gold, loosening her long dark hair and 'crowning' her with a paste tiara that looked as though it had been made for Titania in *A Midsummer Night's Dream*, he had taken in the gown at her waist with pins that dug into her every time she moved.

Oblivious to her discomfort, he ordered her to hold the hem of the skirt off the ground, which meant she had to stretch out her arms at an uncomfortable angle. As a final indignity he'd twisted her head to make it look as though she were glancing over her shoulder at an imaginary suitor.

He then spent five minutes barking commands at her before he had begun to sketch like fury. The only time he broke off was to shout if she moved a fraction of an inch.

'I should have warned Bella that Toby is demented when he's working.' Harry set a tray of drinks that he had carried out of the bar on to one of Alf's garden tables. He had brought beer for his

302

father, uncles, Toby and himself, and lemonade for his mother, aunts and Bella.

'I think Bella's found out for herself what Toby is like when he works. Thanks, Harry.' Lloyd passed around the lemonades to everyone except Bella, before taking a glass of beer.

'I'd forgotten how quiet this valley is.' Megan sat next to them on the wooden bench and looked up at the hill behind the inn. 'No traffic to stop you from hearing the birds, more horses and carts and carriages than cars on the road, more sheep than people everywhere you look, and not a gramophone or radio to be heard for miles.'

'It's certainly peaceful,' Harry agreed.

'Did you find out any more about my family?' she enquired.

Harry looked uneasily at his uncle.

'It's all right, Harry,' Victor reassured him. 'Everyone here can remember Megan's father with the exception of you and Bella. But a word of warning, Megan and I would rather the boys didn't know about him, because we don't want to burden them with the knowledge that their other grandfather is someone they'd be better off not knowing.'

'I meant to tell Dad on the telephone that I met him,' Harry confessed.

'I trust you didn't tell him that you were related to me?' Megan asked.

'No.'

'Where did you see him?' Her hand shook, and Victor took her glass of lemonade from her.

'In chapel.'

'You went to chapel, voluntarily?' Lloyd asked in amusement.

'I passed one of the maids from the sanatorium walking there with her family, and as it was five miles from her house and she wasn't feeling too well, I offered to take them. I waited to take the family back afterwards.'

'Did you enjoy the service?' Joey enquired.

'No,' Harry retorted.

'Was his second wife with him?' Megan continued.

'Yes, and until someone said who she was, I thought she was

your father's granddaughter. I have asked various people about your sisters but no one knows any more than Mrs Edwards told Uncle Victor. One married a railwayman and they think she moved to the north of England. The other married a man from Brecon and died there a few years ago. If your father knows more he hasn't confided in anyone I've spoken to.'

'He never was what you might call the approachable type.' Victor gripped Megan's hand tightly. 'Harry will drive us up to the farm if you want to visit him, Megs.'

'No! I don't want to see him.'

'Then forget him.' He slipped his hand around her waist. 'I know it's easy to say—'

'You, the boys and your family have been family enough and more for me these past thirteen years, Victor.' She looked from him to his brothers and Sali and Rhian. 'Thank you for making enquiries, Harry, but coming back here has rekindled memories best forgotten. I know I had a lucky escape when I left my father and this valley. And now I would like to see this painting of yours that Toby told us about at lunch.'

Alf drove the carriage into the yard. Lloyd helped Sali, Rhian and Megan inside, but when he stepped back to offer Bella his hand, Toby was standing next to her, holding her elbow.

'If you don't mind, Mr Evans, I'll travel to the station with the ladies.' Toby wasted a brilliant smile on Lloyd, who scowled back.

'Does your friend flirt with every young girl he meets?' Lloyd asked Harry after Toby followed Bella into the carriage.

'He's always paying women extravagant compliments.' Harry watched Alf drive away before walking to the barn to get his car.

'He can pay as many compliments to other women as he likes. It's the ones he pays to Bella that concern me.' Lloyd followed him inside, opened the car door and sat in the passenger seat.

'It's difficult to know when Toby's joking and when he's being serious, but he says he's in love with her.'

'That's ridiculous. Bella's a baby!' Lloyd glanced at his brothers as they ducked under the low lintel and joined them.

'She's older than you were when you started courting a certain

304

older woman, big brother.' Joey climbed into the back and moved along to make room for Victor. 'And boys do not mature younger than girls, whatever you'd like to think.' He opened his cigarette case and offered it around. 'In fact, if my experience is anything to go by, I'd say the opposite is true. When I was a boy—'

'You were the talk of Tonypandy and nothing in a skirt was safe from you.' Lloyd flashed a look at Harry, and realized from the grin on his face that his stepson knew more about his and Joey's past than they had told him. 'Leave ancient history where it is, Joey. Compared to you, I lived like a monk before I married Sali. And Bella's still in school. She has college ahead of her. There'll be time enough for her to meet boys after that.'

'Plenty of girls her age and younger are working. Some are even married.' Joey closed his cigarette case after they had all taken one. 'Besides, Bella may change her mind about going to college when the time comes.'

'She won't. She's been planning a career in teaching since she read her first book.' Lloyd took his lighter from his pocket.

'That's what she says now—'

'Stop tormenting Lloyd, Joey.' Victor leaned forward so Lloyd could light his cigarette. 'Don't forget you have three girls of your own and they won't be in primary school for ever. Given your history, I can't wait to see how you'll react the first time a boy comes calling on one of them.'

'I'll lock the front door, shut all three in the attic and set their brothers to guard them while I watch the windows.'

'They'll love you for that, Uncle Joey.' Guessing that the carriage was well ahead of them by now, Harry drove out of the barn.

'As if Rhian will let him do anything of the kind.' Lloyd returned his lighter to his pocket. 'Do you know that your mother invited Toby to stay with us?'

'Yes. But Toby is hardly likely to do anything untoward with you and Mam in the house.'

'If he comes, I'll warn your mother not to leave him alone with Bella.'

'Don't you think you're over-reacting, Lloyd?' Victor asked.

'Bella's a sensible girl and well able to put any boy in his place, if she's a mind to.'

'It's the "if she's a mind to" that bothers me. She wouldn't be the first sensible girl to accept the attentions of a man not worth bothering with,' Lloyd answered tersely.

'I know three sensible women in our family who prove that point, Lloyd,' Joey laughed.

Harry dropped his speed when he saw the carriage on the road ahead of them. 'None of you have said anything about Granddad.'

'You see Dad most days, so you know his condition better than us.' Victor flicked the ash from his cigarette outside the car. 'Although I'm surprised how much weaker he's become in seven days.'

'He wasn't cut out for an invalid's life,' Lloyd said seriously.

'He's certainly not making it easy for the nurses to look after him,' Joey chipped in.

'Despite the banter, they're fond of him and they don't take his grumblings any more seriously than he takes theirs. After I've visited him tomorrow, I'll telephone to let you know how he is.' Harry parked alongside the carriage in the station yard.

'Please telephone every day from now on, Harry.' Joey left the car and held the door open for Victor. They went to the carriage to help their wives but Lloyd stayed behind.

'You should know that Dad told us he doesn't expect to see us again. He also repeated what he said he's already told you.'

'That he has nothing to say to any of us that he hasn't already?' Harry guessed.

'You took on a man's load, Harry, and you've carried it well. You'll telephone?'

'Every day, and the moment I've any news, I promise.'

'It's going to be odd without him.' Lloyd ground out his cigarette in the ashtray. 'He's been part of mine and your uncles' lives ever since we can remember. And unlike most men with their fathers, we've remained close. I can't imagine making a decision without discussing it with him first.'

'Neither can I.'

'There's no point in facing tragedy until we have to, or railing against what can't be changed.' Lloyd moved the conversation on. 'When you're no longer needed here, you'll go to Paris?'

'I don't know.' Harry took a last puff of his cigarette. 'I have to do some serious thinking about my future.'

'I know I've been nagging you to work in your businesses, but I took a good long look at that painting you did today. It's very good, as are your sketches. So, if you're serious about becoming an artist, perhaps you should follow your dream. And that, by the way, is as close to an apology as you'll get for all the pep talks I've given you over the years.'

Harry thought of the plans he'd made only the night before to marry Mary Ellis. The domestic bliss he'd imagined and the problem of finding the ideal profession for himself. 'I don't know what I want to do.'

'It is time to make a choice, Harry.' Lloyd didn't raise his voice but Harry knew he was irritated by his indecisiveness. 'Like it or not, they are your businesses and hundreds of people depend on them to pay their wages.'

'The trustees run everything perfectly well.'

'To the best of their ability – yes, they do. But the people appointed by the bank and the solicitor's office hardly have a personal interest,' Lloyd observed. 'And you can't expect the board to look after your affairs for ever. In nine years they will be disbanded, and some of the members appointed by your mother's Great-aunt Edyth may not live that long. Apart from your mother and Joey, most of them are well over seventy. I doubt you'll find anyone with the same sense of dedication to replace them if you do try to keep the board going.'

'I wasn't thinking of doing that.'

'Nine years can go very quickly,' Lloyd advised. 'Especially when you are learning how to manage something you're not familiar with. I hate to keep lecturing you, but it's time to face your responsibilities, and as I see it, you can do one of two things. Either call a meeting of the board of trustees, tell them that you aren't interested in running the companies and ask them to sell them to someone who is.'

'*Sell* them?' It was the first time Lloyd had suggested he sell

Gwilym James and the subsidiary companies he owned, and Harry was shocked by the idea.

'Or you can go into the office and make an effort to get to know the people you employ and learn enough to take control.'

'I promise you, I will begin to think seriously about my future.' Harry was still reeling at Lloyd's proposal that he sell the businesses.

'Thank you. And I'll thank you even more if you don't tell your mother how much I have badgered you and keep on badgering you about this. You know how protective she is of all you children.'

'Yes.' Harry smiled. 'Which I why I appreciate you giving me a kick in the right direction now and again.'

'No hard feelings?'

'None,' Harry said sincerely.

'I trust you to make the right decision.'

'Really?' Harry eyed Lloyd sceptically.

'Put it this way, I'll tell you if you don't.'

'I'm sure you will.'

'And if I don't get a move on, I'll miss the train.'

They left the car and followed the rest of the family into the station and on to the platform. To Lloyd's annoyance, Toby was holding Bella's hand and gazing into her eyes.

'Let me,' Harry whispered, 'Checking the colour of Bella's eyes, Toby?' he asked slyly.

'It's going to be difficult to capture that exact shade of ripe mulberry,' Toby replied implausibly.

'I could mix it for you.'

'Bella, the train's coming,' Lloyd called out, when it rounded the curve in the tracks and steamed into view.

The next few moments passed in a blur of kisses, handshakes and goodbyes. The stationmaster had finished closing all the doors to the carriages and was lifting his whistle to his lips when Lloyd leaned out of the window.

'Don't forget to telephone, Harry.'

'Every day,' Harry called back.

'We'll see you next week.'

If he's still alive. It remained unspoken but Harry sensed that every one of them was thinking the same thing. He lifted his hat. 'Give my love to Glyn, the girls and my cousins.'

'Take care of him, Harry.' Bella stuck her head out alongside Lloyd's. 'Promise me that you will take care of him.'

'So, my mother invited you to visit us?' Harry waved to Alf, who had picked up two passengers for the village and was turning his carriage in the yard.

'Yes,' Toby confirmed smugly. 'It was kind of her. She did say "anytime I can make it." But I told her it wouldn't be until after I finish all the illustrations. And then I can't really leave Frank, although if I visit him early in the morning, say eight o'clock I should be able to catch the nine o'clock train to Swansea. Supposing there's a train within half an hour or so, what time will I reach Pontypridd?'

'With luck you'll be there by half past eleven or twelve.'

'So maybe I could visit for just a day and a night, and provided I came back early enough the following morning to visit Frank, I wouldn't miss seeing him.'

'Did Bella comment on the invitation?' Harry probed.

'She said any Wednesday or Thursday would suit her.'

'Did she?'

'Why the all-knowing smirk?' Toby questioned suspiciously.

'I knew she wouldn't invite you at the weekend. Saturday night is *the* night in Pontypridd for concerts, dances and parties. Bella's been booked months ahead since she turned fifteen. And take a tip: if you ever want to paint her again don't make it quite so obvious that you're mooning over her.'

'It was noticeable?'

'My father asked if you were always like that. And if so, what I thought he should do about it. Bella is only—'

'Sixteen,' Toby chimed in irritably. 'But hell, a fellow can make friends with a girl, can't he?'

'He can, but he can't blame her family for being wary when he's already told her brother that he's in love with her.' Harry opened the car.

'All right, I got a bit ahead of myself, but supposing that friendship turns to something more—'

'I agree with my father. The "something more" can wait five years until Bella is twenty-one.'

'That's ridiculous!' Toby exclaimed.

'I warned you that my father will never give his consent to Bella marrying anyone until she reaches her majority.'

'When he gets to know me and discovers what a thoroughly nice and charming chap I am, he'll change his mind.'

'Or lock Bella up.' Tired of the conversation Harry changed it. 'I'm going up to see the Ellises. Do you want me to drop you back at the inn?'

'More reading and writing lessons, and on a Saturday night too, when Doctor and Mrs Adams will be in Swansea,' Toby mocked. 'I thought you'd be haunting the bar, waiting for a telephone call from the love of your life.'

'If you're talking about Diana Adams, she's going back to London soon and we've agreed not to see one another again.'

'You quarrelled?'

'On the contrary.'

'Yet you stayed out all night. And Enfys noticed that your bed hadn't been slept in and you weren't at breakfast this morning.'

'Enfys wouldn't notice if a crocodile came down for breakfast instead of me.'

'Perhaps we should go to Bristol zoo and steal one just to find out. So, tell Uncle Toby all about the problems between you and the Snow Queen.'

'There are absolutely none,' Harry replied airily.

'Then you lied and you will be seeing the gorgeous Diana again.'

'Tomorrow morning at the sanatorium.'

'That's not what I mean, and you know it.'

'Then what did you mean?' Harry changed up a gear.

'I meant privately – the two of you alone, in the romantic sense.'

'I told you, she's going back to London.'

'What about my Guinevere?' Toby sounded alarmed.

'You have a few days left to persuade Diana to sit – or stand – for you, depending on how you want to paint her.'

'You could—'

'Do absolutely nothing,' Harry interrupted. 'You're the one who wants her to model for you.'

'I was about to say, if you'd let a fellow get a word in edgewise, that you're footloose and fancy-free. Why don't you follow her up to the Smoke? You could see the sights, study at the Slade—'

'One, I haven't applied to the Slade. Two, I don't want to follow Diana Adams anywhere.'

'Tetchy, aren't we.' Realizing that Harry was probably on edge because of the deterioration in his grandfather's condition, Toby said, 'All right, you've talked me into it. I've done enough work for one day to earn a reward and a walk down to my Arthurian lake would probably do me good.'

'I thought you'd finished both lake paintings.' Harry turned right and drove up the valley towards the hills.

'I have, but there's something about the archway into the farmyard.'

'I love it,' Harry enthused. 'It's as if it's part of a time warp. Step through it and you're back in—'

'Sixteen twenty-four, when the first David Ellis built it.'

'I doubt he was the first, given the number of Ellis graves in the churchyard.'

'I want to take another look at it. I'm not at all sure where it would fit into Camelot, or even if it will, but given time I might think of something or someone relevant that I could put in the foreground.' Toby took a threepenny bar of chocolate from his pocket. 'If you are going to give the children lessons, you can reward them with this.'

'Chocolate from the man who warned me about distributing largesse?' Harry couldn't resist sticking a pin.

'It is only chocolate and a very small bar for five children at that.'

'I might give them a lesson, but I'm going there because I told Mary that I would call in after I had taken my parents to the station.'

'First Diana Adams, now Mary Ellis. And you told me you were no good at seducing women.'

'If I thought it would have the slightest effect, I'd ask you to stop talking about Diana and Mary. Instead, I'll draw your attention to the afternoon. Glorious, isn't it?' Harry gazed at the hill that rose steeply on their right.

'Yes, it is.' Toby looked up and fell in with his mood. 'It really is. Have you ever seen such a pale-washed sky? It could have been painted by a water colourist.' He slid down in the seat and studied the expanse of blue. 'What would you call those wisps of water vapour? They're too thin and gauzelike to be graced by the name of clouds.'

'I have no idea.'

'Don't you just *know* that it was on an early evening exactly like this that Guinevere first rode into Camelot with Lancelot at her side? You can just see King Arthur standing on the battlements as the first delicate red-gold fingers of the dying sun smudged the western horizon behind them, touching the—'

'You've overdosed on *Le Morte d'Arthur.*'

'Philistine!' Toby bit back before falling serious. 'Do you think more about your grandfather at this time of day than any other?'

'How do you know?'

'Because I tend to picture Frank about this time every day. I think it's association. Evening of day – evening of life. I imagine him lying out on the balcony of his room, looking at the garden and thinking of all the paintings he will never create.'

'Why not concentrate on all the paintings he has completed that have given so much pleasure to so many people and will continue to do so for hundreds of years?'

'You're right; I should dwell on his achievements, not the might-have-beens. Did you know that your grandfather used to talk to him when he was still strong enough to leave his room?'

'Yes, he told me.'

'They – I mean, their situation – makes you think seriously about life, doesn't it? Frank is only eight years older than me, yet he's dying. And even seeing him every day hasn't woken me up to the fact of my own mortality. I carry on as if I am going to live for ever.'

'According to my grandfather, that's the only way.'

'You're right, I should console myself with the thought that Frank has achieved his ambitions and left a legacy that will last as long as there are people who appreciate art.'

'As will you,' Harry said. 'The illustrations in *Le Morte d'Arthur* are as much yours as Frank's.'

'They are Frank's swansong, the culmination of years of study that will put him up there with the greatest painters of his generation. I'm dreading the completion of this book because Frank won't have anything left to live for and I'll be left to find my own commissions.' He glanced across at Harry. 'I'm terrified at the prospect. What if no one gives me any?'

'Come on, Toby, that's false modesty. I've seen what you can do.'

'As a draughtsman. The actual painting and execution of an illustration is the easy part, Frank taught me that much. It's the putting together and the creation of a scene that carries the truth and essence of a book and stays with the reader long after they've looked at it that's the difficult part.'

'The publishers know how much you've put into this project.'

'The publishers are Frank's publishers, and I couldn't bear to think that I only received a commission from them because I'm Frank's nephew. I need to make it on my own, Harry. I need to know that I am my own person, with my own talent. That I have something to give to life, and – the woman I love.'

'Please, tell me you're not thinking of Bella?'

'I promise I'll wait until she's old enough before I tell her how I feel about her.'

'What do you call old enough?'

'Younger than twenty-one.'

'I was afraid you'd say that.'

Toby looked up at the hills and, from the faraway look in his eyes, Harry could see that he was either imagining a painting or picturing his sister.

His thoughts turned to his own future and the embryonic plans he had made and discarded. What did he have to give a woman except his money? Money he hadn't even earned. And what would he leave behind when he died? Not superb illustrations for classical books, or a legacy of union work like his grandfather who had changed so many colliers' lives for the better. Billy Evans had won a place in history as a fighter for workers' rights. Maybe, in the vast scale of the world, it wasn't as big a place as he deserved but he would be remembered fondly by hundreds, if not thousands of people in the Rhondda and Wales. He wondered if he would even be remembered by anyone when he died, and if so, what for.

Toby's voice broke in on his thoughts. 'There's a lot of activity around the farmhouse.'

Harry looked ahead. 'I've never seen so many vehicles parked on this road.'

'Perhaps the Ellises are having a party,' Toby suggested flippantly.

Harry made out a police car, half a dozen farm and livestock carts, a closed, high-sided black van with 'Brecon Workhouse' on the side painted in large white letters – and a trap. Although he couldn't be absolutely certain it was the one he'd seen in the archway in the early hours of the morning, it looked suspiciously like it.

'What's the matter, Harry? You've gone the exact shade of white I painted my ghost lady.'

Harry didn't answer. He stopped the car behind the trap, pulled on the handbrake, switched off the ignition, jumped out and started running.

Chapter 19

HARRY DODGED a bruiser with the height and build of a heavyweight boxer, and bolted into the farmyard in time to see David Ellis break free from a policeman.

'Let go of my sister!' David hurled himself at two men who were dragging Mary through the door of the farmhouse. Kicking one on the shins, he hit the other in the chest with his fist. 'Let go of her, you swine—'

'I told you he was out of control.'

Harry recognized the voice from the night in the stable. The owner, a square-shouldered, middle-aged man running to fat, lashed out and slapped David across the head. Harry flinched when he heard the blow. The boy reeled and Harry dived forward, catching him before he hit the cobbles.

Knowing that losing his temper would achieve absolutely nothing with a figure of authority, Harry looked to Mary as he helped David to his feet. 'What's going on?'

The two men flanking her tightened their grip on her arms and she winced. Her dark eyes glittered, dry and enormous, in her pale, thin face. Harry had seen a similar expression when, against his better judgement, he had joined a stag hunt at a friend's house. Mary looked just as the animal had done when it realized it was cornered and had nowhere to run.

'Let go of her. You're hurting her.' Harry stepped forward but the men pulled her back, away from him.

'Who are you?' the constable demanded.

The man who had hit David answered the officer before Harry could. 'I don't know his name, but I can tell you that he's the same thug who attacked me last night. He did this.' He pointed to a bloodstained bandage wrapped around his head.

'Is that right?' the policeman asked Harry.

Harry glared at his accuser. 'You're the agent, Robert Pritchard?'

'What's it to you who I am?'

Fighting the impulse to thump him as soundly as he had hit David, Harry clenched his fists. It took all the powers of restraint that he had been taught as a child to remain calm. Forcing himself to think only of Mary and the Ellis family, he said, 'If you are the agent, then yes, I hit you. But it was in self-defence. It was you who attacked me.'

'A likely story, when I complained about the attack first,' the agent snorted.

'It's the truth, Constable.' Harry appealed directly to the officer.

'Then where are the bruises where I hit you?' Bob Pritchard demanded.

'On my chin, chest and elbow.'

Bob Pritchard turned to the constable. 'If they're there, they're not the result of anything I did.'

'That will be for the court to decide, that's if you want to take it that far, sir,' the officer murmured deferentially.

'I want to, and you will,' the agent snapped, as if he were the constable's superior.

'Your name?' The policeman removed his notebook from his top pocket.

'Harry Evans.' Harry saw Toby fighting to get into the yard.

'I'm a friend of Harry Evans and the Ellises,' Toby shouted. 'These idiots tried to stop me from following you, Harry' He looked around. Two men were working in the barn, busily crating all the live poultry. Another was walking around the pigsties, scribbling numbers in a book. A third was stacking the utensils in the dairy. 'What's going on here? Who are all these people?'

'That's what I'm trying to find out.' Harry looked to the constable but it was the agent who answered him.

'This family is being evicted for non-payment of rent. Their goods are forfeit to the landlord, not that they'll cover a fraction of their debts, and the constable is here to see that everything is done according to the law.'

'Whatever the arrears, I'll pay them,' Harry offered impetuously.

'They owe hundreds of pounds,' the constable replied. 'You couldn't possibly pay them.'

'I have money.' Harry knew he'd said the worst thing that he could have once the words were out of his mouth.

'Enough to buy yourself a whore,' Bob Pritchard mocked. 'I saw your car parked outside here last night. It's just like I told you, master,' he called across to a man in a black three-piece suit and a bowler hat who was standing in the doorway of the house. 'The girl is a moral degenerate. This,' he gave Harry a disparaging look, 'is one of her customers.'

Screams filled the air and a man in a khaki work jacket hauled Martha and Matthew out of the house. Both were yelling at the top of their voices. They saw Mary and tried to run to her but he held them firmly by their wrists. Martha struggled and fell to her knees.

'Please, don't hurt them, they're children,' Harry said.

A cry, shriller and more anguished than Matthew and Martha's, cut Harry short. A woman wearing a grey, hospital uniform followed the man. She was having difficulty holding Luke. He was red-faced, and hysterical, and stretched his small arms out to Mary as soon as he saw her.

Mary tried to lift her hands but the men pinned them to her sides.

The workhouse master waved to one of the men standing in the archway. 'Bring the van.'

'No . . . I won't go . . . I won't go . . . not to no workhouse . . .' David wriggled free from Harry's grip only to be floored by the agent who lifted him unceremoniously from the ground by his hair before handing him back to the constable.

'I warned you he'd be too much for the workhouse, master. He may be fourteen but you'd be better off sending him to a correctional facility, or a prison first as last,' the agent said coldly.

'David,' Mary appealed to her brother, 'go quietly with the little ones, they need someone to look out for them.'

'And you?' David fought back his tears.

'I'll be all right as long as I know that you will be caring for the others.'

'You can't just take this family to the workhouse!' Harry exclaimed. 'It's inhuman when they have friends.'

'What friends?' The agent stepped even closer to Harry. 'You?' he mocked. 'It's like I said to the police sergeant this morning. Mary Ellis is under-age and in need of moral guidance. The only place for a girl with that failing is the workhouse. And the children will be better off in the orphanage wing where they'll be kept away from her.'

'How can you sleep at night?' Harry asked in disgust.

'With a clear conscience. The same conscience that led me to call in the authorities. I gave Mary Ellis every chance to take over the rent book on this farm but rather than work, she turned the house into a brothel. I came here last night to find you,' he jabbed his forefinger into Harry's chest, 'alone with her in the stable doing things that as a Christian man I'd rather not mention. And the younger children left alone in the farmhouse. Anything could have happened. A fire could have broken out, they could have burned to death in their beds.'

'You're a liar, Mr Pritchard.' There was no emotion in Mary's voice. Her worst nightmare had been realized and she felt oddly detached, almost as though the proceedings were happening to another family, not hers. 'You raped my mother, me, and all the women around here who couldn't pay their rent. Mr Evans only tried to help us.'

'She is telling the truth,' Harry said strongly, aware that two men had moved in behind him.

'You don't want to go making any more accusations like that, either of you,' the constable warned. 'Perjury is a serious crime. You could both find yourself in gaol for that. And a women's prison is worse than the workhouse, Miss Ellis.'

'I know what really happened,' she asserted, staring at the agent, 'and so does Mr Pritchard.'

The constable poised his pencil over his notebook. 'I'm asking you formally, Harry Evans. Did you attack Mr Pritchard last night?'

'In self-defence,' Harry replied.

'I'm making notes that could be used as evidence against you.'

'Are you charging me with a crime?' Harry demanded.

One of the bailiffs opened an upstairs window. 'Mr Pritchard, sir.'

'What is it, Fred?'

'We'll be able to get all the saleable furniture into two carts; there are only the beds, bedding, kitchen table, and pots and pans. It's not worth taking the benches in the kitchen unless you're short of firewood.'

'Tell them to bring the carts into the yard,' the agent called to the man who was standing next to Toby in the archway.

'And find out what the hold-up is with the workhouse van,' the constable added. 'The sooner we get these children out of here the sooner we can hear ourselves think.' He glared at Martha, Matthew and Luke, who were still sobbing.

'I can take the children with me,' Harry offered when three carts rumbled through the archway into the cobbled yard.

'You a married man, sir?' the constable asked.

'No.'

'You have a house.'

'In Pontypridd.'

'A likely story. The man can't stop lying,' Bob sneered. 'I told you, he's one of her,' he pointed at Mary, 'fancy men.'

'I can't hand these children over to someone I know nothing about who lives out of the area. It's for the magistrates to decide what will happen to them,' the constable declared.

'I'm lodging at the inn in Abercrave. My landlady would vouch for me and help me to find suitable accommodation for them,' Harry pleaded.

'You think a public house a suitable place for children?' the workhouse master enquired coldly.

'Plenty of children grow up with parents who run public houses,' Harry retorted.

'And we all know what happens to those who are brought up in a dissolute, licentious atmosphere.'

'I'll take a cottage for them. Hire any woman you approve of who is willing to look after them.'

'You won't be in a position to do any such thing, Harry Evans.' The constable snapped his notebook shut. 'On your own admittance you assaulted Mr Pritchard—'

'In self-defence,' Harry reiterated.

'Harry Evans, I am arresting you . . .'

The men standing behind Harry caught his upper and lower arms in an iron grip while the constable read him his rights. Harry could see the constable's lips moving but he couldn't hear a word the man was saying for Matthew, Martha and Luke's wails and David's curses, as all four were bundled unceremoniously into the workhouse van.

David stuck his head out of the back and, for the first time, Harry saw real fear in the boy's eyes. 'Do what you can to get the little ones out, Harry. I won't be in the workhouse long enough to take care of them. Any farmer in need of an unpaid servant can take Martha and me, and then Matthew and Luke won't have anyone. Please . . .' A cuff from one of the bailiffs sent him hurling back.

Harry heard a bang and hoped it wasn't David's head. 'I'll get you all out, David. I promise,' he shouted, hoping the boy could still hear him.

'No, he won't, Ellis,' the agent taunted. 'The sooner you get used to the workhouse, the better it will go for you.'

'This is ridiculous,' Toby protested. 'Harry wouldn't assault anyone.'

'And who might you be?' The constable opened his book again.

'Ross, Toby Ross.'

'Address?'

'I'm staying at the inn in Abercrave with Mr Evans.'

Matthew, Luke and Martha's cries escalated. The bailiffs slammed the doors on the van and locked them on the outside. The woman who had lifted Luke into the back climbed into the cab beside the driver, and he drove the van out of the yard.

The workhouse master beckoned to the three waiting carts. The horses pulled them over the cobbles close to the door.

'Please, allow me to take care of this family.' Even as Harry begged, he knew he was wasting his breath.

The workhouse master opened the back of the second closed cart. He looked Mary up and down. 'Put her in.'

The men holding Mary hoisted her into the iron cage that filled the back of the cart, one of the men deliberately hitching her skirt up.

'Damn you!' Harry shouted.

'There's no need for that,' the constable said to the man.

'She's too skinny for my liking, anyway.' He laughed, slammed the door shut and locked the door.

Once again, Harry had no choice but to stand back and watch. There wasn't even a window in the back of the cart, and he imagined how Mary must be feeling.

'Put your hands out.'

Harry looked blankly at the constable.

'Hands out!'

The bailiffs grabbed Harry's wrists and held out his hands. The constable snapped a pair of handcuffs on to him.

'I want you to press charges and I want to see him in court.' The agent was speaking to the constable but he was watching Harry.

'Toby,' Harry shouted to his friend as the police van was driven into the yard, 'drive to the inn and telephone my father as soon as you get there. The number is in my diary in my room. Tell him what's happened.' He turned to the constable. 'Where are you taking me?'

'Brecon.'

'You heard that, Toby?'

'Brecon,' Toby repeated.

'Ask him to do whatever it takes to get me out.'

Something fell from one of the windows. Harry ducked, before he realized it was a bundle of sheets. Pillows, blankets and hand-stitched quilted bedspreads followed, and landed on the muck-stained cobbles.

'How would you like someone to treat your family's belongings

321

this way?' Harry asked a bailiff who was making lewd comments as he threw out Mary's underclothes.

Iestyn Williams walked through the bottom gate of the yard that led to the cow pastures. He stared at Harry. 'I know you. You're Mary Ellis's fancy man.'

'We've established that, Iestyn,' Bob Pritchard replied.

Ignoring Harry, Iestyn turned to the agent. 'There's no need to go to the expense of carting all the livestock to market, Bob. I'll take the lot off your hands, same price as before.'

'And that makes you, as well as Robert Pritchard, a thief and a fraudster,' Harry pronounced angrily.

'Get him out of my sight, Constable,' Bob Pritchard ordered.

Harry was pushed into the back of the police van. Caged like an animal, the last thing he saw through the wire-mesh window in the back door was the farmhouse receding slowly behind him and a man climbing a ladder that had been propped against the front wall of the house, a sheet of board under his arm ready to cover the windows.

Toby tried to appear nonchalant as he left the farmyard and walked to Harry's car. After checking that the police van was a diminutive dot on the road to Brecon, he looked over the door on the driver's side and breathed a sigh of relief. Harry had left his keys on the seat. He wished Harry had also left a handbook on how to drive the Crossley. He had seen his friend hit the ignition button enough times to know how to start the engine but he had never driven a car in his life and he was aware that the agent, who was ostensibly supervising the men boarding up the house, was watching him.

He believed Harry's story that he had hit the man in self-defence, but the fact that the constable had summarily arrested Harry without further investigation suggested that Robert Pritchard had rather more authority than his position as a rent collector warranted. And he suspected that the man would have absolutely no compunction in getting him arrested by informing the police that he wasn't fit to drive.

He waited. His chance came when a bailiff called the agent back into the farmyard. As soon as he disappeared through the arch,

Toby jumped into the front seat and started the car. It leapt forward, hitting the back of the trap in front. The horse whinnied and bolted.

'Hey, here, boy! Here, boy.' A young man jumped off a waiting cart and grabbed the pony's head, wrestling it to a standstill.

'Sorry, didn't mean to spook the horse,' Toby apologized.

'Not used to the car?' the boy asked, still holding the pony.

'It's my friend's.'

'You should always check the engine's out of gear before pressing the ignition. That's what my dad says.'

'You know how to drive?' Toby asked hopefully.

'Tractors. The farmer my father works for has one.'

Toby thrust his hand into his pocket. 'I'll give you half a crown to turn this car around, point it in the other direction and show me what I have to do to get it to Abercrave.'

The young man glanced over his shoulder. There was no sign of the agent. He held out his hand. 'You have a deal, sir.'

'That's right, Mr Evans.' Toby raised his voice in the hope that Lloyd could hear him above the irritating drone on the line. 'Harry has been arrested . . . He is in the police station in Brecon. He asked me to telephone you . . . No, of course he hasn't done anything wrong . . . All he was trying to do was help a family who were being evicted . . . The man who put the bruises on Harry's face that you saw today told the police Harry attacked him . . . Harry said it was self-defence . . .' The line went dead. Toby hit the receiver and when it remained dead hung up.

'Two and a half minutes is all we're allowed, Mr Ross. There's only one line and the sanatorium takes precedence,' Mrs Edwards reminded him from the doorway.

'That is stupid. Especially as it took me three hours to get through.' He glanced at the clock above the bar. It was after nine and he doubted that Harry's father would be able to do anything to help him immediately, which probably meant Harry would be spending at least one night behind bars.

'Your dinner is ready. Shall I ask Enfys to put it on the table?'

It seemed wrong to eat when Harry was incarcerated in a cell, but Toby reflected that starving himself wouldn't help. 'Please, Mrs Edwards.' He walked past her and went into the dining room.

'Enfys, Mr Ross is waiting for his dinner,' Mrs Edwards called into the kitchen as she carried Toby's customary pint of beer and whisky chaser from the bar. She set them in front of him. 'Poor Mr Evans, I do hope someone will give him dinner in the police station.'

'I don't think the police are allowed to starve their prisoners,' Toby commented grimly.

'Such a nice, polite young man. Thoughtful too, but I warned him not to get mixed up with the Ellises when he was talking to their old shepherd, Dic, in the bar the other night. The family's bad news, Mr Ross,' she declared emphatically. 'They don't mean to be and can't help it, bless them, but it's like people say: the Ellises are cursed and have been ever since David Ellis hung himself. The Lord doesn't forgive murderers. And he was a self-murderer. It's not right to take a life.'

'It was their father, not them, who took the life, Mrs Edwards. And if you could have seen them being carted off to the workhouse today, I'm sure you would have tried to help them.'

'I would have cried my eyes out, not that it would have done them any good,' she qualified. 'But I wouldn't have done anything to get myself arrested. There's no quarrelling with the law of the land and Mr Evans shouldn't have tried, however upset the Ellises were.'

Toby knew the story he had told Mrs Edwards about Harry arguing with a policeman and being arrested for trying to help the Ellises wouldn't hold for long. But he couldn't bear to repeat the foul things the agent had said about Mary Ellis and Harry. He wasn't sure whether Harry was attracted to the girl or not, but he was prepared to swear – and in court, if necessary – that she wasn't a prostitute.

Enfys brought Toby's meal, and Mrs Edwards looked critically at the roast chicken dinner she laid in front of him. 'Mr Ross doesn't want a dinner as dry as that, Enfys. Bring a jug of gravy.'

'It's reasonably quiet in the bar, Mrs Edwards, so why don't you sit with me and have a drink. On my account?' Toby said, not wanting to eat alone.

'Thank you, I will. You can bring me a sherry when you bring Mr Ross's gravy, Enfys.' She sat at the table, avoiding the chair Harry usually occupied.

'You're from around here, Mrs Edwards, you know the way things work,' Toby said thoughtfully. 'There has to be something that we can do to help the Ellis family.'

'Nothing I can think of. They're not the first farming tenants to be evicted and dumped on the parish. And the way things are,' she grimaced, 'there are plenty more around here headed the same way.'

'Before he was taken away, David Ellis mentioned that people can take children from the workhouse.'

'If they need workers for their farms, some families round here take the older ones,' she replied cautiously.

'And the younger ones?'

'Some are adopted by people who have no children. But not many.' She passed him the salt cellar. 'Not in an area like this. Times are hard and people have trouble enough feeding their own.'

'Will they be kept together as a family in the workhouse?' Toby asked.

'Bless you, Mr Ross, I can see you've no experience of the poor house. The orphanage wards only take children under sixteen and they separate girls from boys. They won't see one another or the adults, and Mary Ellis will be put in a block with the adults.'

'Can we get her out?' Toby asked.

'That depends,' she said dubiously.

'On what?'

'On whether someone's prepared to take a girl with her reputation as a maid. Thank you, Enfys. You can go back to the kitchen now. I'll get Mr Ross's afters and anything else he wants.' She took the sherry and gravy jug from the girl and put them on the table.

'What reputation does Mary Ellis have, Mrs Edwards?' Toby asked bluntly.

'I've only heard rumours,' she replied guardedly. 'And I'd soon have no customers if I went round repeating everything I heard.'

'The agent said Mary Ellis was "a degenerate in need of moral guidance" but she's always behaved impeccably whenever Harry and I have seen her. In my opinion she's simply a nice girl with more problems than anyone her age should have to cope with.'

'I run an inn, Mr Ross. I can't afford to alienate anyone.'

Toby glanced through the open door.The passage was empty. He left his seat and closed the door. 'You have my word, Mrs Edwards; nothing you say to me will go any further than this room.'

'All I will say is that if Mary Ellis has a reputation, it's the same one as all the wives and daughters of the tenants Bob the Gob collects rent from.'

'If I paid you, would you go to the workhouse and offer Mary a job?'

'I would, if I thought that it would do any good. But if she's been admitted as a moral degenerate they won't allow anyone to take her out. I've known girls with better reputations than Mary Ellis who went in there forty years ago with that label and haven't been seen in the outside world since.'

The workhouse nurse walked down a long corridor ahead of Mary. The walls were covered to shoulder-height with brick-shaped, dark-green tiles. Above them, the plaster was painted a sickly yellow. The floor was wooden-blocked and the nurse's rubber-soled shoes squeaked when she halted outside a door panelled in opaque glass. She opened it.

'In here,' she ordered sharply.

The first thing that struck Mary when she entered the enormous bathroom was the stench. A nauseating mixture of stale sweat, dirt, carbolic soap, urine and faeces. A row of six sinks filled the long wall opposite the door. Two toilets stood side by side on the short wall to her right, and two baths, also set side by side, filled the remaining space. One was half-full, and clumps of dirt, hair and lice floated, black islands on a sea of crusted grey scum.

'Strip off, bag your clothes and shoes.' The nurse opened a cupboard and handed Mary a linen bag. 'Then get into that bath and start scrubbing.'

'In that?' Mary stared at the bath in horror. 'The water's filthy.'

'That's what you get for being the last admittance today.' She took a grey Welsh flannel smock from the cupboard and hung it on a peg. After glancing at Mary's feet she placed a pair of wooden clogs on the floor beneath it. 'Get a move on,' she snapped. 'I haven't all day.'

'I will not get into that water.' For the first time Mary was glad that her brothers and sister weren't with her. If they had been, she would never have found the courage to refuse to obey someone in authority lest they suffered for her defiance.

The nurse whirled around. 'What did you say?'

'I will not get into that water. It is full of dirt and vermin.'

'I know what you young farm girls are like. Dirty to bed and dirty to rise. You've probably never had a bath in your life. Well, you're going to have one now. The rules state that everyone who comes into the workhouse has to have a bath before being issued with a uniform and that is exactly what you are going to do.'

'I bathed every day at home, including this morning. We have a stone sink large enough for a grown-up to lie down in.'

'You bathe every day, where?' the nurse jeered.

Mary tensed herself and bit her lip. Until that moment she hadn't allowed herself to think further than the next few minutes. That way it had been easier to fool herself that her situation was temporary. That tomorrow morning she would wake up back in her own bed next to Martha and Luke with the boys sleeping in the room next door. She recalled something Mr Pritchard had said about a woman whose children had been taken to the orphanage: *She'll probably never see them again in this life.*

David had been right in what he had said to Harry. He and Martha were accustomed to hard work. A farmer looking for free labour would soon snap them up. And that would leave Matthew and Luke all alone with strangers who wouldn't care for them.

'You don't want to start your life here by drawing the wrong kind of attention to yourself,' the nurse warned. 'We've ways of dealing with young girls who try to get above their station. You're here because you're worse than a penniless, pauper degenerate, Ellis. You're a debtor! The lowest of the low, and if the master gets to hear of your refusal, make no mistake, you will be punished – and severely. Now get in that bath.'

Mary shook her head, backed away and whispered, 'No.'

'What's going on in here, Staff?' The ward sister, wearing an apron and veil that crackled with starch, entered and looked from the nurse to Mary.

'This new inmate is refusing to get in the bath.'

'Are we running a hotel or a workhouse, Staff?' The sister's voice was high-pitched in indignation.

'A workhouse, Sister. I have informed her of the rules.'

'Not firmly enough, by the look of it.' The sister addressed Mary. 'Strip off and get in that bath, girl.'

'There are fleas and lice in it.' Mary pointed to the water.

'One bath of warm water is to be drawn for morning admissions, one for evening. You are the last admission this evening and you will get in it.'

'Please, allow me to let out the water and scrub the bath and I will wash in cold,' Mary pleaded.

The sister crossed her arms over her thin chest and pursed her lips. 'You think we don't know what you are up to, Ellis? You want a cold bath so you can catch bronchitis, or even better, pneumonia. That way you won't have to work and contribute to your keep. You'd rather do what you and your family have done all your lives – run up debts and expect others to keep you.'

'No—'

'You will address me at all times as "Sister". Strip and get in that bath. Now!'

Mary was trembling but she stood her ground. 'I will not get into dirty water.'

'Then on your own head be it.' The sister stepped back into the corridor and called, 'Porters!'

Two burly men in khaki coats appeared. 'Sister?'

'Strip her, put her in the bath and scrub her. With the brushes we use for the floor.'

'Please, no, I'll get in—'

'You had your chance. You refused.' The sister nodded to the staff nurse. 'Afterwards, take her to the ward. Tell the sister there she is to be put on scrubbing duty and bread and water for three days. That should teach her manners.'

'Yes, Sister.'

The sister glanced at the linen bag. 'And there's no need to keep her clothes or boots. She won't be going anywhere. Incinerate them.'

David sat curled on a tiny high windowsill of the workhouse dormitory. It wasn't late – eight o'clock or thereabouts, he guessed, from the sun sinking over the narrow sliver of hill that was all he could see. He, Matthew and twenty-two other boys had been marched into the room half an hour earlier by a man who had locked his fingers into his curly hair and pulled hard when he hadn't called him 'Sir'.

Sir had given them five minutes to change out of the institution uniforms of grey flannel shirts, short trousers, grey woollen under-wear and socks, and into sackcloth nightshirts. Afraid of what Sir would do to Matthew if he didn't do as he was told, David had complied along with the other boys.

When they had all changed, Sir had ordered them to stand, barefoot, eyes closed at the foot of their beds while he had gabbled a hasty, unintelligible prayer. Finally he had ordered them into their beds and, after leaving strict instructions that they remain in there until they were woken by the bell at six, locked them in for the night.

Ignoring the whispered warnings of the other boys, he had climbed out of his bed as soon as he heard the key turn. It was the first time that he had slept behind a locked door, and he felt like a hen in a coop waiting to be slaughtered. He remembered what the agent had said about Mary leaving him and the others in the house and going to the stable – not that he had believed him: *They could have burned to death in their beds.*

Well, he and Matthew were in the orphanage wing of the workhouse, supposedly being looked after by their 'betters', and they were in more danger of being burned to death than they had ever been at home. *Home.* Hoping no one was watching him, he wiped the tears from his eyes with the back of his hand, smearing his face with stinging salt water.

He gripped the thick iron bars in front of him that covered the glass window pane and, using all his strength, tried to pull them apart. They didn't give a fraction of an inch. He continued to gaze at the small slice of sky and hills, and wished he were free – but only if the rest of his family were too.

He looked down at the two dozen beds in the room. Matthew's was directly below him. Even in the subdued light that came from the small windows he could see that his brother's eyes were closed, but his shoulders were shaking and he knew he was crying. A piercing wail echoed faintly from another part of the building. He couldn't be certain but he thought he recognized Martha's voice and he blanched at the thought of her misery – and Luke's.

It had taken him half an hour of the journey to the workhouse to quieten the toddler. But the moment he had stepped down into the yard outside the building, his brother had been snatched from his arms by the woman who had sat next to the driver. Luke had howled like a dog when she carried him away, and in between howls had held his breath for so long that his face had almost turned black. But when he had run after the woman and tried to comfort Luke, two men had beaten him back.

He wondered if Luke was still crying, or if he had finally worn himself out enough to sleep. He might be as frightened as the rest of them but at least he was too young to understand what was happening. He shivered when he thought of Mary. He hated this place but he suspected the adult block was worse. Bob the Gob had called her 'a moral degenerate'. He didn't understand what the words meant but he knew they were bad. Everything Bob Pritchard had ever said or done to them had been bad.

So much for him being 'the man' of the family. He hadn't been able to stop the bailiffs from evicting them and he had been forced to stand back and watch Luke and Martha being taken away from him to the babies' and girls' parts of the workhouse.

When he had asked that he and Matthew be allowed to keep their own clothes, not only him but also his brother had received painful clips around the ear, and he'd realized that if they couldn't control him by beating him, they'd do it by punishing his brother.

'Please, Harry . . . Please, Harry . . .' He murmured his

friend's name over and over again as if it were a prayer. Harry was the first adult apart from Diana Adams who had tried to help his family since his parents had died. He'd never understood why. But whatever Harry's motives, he was their only hope of getting out of the workhouse. But would Harry even dare try now that he had seen what Bob the Gob could do?

He locked his hands around his knees and sank into despair. His family had been broken up, and somewhere on the journey between the Ellis Estate and the workhouse he had lost the hope that one day life might get better. All that was left to him now was this tiny glimpse of the world, framed by an iron-barred window.

Chapter 20

'I AM entitled to a telephone call.'

'You're a prisoner and, as such, entitled to precisely nothing.' The constable grabbed the chain that linked Harry's handcuffs and yanked him out of the back of the van. Harry blinked and looked around. He barely had time to register the sign 'Police Station' before being shoved through the door of a grey, forbidding building.

A middle-aged, portly constable, who looked as though he was about to burst out of the uniform that strained over his chest, was sitting on a stool behind a high desk in the reception area, reading a copy of the *Brecon and Radnor* and dunking a jumble biscuit into a mug of tea.

'One Harry Evans for the cells, Smith.' The constable pushed Harry in front of the desk. 'I've read him his rights and charged him with assault and battery on Mr Robert Pritchard.'

'Bob the Gob?' Constable Smith bit into the soggy jumble, spraying his chin and uniform collar with wet crumbs.

'Yes. And seeing as how Mr Pritchard's head is all bloodied and bandaged, he wants us to press charges,' the officer confirmed.

'Mr Pritchard's an important man. I wouldn't like to be in your shoes, Harry Evans.' Smith rose to his feet. 'Empty your pockets.'

'This is ridiculous—'

'Your pockets.'

'How can I empty anything with these on?' Harry held up his cuffed wrists.

'He has a point,' Constable Smith said. 'I'll get a truncheon in case he tries any funny business while you're removing the cuffs, Constable Porter.'

Porter waited until Smith had set a wooden truncheon on the desk, before producing a key and unlocking the handcuffs. Harry reluctantly plunged his hands into his pockets and proceeded to remove the contents. Constable Smith took a large brown paper bag from a cupboard behind the desk, opened a book out on the counter, dipped a pen into an inkwell and proceeded to list Harry's possessions.

'Effects of Harry Evans.' He picked up the first object Harry had placed on the counter and opened it. 'One gold cigarette case, holding one . . . ten . . . fifteen . . . nineteen cigarettes. Engraved, "To Harry with love on your twenty-first birthday from Bella, Edyth, Maggie, Beth, Susie and Glyn" – that's quite a harem of women you have there.' He felt the weight of the case in his hand. 'Is this real gold?'

'It is,' Harry replied tersely. 'As is the lighter.'

The constable held it up to the electric light and read, ' "To Harry with love from your parents on your twenty-first birthday." Who was a lucky boy, then?'

'Get on with it, Smith,' Porter snapped. 'You've had your tea break. I haven't had a bite since breakfast. My stomach thinks my throat's cut.'

'One wallet, looks like crocodile skin stiffened by gold corners . . .' He looked enquiringly at Harry.

'Yes, they're real gold,' Harry confirmed brusquely.

Smith's pen scratched over the page. The nib split, blotted the paper and scraped a small hole. 'Wallet contains.' He opened it and whistled. 'Four five-pound notes, three one-pound notes, one ten-shilling note . . . you rob a bank, Harry Evans?'

'That is my money and I'll expect it to be there when I get my wallet back,' Harry said tersely.

'*If* you get it back,' Smith corrected. 'How did you earn it?'

Harry hesitated. The point was he hadn't earned it, but the last thing he wanted to say was, 'I'm idle rich.' He settled for, 'I'm a businessman.'

'And what kind of business would that be?' Constable Porter leaned over the counter and looked Harry in the eye.

'I own property and shops.'

'I can't wait until the sergeant questions you, Harry Evans,' he grinned. 'I'll bet a week's wages on you getting ten years, and that's just for what we know you've done.'

'One card case – silver – the family let you down there.' Constable Smith flicked it open. 'Cards in the name of Harry Evans, Pontypridd address and telephone number.' He tossed it to his colleague. 'Name mean anything to you, Porter?'

Porter shook his head. 'Nothing.'

'One linen handkerchief monogrammed H.E. One fountain pen, bearing a gold hallmark.' Smith pushed it into the bag.

'That's all I have apart from this.' Harry dropped a handful of silver and copper coins on to the counter.

Smith started counting it, making notes as he went along. 'Two half-crowns, three florins, one shilling, four silver sixpences, two silver joeys, three pennies, three halfpennies, a farthing.'

'Happy now you have everything?' Harry demanded caustically.

'Not everything.' Porter lifted his wrist. 'Your watch, tiepin, collar studs and cufflinks.'

Harry reluctantly unbuckled his wristwatch and removed the jewellery the officer had listed.

'Shoelaces, sock suspenders, braces and belt,' Porter demanded.

'I'm hardly likely to hang myself.'

'Regulations, *Mr* Evans.'

'We've a real dandy here; I take it they're all real gold?' Smith dropped Harry's studs and cufflinks into the bag, and glanced down at Harry, who was pulling his laces from his shoes.

Harry finally lost his temper. 'You clearly don't recognize quality when you see it, Constable.'

'Not on what I earn. In my experience, it's only criminals who can afford gee-gaws like this. One pair of laces,' he wrote when Harry laid them on the counter, 'one belt, one pair of sock suspenders and one pair of braces.'

'Arms and legs out so I can check if you have anything else on you.' Porter patted Harry down professionally. 'And what have we here?' He pulled another handkerchief from Harry's back pocket and a pocket watch.

'I forgot they were there, I don't usually keep anything in my back pocket. It spoils the hang of the trousers.'

'Does it now?' Porter enquired sceptically. 'I wouldn't know.'

'Second handkerchief, linen, monogrammed H.E. . . . and one pocket watch, silver. Nice, expensive-looking workmanship.' Smith eyed his colleague quizzically. 'Now why do you suppose a man would need a pocket watch *and* a wristwatch?'

'That is Robert Pritchard's watch,' Harry explained, realizing instantly that possession of it would appear suspicious. 'I picked it up from the floor of the Ellises' stables. He must have dropped it when he attacked Mary Ellis.'

Smith opened the watch. 'It's Mr Pritchard's all right.' He continued to write. 'One pocket watch, silver, engraved "For Robert Pritchard in return for ten years of faithful and loyal service, E&G Estates" Tell me again, Harry Evans: how did you come by this?'

'I told you. I picked it up from the floor of the stable. Robert Pritchard must have dropped it when he attacked Mary Ellis.'

'And you expect us to believe that cock and bull story?' Smith looked at Porter.

'It's the truth.'

'And I'm Tinkerbell.' Porter pushed Harry past the desk towards a door in the back wall. 'Now I'm taking you down for a nice little rest in the cells until the sergeant comes in to question you.' He opened the door. 'After you, Harry Evans.'

'It's dark.'

'Go on, I'll put the light on.'

Unable to see where he was going, Harry moved forward tentatively. He stumbled, and tried to regain his balance, but his feet twisted awkwardly in his unlaced shoes and as he was more concerned with trying to hold up his trousers than saving himself, it took him a few seconds to straighten upright. Just as he did, a blow to the back of his knees sent him tumbling down the steep flight of stone steps. He slammed face-first into a metal door.

Light flooded down the stairs after him. He heard Constable Porter descend the steps.

'Are you all right, Mr Evans?'

'I'll live.' Harry struggled to his feet only to be pushed forward a second time. His face collided with the door again, and when he looked at it, he saw blood on the steel panels.

Footsteps sounded in the corridor outside the boys' ward in the workhouse. Gripping the bars in front of the window, David lowered himself swiftly to the floor, ran to his bed and pulled the single blanket over himself just before the door opened. He wrapped both arms around his head, and opened his eyes a fraction beneath the cover of his fingers.

Sir walked in and headed straight for his bed. He closed his eyes tightly and pretended to be asleep.

'David Ellis?' Sir shook him by the shoulder.

David opened his eyes warily.

'You're wanted downstairs.'

'Why?' David didn't bother to lower his voice.

'Quiet!' The man yanked back the blanket and pulled it off him.

'Why?' David repeated, earning himself a clout on the ear.

'You'll find out. Get dressed. Quickly!'

David sat up and pulled off the sackcloth nightshirt. He thrust his legs into the grey institution pants and trousers. The woollen underclothes were too tight, the trousers and shirt too short, the socks too large.

Sir watched him dress. 'Carry the clogs. You don't want to go waking any of the other boys.'

Matthew sat up. 'Where you taking my brother?' he cried out in alarm. Like David he didn't bother to lower his voice.

'That, young man, is none of your business. But if you don't want a beating you'd better close your eyes and get to sleep. And the same goes for the rest of you boys,' he ordered sternly as they started turning restlessly in their beds.

'Davy,' Matthew wailed.

'I'll be fine, Matthew. And I'll get you, Mary, Martha and Luke out of here, I swear it. No matter how long it takes me, I will get you out.'

'Promise?'

'I promise.' David considered the extra thump he received a

336

small price to pay to be able to reassure Matthew. He only wished he could believe what he'd said himself. 'If I'm not here in the morning, don't worry about me, just look after Martha and Luke if you can,' he added before Sir slammed the door.

'You don't give up, do you, boy?' Sir shoved David ahead of him down the stairs. David clutched at the banister and held on tight as he received another blow in the small of his back.

'Into the office.' He pushed David into a small cosy room.

A fire burned in the grate, books lined the walls, and a folded newspaper, a cup of tea and plate of shop-bought biscuits lay on the desk. The workhouse master who had been at their eviction, now minus his bowler hat, sat behind it, smoking a cigarette and talking to someone sitting in front of him in a high-backed chair.

'This the boy you want, master?'

'You'd better ask our guest that question,' the master replied.

Iestyn Williams, cup of tea in hand and also smoking a cigarette, turned and looked at David standing in the doorway. 'That's the boy.'

'You sure, Mr Williams? He's a defiant, insubordinate creature. He'll need a firm hand.' Sir yanked David forward.

'Then it's just as well I have one.' Iestyn Williams smiled coldly.

'You are fortunate, Ellis.' The workhouse master squashed his cigarette stub in an ash tray. 'Mr Williams has offered you a home in exchange for your help around his farm.'

'I want to stay here with my brother and sister,' David protested.

'You want?' the master repeated scornfully. 'What you want is of absolutely no concern to the parish, me or Mr Williams, Ellis. You are a lucky boy to find someone willing to put a roof over your head and food on your plate. And the parish is grateful that there's one less useless Ellis to be housed and fed.'

'I won't go . . .' David gasped, Sir twisted his ear.

'See what I mean, Mr Williams,' Sir said flatly.

'You'll have to watch that he doesn't run off, Mr Williams,' the master warned. 'Especially at night.'

'I have a cellar that I can lock him into.' Iestyn Williams tossed his cigarette end into the fire, placed his empty cup on the desk and rose from his chair.

'Ellis,' the master looked David in the eye, 'this could be a chance for you to make something of yourself. But be warned, if you run away from Mr Williams, or don't do exactly as he tells you, your brothers and sisters will be punished for your crimes. Do I make myself clear?'

Sickened by pain and humiliation, David nodded sullenly.

'If we have to beat it into you, Ellis, you will learn that you and your family owe a debt of gratitude to the charitable people who have been forced to hand over taxes from their hard-earned money to pay for your feckless family's board and keep.' The master held out his hand to Iestyn Williams. 'I wish you luck with him. Any problems, bring him back.'

'There won't be any.' Iestyn Williams prodded David with the end of his riding whip. 'Outside and untether my horse; you can walk alongside it back to my farm.'

'Stay still, girl,' the staff nurse ordered abruptly.

Mary tensed her muscles and sat rigidly upright on the wooden stool. The shears the nurse wielded snapped loudly and she was aware of a cool draught blowing across her neck as her long curls fell in great clumps to the floor. She glanced down without moving her head and watched the pile of black hair at her feet grow steadily higher.

'Finished.' The staff nurse removed the towel she had placed around Mary's shoulders and shook it over the heap at her feet. 'You have five minutes to clear that mess, wash the floor and clean out the bath. There's a brush, scrubbing brush, bucket, powdered bath brick and bin under the sink. I will return in five minutes to inspect what you've done. If it's satisfactory I'll take you to the dormitory. You're too late for supper.'

Mary rose to her feet.

'When you're spoken to, Ellis, you answer, "Yes, Nurse or Sister," or "no, Nurse or Sister," as appropriate. Understood?'

'Yes, Nurse.'

'Five minutes.' The woman left, closing the door behind her.

Mary went to the sink and found everything just as the nurse said she would. She carried the bin over to the heap of hair on the floor and knelt beside it. Unable to resist the impulse, although she knew it would upset her, she ran her fingers gingerly over her head. The nurse had shorn her, as completely as David did the sheep in shearing season.

Grateful there was no mirror so she didn't have to look at herself, she grabbed handfuls of hair and dropped them into the bin. When she had picked up as much as she could with her fingers, she tried to sweep up the rest with the brush, but it was hopeless. The strands became entwined in the coarse bristles, and it was almost impossible to pull them out.

She returned to the sink, filled the bucket, threw in an evil-smelling floor cloth and carried it over to the mess. Trying not to think what the cloth might have mopped up the last time it had been used, she wiped up the last vestiges of hair. She gritted her teeth and fought back tears, determined not to give the nurse the pleasure of seeing her cry when she returned.

She had lost her family and control of their lives as well as her own. The authorities had humiliated her by sending men in to strip her and scrub her in filthy water. Her hair had been shaved off, and the sister had threatened to starve her, but she was determined not to be broken.

She would cling to her memories of the good times when her father and mother had been alive. She would think of her brothers and sister every minute of every day. And she would never – *never* – allow the nurses or the sister to see just how much they had hurt her. Above all, she would try to find a way that would enable her to bring what was left of her family together again.

Just not now. She was too tired to think, let alone make plans. She carried on picking up every single hair from the floor then started on the bath. It had looked shabby when it was full, empty it was worse. The porcelain had worn away in places allowing the black cast iron to show through. But she smeared bath brick over every speck of dirt and scrubbed and scrubbed, working herself into a frenzy, as though her life depended on the degree of cleanliness she could achieve. She would show them that she wasn't lazy. She would scrub and clean and . . .

An image of David and the others as she had last seen them flooded her mind. She could bear any amount of shame and humiliation if only she knew for certain that they were safe and being cared for. If they tried to treat David as they had treated her he would fight back and . . .

She couldn't stand the thought of him – of any of the little ones – being beaten, shorn and ill-treated. And Luke? She could still hear his cries, piercing and heartbreaking. Matthew, Martha . . .

She uttered a silent prayer for all four of them. Then, afraid of driving herself insane with worry, she deliberately shut her mind and concentrated every ounce of energy that she could summon on scraping the dirt from the bath.

Harry's hands and face were burning. He was loath to open his eyes because he suspected that the pain would be intolerable. He couldn't even recall where he was. There was a peculiarly unpleasant smell, a mix of institution disinfectant, male changing room and dirty lavatories. And although his exposed skin was on fire, his limbs were freezing. Just as they had been the winter the heating had broken down in his rooms in college.

He couldn't hear a sound. Steeling himself for pain, he tried to force his eyes open but his eyelids were glued shut. He moved his hand over them, rubbing at the crust that gummed his lashes, and caught a glimpse of a shadowy, unfocused world. He ran his fingers over the surface he was lying on. It was rough stone – flagstone. Then he remembered.

He was in the police station in Brecon, and Constable Porter had thrown him into a cell. The only light was fading fast. It came from a tiny sliver of skylight bordering the high ceiling, and even that was grated by iron bars. He moved tentatively. His back, arms and legs hurt, but not as much as his face, especially his nose and eyes. He crawled to the steel door and banged on it, but the sound echoed into silence.

The police had been hostile, but logic told him that they wouldn't have left him to starve to death. It was a Saturday night

— the traditional night for drinking and drunks in every Welsh town. They were probably out on patrol. It was the most likely explanation, but it didn't stop him from feeling any the less vulnerable and abandoned.

Something warm and sticky slunk down his face. He hit it and when he looked at his fingers they were dark with clotted blood. A lidded bucket stood in the corner of the cell. No need to guess what that was for.

Above it and to the side was a metal shelf. He crawled towards it, stretched up, gripped the sides and used it to haul himself upright. His trousers slipped and he recalled handing over his belt and braces. He grabbed the waistband. The shelf held an enamel jug of water and a small tin cup. He filled the cup and fumbled in his pockets. He didn't even have a handkerchief left to wipe his face and there was no sign of a cloth.

Leaning heavily with one arm, he managed to pull the other out of the sleeve of his jacket. He dipped the cuff in the water and gently sponged his face. His skin felt stiff when he tried to move his muscles, and he realized that his bruises were caked with dried blood. Judging by the light, he must have been lying on the floor for hours.

Dizzy and faint, he continued to cling to the shelf. He felt as though a herd of miniature bullocks was pounding through his head. A tide of bile rose from his stomach. He looked for something other than the cold floor that he could lie on. A long metal shelf, reinforced by two chains, was bolted to the wall behind him, a blanket folded at one end. Even in the receding light he could see that some parts of it were stained darker than others. He swept the blanket to the floor with his forearm. Shrugging his other arm out of his jacket, he folded the damp part inside and made a pillow for his head. Clutching it, he sat on the bunk, lifted up his legs, lay back and waited for someone to come.

When he next opened his eyes, he found himself in darkness as unrelenting as the coal store in Ynysangharad House, which, to Mari's annoyance, he and Bella had occasionally used as a hiding place when they'd been children. He touched the sheet of steel beneath him and recalled where he was before slipping back into unconsciousness.

A loud clatter woke him some time later, he had no way of knowing whether it was hours or minutes, and later still he heard a drunk belting out 'Alexander's Ragtime Band' at the top of his voice.

He considered banging the door of his cell to attract attention. He was thirsty and in pain. But it hurt to move and it was easier to close his eyes. The next time he opened them, the thin grey light of dawn had lightened the skylight above his head. A key turned in the lock, the door opened and Constable Smith, freshly shaved and smelling of soap, stood, steaming mug in one hand and a plate holding a sandwich the size of a doorstep in the other. His eyes rounded when he saw Harry.

'You all right?'

'Do I look all right?' Harry swung his legs over the side of the bunk, sat forward and cradled his head. 'I need a doctor.'

'You hurt yourself in the night?'

Harry sensed it wasn't so much a question as a plea for reassurance that his injuries were self-inflicted. 'Didn't your colleague tell you?'

'He said you fell against the door, but that happens quite often here. Well, it would, wouldn't it?' Smith muttered defensively. 'It's difficult to walk down a flight of steps when you have to hold up your trousers and keep your shoes on without laces.'

'It's even more difficult when you're pushed from behind.'

'You making an accusation?'

'Do you really think that I fell, Constable Smith?' Harry enquired heavily.

'That's what Constable Porter said, and I've never known him tell a lie.'

'Well, I suppose you could say I did fall, in a manner of speaking.' Harry took the mug of tea Smith handed him, and wrapped his hands around it.

'There you are, then.' Constable Smith was clearly relieved.

'But I wouldn't have if Constable Porter hadn't put his boot behind my knees.'

'That's slander, and I wouldn't repeat it if I were you. You could face even more charges—'

'Can I or can I not see a doctor?' Harry repeated, suffering too much pain from what he suspected was a broken nose to be diplomatic.

'I'll ask the sergeant when he comes in.'

'And when will that be?' Harry enquired testily.

'It's Sunday. His wife likes to go to morning mass – she's Catholic, he's not, but sometimes he goes with her. It's difficult to know when he'll be in because we don't have what you might call a regular routine on Sundays, but he usually calls here during the afternoon.'

'Can I at least have my handkerchief?' Harry lifted his jacket and unfolded it. The right sleeve was crimson with blood.

'It's against regulations. A man can hang himself with a handkerchief.'

'Not this man. That is unless Constable Porter chooses to join me in this cell,' Harry added acerbically.

'I've warned you before. It's slander to make accusations against an officer of the law.'

Harry held up his blood-stained jacket. 'Do you want me to bleed to death?' When Smith didn't move, he said, 'If it helps, you have my permission to cut my handkerchief into four quarters. And I'd like some fresh water, if it's not too much trouble. To wash with as well as drink,' he shouted as Smith finally retreated and locked the door.

Smith returned a few minutes later with Constable Porter. He set Harry's handkerchief, which had been duly quartered, and a fresh jug of water next to the sandwich on the narrow shelf.

'Can I see a doctor?' Harry raised his eyes to Porter's.

'I've no authority to call one on Sunday. They charge more.'

'I'll pay.'

'We have to return your money to you, intact.'

'I'll sign a waiver,' Harry offered.

'Not allowed,' Porter snapped officiously.

'If you're hoping the cuts and bruises will fade by tomorrow, forget it,' Harry advised. 'The way they feel right now they will be there for months and I'll take care to tell your superiors that they are entirely your work, Constable Porter.'

'The blood under his nose is bright red; that means it's still bleeding,' Smith observed timidly.

'Only because he's been picking it,' Porter retorted touchily. 'You been picking at your nose?' he demanded of Harry.

'Of course. I love pain so much I can't stop inflicting it on myself,' Harry retorted flippantly.

Smith laughed nervously.

'What's funny?' Porter turned on his colleague.

'Nothing,' Smith muttered, very much Porter's second-in-command although they were the same rank.

'We'll see what the sergeant says when he comes in.' Porter backed out of the door. 'And when he does, the first things he'll see on his desk are Mr Pritchard's stolen watch and his sworn statements.'

'I *found* the watch.' Harry felt as though he were talking to a deaf man.

'Even if you did, you didn't turn it in. And for that you'll be charged with stealing by finding. The sergeant thinks very highly of Mr Pritchard, Harry Evans,' Porter warned.

'Can I make a telephone call?' Harry leaned weakly against the wall. 'This situation is new to me but I believe that I'm entitled to one.'

'Who would you want to telephone?' Porter demanded aggressively.

It was on the tip of Harry's tongue to correct Porter's grammar and say, Whom would you wish to telephone? but he'd lost the will to fight. Locked in a cell with a bloody nose and thumping head, he felt powerless. And what was worse, he didn't even know whether Toby had managed to speak to his stepfather the night before. It would have depended on what time his parents reached Pontypridd. And his Uncle Joey's house was closest to the station. Knowing his father and uncles, they could have sat up half the night talking.

Mari and the rest of his sisters would have been at home to take a message, but his father's workload was heavy, even more so since the miners' strike. However much Lloyd would have wanted to drop everything to help him, he knew that his stepfather might not be in a position to do so.

'I would like to let my family know where I am. They will be worried about me.'

'You said you were staying at an inn,' Porter prompted.

'I telephone them every night.'

'Proper mammy's boy sissy, aren't you?'

'You can't keep me here another day.'

'I'm the officer of the day and I can do exactly that,' Porter contradicted. 'You've been formally arrested so we can keep you here until you go before the magistrates' court. And there won't be one of those until Monday morning.'

'I'm entitled to legal representation.'

'Not on a Sunday in Brecon you're not. It's my guess that the sergeant will keep you on ice for another twenty-four hours. He'll want to talk to you before you go to court, but there's plenty of time. All day, in fact. Not that you'll be able to add much of any interest to Mr Pritchard's sworn statements. We've all the evidence we need to send you down. The only thing left for the magistrate to do is sentence you. And my money's on five to ten years' hard labour.'

'Doesn't "innocent until proven guilty" apply in Brecon?' Harry closed his eyes momentarily against the pain.

'We have the crache, we have hardworking ordinary people, we have layabouts and, at the bottom of the pile, we have incoming thieving scum who strut around wearing gold cufflinks and tiepins.' Porter nodded to the tea and sandwich. 'Eat your breakfast.'

Constable Smith murmured, 'Perhaps we should—'

'Eat our own breakfast, Smith,' Porter interrupted. 'Good idea. Lock him in.'

Harry shuddered when he heard the key grate in the lock again. He jumped down from the bunk and leaned unsteadily against the small shelf. He tipped the blood-stained water from the cup into the bucket, rinsed it out and filled it with clean from the jug. Dipping a square of handkerchief in, he bathed his face again. The water was tepid, and soon it was as red as the water he had discarded.

Holding a dry piece of handkerchief over his nostrils, he pinched them in an effort to stop the blood from flowing. He wasn't hungry but he was thirsty. His cup of tea had cooled, and there were greenish lumps of discoloured milk floating on the surface. He placed it back, untouched, on the saucer and poked the sandwich. It was hard and stale. He opened the enormous slices. A thin layer of peculiar pink meat lay between the pieces; there was no butter.

He returned to the steel shelf, bundled his jacket back into a makeshift pillow again, lay down and, having nothing better to do, tried to formulate a plan of action.

Top of the list was to get himself out of the cell, he reflected grimly. Then he would find Brecon Workhouse, and get the Ellises released, if not into his care, then into his parents'.

And once he'd taken them out? What then? Find out who owned the Ellis Estate and employed Bob Pritchard, and take them to task. He wondered what kind of unprincipled individual or organization would employ a criminal so devoid of principles that he'd rape and steal from defenceless people?

If he could track down enough current or past tenants to speak out against the agent, he'd ask his solicitors to make a case against the man. But would any of the women admit to being raped when it would be their reputations that would suffer, not Bob Pritchard's?

He didn't doubt that his mother would help him to get Mary out of the workhouse and the children out of the orphanage wing, but even if he paid all their debts he might not be able to get the Ellis Estate back for them, and that left him with the problem of finding somewhere for the family to live and some way for them to earn their keep.

He imagined Mary Ellis in the grey uniform dress and wooden clogs he had seen the inmates wearing in Pontypridd Workhouse. She was used to hard work but not the mind-destroying scrubbing of outside yards and paving, which he had seen the female inmates being forced to do on the rare occasions when the huge double doors at the side of the building had been left open. And he could only imagine how desperate she felt at being separated from her brothers and sister.

His nose hurt and his head ached, but he was too restless to continue lying on the bunk. He started pacing the cell. Seven steps one way, three the other, and they weren't big steps. He looked up at the narrow window. The sill began about a foot above his head. He reached up, locked his fingers around the bars and pulled himself up. The pavement was at eye level.

'What a way to spend a Sunday morning,' he muttered. He lowered himself to the floor and pulled himself up again – and again and again – in an effort to work off the frustration and the anger he felt towards Porter for pushing him downstairs, the authorities for allowing a hardworking family like the Ellises to be separated and destroyed, but most of all, towards Robert Pritchard, who had abused the power with which he'd been entrusted.

He started counting the number of times he pulled himself up – one, two – and when he reached sixty the key turned in the lock. He dropped to the floor.

Constable Smith coughed in embarrassment. 'Your solicitor and your father are here. Why didn't you tell us that your father is an MP?'

'Because it shouldn't have made any difference. Every man is innocent until proven guilty – that is the law of this country, isn't it? The one you swore to uphold.' Harry walked to the bunk and picked up his jacket.

The officer shifted his weight uneasily from one foot to the other. 'The sergeant's with them. They're waiting in his office.' He held out Harry's belt, braces, sock suspenders and shoelaces. 'Do you want me to help you to put them on?'

Harry took them from him and handed him the jug. 'I can manage but I'd appreciate some clean water and a towel so I can clean up my face. A mirror might be useful as well,' he called after Smith.

Chapter 21

LLOYD JUMPED up in horror when Harry walked through the door. 'You had a few bruises yesterday but nothing like this. What happened?'

'Should we send for a doctor, Harry?' Mr Richards asked. The elderly man had been his mother's solicitor and their closest family friend ever since Harry could remember.

'I asked if I could see one earlier. Constable Porter told me that he didn't have the authority to send for one on a Sunday.' Suddenly dizzy, Harry almost fell into the chair Lloyd vacated for him.

'Is this indicative of the treatment you mete out to people you arrest, Sergeant?' Lloyd enquired icily.

'Constable Porter?' the sergeant shouted. The officer came running. 'You refused to call a doctor for Mr Evans?'

'I didn't think his injuries were serious enough to call the doctor out on a Sunday, Sergeant,' the constable muttered.

'And how did Mr Evans come by his injuries?'

'Mr Evans fell down the steps when I was escorting him to the cells.'

Harry gazed at Porter as coolly as someone with two black eyes and a bloody nose could. 'I was pushed.'

'Is that right, Constable?' the sergeant asked the officer in an ominously low voice.

'If I touched Mr Evans it was to help him to his feet, sir.'

'I am so sorry that I misunderstood your actions, Constable. Perhaps it was the second blow that made me warier of you than I should have been,' Harry said sarcastically.

'Do you want to make a formal complaint, Mr Evans?' the sergeant enquired officiously.

'I most certainly do,' Harry answered decisively. 'If only to prevent similar accidents happening to other unfortunates on their way to the cells.'

'You do realize that a formal complaint would mean putting a man's job on the line,' the sergeant warned.

'Yes,' Harry replied shortly.

The sergeant saw Constable Porter still standing in the doorway. 'That will be all, Constable.'

'Sergeant.' The officer disappeared down the corridor.

'However, whether you make a complaint against Constable Porter or not is immaterial to the cause of your arrest, Mr Evans.' The sergeant pulled a sheaf of papers in front of him. 'You will appear before the magistrates tomorrow morning to answer to the charges of theft of one silver pocket watch, property of Mr Robert Pritchard, and assault on the same Mr Robert Pritchard. Both the assault and theft having taken place in the early hours on the morning of Saturday, the seventh of August at the Ellis Estate. Mr Robert Prichard has made a statement to the effect that you attacked him without provocation and hit him severely about the head when he was engaged in legitimate business on behalf of the owners of the Ellis Estate, E and G Estates. Do you have anything to say at this time, Mr Evans?'

'Mr Robert Pritchard is the agent for E and G Estates?' Mr Richards asked.

'Yes, they are the largest landowners in Breconshire, which makes Mr Robert Prichard an important man in the town,' the sergeant declared. If he'd hoped to intimidate Harry, Lloyd or Mr Evans, he was disappointed.

'You have heard of E and G Estates, Mr Richards?' Harry asked.

'I have.'

'Then you will probably be aware of the respect their agent commands in this town, sir,' said the sergeant. 'Mr Pritchard doesn't simply collect rents. He sells livestock, feed, crops and the produce from Estate properties on behalf of the tenants. He is highly respected by the auctioneers and market traders, and his activities are vitally important to the commercial life of the town—'

'We understand the gist of what you are telling us, Sergeant,' Mr Richards interrupted.

Rebuked, the sergeant addressed Harry again. 'Do you or do you not want to comment on the charges at this time, Mr Evans?'

'Only to say that it was Robert Pritchard who attacked me when I stopped him from assaulting Mary Ellis.'

'That is a grave accusation for anyone to make, especially against a respected member of the community,' the sergeant said heavily. 'I advise you to consider your position very carefully, Mr Evans. If you hope to draw attention away from the charges levelled at you by making counter-accusations of a more serious nature against Mr Pritchard or Constable Porter, your ploy could backfire with adverse and severe consequences for yourself.'

'I suggest you contact Mary Ellis who will verify my version of the events of that night.'

'According to Constable Porter's report, Mary Ellis is a moral degenerate who has been placed in the workhouse.'

'She is no more degenerate than any other respectable, family-loving woman I know,' Harry countered angrily, 'and the last place she and her family should be is a workhouse.'

'I can see that we are not going to make any progress this morning, Mr Evans.' The sergeant pushed a piece of paper in front of Lloyd. 'Will you sign this assurance that your son will appear before the magistrates tomorrow morning at nine o'clock? And that he will not leave town before then?'

'I have taken a suite at the Castle Hotel; we will be there until this matter is cleared up,' Lloyd pulled a fountain pen from his top pocket and scribbled his signature at the bottom of the form, 'speedily, I trust. I have urgent parliamentary business to attend to.'

Mr Richards took Harry's arm as he left his seat. 'We'll call for a doctor as soon as we reach the hotel.'

'I'm sorry to put you to all this trouble.' Harry was touched by the old man's concern. Given Mr Richards's age and frailty, he felt that he should be the one assisting him.

'I have a feeling that you are going to be sorrier still before the day is out,' Mr Richards commented enigmatically. 'Your father and I took a taxi from the station, and asked the driver to wait. Looking at you, I think it is just as well that we did.'

'There is something that I have to do before I leave.' Harry went to the desk. 'Constable Smith, my property, if you please. And I recall exactly what I had when I came in here.'

'You may have problems breathing through your nose for a while, young man, and your bruises could inspire another verse of "*Two Lovely Black Eyes*", but you'll live to fight another day.' The doctor closed his bag and reached for his coat.

'I hope not, Doctor,' Lloyd left his chair. 'I think my son's done enough fighting in the last week to last him a year or two.'

Harry shook the doctor's hand. 'Thank you, I feel better already.'

'These may help.' The doctor placed a bottle of pills on the table. 'If the pain gets too much, you can take two with water, but not more than every four hours. On the other hand, should you prefer to imbibe, a glass of brandy would probably have the same effect.'

'I'll see you out and pay your bill, Doctor.' Lloyd shrugged on his coat. 'I'll meet you in the bar Mr Richards; we'll have a quick one before lunch. I promised Sali I would telephone to let her and the girls know what was happening. You have no idea of the worry you have caused, Harry.'

'I'd argue with you there, Dad.'

'Brandy or pills, Harry?' Mr Richards asked after Lloyd left the hotel suite with the doctor.

'Brandy.' Harry tried to smile but every muscle in his face hurt and his nose felt numb and stiff.

'Then let's go downstairs. Given the state of your jacket, it will have to be the "Gentlemen only". They won't mind you sitting in shirt-sleeves. I'm glad we have these few minutes to ourselves, there's something that I want to talk to you about.'

Harry knew better than to hurry the old man, and Mr Richards waited until they were comfortably settled in the bar with two double brandies in front of them before broaching the subject again.

'Your father was telling me on the journey here that you may not go to Paris after all.'

'It is a possibility.' Harry sat back and savoured the sensation of warming brandy hitting his empty stomach.

'But you're not sure about running the businesses that you have inherited.'

'No, I'm not.' Harry stared into his brandy glass. 'I told Dad that I would think about it, but with everything's that been happening I haven't had time.'

'Cigar?' Mr Richards opened his cigar case and offered Harry one. They were thin and black, his favourite small Havanas.

'Thank you, but I'd prefer to have one after the meal if I may. I feel light-headed enough after the brandy.'

'I should imagine you do, given your injuries. Tell me, do you have an opinion on E and G Estates?'

'They are a disgrace to the name of the landlord, and whoever owns it should be ashamed of themselves for employing an agent like Robert Pritchard and not monitoring his activities,' he said heatedly. 'They have caused untold misery to dozens if not a hundred or more families around here. They handed their agent the power and the means to assault and thieve from helpless people, and all in the name of profit.'

'Unfortunately, I agree with you, Harry.'

'Why unfortunately?' Harry asked suspiciously.

Mr Richards met Harry's eye. 'E and G Estates was set up by Edyth and Gwilym James. You own it.'

'I . . .' Harry stammered into silence, barely able to comprehend the gravity of what Mr Richards had told him. He thought of all the lectures Lloyd had given him on the responsibilities of wealth and being an employer. How families depended on the wages his companies paid their breadwinners. And how tiresome he had found them. And now . . . 'Does anyone else know I own it?' he croaked, hoarse with shock.

'The entire board and the trustees who work in the Capital and Counties Bank, and my office, which is nominally in charge of the firm.'

'My father?' Harry asked.

'You know that he has deliberately distanced himself from the day-to-day running of your businesses and your money.'

'I wish he hadn't,' Harry said feelingly.

'So he could have done what you should have?' Mr Richards questioned. 'If he had spent his time overseeing your estate, Harry, he wouldn't have been able to stand as an MP or work for the miners' unions.'

Harry recalled the pocket watch he had found. 'Robert Pritchard has been working for E and G Estates for over ten years. He was given his job when I was still in school.'

'And in short trousers,' Mr Richards said. 'No one can blame you for hiring him then, Harry.'

'I *can* blame myself for not finding out about him since. Did you know that the estate sold the farms to the tenant farmers in nineteen nineteen only to buy them back for half the price they paid for them when the slump came and the banks that held their mortgages foreclosed?'

'Yes.'

'And you did nothing to stop it!'

'Harry, I am your mother's adviser and solicitor. I am not and never have been one of your trustees. And even if I had been, and had seen fit to question what E and G Estates were doing on moral grounds, the bankers would have reminded me that someone had to buy up the bankrupt farms, so why not E and G Estates? They would have also shown me a balance sheet to prove that your money was doing exactly what money should – making more money. You may not be aware of it but you are a millionaire, Harry. I doubt there are more than ten in Wales.'

'But my mother, Uncle Joey, they are on the board—'

'And they know everything there is to know about Gwilym James the department stores. They have ensured that all six are managed the way ideal businesses should be, with profit, customers and – very importantly – employees in mind. The staff are treated fairly and paid well in return for hard work. The conditions and contracts of employments are excellent, and the side benefits of paid holidays, medical care, subsidized canteens and retirement pensions among the best in Britain. All of that is down to your

353

mother and uncle. But they only oversee the stores. E and G Estates is the province of the bankers and solicitors on the board.'

'And they don't care how they make their money?' Harry asked furiously.

'*Your* money, Harry,' Mr Richards corrected. 'And in answer to your question, all they care about is doing their job to the best of their ability, making their employer rich and seeing a balance sheet in the black at the end of the year.'

'As if all I care about is money,' Harry declared bitterly.

'Now that you know about the situation, you can put it right.'

'It's too late for the Ellises and all the other families who have been broken up and dispersed in workhouses.'

'Is it, Harry?' Mr Richards said.

Harry glanced up as Lloyd entered the bar. 'Dad, what's wrong?'

White-faced, Lloyd sank down on to the chair next to Harry's. 'Craig y Nos telephoned the house this morning when they couldn't get through to you at the inn. Dad . . .'

Harry gripped his father's hand. 'I should have been there.'

'He died in his sleep, Harry, in the early hours. Doctor Adams told your mother that the end was quiet and peaceful. He never woke. It was what he wanted. We have to comfort ourselves with that thought.'

The next hour passed in a flurry of activity and telephone calls. Lloyd telephoned his brothers and agreed to meet them at the sanatorium so they could make arrangements to accompany their father's body back to Pontypridd.

Mr Richards contacted the senior staff in his office – judging by the sharp words he exchanged with them, they weren't happy at being disturbed on a Sunday – but they arranged for a clerk to bring all the papers he could find pertaining to E and G Estates on the first available train to Brecon.

Lloyd checked the time of the next train to Craig y Nos, and discovered he had time for lunch with Harry and Mr Richards, but none of them had much appetite, not even Harry who hadn't eaten for twenty-four hours. And they were all relieved when the taxi arrived to take Lloyd to the station.

'I only wish I could go with you,' Harry said, when he and Mr Richards accompanied Lloyd on to the platform.

'And I wish that I could stay here with you.'

'Don't worry about him, Lloyd. He won't be returning to any police cells,' Mr Richards stated confidently.

'Joey and Victor and I won't have anything to do other than make the necessary arrangements with the undertaker, and it won't take three of us to do that. If you did come you'd just be sitting around the inn with us, Harry.' Lloyd picked up his overnight case when the train drew in.

'I paid for my room on Friday and told Mrs Edwards that I'd be needing it for at least another week.'

'Do you want me to clear it for you and settle up with her?' Lloyd asked.

'No. If they let me go in the morning I'll come straight home, but afterwards – after Granddad is buried – I'll go back there. I would like to say goodbye to a few people.'

'See you soon, Harry. Mr Richards, thank you for coming up with me this morning and volunteering to stay with Harry.' Lloyd entered the nearest carriage.

'Tell everyone that I'll be home the moment this mess is cleared up,' Harry called out.

'I will.'

Mr Richards and Harry were standing watching the train pull out when a man walked up behind them and coughed diffidently.

'Mr Richards?'

Mr Richards turned around. 'Mr Beatty.' He shook his hand. 'You made good time. You have brought everything I asked for?'

'Yes, sir, all the files on E and G Estates.'

'Harry Evans, allow me to introduce Anthony Beatty, one of our clerks, who has been working on the E and G portfolio for three years. Have you lunched, Mr Beatty?'

'No, sir, there wasn't time,' the young man replied shyly.

'I'm sure they will be able to find you something at the hotel. I suggest we retire there, order refreshments and take a look at what you have in that briefcase.'

'No! Don't!' David Ellis flung himself between Iestyn Williams and Merlyn, the dog that had been his inseparable companion until the day before, when Iestyn had moved all the livestock from the Ellis Estate to his own farm.

'The dog went for me. He needs to be taught who's master.' Iestyn unfurled his horsewhip.

David struggled with the chain that fastened one end of Merlyn's collar to the wooden post in the centre of the farmyard. Iestyn unfurled the whip, lashed it and caught the dog's ear. Blood flowed. David unbuckled the dog's collar. 'Go, Merlyn, go, run . . . run . . .'

The dog hesitated and licked David's hand.

'Run, Merlyn!' David screamed. 'Run!'

The dog still lingered, crouching low, watching Iestyn furl his whip again.

'Run!' David struggled to his knees and slapped the dog's rump. Merlyn finally charged off, seconds before Iestyn cracked his whip short of his heels.

'Call him back,' Iestyn shouted.

'No.' David glared defiantly at his new employer.

'A shepherd's no good without his dog; call him back.'

'So you can whip him again?' David asked. 'No!'

The whip cracked, and caught David across the face. He grabbed it. The leather cut his hand, but he wrapped it around his fingers and tried to pull it from Iestyn.

'Let go.'

'No.' David tugged it, and Iestyn stumbled forward.

'Let go or I will complain to the workhouse master and it will go badly with your brothers and sisters,' Iestyn threatened.

David reluctantly released his hold. Iestyn cracked the whip again and caught David across the shoulders.

'I'll teach you to disobey me. That thieving son-in-law of mine will make me pay for that dog and you've sent it the devil only knows where. I should have left you in that workhouse. You spit on my Christian charity . . .'

David crouched on hands and knees, curling himself as small as he could to lessen the impact of the blows. When the pain began to consume him, he thought of Martha and Matthew, and the look of bewilderment on Matthew's face when he had sat up in the dormitory bed.

'Iestyn?'

David heard Mrs Williams. He opened his eyes and watched her long, thin feet, encased in pale-blue leather shoes, cross the farm-yard. A weakening tide of relief washed over him. No woman would stand by and watch her husband whip a helpless boy without lifting a finger to help the victim . . .

'You'll have to leave that until later. It's time to go to chapel.'

'I'll put him in the cellar.' Iestyn dropped the whip on to a stone wall. He walked up to David and kicked him in the ribs. 'Get up.'

David struggled to his knees only to fall back again. He had been locked into the dank cellar the night before and was in no hurry to return there.

'Get up!' Iestyn kicked him again.

'I can't stand,' David mumbled.

'Then crawl.'

David did just that. He struggled to the door behind the kitchen. Hauling himself up on the metal rail set in the stone wall, he inched his way down the steps. Before he reached the bottom Iestyn Williams slammed and locked the door.

He was back in the cold and dark. But he had never been afraid of the dark and he was used to the cold winters on the mountain. The pain was bad but he had two good thoughts to cling to. He had prevented Matthew and Martha from being thrashed. And he was alone with his memories – the happy ones.

The grief at his grandfather's death, so long anticipated yet so sudden at the end, consumed Harry. It was a raw and constant pain that was almost physical. But Mr Richards forced him to con-centrate on the task in hand. And the first papers he handed to him were Robert Pritchard's balance sheets.

Harry was shocked to see that the agent had banked less than twenty pounds against the Ellis Estate's arrears of rent in the last year. He recalled the back-breaking work he and David had put into carting the 120 fleeces that the Ellises had put aside to sell to the wool merchant – and they had been a fraction of what Robert Pritchard had taken from the sheep pens. He thought of the long hours Mary spent making cheeses, churning butter, scouring milk churns, trussing poultry. Even little Matthew collecting eggs. To his own knowledge, the agent had taken cartloads of fleeces, dairy produce, poultry, eggs, sheep and bullocks that had had to be worth twenty times that amount.

And it wasn't only the Ellises. Some of the other farms that the agent collected rents from seemed to produce absolutely nothing, or were boarded and derelict.

Harry set his coffee cup back on the tray of refreshments that Mr Richards had ordered to be brought to their suite. 'I don't understand, Mr Beatty.' He rifled through the papers on his lap. 'How can E and G Estates be making any money when the agent collects so little in rent?'

'A proportion of E and G Estates holdings are a tax loss, Mr Evans.' Mr Beatty held out his cup when Mr Richards offered to refill it. 'Basically, the company has so many assets it doesn't matter if a quarter, or even half, don't make any profit, or even if they lose money, because the loss can be offset against the returns on the more lucrative properties. And E and G makes thousands of pounds from the buildings you own and rent out in the centre of Cardiff and London.'

'London?'

'Yes, Harry, London,' Mr Richards affirmed. 'I did tell you that you are an extremely wealthy young man.'

'As I was saying, Mr Evans, sir, the farms might be idle but we can offset the cost of keeping the houses boarded up and maintaining the land for possible future cultivation against the profits of your urban rentals. All the bankers want to see is an account sheet that balances. And E and G Estates has always had one of those. It is only the bottom figure that counts, and that is, and always has been, black not red.'

'I know how much the agent has taken from the Ellis Estate in the last month and barely a fraction of it is detailed on this sheet.' Harry tapped the paper in his hand. 'Do you know the agent, Robert Pritchard?'

'No, sir, I don't,' Anthony Beatty replied.

'Have you ever met him?'

'No, sir.'

'Who appointed him?'

'I believe the directors of the Capital and Counties Bank advertised and interviewed for the post, sir. That is the usual way of filling a vacancy.'

'It is, Harry.' Mr Richards offered his cigar case around, and this time Harry took one.

'You didn't sit on the interview panel?' Harry asked the clerk.

'No, sir. Someone in my position in the firm wouldn't. And as you see from this letter offering Mr Pritchard a contract, he started working for the company over ten years ago. I only joined the firm four years ago.'

'What do you want to do, Harry?' Mr Richards asked.

Harry shuffled the papers together. 'These prove the agent has defrauded one tenant and – when we track down and interview the others, especially the ones he has evicted – I'm certain that we'll be able to prove that he has defrauded more. Not to mention E and G Estates, because it appears that very little of what he collected from the tenants found its way into the company account. Given the fraud and the amount of produce he purloined from the Ellises, we can also prove that he perjured himself by stating that the family were in serious arrears. He had absolutely no right to evict them. And when we find Mary Ellis she will corroborate my story and confirm that Robert Pritchard assaulted me, not the other way around. Hopefully that will persuade the police to drop the charges that led to my arrest.'

'Arrest, Mr Evans, sir?' Anthony Beatty exclaimed.

'It's a long story, Mr Beatty. I also need to look into Iestyn Williams's affairs. I heard him tell Robert Pritchard that there was no need to send the Ellises' stock to market, and that he would take the lot off his hands. That also sounds suspiciously like fraud to me.

Perhaps we can employ a detective to investigate the dealings of both men. I would do it myself, but my first priority has to be to my family. And I would like to return to Pontypridd as soon as possible.'

'May I suggest that we pay Robert Pritchard a visit so he can drop the charges against you?' Mr Richards placed his cigar in the ashtray.

'That would be a start, and my second priority has to be to get the Ellis children and Mary Ellis out of the workhouse.'

'That may take some time, Harry,' Mr Richards warned. 'But our visit to Mr Pritchard can be made right away.'

Bob the Gob lived in an impressive four-storey, doubled-fronted Georgian house in Wheat Street, in the centre of Brecon. The taxi cab that Mr Richards had insisted on calling for Harry's sake stopped outside the front door. Harry looked up and saw fine lace fluttering out of the open windows and the sound of a piano being played.

'Mr Beatty?' Mr Richards took the briefcase from the clerk. 'Would you be kind enough to knock on the door and inform whoever answers it that the owner of E and G Estates wishes to see Mr Pritchard on urgent business? When you have done that, would you please take this taxi and go to the police station. Ask to see the sergeant, not a constable. I warn you that may mean a longish wait. Ask him to send an officer to arrest Mr Pritchard for fraud. Tell him we have all the evidence he needs. If he should argue with you, mention Mr Lloyd Evans's name and warn him that the MP is a personal friend of the chief constable.'

Anthony Beatty left the taxi and knocked at the door. Harry sat back, away from the taxi window, and watched. A maid in a black dress, lace afternoon cap and apron opened it. She bobbed a curtsy. Anthony Beatty raised his bowler and spoke to her.

She listened, turned and ran back up a staircase carpeted in red plush. A few minutes later Robert Pritchard walked down the stairs, buttoning his jacket and straightening his tie. He offered his hand. The clerk shook it and returned to the taxi.

'Are you sure that you want to face the man now, Harry? We

can wait for the police.' Mr Richards lifted the briefcase from the seat.

Harry wasn't at all sure, but said, 'Let's get it over with.' He left the back of the cab and held the door open for Anthony to get in.

Robert Pritchard was shaking hands with Mr Richards when he caught sight of Harry. 'I don't know what you are doing out of your cell, but I don't allow filth over my doorstep.'

'Oh, I think you'll make an exception for me, Pritchard,' Harry said curtly. 'I own E and G Estates.'

The agent opened and shut his mouth like a goldfish scooped out of water.

'Mr Evans is correct, Mr Pritchard,' Mr Richards confirmed. 'And, as we have business to conduct, I believe it would be better if we discussed it inside.'

Unable to look either Harry or Mr Richard in the eye, the agent focused on an indeterminate point across the street. Eventually, he stepped back and opened the door wider. 'If you want to discuss business, you had better come into my office,' he muttered. 'Close the front door behind you.'

He led the way, walking to the right of the staircase and down a dark, narrow passageway. He opened a door in the back wall to reveal a large room that overlooked the yard behind the house. The only window faced a brick wall, and Harry had the feeling that he had walked from bright afternoon into evening twilight.

It didn't help that the office was furnished in age-blackened oak and the walls painted a sombre dark green. The fireplace filled one half of the longest wall on their left. It was heavily carved in Jacobean style, whether real or reproduction, Harry couldn't tell. He knew very little about antiques, but he placed it in a different era to the house.

A glass-framed tapestry firescreen hid the fire basket and chimney. The fire irons in the hearth resembled the instruments of torture Harry had seen in continental museums, and he wondered if they had been made by a local blacksmith who had overdosed on Gothic novels. A red-and-green Turkish rug covered most of the floor. In the exact centre of the room, and dominating it, stood an antique oak desk, the largest Harry had ever seen.

He recalled the desk Mary and David had mentioned when he had told them about quill pens, and wondered if the agent had earmarked the Ellis property for his own use. After seeing Iestyn Williams's wife wearing Mrs Ellis's jewellery, and eavesdropping on the conversation between Iestyn Williams and Robert Pritchard, he was certain the family's possessions hadn't been put into a fair and open auction. If they had raised any money at all, and not been stolen as he suspected, he was equally certain that the proceeds hadn't been deposited in either the Ellises' debit account or declared to E&G Estates.

Two enormous leather chairs on the same scale as the desk stood either side of the fireplace. A matching, lower-back sofa faced the hearth between them. There were various corner cupboards and sideboards, all in the same dark carved oak, but Harry's attention was drawn to four bureau bookcases. The glass doors above the drop-down desks appeared to be locked, but behind them he could see files and notebooks, some clearly marked E&G Estates.

There were more oil paintings on the walls than there were in the average gallery. Most were old, and Harry recognized that a couple were the result of creative inspiration, a few were very good, the majority mediocre and a handful indescribably bad. Slightly more than half were of local scenes. The rest were mainly portraits of stolid-looking men and women dressed in bygone fashions that weren't rich or ornamental enough to be aristocratic dress.

The room might be Robert Pritchard's office but Harry had the feeling that it served a double purpose as a clearing house for the goods that the agent appropriated from farmhouses 'in lieu of debt'.

Bob the Gob sat behind his desk. He pointed to two wooden upright chairs set in front of it but Mr Richards wasn't to be so easily manipulated.

'As we have serious matters to discuss, it might be as well if we sit over here.' Mr Richards took the left-hand leather chair, Harry the right, leaving Bob Pritchard with no choice but to sit on the low sofa between them.

'You said that you own E and G Estates. I find that difficult to believe,' Bob challenged, with less arrogance that he had exhibited when he had evicted the Ellises. 'I have worked for the company for eleven years, ever since I was invalided out of the army.' He paused, clearly hoping that they would ask about his heroic exploits on the Western Front. When they didn't, he continued. 'In all that time I have dealt with Mr Owens at the Capital and Counties Bank, and he has never mentioned a Harry Evans to me.'

'E and G Estates is part of a substantial trust—' Mr Richards began.

'Then you don't own it.' Pritchard turned on Harry. 'You have wormed your way into my house under false pretences and I am going to call the police.' He rose to his feet.

'I wouldn't if I were you, Mr Pritchard,' Mr Richards cautioned. 'And I wouldn't interrupt either Mr Evans or myself when we are speaking again. Mr Evans is set to inherit E and G Estates along with other holdings when he reaches his majority. Until that time, he will continue to receive the full support of every member of the board of trustees of his estate, just as he has done since he was named sole heir to the trust.'

The agent stopped in his tracks and turned to Harry. 'You really do own E and G Estates?'

'It is not the largest company I own, but it is one of them,' Harry confirmed.

Bob Pritchard continued to stand, transfixed, in the centre of the room, too stunned to move. 'It really is yours,' he muttered when he could finally speak again.

'It is. And I will never forgive myself for allowing a man like you to be given the authority to assault and rape helpless women, terrorize families, steal their possessions, evict them from their homes and ruin people's lives.'

For once, Bob Pritchard didn't deny the accusations levelled at him. 'You should have said. If you had said—'

'You wouldn't have raped Mary Ellis, intimidated her and her family, evicted them, attacked me or asked your policeman friend to arrest me?' Harry enquired coldly.

'I . . . I . . .'

'Sit down, Mr Pritchard. As employer and employee, you and I have a great deal to discuss.'

It had taken Harry a long time, but he felt that Lloyd would have been proud of him. He had finally begun to assume the responsibility of running one of his own companies.

Chapter 22

MR RICHARDS opened the discussion. He spoke softly, yet every word was precise, businesslike and to the point. Even when the solicitor had been a guest at their private family occasions, Harry had never seen him speak otherwise.

'We are here, Mr Pritchard, because we have been alerted to irregularities and discrepancies in the accounts that you have submitted to E and G Estates.' The old man looked intently at the agent, who still appeared to be in shock. 'You do understand what I am saying to you, Mr Pritchard?'

'There are no irregularities or discrepancies in the figures that I presented to Mr Owens.' The agent regained his composure sufficiently to raise his chin but Harry thought he detected a flicker of fear in his eyes.

'I'm afraid there are,' Harry contradicted. 'Mr Richards, if you'd be kind enough to show Mr Pritchard the evidence.'

The solicitor opened the briefcase he'd carried into the house and produced the records that Anthony Beatty had brought up from Pontypridd. He opened the topmost file and extracted a sheet of paper. 'I believe this to be a copy of the account you sent at the end of last month to the Capital and Counties Bank, detailing the produce – or lack of it – that you received from the Ellis Estate in the last quarter.'

'It could be, I don't know.' The agent shifted uneasily on the sofa.

'That is your signature.' Mr Richards held up the sheet of paper.

Robert Pritchard peered at it. 'It looks like it, but you can't expect me to remember everything I took as payment from the Ellises.'

'Then that balance sheet isn't accurate?' Harry challenged.

'Of course it is.'

'Either it is, or it isn't, Mr Pritchard, which is it?' Harry was surprised at his own insistence.

'If I signed it, it must be accurate.'

'If? You just admitted that the signature looked like yours.' Harry took the sheet from Mr Richards. 'I have seen for myself the amount of farm produce and livestock that you have taken from the Ellis Estate in the last quarter. None of it is mentioned here, yet I was assured by my clerk that these accounts are up to date, as of last Friday. I have also seen the records of the produce the Ellis family have given you over the last eight years, since the Ellis Estate was bought back by E and G Estates. None of it has appeared on any of the balance sheets you sent to the bank.'

'What records? None of the Ellises can read or write,' the agent said scornfully.

'Nevertheless, they have invented a system that records the productivity of the farm and the produce they give you or – to be more accurate – you take.'

'Anyone who says that I have taken anything from the Ellis Estate in the last quarters is lying.' Pritchard blustered. 'The Ellises are idle beggars. They're incapable of running a small farm, let alone one the size of the Ellis Estate. That's why I turned them off it. And I didn't go to all the trouble of arranging the eviction with the police, the workhouse master and hiring the bailiffs for my own benefit. I did it for E and G Estates. The Ellises haven't paid a penny off their rent arrears for months—'

'Yes, they have,' Harry countered baldly.

'Are you accusing me of lying?'

'Yes.'

Bob Pritchard rose to his feet and loomed threateningly over Harry. 'Is this all the gratitude I'm going to get for giving E and G Estates my undivided loyalty? For devoting the best years of my life to the company?'

'The Ellises are not the only family that you have cheated, robbed and evicted. There are others, and I intend to speak to all of my present and as many of my previous tenants as I can. I am certain that once we get them into a court of law, and ask them to swear to "tell the truth, the whole truth and nothing but the truth" on a Bible, they will have some interesting things to say about you and your methods of collecting rent, Mr Pritchard.'

'You have nothing but hearsay—'

Mr Richards tapped the briefcase. 'We have a great deal more, Mr Pritchard. And I suspect that the account books, ledgers and files in those bureau bookcases will also make interesting reading.'

'Those are my personal and private papers.'

'Marked E and G Estates,' Mr Richards said.

'They are personal observations.' The agent's face reddened. 'You have no right to come into my house and look at my personal papers—'

'I have every right, as your employer, to look at papers pertaining to the company *I* own. And when they arrive, the police will agree with me.'

'If that's a threat, it's not going to work,' Bob blustered. 'I *know* the local police.'

'Then you admit you bribe them?' Harry enquired coolly.

'I admit nothing of the kind. They are sensible men. They know the truth when it's staring them in the face.' The agent paced to the desk. 'They'll realize that you've concocted a pack of lies.'

'We have sent Mr Beatty to the police station to request that the police arrest you for fraud, Mr Pritchard. All the evidence the officers will need is here.' Mr Richards held up the briefcase again. 'Coupled with the sworn statement that Mr Evans is prepared to make, I think that you'll find the case against you overwhelming.'

The agent made one last desperate attempt to unnerve them. 'It will be Mr Evans's word against mine. He may be someone in Pontypridd but he is no one in Brecon.'

'He is your employer and the owner of half the farms in the county, Mr Pritchard,' Mr Richards reminded him.

'I believe I have only uncovered the tip of an iceberg of deceit, fraud and crime perpetrated by you and your associates,' Harry informed the agent icily. 'And I am confident that a full investigation will discover a great deal more. If the local police do not have the resources to organize one, then I am prepared to pay private detectives to carry out the work for them.'

The colour drained from Bob Pritchard's face. He fell into the chair behind his desk.

'I suggest you think very carefully about your situation, Mr Pritchard,' Mr Richards cautioned. 'We know that you have defrauded tenants and E and G Estates. However, there are still a few things that you can do to lessen the prison sentence you will undoubtedly receive and possibly even the number of charges you will face.'

'Prison?' the agent croaked.

'If you make a full and comprehensive confession, and produce your private account books – that's if you kept any – and your personal bank statements and a breakdown of all the money and goods that you have stolen from the tenants as well as the company, it is possible that the trustees and Mr Evans may look more leniently at your case and not press every charge against you. Am I correct in that assertion, Mr Evans?'

'The most important thing at the moment is to calculate the exact amount that you have stolen from my tenants so they can be recompensed,' Harry said firmly. 'That takes precedence over the money you have stolen from me.'

'Stolen—'

'I can't think of any other word that describes what you have done,' Harry interrupted. 'I would also like an exact account of the business dealings and relationship between Iestyn Williams and yourself. I heard him offer to take the Ellis livestock off your hands "to save you going to market". Was that the normal arrangement at evictions?'

The agent sank his head in his hands. Harry glanced across at Mr Richard who was sitting as calm and composed as if he were in his own sitting room in Pontypridd.

Footsteps sounded on the stairs and along the corridor. There was a knock at the door, followed a few seconds later by another.

'Shouldn't you see who that is, Mr Pritchard?' Mr Richards prompted.

The agent left the sofa, walked to the door and opened it.

A young woman stood framed in the doorway. She was a little below average height, with white-gold hair and grey eyes.

'Excuse me, gentlemen,' she smiled. 'The girl told me that you have visitors, Robert. I would like to offer them some refreshment.'

Her husband continued to stare at her, dumbstruck.

Mr Richards rose from his seat. 'I am Mr Richards and this is Mr Evans, the owner of E and G Estates.' Mr Richards offered the woman his hand, and Harry followed suit.

She shook their hands and waited for her husband to effect the introductions. When he didn't, she introduced herself. 'I am Carys Pritchard, Robert's wife.' She blushed. 'I am sorry, I should have liked to have met Robert's employer before now, Mr Evans, but then you must know that Robert and I have only been married three weeks.'

'I didn't, Mrs Pritchard.' Harry couldn't bring himself to be hypocritical enough to offer the usual congratulations. 'I am pleased to make your acquaintance.'

'I only wish we could have met under better circumstances, Mrs Pritchard,' Mr Richards apologized.

'Better circumstances?' She looked from Mr Richards to Harry in alarm.

'I think we should leave Mr Pritchard with his wife so he can explain matters to her in private, Mr Evans. We will wait for you in the hall, Mr Pritchard. Mr Evans has urgent family business in Pontypridd. I trust that you will drop the charge of assault against him as soon as the police arrive.'

Carys Pritchard, who had only heard her husband's version of events, looked at Bob in amazement when he nodded agreement.

'One more thing, Mr Pritchard.' Harry avoided Carys Pritchard's eye. 'As of now, you are no longer E and G's agent.' He followed Mr Richards into the passageway and closed the door. A few seconds later they heard a woman cry.

Harry stepped off the Pontypridd train, handed his ticket to the collector in his box and ran down into Station Yard. His mother had parked her car close to the entrance so he wouldn't miss her. Her hand flew to her mouth when she saw him.

'Harry, your face!'

He glanced at the jacket of his suit that he'd folded over his arm to make sure that the bloodstains couldn't be seen. 'I'm fine, Mam, it looks worse than it is.'

She wrapped her arms around him and hugged him. 'Why are you in shirt-sleeves in the middle of town? You didn't travel that way, I hope.'

'I used my jacket to clean my face.' Harry tried to smile and it hurt. 'Towels and flannels appear to be in short supply in police stations.'

'I should have given Lloyd some clothes for you.'

'It doesn't matter; I'll have a bath and change as soon as I get home. How's Edyth?'

Sali gave a small smile. 'The doctors have said they'll allow her home for Granddad's funeral, provided she stays with the mourners in the house and takes life quietly for a month or two.'

'So, you're going to tie her to her bed?'

'I'm considering it.'

'Is Dad back yet?'

'He telephoned from the Swansea Valley before I left to meet you. He and your uncles are staying at the inn overnight and won't be home until tomorrow.' She opened the car and stepped inside.

Harry closed the door for her and walked around to the passenger side. 'Are they bringing Granddad home?'

'Yes. Mari is clearing our small drawing-room so we can place his coffin in there.'

'A lot of people will want to pay their respects.' Harry sat beside her.

'Lloyd talked it over with Joey and Victor. It made more sense to bring him to our house, because Victor's farm is a good half-hour walk from Tonypandy, and Joey and Rhian's spare parlour can't be shut off from the rest of the house as easily as ours.' She drove out on to Tumble Square and turned left into Taff Street. 'It will be different when the coffin is actually in the house but at the moment I can't believe he's gone. That I will never see him again.' She fought back tears and concentrated on the road.

'I know just how you feel.'

'We've never really talked about our life before I married Lloyd, Harry. Do you remember much?'

'Not a great deal. I can recall living in a horrible dirty house with a woman who beat me and had a son who was bigger and stronger than me and beat me even more. I remember you coming to get me and living with Dad, Granddad and the uncles, and from then on all I remember are good times, except for the strikes when there was a lot of fighting, in school as well as the streets, and never enough to eat. I don't mean in our house, I mean the valley.'

'Your grandfather treated me like a member of the family from the day I started work as his housekeeper.' Sali slowed and drove past a charabanc full of elderly women on their way to chapel. 'It's hard to believe now, but I was too frightened to tell him that I had a child because I thought he wouldn't allow me to stay in his house and then I wouldn't have had the money to pay that vile woman who was supposed to be looking after you. The moment he found out you existed, he sent me and your uncles to get you and from then on he didn't treat you any differently from the way he would have a grandson of his own. That meant a great deal to me because it was two years before I married Lloyd.'

'These past few weeks have been dreadful and wonderful in turns. It was dreadful to watch his health deteriorate but wonderful to have the time to talk to him.' The enormity of Billy's death finally began to sink in, and Harry steeled himself to face his family's grief as well as his own.

'No regrets about giving up the Paris trip to go to the Swansea Valley?'

'None. I only wish I had been with him at the end.'

'You couldn't have done anything if you had been. He died in his sleep,' she consoled.

'I know, Dad told me.'

They fell silent, each lost in their own memories. Eventually Harry asked. 'How are the girls?'

'Broken-hearted like the rest of us. When Mr Richards telephoned and said that you were coming down on this train, I called Rhian and Megan and invited them and your cousins for the evening. Mari's made a cold supper. I thought it might help if we all sat together to eat, drink and share our memories of Granddad.'

Harry laid his hands over his mother's on the steering wheel. 'I think a wake is a wonderful idea and the very best way to honour him.'

'Please, Harry, don't say any more. Not until we reach home. I can barely see the road for tears as it is.'

'I remember the nineteen eleven strike.' Megan looked at her four sons, 'Your poor grandfather had terrible trouble keeping your Uncle Joey and your father under control.'

'And Uncle Lloyd?' Tom, one of her twins, asked.

'Your Uncle Lloyd was the sensible one, even then. There was fighting practically every night in the square, and the police used to chase the strikers through the streets. Your Uncle Joey always used to run and hide under Aunty Betty's parlour table.' She smiled at the widow who had become Billy's housekeeper after Sali and Lloyd had left to live in Ynysangharad House. Betty had moved up to Victor and Megan's farm with Billy when he had decided to help run the farm, and had stayed on to give Megan a hand with the dairy and her children.

'Your grandfather used to spend more time in the police station, trying to bail out his sons, than some of the policemen who worked there,' Betty Morgan declared.

'I remember Granddad giving me my first small glass of beer when I was six,' Harry confided. 'It was Christmas. We were all in Ynysangharad House, and he caught me trying to sneak whisky from a decanter. But instead of telling me off, as I expected him to, he gave me some of his beer and made me promise not to drink whisky until I was a man.'

'He did the same thing with me,' Tom shouted.

'And me,' Tom's twin, Jack, chimed in.

'And me last Christmas.' Eddie, Joey's eldest son, brushed aside a tear and pretended he hadn't.

'And all of you boys thought we women didn't know what was going on.' Rhian hugged Eddie, to his acute embarrassment.

Mari jumped up as the telephone rang in the hall. She returned a few minutes later. 'Master Harry, it's for you. Mr Richards telephoning from Brecon.'

'Trouble?' Sali asked anxiously when Harry rose from his chair.

'Not for me,' Harry reassured her. 'Mr Richards and I went to the police station after they arrested the agent, and he dropped all the charges he made against me. This must be something else. I gave Mr Richards a list as long as my arm of urgent things that need doing for the company. I would have done them myself, but I wanted to be here. No, that's not right.' He ruffled Glyn's curls as he passed him and Bella, who were curled up in the same armchair, 'I needed to be here.' He went out into the hall and closed the door behind him, before picking up the receiver. 'Mr Richards?'

'Are you feeling any better, Harry?'

'Much, Mr Richards. Do you have any news?'

'I have made enquiries about removing the Ellis children from the workhouse. There are obstacles, Harry. They will only be released into the custody of a respectable married couple, widow or spinster.'

'I am sure that my parents will help as soon as they can spare the time.'

'And I doubt that your father will jeopardize his position as an MP,' Mr Richards countered. 'If he should decide to help the Ellis children, he will only do so by complying fully with the regulations laid down by the authorities. And that means more than paying lip service, Harry. To take on a family of five children with no means of support is a serious enterprise. Firstly, you need a guardian to take care of and assume responsibility for them on a daily basis; secondly, you have to find somewhere for them all to live; and thirdly, you have to train them for a vocation or profession so they can find work and support themselves. Your father has six children of his own besides you. It would be totally unreasonable of you to expect him to adopt the Ellises as well.'

'You're right.' Harry realized that if he were to get the Ellis children out of the clutches of the parish he would have to make provision for all their futures, including Luke's, and that meant planning for at least the next thirteen years until the boy could support himself.

'Have you thought where they will live?'

'The Ellis Estate. I intend to give it to them in recompense for everything the agent stole from them.'

'A laudable ambition, Harry, but I warn you, your trustees will never agree. I believe they will vote against you to prevent you from giving away your assets before you even inherit them.'

'Surely not when they hear the facts,' Harry argued. 'After what the agent did to the Ellises that property isn't morally mine.'

'The trustees were appointed to protect your estate until they can hand it over in its entirety on your thirtieth birthday. And they will do just that, Harry, even if it means protecting it against you. However, you can do what you like with it nine years from now. But before you make too many plans for the Ellis Estate. I spoke to one of the bailiffs who stripped what little there was from the house. He told me there is nothing left there, not a table, bed, bedding or, more importantly, livestock. No one can move in there until the farm is re-stocked and the house refurbished.'

'Could you make arrangements to have the place furnished and stocked for me, please, Mr Richards?'

'I have my own business to attend to in Pontypridd, Harry, and I have to return tomorrow. Besides, I think the next family who move in there should be the ones to furnish and stock the place.'

'You are right again, Mr Richards.' Harry realized that the Ellises were one problem he was not going to be able to pass on to someone else. 'My grandfather's funeral is on Saturday. I won't be able to leave here until then. But I'll telephone the inn and see if Mrs Edwards can find a cottage that I can rent for the Ellises until the house is ready for them.'

'That's if you manage to get them released, Harry.'

'I will,' Harry said with more confidence than he felt. 'Thank you for making the enquiries Mr Richards.'

'I will talk to the police again tomorrow before I leave Brecon. The evidence against Mr Pritchard is incontrovertible. As Mr Beatty has a thorough knowledge of E and G Estates and the company's accounts, I have taken the liberty of giving him permission to stay in the town to assist the police with their enquiries and do what he can to redress the damage inflicted on the company and the tenants by Robert Pritchard. But the trustees will need to appoint another agent as soon as possible, and until matters are sorted, I believe he will need an assistant to help him resolve the situation.'

Harry made a swift decision. 'I will call a meeting of the board as soon as possible so they can discuss it. Will you attend with me, Mr Richards?'

'If you think I can be of help, Harry.'

'I do. I can't thank you enough, Mr Richards.'

'You said that your grandfather's funeral will be held on Saturday?'

'Yes, in Trealaw cemetery.'

'Tell your mother that if there is anything – anything at all – that I can do to help with the arrangements, I will be back in Pontypridd tomorrow morning and I would consider it an honour. Oh, just one more thing. I have discovered the connection between Robert Pritchard and Iestyn Williams. The Mrs Pritchard we met is the agent's second wife. His first was Bronwen Williams, Iestyn Williams's daughter—'

'And my Aunty Megan's sister,' Harry breathed, wondering just what kind of a husband Robert Pritchard had been to her.

'She died in childbirth, two years ago.'

'We know.'

'Will you tell your aunt?'

'Yes. We are having a family wake for my grandfather but I will tell her before she leaves at the end of the evening, Mr Richards. Thank you again for everything you have done for me and E and G. I look forward to talking to you tomorrow.' Harry hung up the receiver.

'You will tell who what before she leaves at the end of the evening?' Sali was standing behind him.

'I didn't have much chance to talk to you about the agent who has been defrauding one of my companies.'

'Mr Richards told me a little when he telephoned to say that you were coming home.'

'The man who brought the charges against me, and who has been stealing from the tenants and the company, was married to Aunty Megan's sister, the one who died. Unfortunately, I am fairly sure that her father is also involved in the fraud.'

'Poor Megan,' Sali said feelingly. 'Would you like me to tell her?'

'No, it's my place to do that.'

'If you go into the study I'll send her in.'

'Not until we've finished talking about Granddad.' He slipped his arm around his mother's waist. 'I've discovered so much about him that I didn't know this evening.'

'I think we're all going to find out a lot more about Billy Evans over the next few days. He touched a lot of people's lives, and I've a feeling that there are tales that none of us know yet.'

Megan listened to Harry in silence then reached for her coat. 'I must get the children home. The boy will need help with the milking in the morning.'

'Aunty Megan, I'm sorry, I can't let this man get away with what he's done even though he's your brother-in-law,' he apologized. 'And the same goes for your father. If my suspicions are correct and he is involved in, if not exactly stealing, then taking advantage of people's misery to acquire their livestock at a knock-down price, I will charge him with fraud.'

'I wouldn't want or expect you to make allowances for either of them, Harry. Especially for my sake,' she said in surprise. 'I haven't seen my father, brothers and sisters in over fifteen years. And, after spending the evening talking about your grandfather, I realize that I don't even consider them as my family any more.'

'Don't you want to see your brothers or your one remaining sister?'

'Perhaps, if I ever find out where they are. But the fact that they haven't left their addresses with anyone in the valley suggests that they feel the same way about my father as I do. I need to talk to your Uncle Victor about this. He always comes up with answers to all my problems.'

'You don't want to see your father?' Harry had to be sure.

'Frankly, I wish I could disown him the way some parents do their children. I knew what he was when I was growing up, and I doubt he's changed. There are all sorts of questions I need to ask myself. Like what I would do if I discovered that my late sister played a part in her husband's schemes, and was stealing from people who could least afford it. I'd like to think that she wasn't, but as her widower and my father get along, it looks as though she married a man just like our father. Over the years it's been easier not to think about him than face up to the terrible things he did to try and separate me and your Uncle Victor, and what he succeeded in doing to my mother and brothers.'

'I'm sorry.'

'Don't be.' Megan gave him a brittle smile. 'You're just one of many Evanses I count myself lucky to be related to, Harry. I need to think about what you've just told me, and I won't be free to do that until after we have said goodbye to Dad.'

'This week is going to be a long one.'

'Isn't it?' She hugged him and kissed his cheek. 'Thank you for being tactful and being you, Harry. And for taking care of Dad for us. He was so proud of you.'

Saturday morning dawned dry and warm without a cloud in the sky. Harry stood in front of the open window of his bedroom, buttoning his shirt and waistcoat, his black tie slung around his neck. The garden had only been planted in the spring, but already there were roses on the mature bushes his mother had insisted on moving from Ynysangharad House, and the lavender cuttings had taken well, filling the air with their heady, late-summer scent.

It promised to be a hot day, the kind his grandfather had loved, and Harry resented the weather for being perfect when Billy Evans could no longer see the sun or flowers. Rain would have been easier to bear. He pushed in his stud, fastened his collar and looked at himself in the mirror.

'Harry?' Lloyd knocked the door.

'Come in.' Harry began to knot his tie.

Lloyd saw the grief etched in Harry's eyes. 'It's not too late to change your mind about being a bearer.'

'It seems right for Granddad to be carried to his grave by his sons and his eldest grandson. Although, strictly speaking, I wasn't—'

'You were,' Lloyd contradicted.

'Either way, I feel privileged to be able to help you, Uncle Joey and Victor to do that one small last thing for him.' Harry straightened his collar and peered critically into the mirror.

Lloyd picked up the gold cufflinks from the dressing table. They had belonged to Sali's Great-uncle Gwilym James and were part of Harry's inheritance. Harry only wore them on formal occasions. They were old-fashioned but he didn't mind, although his allowance would have run to modern, more fashionable replacements.

'Thank you.' Harry took them from him. 'Would you mind slipping them into my cuffs?'

'Mari always puts too much starch in our shirts.' Lloyd finally managed to push one of the links through the glossy, stiffened buttonhole. 'I feel so guilty,' he murmured. 'Dad wouldn't have been happy at the thought of being buried by Father Kelly. In fact, it wouldn't surprise me if he comes back to haunt your uncles and me for allowing it to happen.'

'He knew he'd have a Catholic funeral.' Harry held out his other cuff.

'He did?' Lloyd looked at him in amazement.

'He said he'd put up with it for his wife's sake. He also said that Isabella was such a saint she didn't need any more prayers, and he was such a sinner that he could do with all the help he could get to try to reach the same place as her.'

'That sounds like Dad.' Lloyd laughed.

'He also said that Father Kelly would persuade you to go along with him in the end, but that was all right too, because if the man ever found the sense to dump his religion he'd become a decent communist.'

'He and Father Kelly made a strange pair of friends.' Lloyd saw and looked away from the framed photograph of the entire family taken on Harry's twenty-first birthday. It hurt to know that no matter how many other family parties they'd have, his father would not be there.

Harry picked up his black hat, gloves and jacket. 'Father Kelly knows how Granddad felt about religion.'

'Joey, Victor and I have warned him not to overdo the sermonizing. Oh, I came up to tell you that your friend's arrived. He's downstairs.'

'Which friend?'

'The artist from the inn who follows Bella around like a moonstruck lapdog. He turned up with a wreath and asked to see you and Bella so he could offer his condolences.'

'It was good of him to come all this way.'

'I suppose it was.'

'You sound unconvinced.'

'If he's here to offer his sympathy to you, fine. If it's Bella he's after, I might throw a bucket of cold water over him.'

Lloyd and his brothers had arranged for the funeral to take place on a day and at a time that would allow every miner who wasn't actually working on shift an opportunity to pay his respects to Billy Evans. Instead of cars, they had hired an old-fashioned glass-sided hearse, and horse-drawn carriages to follow so that pedestrians would be able to keep up with the procession.

Lloyd, Joey, Victor and Harry carried Billy out of the house for the last time. His coffin was covered with white roses that Megan, Rhian and Sali had picked from their gardens. Lloyd had been forced to hire two more hearses for the flowers that had been arriving all week, sent and brought by neighbours and friends since the day Billy's coffin had arrived back in Pontypridd.

Men stopped and bared their heads, and women lowered their eyes, as the funeral cortège wound slowly through Taff Street in Pontypridd and turned up Mill Street towards the Rhondda. It was only when Harry glanced around that he saw that most of the people who had stopped had joined the procession and were walking behind the last carriage.

He wasn't prepared for the hundreds who joined the mourners but he was stunned by the sight of the enormous throng waiting at Trealaw cemetery gates. The hearse turned inside and the driver drove up the narrow lane that cut through the graves, halting at

Isabella's, which had been opened that morning to take Billy's coffin.

Father Kelly and the undertaker stepped down from the hearse, and, with the undertaker's help, Harry, his father and uncles shouldered the coffin and carried it to the spot where Billy had buried his beloved Isabella nineteen years before.

The open grave was covered with green baize. Beneath it, Harry caught a glimpse of a corner of solid oak coffin and he looked away, feeling as though it were something private belonging to his grandfather that he shouldn't see.

They laid the coffin on the ground next to the grave. The undertaker's assistants unloaded the wreaths and cut flowers. Harry stepped back and placed his arms around Bella's shoulders. She had pleaded to be allowed to attend at the graveside and, overriding Lloyd's reservation that the girls were too young to attend a funeral, Sali had given Bella permission, principally because she was still saddened that she had been prevented from going to her own father's funeral in 1904, when she had been only slightly older than Bella was now.

Father Kelly began to speak and, although not a Catholic, Harry recognized that he kept the religious part of the service mercifully brief. After the coffin had been lowered into the ground, the priest stepped forward and looked down at the sea of mourners who filled the cemetery and overflowed out of the gates.

'Now, if I could get half this number into church on a Sunday I'd be a happy man.'

Harry saw his mother and aunts smile despite their tears. It was the kind of remark Billy had loved to hear Patrick Kelly make.

'I flatter myself that I knew Billy Evans as well as any man outside of his immediate family,' Father Kelly continued. 'I also heard him rail against the Church and organized religion more times than I care to remember. Billy Evans would not thank me for saying this but because he's not here to stop me, I will. And loudly. Billy was the most moral man I have ever met. He lived his entire life by principles, good sound principles that he tried to pretend hadn't been laid down by Christ two thousand years ago.

'He loved his wife, he loved his sons, he loved his daughters-in-law when they joined his family as if they were his own flesh and blood, and he loved their children. He loved his friends, his fellow men and his neighbours. Wherever there was suffering, wherever there was want and wherever there was poverty, you'd find Isabella and Billy Evans. Two people trying to put the entire world to rights with nothing more than their bare hands. And when his Isabella died there was Billy, food basket in one hand, purse with relief money from the miners' union fund in the other and a comic for the children in his pocket.

'He was a man who terrified the authorities so much they imprisoned him, not because he was a criminal, but because he dared to dream of a world where men would be paid a living wage for their labour. A wage that would enable them to bring up their families in decent houses and to educate their children for a better world than they could hope to live in during their lifetime.

'Billy, wherever you are, I'm sure of two things: you are with your beloved Isabella and you are still fighting for right. I won't embarrass you with any more prayers for the soul I know you had.'

He nodded to the choirmaster of the local colliery who raised his hands.

'I can think of a no more fitting tribute than this, and I only hope it will give solace to those who loved him most and those he loved in return.'

The colliery choir began to sing, softly at first and then, as they gained confidence, their voices swelled with all those standing around them and the words and music of 'Bread of Heaven' filled the cemetery, echoing upwards to the blue and perfect sky.

Chapter 23

'CHICKEN AND cress sandwich, Master Harry?' Mari offered Harry the plate, and he took it from her.

'I take it you're hungry?' she commented wryly,

'It's bedlam in here.' He flattened himself against the wall of the drawing-room so a group of elderly matrons could walk through to the dining-room where Mari, with Betty Morgan's help, had laid out a buffet. 'I'm going into the garden.' He signalled across the room to Toby and pointed to the french windows.

'Would you like me to send one of the girls out to you with some drinks and another plate in ten minutes?' Mari asked.

'Please, you're a darling.' Harry would have kissed the house-keeper if a party of union men hadn't separated them.

'I've never seen so many people in one house. Granted it's a large house, but not suitable for the entire town to play sardines in.' Toby joined him in the arbour the gardener had just finished building. Hardy clematis had been planted around its base, but none were more than a foot high, although Sali had great hopes of seeing them flower the following summer.

'Sandwich?' Harry offered him the plate.

'Thanks. You haven't seen Bella, have you?' Toby failed to make his enquiry sound casual.

'She's upstairs with my younger sisters, trying to stop them from crying. Not that she's likely to succeed while all these people are around. Like me she's discovered that endless sympathy, no matter how well meant, is difficult to take.'

'I know.'

Something in the tone of Toby's voice alerted Harry. 'Your uncle?'

'Died early on Thursday morning.'

'Toby, I am so sorry. Why on earth didn't you telephone me? I would have come at once.'

'To do what?' Toby asked logically. 'At least here you could be with your family to offer them some comfort.'

'And there I could have been with you.'

Toby made a wry face. 'Be honest, has anything anyone said comforted you?'

'Not outside of my immediate family,' Harry conceded.

'I would have given ten years of my life to have had someone to grieve with, someone who knew Frank well enough to make jokes about him the way that Catholic priest did today about your grandfather. Mrs Edwards and Alf did their best, so did Doctor Adams, but in the end their muted whispers irritated more than helped.' He shrugged. 'I don't need to tell you how I feel.'

'When is your uncle's funeral?'

'Yesterday.'

'Yesterday! That was quick.'

'And small. Frank wanted it that way,' Toby explained. 'No fuss, no false tears from people who had only known him as a helpless, bedridden invalid. Last Sunday morning, when you were languishing in a cell, he even accused me of dragging out the illustrations to keep him going. When I showed him your sister's Morgan le Fey before sending it to London on Monday morning, he said it was the best work I'd ever done, and not bad considering it was the first composition I'd put together without his help. That may not sound much to you but it was high praise from Frank. On Wednesday morning the print drafts arrived from London, including a rough of Morgan. They must have pulled out all the stops to do it. Doctor Adams bent the rules and allowed me to show them to him on Wednesday afternoon. Frank looked at them, smiled, murmured, "They're not bad after all. I might make an artist of you yet." Then he went to sleep and, like your grandfather, never woke up. You should have seen him, Harry. He looked so peaceful in his coffin.'

'So did my grandfather.' Harry left the plate of sandwiches on the bench, rose to his feet, turned his back to Toby and looked out over the town. 'So, the book is finished?'

'I don't have another single line to paint or draw on that commission. No more alterations – nothing. Frank decided my Morgan should be the centrepiece, not Guinevere. So I didn't need the Snow Queen to model for me after all.'

'When will it be out?'

' "*Le Morte d'Arthur*, illustrated by Frank Ross, will be published in the spring of nineteen twenty-seven. Subscription orders for leather-bound copies are now being taken. Exact date yet to be announced." ' Toby quoted from the publishers' catalogue.

'I'd like to order twenty.'

'There's no need to do that, Harry. Books illustrated by Frank always sell,' Toby took another sandwich.

Harry turned and faced him. 'Bella's in it. Six will make great birthday presents for my brothers and sisters next year. Then there's one for me, one for my parents, two for my uncles and aunts, and nine for my cousins who will fight if I don't give them one each.'

Toby did a quick calculation. 'That's nineteen.'

'And one for the Ellises. They'd like to see their Arthurian lake. And it may encourage Martha and Matthew to persevere with their reading.'

'They won't allow them to keep it in the workhouse.'

'I know, and that's just one more reason why I have to get them out.'

Toby allowed Harry's comment to pass – for the moment. 'Frank left some papers besides his will, which, incidentally, left everything to me. Doctor Adams confiscated the originals in case they harboured germs, so I couldn't take them out of the sanatorium, but Frank planned his funeral down to the last detail. Unbeknown to me, he'd asked to see the local vicar, bought a plot in the churchyard in the valley and asked him to conduct a funeral within twenty-four hours of his death. Said he didn't want to leave me hanging about in the back end of beyond. The only mourners were myself, Doctor Adams, the beautiful Diana, who left for London an hour afterwards, the nurses who weren't on duty and Mrs Edwards and Alf. Frank made me write to the publishers months ago when he was first diagnosed. He said he had no objection to a memorial service, provided it was a happy occasion that would coincide with the publication of the book. And that is exactly what they are arranging, a memorial service followed by a party at the Ritz. Perhaps they should rename the book *Le Morte de Frank Ross*.'

'I'll come to the memorial service and party with you, if I may.'

'I was hoping you would.' He dared to add, 'And Bella in her best party frock – chaperoned by your parents, of course. You've seen me at my worst, Harry. Usually I'm happy-go-lucky, and I have lots of friends to prove it. But when Frank was taken ill, they sort of melted away. I have no doubt that when I go back to London they will materialize again but . . .' Toby fell silent.

'The Swansea Valley is a difficult place to get to,' Harry consoled clumsily.

'It has a railway, so don't go making excuses for them. I feel I've grown close to you and I hope we will remain friends – and before you say anything, that's not just because of Bella. I know it's partly because we've suffered the same experience, watching people we love inch towards death, trying to fight a disease that had already won the battle. But it's not all we have in common. Those evenings we spent together in the pub kept me sane. Those talks about life, love, art—'

'And the drinking.'

'That too.' Toby smiled.

'I hope we remain good friends for the rest of our lives.' Harry waved to a young maid who had carried a tray of drinks and cakes from the house and was standing looking around the garden.

She walked towards them. 'From Mari, Mr Harry.'

'Thank her for me, Ruby.' Harry took the tray from her. 'I won't tell anyone if you return to the house the long way round.'

'The long way, sir?'

'Walk around the garden three times, then go in through the kitchen door.'

'I couldn't do that, sir, not with the number of people waiting to be served,' she giggled, and ran back inside the house.

'Four glasses of wine.' Toby took one. 'And perfectly chilled too.'

'Mari's not only an expert housekeeper, she knows me better than I know myself.' Harry sipped his wine. 'When are you leaving Wales?'

'The inn, a week Monday. I have already given Mrs Edwards notice. I need to sort out Frank's headstone and make arrangements for the grave to be maintained before I move on.'

'To where?'

'I don't know, not yet. Did I mention that the publishers sent me a letter with the proof illustrations?' Toby murmured diffidently. 'They've offered me a commission, in my own name.'

'You know damn well you didn't mention it. Congratulations!' Harry set his wine glass on the bench and shook Toby's hand enthusiastically. 'I told you, you're brilliant. You deserve it after the work you put in on the *Morte*. Is it an entire book?'

'Yes.'

'How many illustrations?'

'Fifteen colour plates, eight black and white.' A note of pride crept into Toby's voice.

'Do I have to drag the name out of you?'

'*Aesop*'s *Fables*, so I'll be looking at animals. The hare, the tortoise, the fox, the crow, the lion . . . perhaps I ought to consider moving next door to a zoo.'

'Are you serious?'

'I must admit the idea doesn't appeal. But a zoo couldn't be a worse neighbour than some of the others Frank and I have had over the years.'

'You said you had no settled home.'

'Not since my parents drowned. Frank rented a studio in Paris but he sold the lease when he was diagnosed with TB. He owns — owned,' Toby corrected himself sharply, 'a house in Chelsea. I suppose it's mine now, but it's never been home, not in the true sense of the word, like this place.' Toby looked wistfully at the villa. 'It was just a base he used whenever he exhibited in London. After my parents died, I joined Frank every school holiday, but we lived like nomads, wandering from one rented house to another. Most were in Cornwall because he liked the sea. The closest I have to a home are the boxes in storage in Frank's attic. What about you? Will you live here now with your family?' He deliberately switched the conversation away from himself.

Harry looked over the garden wall to the house next door. The roof was finished and, as far as he could see, the windows were too. 'The trustees of my estate have bought that house for me.'

'Trustees – don't tell you me that you are heir to a fortune?' Toby laughed.

'I will inherit some businesses when I'm thirty,' Harry divulged, reluctant as ever to talk about his wealth.

'And there's me wondering if you were going to touch up your father when you offered to pay the Ellises' debts.' Toby surveyed the house. 'Very solid, middle-class and respectable – and I mean that in the nicest possible way. I have had enough of the Bohemian existence. When are you moving in?'

'I don't know. What I do know is that I need to return to the Swansea Valley to clear my room, pick up my car and settle a few things. Are you going back up there today?' Harry asked.

'I checked the timetables. There's a train that leaves Pontypridd station at six that will get me into Penwyllt just after nine. If you don't mind me using your telephone I thought I'd call Mrs Edwards from here and ask her to keep me a meal.'

'I have arranged to see my solicitor when everyone's gone, so I won't be able to go to the Swansea Valley until tomorrow. Don't suppose you fancy staying the night? There's a decent guestroom.'

'I haven't even brought a razor.'

'I can lend you whatever you need,' Harry offered.

'In that case, yes. This meeting with your solicitor isn't anything to do with the Ellises by any chance, is it?' Toby asked cautiously.

'And if it is?' Harry challenged.

'Harry, be reasonable. I thought your father performed miracles to get you out of that scrape. You could have knocked me down with a feather when I telephoned here on Sunday and Bella said that vicious agent had dropped the charges against you.'

'I didn't know you spoke to Bella on Sunday.'

'I was worried about you,' Toby said guiltily. 'I didn't know whether to rush up to Brecon to see if I could do something to help, or if I'd only make things worse. But if I'd gone, I would have taken the train. Given the trouble I had getting your car back to the inn I certainly couldn't have driven there.'

'I never thought to ask, can you drive?'

'I can now.' Toby exchanged his empty glass of wine for a full one.

'And my car?' Harry's voice heightened in concern.

'Only has a couple of dents, but Alf's done his best to knock them out and it doesn't look half bad.'

'Toby, is this one of your jokes?'

'It could be, but on the other hand, I did say that Alf has done the best he could,' Toby replied maddeningly.

'That will teach me to get arrested at a moment's notice.'

'All the more reason not to go back to the Swansea Valley. I can pack your things and send them on.'

'I'd rather pack them myself into my dented car, if you don't mind.'

'Alf would drive it here for you if you asked him.'

'No.' Harry finished his second glass of wine, collected the plates and glasses, and stacked them on the tray. 'There are a few things you don't know about me and the agent, Toby. I'll fill you in on the way back tomorrow. Thank the Lord, people are finally beginning to leave,' he said in relief, when he saw guests walking down the drive. He gave Toby a sideways glance. 'I suppose I could find Bella for you. But no talking to her unless all my other sisters are present or you'll incur my father's wrath, and believe me, that is not something you want to do, whether you are serious about wanting to court Bella or not.'

Although some people made a point of paying their respects and then leaving Lloyd's house, those who knew Billy Evans well lingered, wanting to remain with his family and talk about him. Some stayed so long Harry began to wonder if they had homes to go to. His parents had invited Lloyd's brothers and their families as well as Mr Richards, Father Kelly, Betty Morgan and Billy's closest friends to dine with them that evening, which meant that Harry didn't have a chance to talk to Mr Richards about the Ellis children until almost ten o'clock.

Victor took Father Kelly, Megan and the boys back to the Rhondda in his truck, the children riding in the back, which they loved, especially at night. Joey drove Rhian and his family the short distance to his home soon afterwards. To Harry's surprise, Betty Morgan was spending the night and, after dinner, she and Mari disappeared to the housekeeper's room with a bottle of Mari's favourite sherry to toast Billy's memory.

As a special concession, Sali had allowed all the girls to stay up, even Edyth, who was pale and subdued, and nine-year-old Susie, who was sleeping on her feet. Bella commandeered Toby to play cards with them in the library.

Ruby made coffee and carried it to Lloyd's study, and Harry and Mr Richards retreated there as soon as they had waved Joey and Victor off.

'Join us?' Harry asked Sali and Lloyd when they closed the front door and walked down the hall.

'You sure you want us to?' Lloyd looked round the door.

'After what happened to me on Saturday, most definitely. I know that Mr Richards has been trying to work out ways for me to help the Ellis family and, given the problems he's come up against, I need all the advice I can get.'

'Put like that, how can we refuse?' Lloyd pulled up a chair next to Harry. Sali fetched two extra cups from the dining room and set them on the coffee tray. Mr Richards took a notebook from his pocket, opened it and, with his customary businesslike approach, went straight to the point.

'As a single man you won't be allowed to remove the younger children from the children's section of the workhouse, Harry. And, after being labelled a "moral degenerate", it may prove impossible for anyone to sign Mary Ellis out. But let's concentrate on the younger children first. If you were married you wouldn't have a problem either in adopting them or taking them into your home as prospective servants.'

If Harry hadn't known Mr Richards better he would have thought he was joking but much as he respected and loved the old man, in all the years he had known him, he had never seen him exhibit a trace of humour. 'As I'm not about to rush up the aisle,

I'll have to advertise for a respectable married couple to look after them. But I know the Ellises. They'd hate to admit that they can't look after themselves. And they can. They proved it every day between their mother's death and their eviction.'

Mr Richards glanced down at his book. 'The workhouse rules are simple and never waived. No child may be taken out except by a respectable married couple,' he glanced up at Harry, 'spinster or widow.'

'There is a highly respectable widow without a position staying the night in this house,' Sali reminded Harry.

'Of course! Betty Morgan. Why didn't I think of her?' Harry said excitedly. 'Have you asked her?'

'Your mother and I did discuss the idea, but decided against broaching the subject with her until after we had spoken to you, Harry. Finding someone to take the children out of the workhouse is just one of many obstacles,' Mr Richards warned. 'I have approached each of the trustees in turn and after talking to them, have taken it upon myself as your solicitor to call an emergency board meeting for nine o'clock tomorrow morning. You need their permission to set aside sufficient money from your trust fund to care for the family. And I warn you, there is no way that they will vote to allow the Ellis children to return to the Ellis Estate.'

'But the house and the farm are theirs, by right,' Harry protested. 'They have paid for it ten times over. Morally—'

'It's what I said to you last Sunday. The trustees are only concerned with preserving your inheritance until your thirtieth birthday. The Ellis Estate is a large and valuable one. Managed correctly, it could prove extremely lucrative.'

'Then I'll find a farm manager that the trustees will approve of, and he can live there with the Ellises.'

'Any manager worth having would want to live in the house with his family, and he would resent the presence of a family of pauper children. Particularly if they regarded themselves as the rightful tenants.'

'If I explain the situation to the trustees they'll understand and see it the way I do,' Harry persisted.

'Believe me, Harry, I have tried.' Mr Richards took the coffee

Sali had poured for him. 'If you'll forgive me for saying so, you are allowing your heart to rule your head, and the trustees are doing the converse. In my experience, when heart meets head there is never enough common ground to reach a compromise. If you want to take the Ellis children from the workhouse you will have to find somewhere else for them to live.' He filched a sheet of paper from his notebook, leaned forward and handed it to Harry. 'That is a list of modest farms and smallholdings in the Swansea valley owned by E and G Estates that are vacant.'

'All repossessed by Robert Pritchard,' Harry said in disgust.

'And all empty,' Mr Richards emphasized. 'And I mean empty – no furniture, no livestock, not even the bare essentials of a table and bed. I believe that given the way the Ellis family have been treated by the representative of E and G Estates, the trustees might look favourably on a request from you to earmark one of those properties for the family's use. But the problems don't end there, Harry. Should you take the family from the workhouse you will become legally responsible for them. The trustees see that as an onerous and unnecessary burden.'

'Not on an estate the size of mine.'

'Financially, it won't be.' Lloyd finally spoke. 'But the Ellis family might well become an emotional drain on you, Harry. Hopefully, you won't remain a bachelor for ever, and your future wife may resent your involvement with this family.'

'And if she, whoever she may be, asked me to abandon the Ellises, as they have been so many times by people who should have cared for them, I'd walk away from her.'

'You say that now, Harry, but who knows what the future holds? Circumstances change.' Lloyd offered his cigarettes around.

'I don't need reminding that only a few weeks ago I wanted to go to Paris for a year and now I'm not sure that I want to go at all.' Harry set his coffee cup on a sofa table and took one of his father's cigarettes.

'We didn't say that, Harry,' Lloyd said flatly, 'you did. Stop being so hard on yourself, you are only twenty-one. You have your whole life ahead of you, and you have to stop blaming yourself for what Robert Pritchard did. You were in school when he was

391

appointed. And no sooner did you finish university than you left here to take care of Dad.'

Harry quoted the lecture Lloyd had given him so many times. ' "Wealth brings responsibilities. You owe it to the people dependent on the wages your companies pay to make sure that every business you own is run fairly and honestly. And the only way you can do that is by monitoring them. It is time you learned everything there is to know about them and the people who labour for your benefit." '

'I've always been too severe with you, Harry.' Lloyd reached across and gripped Harry's shoulder.

'No, you haven't. All you ever tried to do was make me see that my inheritance was more than a windfall of wealth. That I owed a responsibility to the people who work for the companies held in trust for me. And you were absolutely right to do so. I have done a lot of thinking this week and I've made a few decisions. I want to try to be the kind of man Granddad was. When I reach old age, as I hope I will, I want to be able to look back and say, "I did make a difference. I did manage to make some people's lives better." '

'That's a tall order, Harry.' Lloyd smiled.

'I know, and I also know that I'll never be a fraction of the man Granddad was. But you're right, it is high time that I shouldered my responsibilities and tried to put things right in the companies I will inherit. I know that I haven't done anything to convince you that I have a serious side, not yet,' he said earnestly, 'but the Ellis family wouldn't have lost their home and each other if it hadn't been for my shortcomings.' He looked at Mr Richards. 'I told you what I thought of a man who would employ an agent like Robert Pritchard and it still holds. The Ellises are in desperate straits because of my refusal to take control of my inheritance.'

'Your mother and I are here if you need us to do anything, Harry,' Lloyd offered.

'That's good to know.'

'So, what do you want to do, Harry?' Mr Richards asked.

'Offer Mrs Morgan a job looking after the Ellises and hope she'll take it. Attend the trustees' meeting in the morning and then travel to the inn. Rent a cottage for the Ellises until Mrs Morgan and I can prepare one of these farms for them. As soon as we have some-where to house the family, go to the workhouse and get the Ellises released. When they are settled, I intend to take a good look at E and G Estates. If Mr Beatty is willing, I'd like him to stay in Brecon and work with me to clear up the mess Robert Pritchard made. He knows a great deal more than I do about my own business,' Harry said wryly.

'It may take an increase of salary, but I'm fairly certain that we can persuade Mr Beatty to stay in Brecon, Harry.' Mr Richards closed his notebook and returned it to his pocket.

'You're going to be very busy, Harry. You'll find time to telephone us when you reach the inn tomorrow?' Sali took Mr Richards's empty coffee cup from him.

'Of course.'

'And at least once a week,' she pressed.

'At least, but I've a feeling that it'll be a lot more often than that, given the help I'm going to need. Thank you, Mr Richards, for all your hard work on my behalf.' Harry shook the old man's hand.

'My pleasure, Harry. I only wish that your Great-great-aunt Edyth could see the fine young man you've become. She made a wise decision when she left her estate to you.'

'I'll see you to your car, Mr Richards.' Lloyd opened the door.

'And I'll ask one of the girls to get your coat.' Sali went into the dining-room, where the maids were putting away the silver.

Lloyd laid his hand on Harry's arm to detain him after Sali and Mr Richards had left. 'This Mary Ellis, how old is she?'

'Nineteen,' Harry answered shortly.

'Pretty?'

'No.' Harry met Lloyd's searching gaze. 'Beautiful.'

'And from what Mr Richards said, illiterate and uneducated like most of the women Robert Pritchard raped.'

'Yes, and because she's lived in isolation with her family all her life, she's wild and full of crazy ideas, especially when it comes to caring for her brothers and sisters. And no matter how impossible they are, she tries to carry them out. She will do anything to protect them. Robert Pritchard knew that and used it to hurt her.'

'You love her?' Lloyd asked bluntly.

'With all my heart.' It was a relief to admit it.

'But her lack of education is an obstacle.'

'Only for her. I'd marry her tomorrow if she'd have me.' Harry meant it. Life had battered Mary with more injustices than any one person should suffer in a lifetime, yet she had remained essentially true to herself. And he thought that if he could get her to care for him half as much as she cared for David, Matthew, Martha and Luke, he'd have a love worth more than all the wealth in his trust fund.

'Then good luck with her, but a word of warning: tread carefully. Damaged women are fragile; smother them with kindness and you'll suffocate them.'

Harry looked at Lloyd in confusion. His stepfather sounded as though he was speaking from experience, but he couldn't be . . . He looked to his mother, immaculately and elegantly dressed as usual, as she helped Mr Richards on with his coat.

Toby and Bella walked, hand in hand, out of the library. Edyth, exhibiting the first trace of her old spirit that she'd shown since she'd come home from the infirmary, was making faces at them behind their backs.

'All right, Edyth?' Harry held out his hand, and she went to him.

'Aren't I always?' She smiled up at him, before sticking out her tongue at Bella and Toby's backs when they went into the drawing-room.

'No, you are not,' Sali corrected her fondly. 'And you are supposed to be taking things quietly, young lady. If Bella sees that tongue of yours there'll be ructions.'

'Young Ross going back with you tomorrow, Harry?' Lloyd asked.

'Yes,' Harry confirmed.

Lloyd glanced at him and said just one word: 'Good.'

Harry sat up as straight as he could to compensate for the low chair on which he was sitting, and faced the workhouse master across his desk. 'I believe that I have complied with all the requirements. The regulations state the Ellis children can only be removed from the custody of the parish if they are transferred into the care of a respectable person who will be responsible for their welfare as well as meet the financial obligations of their keep.' He glanced at Betty Morgan, the picture of propriety in her widow's weeds. 'You have seen Mrs Morgan's references from her employer of the last twelve years and her reference from my father,' he couldn't resist adding, 'the MP.'

'Yes, we received them last week and checked them out.' The master squirmed and stared down at his desk rather than meet Harry's eye.

Harry wasn't surprised at the workhouse master's disquiet. Word travelled fast in a small town like Brecon, and everyone who had done business with Robert Prichard either had been or was about to be interviewed by the police. Anthony Beatty, who had worked closely with Harry during the two weeks it had taken him to prepare the cottage he had rented in Abercrave for the Ellises, had told him that the workhouse master was no exception, and there were rumours that Robert Pritchard had sold the master furniture at preferential prices in exchange for the swift removal of families after evictions.

'You found Mrs Morgan's references satisfactory?' Harry challenged.

'Eminently. But the Ellis family will need more than housing; they will need to find work in order to support themselves. Otherwise they could become a burden on the parish again at some future date.'

'They will need educating first,' Harry said firmly. 'You have seen the letter from the trustees of my estate.'

'Offering to support them until such time as they can earn their own keep, yes, Mr Evans, but that sets a precedence. Paupers—'

'They are no longer paupers,' Harry corrected. 'They have a place to live and a guaranteed annual income.'

'Which they may dissipate in a reckless manner.' The master pulled a pack of cigarettes from his pocket. He fiddled with it but made no attempt to open it. 'The parish has to consider their ultimate welfare. This family was taken into the workhouse because they ran up debts.'

'The debt was to a company I owned, and I sincerely doubt it existed outside of the agent's machinations,' Harry retorted. 'I have no doubt whatsoever that Robert Pritchard cheated the Ellises. I have come here with Mrs Morgan today because you assured my solicitor on the telephone yesterday that there would be no obstacle to our removing all four Ellis children today.'

'Ordinarily, yes, Mr Evans,' the workhouse master hedged.

'There are problems?'

'With young David Ellis, yes.'

Harry sensed what was coming. 'You have already found him a job.'

'We found him a place, yes, on a farm.'

'What farm?'

'I'm not at liberty to say.'

'Why didn't you inform my solicitor of this when you spoke to him yesterday?'

'Because I assumed that I could get David Ellis back in time to leave with you today, Mr Evans. The Ellis family are in the care of the parish—'

'So you keep repeating. But as soon as they are removed and placed in Mrs Morgan's care, they will no longer be a burden on the parish. I doubt that I need to remind you, yet again, that they are only here because of the criminal acts of a man who was in my employ. And I am sure that the farmer who has the boy will be equally happy with another. David Ellis couldn't have been with him much more than a week or two.'

'He took him the night he came in.'

'But no one knew . . .' Harry breathed out heavily. 'Iestyn Williams.'

'Someone told you?'

'I didn't need to be told. I saw Iestyn Williams at the Ellis Estate on the day the family were evicted. David Ellis warned me then that he and his younger sister wouldn't be in the workhouse long, that they'd be taken as unpaid servants.'

'We place our inmates with respectable people, Mr Evans.' The master turned crimson and moved his chair back from his desk — and further away from Harry. 'It was a perfectly normal, legal arrangement,' he continued defensively. 'Mr Williams needed a farm labourer; the boy was experienced and suited to the work.'

'I don't doubt it, but now that the Ellises have a home in which they can live together, the boy needs to be reunited with his family.'

The master stared down at his desk again. 'David Ellis has met with an accident.'

'What kind of an accident?' Harry demanded suspiciously.

'I don't know the details. The police went to Mr Williams's farm yesterday to interview him about his dealings with Robert Pritchard. They saw that the boy was ill, and arranged for him to be admitted to the paupers' ward in the infirmary.'

'Here?'

'The infirmary is run as a separate establishment, Mr Evans, but I was told that he had been admitted.'

'Have his sisters and brothers seen him?'

'It is against regulations for workhouse inmates to visit the infirmary,' the master recited officiously.

Harry rose to his feet. 'I wish to see David Ellis and ascertain his condition for myself. When I return, Mrs Morgan and I will expect all three Ellis children to be ready to leave for their new home.'

'Without their brother and sister you risk upsetting them.' The master left his chair.

'The risk of upset will be less if you allow me to remove Mary Ellis so she can help Mrs Morgan care for them,' Harry ventured.

'She is—'

'I am aware what Robert Pritchard called her,' Harry cut in ruthlessly. 'But surely no one here would take the word of a man who has been arrested and remanded in custody?'

'Every man is innocent until found guilty in a court of law, Mr Evans.'

It was then Harry realized that the workhouse master was still hoping that Robert Pritchard would be found innocent, that the entire scandal of the agent's fraudulent business dealings could be swept aside and forgotten. He had the feeling that more than one 'respectable person' in Brecon was holding their breath, waiting for the police to knock on their door.

' "Innocent until proven guilty",' Harry repeated. 'Tell me, master, in what court of law was Mary Ellis found guilty?'

The master rang the bell on his desk. An assistant knocked on the door, opened it and waited for instructions.

'Mr Evans wishes to visit the infirmary,' he informed the man. 'You do realize that the matron will be within her rights to refuse you entry, Mr Evans?'

'Yes.' Harry turned to Betty Morgan. 'You'll wait here for the children?'

'Yes, Mr Evans.' She had difficulty keeping a straight face. She had never called him anything other than Harry since childhood.

Chapter 24

THE INFIRMARY block was situated behind the workhouse. The assistant disappeared as soon as Harry stepped inside. Harry stood and took a few moments to accustom himself to the smell of boiled cabbage and urine mixed with the peculiar rotten odour of institution disinfectant. The corridor was empty and he was debating whether to try the door on his right or left when a woman appeared. She was dressed in a blue cotton gown, starched cuffs, collar and apron, and sister's veil.

'Can I help you?' she enquired briskly.

'I am looking for David Ellis.'

'Police or relative?' she barked.

'Representative of the Ellis children's legal guardians,' he answered cautiously, wondering why the police would want to see David Ellis again after bringing him in.

'Follow me.' She walked past him and led the way towards the door on their right. Harry was used to walking quickly but he had difficulty keeping up with her. She opened the door to a ward that held two dozen beds, ranged exactly opposite one another.

'He's here, Mr . . .'

'Evans, Harry Evans.'

Harry walked towards the bed she pointed out. It was the one nearest to the nurse's desk in the centre of the ward and, when he approached, he could see why. David was lying pale and gaunt, eyes closed, on his stomach. The sheets above his back had been lifted by a cradle.

'What happened to him?' He turned to the sister who was talking to the nurse at the desk.

'You haven't been told?'

'No.' He stretched the truth. 'The workhouse master sent me here when I arrived to pick up David's sister and brothers. He said that he had been brought here by the police.' Harry knelt beside David's bed. The boy opened his eyes. 'David,' he whispered.

'You said you'd help us, Harry,' David croaked accusingly.

'I'm sorry, it took time to organize. But I have a house waiting for you, for all your family, and someone to take care of you.'

David closed his eyes.

Harry rose to his feet. 'What happened to him?' he repeated.

'He was beaten, Mr Evans. With a steel-tipped horsewhip.'

Harry felt as thought the room were moving around him. He clenched his fists and fought to keep his composure. 'Will he recover?'

'Hopefully, in time, with rest, care and good food. He is barely conscious now because he's been sedated to help him cope with the pain.'

'Can I take him with me now?'

'I wouldn't advise it. The doctor—'

'Find him, get him on the telephone,' Harry ordered. 'I don't care what it takes. I want this boy out of here now.'

'He'll need an ambulance and medical care,' she warned.

'I'll pay for the ambulance, there's a doctor in the Swansea Valley and I'll hire a nurse until he has recovered.' Harry clenched and unclenched his fists. He wished he'd knocked Robert Pritchard and all his bailiffs into the dirt and never allowed the workhouse master to take any of the Ellis children out of his sight.

'You,' Harry pointed his finger at the workhouse master's chest, 'You, and no one else, made the decision to hand a defenceless boy over to a man who whipped him within an inch of his life.'

'Mr Iestyn Williams is a respectable member of the community—'

'I am sick to death of hearing that word from you,' Harry shouted. 'Your interpretation of "respectable" and mine are very different.'

'I had no idea—'

'Considering that you have the power to make life and death

400

decisions that affect the people in the care of the parish, you should have,' Harry cut in savagely. 'They told me in the infirmary that the police took Williams into custody when they found the boy lying, more dead than alive, in his cellar. Iestyn Williams is facing serious charges over his treatment of David Ellis. And if the boy dies, he will be facing the most serious charge of all. You knew Williams did business with the agent and that the agent hated the boy. It's no thanks to you, Iestyn Williams or Robert Pritchard that David Ellis is alive. In fact, given what he knew about the agent's thieving, from which the three of you profited, I believe that all of you would prefer to see the boy dead.'

'They were both respectable men and I never profited from any fraud . . . I resent your tone . . . I resent your implications . . . I . . . I . . .'

'I was there, at the eviction of the Ellises, remember?' Harry pressed his advantage for all it was worth. 'I have spoken to the doctor who admitted the boy to the infirmary and I have sent for an ambulance to take the boy to the house I have taken for his family. I want his eldest sister released into my care so she can nurse him. And I want her released *now*!'

'It would be most irregular—'

'You'd prefer to wait for another one of your cronies to come and take her as a kitchen maid, so she can be beaten like her brother or,' he narrowed his eyes and gave the master a look of utter contempt, 'raped.'

'I did my duty—'

Harry had no compunction about interrupting him again. 'I will ask you one more time. Send for Mary Ellis so she can take care of her brother on the journey to the Ellises' new home and during his convalescence. If you refuse to release her along with her brothers and sister, I will call the police.'

'And tell them what, Mr Evans?'

'That I am concerned for her welfare after the way you deliberately placed the Ellis boy in harm's way.'

'I was not to know—'

'You expect me to believe that after I saw you whispering with Iestyn Williams and Robert Pritchard in the farmyard of the Ellis

Estate? What was your share of the goods and livestock that were taken that day?'

The master reached for the bell on his desk and rang it.

Harry hadn't been prepared for the change in Martha and Matthew in three short weeks. Martha's long black hair had been cropped shorter than a boy's, and Matthew's head had been completely shaved. Both were dressed in workhouse smocks as grey, pasty and faded as their complexions. They were huddled in a corner, so close together it was difficult to see where one child began and the other ended. They stared up at him, all terrified eyes and quivering limbs, like puppies that had been locked into a dark kennel for the breaking period shepherds use before training.

They were on the opposite side of the waiting room, as far away from Betty Morgan as they could get. Harry looked questioningly at her. She shook her head. He had long since realized that the Ellis children were wary of strangers and didn't make friends easily, but Betty Morgan was not only one of the kindest women he knew, she was also one of the most adept at thawing shy children. Even the most timid guests at his family's and cousins' birthday parties had blossomed into sociability under Betty's gentle guidance.

Footsteps sounded in the corridor. He turned and saw a nurse carrying a baby wrapped in a blanket of the inevitable grey flannel. Presuming the child was Luke, he stopped her before she reached the office door and held out his arms. 'If that's Luke Ellis, I'm here to pick him up.'

She handed him over, and the smile he'd intended for Luke froze on his lips. The plump, contented toddler had been transformed into a child as thin, weightless and delicate as a bird. His skin was the same ashen shade as his brother and sister's, and beneath the blanket he was dressed in a miniature version of the workhouse smock, fashioned from rough institution flannel. Harry noticed the rough cloth had raised welts and sores on his delicate skin.

'Luke?' Harry whispered but the toddler stared unblinkingly at him without a spark of recognition. He carried him into the waiting room and over to where Matthew and Martha were glued together.

They backed further into the corner. He fell to his knees, setting himself on the same level as them. To his horror, close up he saw bruises on their faces, arms and legs.

'Martha, Matthew?' He held the baby out to them.

They didn't make a move.

'Don't you recognize your brother?'

They tried to press even closer to the wall as if they wanted it to swallow them up.

'Don't you know me?' he persisted. 'I said I'd try to get you out of here.'

Matthew spat full in his face.

'You disgusting, dirty little brat!' The nurse who had remained in the doorway stepped inside the room, but Harry held up his hand to stop her coming any closer.

'They've been through enough, Nurse. Give them time to accept me again. Martha, don't you remember how much you wanted to learn to read and write? The lessons I gave you . . . Martha . . .' He sensed that she had focused on him and was actually looking at him for the first time. 'Martha?' he repeated hopefully.

She uttered an incomprehensible sob before flinging her arms around both him and Luke.

Harry freed the hand on the arm he had wrapped around her and stroked the stubble on her head. 'It's all right, Martha, it is going to be all right. I'm here to take you away from this place.' He continued to kneel, uncomfortably crouched, pinned down by Martha, listening to her cries.

Matthew crept towards them, and Harry reached out, managing to wrap his left arm around both children. They remained, knotted together in the corner, until Harry's muscles began to cramp.

'Do you think we can move now?' He pulled his head back and glanced from Matthew to Martha.

Betty Morgan left her chair and crossed the room. 'I'm sure this young lady and gentleman would like to see the house you've rented for them and the bedrooms we've made up for them, Mr Evans?'

'A house?' Martha's tear-stained eyes rounded in wonder.

'Yes, Martha, a house,' Harry repeated. 'And this is Mrs Morgan. She is going to look after you.'

'Mary looks after us. Where's Mary?' Matthew demanded fractiously.

'I'm not sure, Matthew. But I'm hoping we'll see her soon.' Harry crossed his fingers.

'This house? Is it our house?' Matthew wriggled free from Harry's arms.

'No, Matthew, I'm sorry, I couldn't get you back into your house,' Harry apologized.

'Then who's living in it?' Matthew demanded. 'The agent?'

'Not the agent, Matthew. No one is living in it because there's nothing there,' Harry reminded him gently.

'You let them take all our things. All the chickens, the pigs, the ducks, the cows, even Davy's dogs and the kittens,' Matthew said accusingly.

'I wish I could have stopped them, Matthew. But I couldn't.'

'I want everything back the way it was.'

Harry found himself struggling to contain his emotions. 'So do I, Matthew. But it may not be possible. I won't lie to you, or make promises I can't keep. But I will get you a house that you can live in that will be yours. Just not that one.'

'Don't want any other house,' Matthew retorted, with a trace of his old spirit.

'Yes, you do, young man,' Betty countered firmly. 'And you'll go to the house Mr Evans has rented for you right now.'

'Won't!' Matthew's bottom lip began to tremble.

'You'd rather stay here?'

'No!' Matthew shouted at Betty.

'Then I think it's time that we went and settled you in the back of Mr Evans's car. There are warm blankets waiting for you, and bottles of milk and packets of biscuits. You and you sister can snuggle down, talk to this little one and remind him that he has a family who care for him.' She took Luke from Harry, and held out her free hand.

Matthew stared at it for a full minute before reaching out and clasping it.

'Mary Ellis, the master wants to see you right away.' Joyce Crocker, a recent elevation from inmate to ward maid, shouted as she ran into the yard that separated the entrance block from the building that housed the wards.

Mary dropped her scrubbing brush back into her pail of cold water. A trickle of fear coursed down her spine, momentarily paralysing her. Like every other inmate she knew the master only sent for people when he wanted to punish them.

'You want permission to rise, Ellis,' the supervising orderly prompted.

'Permission to rise, miss?' Mary murmured tremulously.

'Granted. You'd better tidy yourself up,' the middle-aged woman advised brusquely. 'You can't walk into the public areas or see the master looking the way you do right now.'

Mary gazed ruefully at her grimy, dirt-smeared smock as she rose to her feet. She would have liked to have asked, 'How can I tidy myself up when this is all I have to wear?' But every question she had put to people in positions of authority during the last three weeks had culminated in a blow, and she was loath to risk another.

'Come on, I'll take you to the washhouse first, Mary.' Joyce led the way back across the yard to the women's lavatories. Mary trailed behind, stumbling awkwardly and twisting her ankles when she tried to quicken her pace in the rough wooden clogs that were too large for her feet.

'Here.' Joyce handed her a piece of green carbolic soap. 'Wash your hands and face.'

Mary turned on the cold water tap, the only one there was, and held her hands beneath the flow of water, but she didn't use the soap. Her skin was still burning from the over-generous helping of caustic soda that had been tipped into her bucket.

'You'd better rinse your face as well. You've dirt on your forehead and nose.' Joyce picked up one of the rags they used as towels and held it, ready.

'Thank you.' Mary lowered her face to the sink, dipped her hands under the stream of cold water and rubbed her face. Joyce was more sympathetic than most of the orderlies because she knew what it was like to be an inmate. 'Why has the master sent for me?'

'I don't know, but there's a young man in his office, and he was shouting at the master and the master didn't shout back. Your brothers and sister have been sent for as well. It could be that someone in your family has come to take you out,' she suggested optimistically.

'We haven't any relatives.'

'The young man was tall, blond and very good-looking. A real toff. Do you know anyone like that?'

Mary's spirits lifted. She nodded.

'A relative?' Joyce pressed.

'A friend. A good friend.' Mary had hoped and prayed that Harry would try to help them, but even now she was too afraid to believe that it was really him. It could be any young man . . .

'Lucky you to have rich friends. I've give whole worlds,' she said illogically, given her lack of possessions, 'to know someone like him. I saw his posh car parked in front of the reception block. Perhaps his family needs servants, or perhaps he's discovered that you're a long-lost cousin.' She strayed into the realms of romance. 'Or, it could be that he's heard about your brother.'

'My brother! Which brother?' Mary took the towel and wiped her face. It smelled musty, and without thinking, she dropped it on to the basin.

'The only name I heard was "Ellis". Ellen, one of the ward maids in the infirmary, came into the kitchen earlier to get some grease. They sent her because Matron knows that the master and his family have goose for dinner every Sunday. She said that an Ellis boy had been brought in and he was in a bad way.'

'Brought in from where? Wasn't he already here? What's wrong with him?' Questions tumbled out one after the other, but panicked by the thought that one of her brothers was ill, Mary didn't wait for answers.

'All I know is what I've told you. Perhaps no one's come for you. Perhaps the toff's nothing to do with you, and . . .'

'The master sent for me to tell me bad news.' Mary ran headlong out of the door.

'Wait for me,' Joyce shouted. 'I'm supposed to take you. And you haven't hung up this towel. You could be put on bread and water for that.'

'Mr Evans,' the master called to Harry from the corridor outside the waiting room.

Harry looked up at him without rising or relinquishing his hold on Martha and Matthew.

'Mary Ellis is in my office.'

'Mary . . .' Matthew ran forward but Betty caught him by the waist and held him fast. 'I know you want to see your sister but you have to wait here with me, young man.'

'I'll return as quickly as I can.' Harry pushed Martha gently towards Betty and climbed to his feet. 'You two be good for Mrs Morgan and look after Luke until I come back.'

'We'll see Mary then?' Matthew asked plaintively.

Harry felt like a coward when he pretended that he hadn't heard the boy. He crossed the corridor. The office door was open and he walked straight in. The master was sitting behind his desk. A female inmate was standing with her back turned to him. He knew she was a female because her smock was longer than the ones the men wore over their trousers. But her hair had been cut as close as Martha's.

'I have considered your request, Mr Evans,' the master said formally, 'and if Mrs Morgan is prepared to sign all the relevant papers you may take Mary Ellis with you now.'

Harry blanched when he realized that he was looking at Mary. Where she had been slender, she was now broomstick thin, and as he walked to her side he saw she was as pallid and gaunt as her brothers and sister. 'Mary?'

When she didn't respond, he saw that the workhouse had succeeded in doing what none of the other tragedies she'd had to face in her short life had. She'd been cowed, and the fighting spirit he'd so admired had been destroyed. He wondered if the separation from her brothers and sisters had contributed more to her broken state than the punishing regime of the workhouse.

'Mary?' he repeated softly.

She continued to stare down at her feet, unable or unwilling to look him in the eye.

Harry's temper, constrained for so long, finally erupted. Wishing he'd never followed the advice to wait and help the Ellises through official channels, he shouted, 'The condition of the Ellis family is an absolute disgrace. The younger children are malnourished. Miss Ellis has obviously been starved and mistreated, and her brother has been beaten to within an inch of his life. This is not a workhouse. It is a death house. The only wonder to me is that anyone survives here at all.'

'We do the best we can to care for the destitute with the limited means at our disposal, Mr Evans.' The master pretended to study a paper on his desk.

'If you allowed the friends of those human beings you label destitute to take care of them, you wouldn't have to trouble yourself to draw wages from the parish.' Harry said cuttingly. He heard a vehicle halt outside the main entrance and glanced through the window. As he'd hoped, it was the ambulance. 'Mary, we're going.' He offered her his arm as if they were leaving a ballroom.

'Given the circumstance, I am sorry to have to remind you, Mr Evans, but the Ellis family are wearing workhouse property.'

'Where are the clothes they arrived in?' Harry questioned, his temper still simmering at boiling point.

'We burned them. They were verminous.'

'No, they were not,' Harry contradicted baldly.

'It is workhouse policy to burn all prospective inmates' clothes.'

'Why?'

'Our regulations are designed to keep the institution clean and disease-free.'

Harry looked at the smock Mary was wearing. 'Or more likely they were burned because you want to further humiliate the destitute by insisting they wear rags. I wouldn't force a criminal into this cloth, let alone a baby like Luke Ellis.' He opened his wallet, extracted a five-pound note and flung it on the desk. 'That should more than compensate the parish for anything they laid out on the Ellis family's keep. I'll expect an official receipt to be sent to my solicitor's office. If it isn't, I'll know that you appropriated it, the same way you appropriated furniture that was removed by Robert Pritchard's bailiffs.'

'I object to your tone—'

'Send a clerk out to my car with the papers you want signed. Mrs Morgan has already taken the children there.' Harry grasped Mary's hand and practically pulled her through the door and into the courtyard. He glanced over to the corner where he had parked his car. Betty Morgan had already settled the younger children into the back and was sitting in the passenger seat, but he steered Mary out of their sight towards the ambulance. A nurse was sitting on one of the side benches in the back. David was lying face down as he had been in the infirmary, on a stretcher in front of her.

'How is he?' Harry asked.

Mary looked from Harry to the nurse and back and finally spoke. 'David?'

'Yes.' He helped her into the ambulance and the nurse moved up on the bench to make room for her.

'He's been given something to help him sleep through the journey. I doubt he'll wake until tomorrow morning.' The nurse glanced from Harry to Mary. 'I know he looks bad, but he will recover.'

'Mary? Mary?' Harry had to repeat her name twice before he felt he had her attention but she still refused to meet his gaze. 'I have to drive the others down the valley, but I'll see you at the house.'

'House,' she repeated uncomprehendingly. She picked up David's limp hand and held it in her own.

'I have rented a house for you and your family.'

'The others?' She couldn't tear her gaze away from David.

It was then that he realized she hadn't understood a word he'd said. 'Matthew, Martha and Luke are in my car, Mary. I'm going to tell the ambulance driver where to go. He'll drive you to the house I've rented for all of you. I'll see you there.'

'You have them all? Martha, Matthew, Luke . . .' She didn't look away from David.

'They're all safe, Mary. Another hour and you'll be . . .' He would have given a great deal to have been able to say home. 'You'll see them shortly. And,' he looked across at the grim façade of the workhouse, 'I know I let you down but I swear that neither you nor your family will ever have to go into a place like this again.' He stepped down from the ambulance and closed the door.

Martha waved shyly to him from the car. Feeling as though he had been given a greater reward than he deserved, he waved back to her before walking around to the driver's cab.

The road between the workhouse and the inn was interminable, and the whole time Harry drove, his thoughts were with Mary and David in the ambulance. All three children, fell asleep huddled beneath the blankets in the back, before he pulled into the yard of the inn, the nearest place to the cottage that he could park his car.

'Shall I take the children straight into the house, Harry?' Betty asked.

'Please. I'll help you.' Seeing that Martha, unlike her brothers, had woken and was scrambling out, Harry lifted Matthew into his arms, leaving Luke for Betty. He carried him into the kitchen, where, thanks to Enfys, a fire blazed cheerfully in the hearth. He set the boy in an easy chair.

'It's all right, Matthew, you're in that house I told you about,' Harry reassured him when he opened his eyes and looked around in confusion.

'Sit next to Matthew for now, Martha,' Betty suggested when she led Martha inside and set Luke gently on a sofa. 'Then, when we've had a cup of tea and you've woken up a bit, you can have a look at the bedrooms we've prepared for you.'

'I'll be back in a few minutes, Betty. Will you turn down one of the beds in the boys' room, please?' Harry went to the door.

'The boy is seriously hurt?'

'Yes.'

'I'll turn back the bed in the master bedroom.'

'Thank you, Betty, but I think he'd prefer to share a room with his brother, and his brother with him.' Harry smiled at Martha. 'The Ellises like doing everything together. Don't you, Martha?'

She didn't exactly smile but her lips crinkled.

Harry crossed the garden to the car park. The driver had opened

410

the back of the ambulance and Mary was sitting on the floor next to David's stretcher. The nurse stepped down and stood beside Harry.

'He didn't wake during the journey?' Harry asked.

'Not once,' she confirmed. 'But as I said, I wasn't expecting him to.'

Harry saw Alf in his workshop. He waved and shouted, 'Alf, do me a favour, help us to carry David Ellis into the cottage.'

Alf dropped the cigarette jammed between his teeth, ground it under his heel and ran over to the ambulance. 'We heard what happened to him. Couple of constables came in for a swift half after Iestyn Williams was arrested and sent to Brecon.'

Harry took some comfort from the thought that Iestyn Williams might be languishing in the same Spartan cell he had endured. 'When we've got David inside, do me another favour, please, Alf? Go into the inn and ask your mother to call the doctor?'

Harry found Toby in the bar and bought him a drink. He was looking at some sketches Toby had drawn of a hare when the doctor walked in. He rose to meet him.

The doctor set his bag on a chair. 'Mrs Morgan tells me that you are jointly responsible for the Ellises.'

'We are,' Harry answered. 'Can I get you a drink?'

'After seeing that poor boy's back a brandy wouldn't go amiss.' The doctor sat down. Harry bought a double brandy and set it in front of him.

'They told me in the infirmary that he will recover,' Harry said hopefully.

'In time, but he'll have to take it easy for months. There's muscle damage. He'll need a great deal of care, Mr Evans.'

'I'll see that he gets it. You'll visit him again?'

'Tomorrow.' The doctor downed his brandy. 'Do I send my bill to you, Mr Evans?'

'You do.'

'Here, to the inn?'

'Even if I should move on, I'll leave a forwarding address, but I have no intention of leaving for a while.'

The doctor tipped his hat. 'I have two cases of diphtheria up at Bont Farm. Perhaps I'll see you tomorrow.'

'I hope so.' Harry looked out of the window and watched him cross the yard to his car.

Mrs Edwards left the bar and came over to collect the doctor's empty glass. 'Enfys has taken dinner over to the cottage.'

'Thank you, Mrs Edwards. Mrs Morgan will have her hands full with the children for the next few days without worrying about meals.'

'If you don't mind me saying so, Mr Evans, you've taken a lot upon yourself with those Ellis children. Not that they didn't need someone to take care of them, what with David Ellis getting beaten,' she added illogically. 'And your own dinners are ready for you if you'd like to go in the dining-room.'

Harry picked up his pint of bitter and led the way into the back room. Enfys had set out two plates of pork chops, apple sauce, peas, roast and mashed potatoes.

'Penny for them?' Toby asked after Harry had sat toying with his meal in silence for ten minutes.

Harry pushed his plate aside. 'I lost my temper in the workhouse today. I shouldn't have.'

'Did you lose it before or after you saw David Ellis?' Toby sprinkled more salt on to his roast potatoes.

'After.'

'Alf only helped to carry the boy out of the ambulance and into the cottage, but from what he said to me when he came back here, you had every right to be angry.'

'My losing my temper is hardly going to help the Ellises.'

'You paying all their bills and writing off their debts until they can get back on their feet is,' Toby observed wryly, having been taken into Harry's confidence about his inheritance and E and G Estates.

'It's the least I can do.'

Toby pushed his own plate aside. 'As I'm not in the mood for Mrs Edwards's afters—'

'You never are.'

'Fancy a drink in the bar?'

Harry shook his head. 'The children have nothing except those damned workhouse smocks.' He glanced at his wristwatch. 'It's nine o'clock. The younger ones were sleeping on their feet earlier. Betty should have got them into bed by now. I'll have to buy them some essentials tomorrow in Pontardawe but I asked Betty to check their sizes so I can order most of what they need with my mother to be sent down from Gwilym James. I won't be long.'

'Now where have I heard that before?' Toby enquired sceptically.

'I'm sorry I've not been good company lately.'

'You can say that again.'

'I'm sorry I've not been good company—'

'You're getting more like me every day. Do you realize that I came back here to spend a week and I've been here three?'

'But you're painting,' Harry reminded him. 'And producing work well within your deadline.'

'Next thing you'll be telling me is that this is as good a place as any in the world to paint.'

'Isn't it?' Harry asked.

'I suppose so, as I'm in no hurry to go anywhere else,' Toby said philosophically. 'If you think that I can help with the Ellises—'

'I'll come and find you in the bar.'

Chapter 25

BETTY MORGAN was sitting at the kitchen table – pencil in hand, a teacup and notebook in front of her – when Harry knocked on the open door.

'Harry, I was hoping I'd see you again this evening. Tea?' She left her chair and lifted down another cup from the dresser.

'Please, if there's one in the pot.' Like the doctor, Harry would have preferred brandy after the day he'd had. He made a mental note to have one when he joined Toby in the bar later. 'How's David?'

'Still asleep. He didn't even wake when the doctor examined him, or when I helped his poor sister to change his dressings afterwards. She cried like a baby when she saw his injuries. I'd like to take the birch to the man who flayed the skin from his back.' She poured milk into the cup and added tea.

'You and me both, Betty. It was Megan's father.'

'Was it?' She set the tea in front of him.

'You don't seem surprised.'

'I met him once. He was an evil man. What he tried to do to your poor Uncle Victor and his own daughter beggared belief.'

'Dad told me that he tried to stop them from marrying.' Harry sat at the table and spooned sugar into his tea.

'He practically sold Megan to an asylum in North Wales as a maid. It took your mother months to find out where she was. But you know Sali Evans: as soon as she discovered where Megan was, she went there and, somehow or other, got her out of the place, even though they'd paid Megan's father her year's salary in advance. But then,' she shook her head, 'it's water long gone down the Taff now. Your Aunty Megan and Uncle Victor are healthy and happy, and so are their boys; that's what counts. All we should be thinking about at the moment are those poor mites upstairs. You're a proper Evans, Harry, for all that your real father was crache.'

'A proper Evans?' Harry repeated quizzically.

'Champion of the underdog, just like Lloyd and Billy, God rest and bless his soul.'

His grandfather's death was still too painful for him to want to talk about it. 'You've checked the children's sizes?'

'Yes, and I've made a list of what they need. Do you know they don't even have a set of underclothes between them?'

'If you give it to me I'll go into Pontardawe in the morning and buy enough to tide them over for a day or two. But I'll telephone my mother tonight and ask her to send down most of what they need from Gwilym James.' He looked around the kitchen. Apart from one plate covered with a lid set on top of a saucepan on the stove, the room was immaculate. 'As a housekeeper you amaze me, Betty. You'd never think that there are three children and a baby in the house.'

'Poor mites don't have any toys or books to leave lying around. And it's just as well I bought those nappies last week in Pontardawe. I should have thought and bought a couple of babies' nightgowns as well. I never realized that they'd put a poor scrap of a toddler into a workhouse smock.'

'Are they all sleeping?' Harry asked.

'Except Mary. She's sitting with her brother. She won't leave him.'

'You have everything you need?'

'And more, Harry. The things you've bought for this place—'

'Will come in handy for the next one.' He pulled out his cigarette case, and lit one. 'Has Mary eaten?'

Betty shook her head and pointed to the plate on the saucepan. 'I tried to get her to eat. She wouldn't even listen to the doctor when he told her that her brother won't wake before morning. He advised her to get some rest while she can but he might as well have saved his breath. She's a stubborn girl.'

'She is when it comes to her family,' Harry agreed.

'You sweet on her?' Betty fished.

'Please, would you go up and see her? Tell her that I need to talk to her for ten minutes. If she still won't leave David, offer to sit with him.'

'It would be easier to change coal into diamonds than get a straight answer to a personal question put to an Evans.' Betty eased her bulk out of the chair. 'I'll ask her, but don't hold out too much hope. If by some miracle she should come down, try to get her to do more than look at that dinner, will you? I doubt she's seen a square meal in months. And don't forget this.' She tore the list from the book and handed it to him.

Harry pocketed the sheet of paper and, anticipating that Betty would succeed, he opened a hotplate on the stove and moved the saucepan of water that held the dinner on to it. The walls were thick but the floorboards weren't insulated, and he could hear Betty's voice, muted, muffled but unmistakably pleading.

A few minutes later Mary walked barefoot down the staircase that led directly into the kitchen. Betty had loaned her one of her flowered work overalls and she had tied it on over her workhouse smock.

'Mrs Morgan said you wanted to talk to me.' She still refused to look at him and he wondered if the wild spirit that he had loved so much had been extinguished forever.

'Yes, I do.' He pulled a chair out from the table. 'Please sit down. I'm heating up your dinner and Betty's not long made tea.'

'I'm not hungry.'

'You don't want to help your brothers and sister?' he asked.

'You know I'd do anything for them,' she cried out in anguish.

He hated himself for hurting her more than she already had been. 'Then eat so you can be strong enough to take care of them. Because if you don't, they are going to be the ones taking care of you.'

'David's not in a fit state to take care of anyone.' She sat at the table and stared down at her hands.

'But he will be.'

'The doctor said he'll get better but have you seen his back?'

'He's young, strong and pigheaded enough to make a full recovery just to spite Iestyn Williams.'

416

'I hope you're right.'

'You know I am.' He sat beside her and took her hands into his. 'Mary, they're feeling every bit as wretched as you are,' he murmured in a softer tone. 'They all need you, especially David. I'll do what I can, but they are your family, and if you are going to help them, you have to look after yourself. Your first priority has to be getting your own strength back.'

The water in the saucepan started bubbling. He went to the stove and placed his finger on the edge of the plate. It wasn't quite hot enough. He took a cork placemat from a shelf on the dresser, and a knife and fork from the drawer, and laid them on the table in front of her. She continued to sit, so still and desolate that he felt guilty for lecturing her.

'I know you've had a terrible time——'

'You haven't any idea what's happened to me since I last saw you.'

'If you want to talk about it, I'll try to understand.'

'Will you, Mr Evans?' She finally looked at him.

'You used to call me Harry.'

Her eyes were dark, anguished and so deeply shadowed they appeared to be bruised. 'Have you the faintest idea what it's like to live – no, not live, you can't call what goes on in the workhouse living – to try to exist, day in day out, within those grim walls? To be given slops to eat, to be forced to do endless, meaningless scrubbing because the floor you've been ordered to clean was cleaned only ten minutes before by another inmate?' She plucked at her smock. 'To be given filthy rags to wear, but worse of all, to have to get through every day not knowing what is happening to your family or even where they are?'

'No,' he replied evenly, 'I have no idea. And, as I'm not as brave as you, I hope I never find out. But courtesy of Robert Pritchard I do know what it's like to spend the best part of two days and a night in the police cells.'

'Then they did arrest you for trying to help us?'

'Yes.' The meal was finally warm enough. He took an oven cloth, lifted it from the saucepan, carried it to the table and set it in front of her. 'Careful, the plate is hot.'

'But they let you out,' she said. 'They must have, you're here now.'

'Yes, they let me out, or rather my father came with a solicitor who made them release me.' He sat beside her. 'Eat, and I'll tell you what's happened since you were evicted.'

Mary barely ate a third of her meal but he knew from his childhood illnesses that it wasn't easy to start eating again after a period of fasting so he didn't try to force her to eat more. And while she picked at the food, he told her about Robert Pritchard's arrest, the ongoing police investigation, his suspicions that the agent had defrauded not only them but all the tenants of E&G Estates but, uncertain how she'd take the news, he kept the fact that he owned E&G Estates until last. When he finished speaking, a silence settled over the kitchen, stifling the atmosphere until he felt he could no longer draw breath.

'Haven't you anything to say?' he said.

When she spoke her voice was flat, devoid of expression. 'So you own the Ellis Estate?'

'Not morally, it was built by your family and they – or rather you, David and the others as their direct descendants – are the rightful owners. But as I explained, like everything else I will inherit, it's being held in trust and I won't be in possession of it until I'm thirty. But I promise you that I will give you and your family the Estate as soon as I am able to.'

'Then it's like David and Martha always said, you are very rich?' She turned and finally looked at him but he couldn't decipher the expression in her eyes.

'I will be, yes.'

She left her chair and headed for the stairs.

'Mary?'

She stopped and turned back. 'You said that you would help us, and you kept your word. Thank you, Mr Evans.'

'I'm only sorry that I couldn't do it sooner, Mary. I might have saved David from a thrashing and the rest of you time in the workhouse.'

'The women there told me that I would never get out. That

being a moral degenerate was as bad as being an unmarried mother. You managed the impossible. You took me out.'

'You were never a moral degenerate.'

'No?' she challenged. 'After what the agent did to me?'

'He raped you, Mary.'

'And there was you . . . you said you liked me. I liked you, and if you'd asked, I would have done what he made me do and willingly – and now . . .' The tears she'd held in check for so long finally began to flow. 'I'm bald and ugly and . . .'

He went to her and held her. She struggled but he tightened his grip. 'You are none of those things, Mary.'

'The men, the orderlies in the workhouse, they used to point at us women and laugh. Call us names—'

'Forget them, Mary, I don't want to hear what they called you, it's not important. I want to talk to you about the future, but there are things that need to be said about the past first. It's not going to be easy, but you must try to forget this awful time, for the sake of your brothers and sister. My solicitor has given me a list of small farms owned by E and G that are empty. I'll drive you around them tomorrow afternoon, if you're up to it and prepared to leave David, so you can choose which one you want. And then I'll furnish and stock it for you. Unfortunately, because you're all underage, the only way I could get you out of the workhouse was to arrange for Mrs Morgan to look after you. They wouldn't have released you otherwise. And I chose Mrs Morgan because I have known her most of my life. She is a kind woman. She was my grandfather's housekeeper for years.'

'I should have asked,' she murmured distantly. 'How is your grandfather?'

'He was buried two weeks ago.'

'I am sorry.'

'Mary, you're exhausted and so am I. I'll come back tomorrow morning before I drive down into Pontardawe to buy clothes for you. We'll talk some more and you can give me a list of the other things that you and your brothers and sister need.'

'Why are you doing all this for us?' She struggled to free herself and when he released her, she sat back at the table.

'You know why.'

Her hands went to her bald head. 'You can't still like me?' she whispered. 'Not when I look like this.'

'How can I not still like you? You're the same person you've always been, Mary. Hurt and a little battered and bruised, but still you.' He crouched beside her. 'I'm not far away. I'm staying at the inn in front of the cottage. In fact, you can see my window from here. It's the one over the door.'

'It's almost dark.' She looked out through the open door. 'Do you know what I missed most in the workhouse, apart from Martha, David, Matthew and Luke, that is? The mountains, the trees and the grass – You could see the hills, but we were penned in concrete yards like animals. The walls were so high there was never any fresh air even outside the buildings.'

'Mrs Morgan will stay with David if we ask her to. Why don't you walk outside with me for a couple of minutes now to get a breath of air? We could both do with it after spending most of the day indoors. There's an orchard just behind the house that belongs to the inn. It's pretty and full of apples and pears.'

'I don't want anyone to see me in this smock.'

'There's no one to see you except me, and I've already seen you in it.'

'I need to check on David first.'

'I'll wait for you outside.' He went into the garden, not really expecting her to join him. But she came out a few minutes later with a shawl he recognized as Betty's draped around her shaved head.

He slowed his steps to hers and they walked up to the orchard in silence. At the top, set in a copse of low bushes, was a rickety bench that he suspected was one of Alf's early attempts at carpentry.

The branches of the trees on the gently sloping hillside below them were bowed, heavy with green, red and gold fruit. Twilight had fallen, a purple mist that heralded the close of a fine, late-summer evening and portended an equally good day to come. He could almost feel the last traces of warmth leaving the air and the first cool breaths of autumn wafting in on the night breeze.

'Why don't we sit for a few minutes?' He perched on the rickety bench and Mary sat the other end, leaving a gap between them that he was beginning to feel was unbridgeable. 'You're cold.' He took off his jacket and draped it around her shoulders when he saw her shiver.

She seemed oblivious to his attentions. 'I never thought I'd be able to walk and breathe in the fresh air again.'

'Stop thinking about the workhouse. I promise you that neither you nor your family will ever go back there.'

'You said that before. The morning after you fought Robert Pritchard in the yard.'

'I know, and I'm sorry I couldn't prevent it from happening. But it is behind you now, Mary. You have to believe that.' He took her hand into his. She looked at him and he gripped it tighter. 'I was terrified that I'd never see you again.'

'I thought I'd ever see anyone outside of the workhouse again,' she murmured.

'I order you to forget that place.'

'I don't think I'll ever be able to. Look what they did to me. I wasn't pretty before but now . . .' She bit her lips hard to stop tears coming into her eyes.

'You were never pretty, but you were beautiful, and that's the way I'll always see you. I told my father about you.'

'What did you say?'

'That I loved you.'

'You love me?' she echoed in wonder.

He moved closer to her. 'I think I fell in love with you the first time I saw you when you skinned my face.'

'I hurt you, I treated you so badly.'

'You were being the protective older sister and you had every right to do what you did to me,' he said softly.

'You really love me?'

'I truly love you.' He reached out and touched her face with his fingertips. 'I love your wildness, the single-minded way you love and care for your brothers and sister, and the way you have fought to protect them. I love your dark, beautiful eyes, and I want to spend my whole life caring for you. I want to give you all the things you deserve and above all I want to make you happy. But the question is, could you ever love me?'

'I already do.'

He smiled at her. 'Really?'

'I never thought anyone would love me, not looking the way I do, my hair—'

'It will grow again, Mary.'

'But it's still impossible. I could never leave Martha and my brothers.'

'I know you would never leave them.' His smile broadened. 'It might be fun to start married life with a ready-made family.'

'You want to marry me?' She stared at him incredulously.

'What have we been talking about, if not marriage, Mary?'

'I don't know . . . I . . . the agent . . . I thought perhaps you'd visit sometimes like him . . .'

He laid his finger across her lips. 'I'm not him and I never want to hear you mention his name again. He's gone from our life for good. I'm not usually vindictive, but I hope they lock him and Iestyn Williams up for years.' He opened his arms and she went to him.

He'd intended to hold her gently, but when she relaxed against him and responded to his touch, he drew her even closer, and when he kissed her, it was passionately with a longing born out of love, not lust as it had been with Diana Adams. She clung to him, and tentatively returned his caresses, cradling his head in her hands and running her fingers through his hair.

'Mary, you have no idea what you are doing to me,' he murmured thickly when she pressed her body against the length of his.

'You love me, but you don't want to make love to me?' she asked.

'More than anything, but I'm terrified of hurting you. You need time to recover, you're so fragile . . .'

'So skinny.'

'I warn you, I intend to spend a lifetime feeding you until you grow plump.'

She kissed him again and thrust her chest against his. He cupped her small, hard breasts and remembered what his father had said: *Tread carefully. Damaged women are fragile: smother them with kindness and you'll suffocate them.*

He hoped Lloyd was right, because he had lost all self-control. He raised her from the seat, lay on the grass and lifted her on top of him. Untying her overall, he pulled it away from her before peeling the hated smock over her head. She lifted her arms to help him and to his astonishment she was naked beneath it.

He unbuttoned his shirt and trousers, and tossed aside his own clothes. Moments later he entered her and soon they were both lost in a world where the only thing that mattered was the overwhelming tide of emotion that engulfed them both.

Afterwards they lay, hidden by the long grass and the darkness. He ran his fingertips lightly over her naked back and reached for his jacket and shirt. He covered her with them as she lay on him, not from any sense of false modesty but because the chill in the air had brought goosebumps to her flesh.

She lifted her head away from his and looked down at him. 'So that is what my mother meant when she said that love between a man and a woman could be beautiful.'

'I never understood how it could be either, until now,' he confessed.

'You've never felt like this before?'

'Never. I won't lie to you, Mary. There have been other women—'

'Like Miss Adams.'

'Like Miss Adams,' he said, 'but I now know that what happened between us was meaningless. This is my first true love affair and, my darling, I promise you it will be my last.'

'I wish we could lie like this together for ever.' She snuggled close to him but he could feel the cold seeping up from the ground.

'So do I, but not here. And much as this has been a night I'll remember all my life, I wish we'd waited until we were in a warm room under bedcovers.'

'It is cold, but it didn't seem to matter.'

'It does now.' He kissed her and tried to rise, but she locked her hands around his neck and pressed her body against his again. And once more, he lost all control.

'You've bewitched me,' he said much later, 'but no more, my sweet, not tonight or we'll both catch pneumonia.'

'You're right, I can feel the cold now,' she admitted, when he lifted her away from him. 'Autumn is coming.'

'We'll be married before it begins.'

'Married? You mean it, Harry?' She reached for her smock when he pulled on his trousers.

'I have a house. A large new house in Pontypridd big enough for us and your brothers and sister. I know you're not used to town life. But my parents and my sisters and brother live next door. They'll welcome you with open arms and help you to settle down.'

Once he had begun to outline the plans he had made for them, he couldn't stop. Carried away by describing the life he had spent so many hours dreaming about, he failed to notice that she had fallen silent again.

'You will be able to go into the shops I own and get anything you want. Clothes, furniture, things for the house and whatever the boys and Martha want. We'll go on holidays, stay in hotels and eat in restaurants. I'll take you to the theatre and picture houses. We'll go to London – Mary, if you thought Swansea was big, wait until you see London. It's huge. There are dozens of theatres and hundreds of shops there. I'll show you and your brothers and Martha all the sights – the Tower, Buckingham Palace – and we'll go on holidays abroad, as well as in this country. I'll take you all to France and Germany, Spain, Italy – Italy is beautiful, Mary, you'll love it. I'll find a tutor for your brothers and Martha; they're bright, they'll soon catch up and learn enough to attend school. You'll have maids to do all the housework. You'll never have to wash, cook, clean or scrub ever again—'

'Then what would I do?' she interrupted.

'You'd run the house, supervise the maids. There'll be tea parties, coffee mornings.' He racked his brains, wondering what women who had servants did with their time. His mother worked in Gwilym James, Aunty Megan ran the dairy on his uncle's farm and Aunty Rhian managed a china shop she owned in her own right.

'You expect me and my family to move to a town, Harry?'

He heard the apprehension in her voice but chose to ignore it. 'Pontypridd has picture houses, theatres, shops, a market and a fantastic library. I promise you, Mary, that all of you will love town life once you get used to it.'

'But I'm a farmer's daughter,' she protested. 'The only thing I know is farming. And that goes for the others too. We could never be happy in a town,' she said decisively.

'But my house is in Pontypridd.'

'And my family's future is here, where the Ellises have lived for generations.'

'Be reasonable, Mary. You've lost the Estate and I told you I can't get it back for you for nine years—'

'But you promised you'd help us to find another farm.'

'You want to work all the hours God sends and be a skivvy all your life?'

'I want to work to build a future for David, Matthew and Luke,' she broke in fervently. 'I want to be able to save money so Martha can do whatever she wants with her life. I want to *earn* enough to buy a place that will belong to us – all of us. A home that will always be there when any of us need it.'

'In that case, I'll buy you a farm near Pontypridd. We'll put in a manager and you can visit it whenever you like.' He picked up the shirt that she had dropped when she had put on her smock.

'You can't visit a farm, you have to run it.' She fastened Betty's overall over her smock again.

'Not if you've hired a manager to do all the work.'

'Then it will be his farm not ours. I don't want to visit a farm the way people visit a hotel or a theatre, Harry. I want to run one.'

'I'm not a farmer, I'm a businessman,' he said flatly.

'I know nothing about business, or town living, and I don't want to.'

'Then you won't live with me in Pontypridd?'

Tight-lipped, she shook her head.

'Mary, I'm offering you and your family the chance of a lifetime.'

'You're offering us a life as your pets. You want to break us and train us the way David does his dogs.'

'That's ridiculous. I want to marry you because I love you. Isn't it only natural that I want you to live with me in my house?' he demanded.

'I won't let you turn us into something we're not,' she persisted.

'You can still do whatever you want to. All of you.'

'In Pontypridd?' Even in the thickening gloom her eyes glittered, and he realized that although the workhouse had momentarily cowed her, she had lost none of her spirit.

'Yes, in Pontypridd,' he said in exasperation.

'I can't go to Pontypridd with you when I have to look after the others.'

'I told you, I'll look after them for you.'

'But we belong here, in the Swansea Valley, not Pontypridd. It's kind of you to want to help, but my family are my responsibility, Harry, not yours. If you're serious about renting us another farm, we'll take it. But I'd like one as close to the Ellis Estate as I can get.'

'You stubborn—'

'But I love you and I'll always be here whenever you come to see me. And you can make love to me whenever you want.'

'I'm not Robert Pritchard,' he said acidly. 'You don't have to pay me off, Mary Ellis.'

'I love you.' There was sadness in her declaration.

'So you keep saying, but you won't marry me or live with me in Pontypridd.'

'That doesn't mean I'm not grateful to you for loving me. No one has ever done anything for us before, Harry.'

'Damn you, can't you see that I'm not being kind,' he shouted, his anger getting the better of him for the second time that day. 'Don't you understand that I love you? I want to make you my wife? That I want to give you everything—'

'And make me and my family live your way?'

Furious, he said the most vicious thing he could think of. 'All you want is the Ellis Estate.'

She wanted to tell him that she didn't. Not any more. That she loved him and longed to spend the rest of her life with him, but she couldn't pay a price that she knew would crush and destroy her family. She wanted to tell him that she had made love to him because it was something she had burned to do ever since she realized how much she cared for him. She wanted to explain how much his declaration of love and lovemaking meant to her when she felt ugly and needed reassurance that she was still a woman – and desirable. But she simply couldn't find the words to express her feelings.

She placed her hand on the back of his neck, reached across and kissed him. He pulled her close and she clung to him.

'I love you, Harry.'

The blood pounded headily in his veins. Another few moments and he knew he'd lose his head again. He pushed her away from him while he was still able to release her.

'And I wish that I could believe that you love me. But I know you love the Ellis Estate more.'

'Not the Estate, my family.'

'You'll be fine with Mrs Morgan. She knows how to get in touch with me and she has enough money to buy everything you need. I'll get Alf to take you around the farms tomorrow. I hope David soon recovers, and until he does, I'll ask Mrs Edwards to find someone who can help you to run the farm.'

'Harry, I'm sorry I can't be what you want me to be, or live the way you'd like me to.'

'It's just as well that we found out now, before we married,' he said abruptly, turning on his heel and walking away from her while he still had the strength and the will to do so.

Chapter 26

'SO SHE turned you down. Hasn't a girl ever done that before?' Toby asked irritably, after listening to Harry complain about Mary's refusal to marry him for a solid hour.

'No. How many girls have turned you down?' Harry snapped.

'Just one,' Toby said easily, 'but then, that's all it takes, doesn't it? We young men aren't built for rejection. Our egos are too large.' He reached for the bottle of whisky beside his chair, re-filled Harry's glass and then his own.

'Will you ever tell me that story?' Harry offered Toby his cigarettes and, when he took one, removed his lighter from his pocket. 'Is she the reason you tried to warn me not to get involved with the Ellises?'

'Yes.' Toby pushed the cigarette into his mouth and leaned forward to light it when Harry flicked the flame.

'And you're not going to tell me any more?'

'Not to satisfy your idle curiosity. Besides it's the old story. It doesn't need embellishment. Boy found girl, boy loved girl, boy didn't have the sense to keep girl. It's the Ross tragedy. It happened to my uncle, it happened to me. Why do you think I'm so keen on not letting your sister out of my sight for the next five years, that's if your father is mean enough to make me wait that long. Finders keepers—'

'Losers weepers.' Harry drew heavily on his cigarette.

'I have a feeling that you'll be weeping a long time over Mary Ellis if you're stupid enough to let her go.'

'What do you mean, let her go?' Harry demanded. 'I let her do nothing. I told you she refused my proposal of marriage.'

'Did she?'

'Of course she did.' Harry insisted angrily. 'I told you I asked her to marry me and she said no.'

'I heard you say that she turned down your house, the life you offered her as the ornamental wife of a rich businessman in Pontypridd and the fancy educations you offered her brothers and sister.'

'What do you think I should do, move into a farm with her? Take up mucking out cows, repairing sheep pens and helping David with the shearing? Sitting around the kitchen table in the evenings teaching Mary and the children to read and write? And on high days and holidays driving her and her family into Pontardawe for the highlight of the year, a magic lantern show in a church hall?'

'Doesn't sound like a bad life, does it?' Toby said quietly. 'Not when you have what you really want – the woman you love. Out of all the women in the world you've been fortunate to find the right one for you, Harry. But will you be doubly blessed and fortunate enough to keep her? I know if I had the chance, I'd hold on to my woman with both hands. But if you really can't bear the thought of living her life instead of the one of importance you imagined living in Pontypridd, then you've no choice but to walk away from her.' He held up the whisky bottle again. 'Have you?'

Toby's words came back to haunt Harry several times during that night when sleep eluded him. *Out of all the women in the world you've been fortunate to find the right one for you, Harry. But will you be doubly blessed and fortunate enough to keep her?*

When dawn broke, he slipped the letter he'd written Toby under his door and left the one containing a week's money for Mrs Edwards propped up against the telephone in her office. He carried the cases he'd packed to his car and dropped them into the boot before walking to the cottage. He looked up. A light burned in David's bedroom and he knew that Mary was still sitting up nursing him.

He pressed the latch lightly on the door and walked into the kitchen. Betty was in the easy chair next to the fire, a shawl thrown around her winceyette nightgown. She was staring into the flames, a forgotten cup of tea set in the hearth at her feet.

She looked up at him reproachfully. 'That poor girl has been crying all night. Maybe she hasn't made much noise but then someone whose heart is breaking rarely does.'

Harry pulled a chair out from under the table and set it on the rug next to her. 'You know?'

'That you two are head over heels in love? It's as plain as the nose on your face,' she sniffed. 'The only question is, without your grandfather here to order you to do the sensible thing, just what are you going to do about it?'

'That's a big "what", Betty.'

'Dear God, you sounded just like Billy then.'

'I am going to do something about it. But give me time.' He took his wallet from his inside pocket, opened it and removed all the notes it contained. 'There's fifty pounds there.'

'Fifty pounds! What do I need that kind of money for?' she said indignantly.

'Expenses, doctor's bills – he'll be sending them to the inn.'

'Where are you going?' she asked as he rose to his feet and went to the door.

'Pontypridd. You know what my father's been telling me to do for years. Well, I'm about to do it, and take my responsibilities seriously for once.'

'And that poor girl upstairs, what am I supposed to tell her?'

'That I'll see her again just as soon as I can.'

Lloyd, Sali and Mr Richards listened in silence to Harry. When he stopped talking, Lloyd poured the after-dinner drinks and handed them around.

'I'm not telling you how to live your life, Harry, but you know nothing about farming,' his stepfather warned.

'That's why I want to see if the Ellises' stockman and his wife are still in the workhouse.'

'And if they are?' Mr Richards asked.

'I'll open up the two cottages. Bring the shepherd back as well and employ all the help I need to run the Ellis Estate. I'll have no trouble finding good people. Not given the number of farmers Pritchard evicted during the last few years. I accept that I know

430

nothing about farming, but I'm a quick learner, and in the mean-time David Ellis can tell me if the workers are making any mistakes.'

'A fourteen-year-old boy?' Lloyd exclaimed.

'Who has an old farming head on his shoulders.'

'And what will you do, Harry?' Sali asked quietly.

'Start learning all I can about farming and the businesses that I will inherit in nine years' time. I'll attend the trustees meetings every month, and take whatever books I need to study the other company accounts. But I'll begin with E and G Estates. The Ellis Estate house is huge; I'll set up an office in one wing and put in a telephone.'

'It will cost the earth,' Lloyd remonstrated.

'Probably,' Harry said cheerfully, 'but the company can stand it. I'll open a permanent office in Brecon as well. Mr Beatty can man it. We'll find good tenants for all the empty properties, hopefully the same ones who were evicted by Robert Pritchard, rent out everything on the books and, by judicial and fair management, see if we can turn our tax loss into a living for some of the displaced tenant farmers in Breconshire. I know it will only be a drop in the ocean and we're not going to turn the tide and save the countryside from depopulation, but at least I'll be able to sleep at night.'

'And when you've put E and G Estates to right?' Mr Richards enquired.

'In nine years' time, Mary's younger brother David will be twenty-three and of an age to take over the Ellis Estate. Perhaps then I'll manage to talk Mary into at least giving life in Pontypridd a try for a month or two.'

Sali studied her son for a moment. 'You are serious about this, aren't you, Harry?'

'I've never been more serious about anything in my life.'

'And you love this girl?'

'I can't live without her,' he said simply.

'And Paris and your art?' Lloyd asked.

'I still might paint the odd watercolour, but after seeing Toby's work, I know I'll never make the grade as a professional. Not because I haven't the talent, but I haven't the dedication or will to work at it. On the other hand, I intend to become a reasonable amateur and every man needs a hobby.'

'Sweetheart,' Lloyd took Sali's hand, 'I don't think we could stop the boy from turning farmer even if we wanted to.'

'Just one thing, Harry,' Sali cautioned. 'Don't invite your brother and sisters to the Ellis Estate too often. I dread to think of the mischief Edyth could get up to in a farm yard.'

'We've brought back all the original furniture we could track down, Mr Evans,' Albert Jones said to Harry as they walked from room to room in the Ellis Estate farmhouse.

'And the stock?' Harry asked.

'Master David's dog, Merlyn, was found running wild in the hills. A fair number of milking cows and the bull have been brought back from Iestyn Williams's farm, along with a couple of pigs, but all the poultry will need replacing. Most of the sheep were never moved from the fields belonging to the Estate. So I'd say we have about a third of the livestock we need to bring the farm back to scratch. And of course, you'll need to buy horses.'

'And a tractor,' Harry mused. 'David will want to pick the stock and horses himself.'

'That he will,' Mr Jones agreed.

Harry had furnished one room on the ground floor of the wing the Ellises had never used as an office for himself, and moved a few pieces of furniture that he had bought in Gwilym James into two others. One held a bedroom suite, table, chair, and wash-stand – which he would need until the bathroom and hot water system he had ordered was operational. The other was a sitting-room.

But he had expended far more care on the wing that the Ellises had occupied. He walked from the huge farmhouse kitchen, which was now dominated by an enormous dresser filled with antique china, and a solid pine table that could seat twelve, with chairs to match, and looked into the formal dining- and drawing-rooms. It was odd to be in rooms that he had had last seen bare and walk on the rugs that had been laid on the flagstoned floors. He ran his fingers over the carvings on the old oak cupboards, chairs and table before pointing to the set of gleaming brass fire-irons next to the hearth.

'These are all original, Mrs Jones?' he asked the stockman's wife.

'Yes, sir, I'd stake my life on it after spending five years cleaning the place for Mrs Ellis, God rest her soul. The bedroom suites upstairs are all original too. The carter said they all came from Mr Pritchard's house.'

'Do me a favour please, Mrs Jones, never mention that man's name to me again.' Harry turned to the clerk who was following him. 'Fine, Mr Beatty, you know what to do. Go down to the inn and bring the Ellises here.'

'Yes, sir. And what am I to say if they ask me where you are?'

'That I'm seeing to business in Brecon that might keep me there for the next few days. If they want anything, there's the telephone. Give Mrs Morgan Mr Richard's number and the number of the office in Brecon.'

'Yes, sir.'

Harry drove back to Brecon and unlocked the door of the house that he and Anthony Beatty had moved into. Yet another empty property on the books of E&G Estates. The housekeeper he employed to take care of the place had left a cold ham and chicken pie and a bowl of potato salad. He poured himself a drink and took it into the living-room.

There was a small parcel on his desk. He opened it. It held the Victorian gold and blue enamelled fob watch and the unusual antique gold locket he had seen Iestyn Williams's wife wearing. There was also an old-fashioned heavy gold wedding ring that one of the bailiffs had handed to the police after admitting he had found it in Mary's bedroom.

He could have bought Mary any jewellery she wanted but he sensed she'd prefer these pieces. He read the accompanying note from the police, short and officious, as all their communications. 'Voluntarily given up by Robert Pritchard and Iestyn Williams.' He slipped them back into the cloth bag and went up to bed. His future would be settled one way or another in the next twenty-four hours and he wanted a good night's sleep.

'Harry, you're quite the stranger round here,' Toby said when he walked into the inn late the following afternoon. 'If you've come to see the Ellises, they moved out yesterday.'

'I know.'

'Dic came in. He told me they're back in the Ellis Estate,' Mrs Edward said artfully, hoping Harry would tell her more about his wealth and ownership of local farms than Dic had been able to. She took down a pint mug and held it up in front of him.

'Yes, please, Mrs Edwards, a pint of ale would go down a treat.' Harry pulled some money from his pocket. He turned to Toby. 'Do you want to rent my house in Pontypridd?'

'Next door to Bella? I'll pay twice the going rate,' Toby burst out enthusiastically.

'The going rate will be fine. I warn you my father is not thrilled with the idea but if you promise not to be too intrusive he'll put up with you. And I'll let you into a secret: Bella pleaded your cause with me.'

'The angel. You sharing it with me?'

'I hope not.' Harry took a long pull at his pint.

'She loves you, Harry, I'm sure of it.'

'Anthony Beatty said that David's up and about.' Harry deliberately ignored Toby's comment.

'He is. But the doctor's warned him to take it slowly. His back muscles have been damaged and he won't be able to do any heavy work for a year or two.'

'He won't have to,' Harry said.

'Perhaps you should go and see him for yourself,' Toby hinted.

'Perhaps I will,' he said casually. 'I'll drive you up to Pontypridd when you're ready to move. You know the number of the Brecon office?'

'I do.'

'See you, Toby. Thanks for the pint, Mrs Edwards.'

'That's a close-lipped young man.' Mrs Edwards took Harry's mug and put it on the tray of glasses waiting to be carried into the kitchen for washing. 'I never thought when he came to Abercrave that he owned most of the farms around here. Did you, Mr Ross?'

Harry drove up the valley as he had done so many times before. He tried very hard not to look at Craig y Nos, but the castle was so massive it was impossible. It was going to be hard to live so close to the sanatorium but he hoped that eventually time would soften the pain associated with the building.

The two cottages nearest the Ellis Estate, which had been boarded up, were newly painted. Curtains hung at the windows and fluttered out in the breeze, and children played in front of the doors. The sun was already setting, an hour and half earlier than when he had first driven up the road that rainy afternoon in July when he had knocked Martha down. Two months ago yet so much had happened since then, it seemed like half a lifetime.

He pictured the farmhouse kitchen, and Mary cooking at the stove. Matthew would be bringing in the cows – he guessed David would find the limitations imposed by his injuries irksome. Martha, who according to Betty had progressed well with her reading and writing under her tutelage, would be teaching Matthew and possibly even David to read as well. And Luke would be crawling on the rug, playing with the toys he'd bought in Brecon and left in the farmhouse for him.

He slowed down when he drew close to the farmhouse. Twlight had fallen. He drove in through the arch. A lantern had been lit in the cowshed. Mr Jones, David and Matthew turned and looked out of the door, but David was standing back with his hands in his pockets. Even from a distance Harry could see that he resented being relegated to the role of bystander.

Harry left the car and touched his hat as the cowman and David did the same. Merlyn barked at him and bounded over. He ruffled the dog's fur.

'Harry?' David called.

'I'll see you inside.'

David nodded and disappeared back into the shed.

Harry went to the kitchen door, knocked as Diana had done and walked straight in.

'Harry! Where have you been?' Martha left the table, ran to him and threw her arms around him. 'We haven't seen you for ages,' she complained. 'And my letters are so much better.'

'And mine,' Matthew shouted. 'We've been practising and practising, and Mrs Morgan has been teaching us and—'

Betty looked from Harry to Mary, before scooping Luke up from the hearthrug. 'And Mrs Morgan is about to put Luke to bed so Mary can cook the supper. If you two come up with me, I'll read you another chapter of *Treasure Island*.'

'But Harry's just got here—'

'And I'll still be here when you come down, Matthew.' Harry dropped the bag of books he'd brought for the children on to a chair. He waited until Betty had shepherded the children upstairs before walking over to Mary. 'Hello.'

'Hello.' She stirred the soup she'd made. 'You've come for supper?'

'No.' He took the spoon from her, opened her hand and put the bag of jewellery into it.

'What's this?'

'Jewellery, the kind a rich man gives to his wife.'

'Harry, I told you—'

'Open the bag.'

She did as he'd asked, and cried out, 'Wherever did you get them?'

'The police retrieved them. I could buy you new, but I thought that you might prefer these. Especially the wedding ring. I see it has your mother's and father's name engraved inside it. We could add ours – or get a new one.'

'Harry.' David limped in. He was walking stiffly but was smiling.

'How are you, David?'

'Getting better. The doctor said I can walk as far as I like as long as I don't do any heavy lifting.' He saw his sister lay an extra bowl on the table 'You come for supper, Harry?'

'No.' Harry looked at Mary, and she nodded. 'Not for supper, David.' He took the wedding ring from Mary and slipped it on to her finger. 'I've come home.'